The Accidental Summoner

The Accidental Summoner

R.E. Carr

FALSTAFF
BOOKS
WWW.FALSTAFFBOOKS.COM

To everyone out there who feels lonely. Go on, have that burrito...

Episode One

Pilot

Chapter 1

A Girl Named Meg

"That is a really big dragon," Meg deadpanned as she skidded into position with the other ranged DPS players. "Really, *really*, big."

"*Stay frosty, folks. It's time for a server first.*"

Meg held her breath as the countdown started. Pixelated numbers flashed over the torso of an enormous golden serpent filling the screen. Meg gulped. One hand quivered over her mouse, the other snatched the soda by her monitor. She managed one quick sip before the main tank rushed headfirst into Voldara—The World Slayer. "*Give me five seconds for aggro then light it up, deeps,*" echoed in Meg's headset.

Meg clicked and tapped furiously while sidestepping pesky flames under her onscreen feet. Her heart pounded as she fell into a rotation of magic missiles, arcane explosions, and her mana restoration spells. She kept her gaze darting between the countdown add-on on the left, her damage meter, and the dizzying array of spell effects flashing. Her raid leader constantly barked over the headset, demanding people to spread apart and then clump together, all while a big blue bar continued to fill on the top of her UI, while the green health bar of the boss continued to deplete.

"*We've got this...oh my God...oh my God—*"

Meg began bouncing in her chair, hands shaking and breath racing.

"We've got this. We've got this!" She eyed the ultimate attack meter just millimeters from filling.

"*OK, one mage drop the bomb. One percent and almost to enrage,*" her raid leader commanded. "*Zazzy, you cast!*"

"That's me!" Meg cried, blinking like a deer in headlights as she looked at her name plate on the screen. "It's me."

"*Drop it. Drop it.* Drop It!" filled her headset. Meg gulped and slammed her index finger into her bound hotkey for the ultimate attack. The screen lit up with a giant meteor animation while all manner of excited profanity filled both the screen and the voice chat. Meg squealed as the screen flickered and went white. Her heart plummeted in her chest as *her* hit points dropped to zero instead of the boss's and the meteor landed harmlessly against the background.

"No way," Meg mouthed as she popped up her character screen and looked at her accuracy percentage against the boss—99.9%. The words in her headset were not nearly as kind.

"*How did it miss? Zazz, what the fuck is your accuracy percent?*"

"Ninety-nine-point-nine," she squeaked as the rage-quitting began from the raid. She gave a sideways glance to her phone. The 12:59 glared back at her.

"*I thought you were capped,*" showed up in a tell. Another line of text popped up with "*Go back to WoW, cow.*"

Tears welled up in Meg's eyes as she pulled off her headset to avoid the tide of toxic disappointment. She held her breath as she tried to say all the words she wanted to say, but every sentiment became tangled on her tongue. "They don't want my excuses."

She logged out of her *Lands of Eternaquest* MMORPG before it could get too much worse. She could just see one last, "*Not your fault, Zazzy,*" private message before the screen went black. "*I know you were helping everyone else farm—*"

"But it *was* my fault," Meg muttered as everything shut down. She rubbed her eyes, flipping her glasses off the bridge of her nose—disaster only averted by a temple getting tangled in one of her curls. She grimaced as she had to rip out a few dark strands to get free. Meg groaned and plopped her specs on the nightstand, sending an empty black and white can clattering to the floor. The soulless eyes of the woman on her soda promised her it would be "OK," but in reality, it only made Meg worse as she saw a few new drops of cola staining her belea-guered carpet. She only bothered with yanking her jeans down to her ankles before flopping on top of her comforter. "I suck. I always suck, and I'm always gonna suck."

Eventually Meg managed to kick off her pants and roll into a blanket burrito. Her eyes refused to close as she replayed ninety-nine other scenarios where the gamer God of RNJesus decided to bless her for the night. The notification light flashed furiously on her phone, but she fought the urge to swipe the screen, and instead buried her face in the pillow as tears fell. "I really, *really* suck."

Her night consisted of tossing and turning, moaning, and bemoaning her nearly maxed out accuracy. The other potential scenarios mixed with the remnants of caffeine and high-fructose corn syrup in her bloodstream, until she buried her head completely under her pillow. Just as she entered REM, her phone erupted with an old-school electronica ringtone, and it vibrated to remind Meg that Monday comes for us all. "Five more minutes," she mumbled as she fumbled for the snooze.

Twenty minutes later and her alarm refused to give in to Meg's persuasion. Her eyes snapped open to see 08:05 flashing in her face. She flicked her comforter to the floor in record speed but joined it on the carpet in her haste to get out of bed. "Ugh!"

Meg scrambled through the remains of her raid-night snack binge, tossing aside wrappers to snag a sensible pair of slacks from her dresser. She then stumbled for the shower, nearly forgetting her shower cap, and keeping her glasses on until the steam made her pause. "Oh, come on! What next?" She set her eyeglasses on the vanity and managed to tuck her mess of curls under the blue plastic before she became completely drenched. One speedy scrub session happened while she multitasked brushing her teeth with one hand and furiously shaved her calves with the other. Three painful nicks later and she rinsed before she ended up looking like vampire bait.

"Diet starts today." Her tummy folded over her waistband in a muffin top. She ditched any hope of makeup beyond a little lip gloss and yanked all her curls into a bun. She winced as she could feel hairs tearing from her already fuzzy hairline. The finishing touch involved grabbing a blouse from her closet. As soon as she got to her third button, she lamented the obvious gap showing off her bra to the world. *"Defi-nitely* dieting today."

She eyed the clock on her phone and made a beeline for the kitchen. Meg snatched a packet of toaster pastries and her purse, grumbling under her breath as she saw the coffee pot left empty on the counter alongside some dirty dishes. She yanked open the fridge with a sigh and grabbed a bottle of soda to get her through her morning commute. "Diet starts at lunchtime."

Meg hustled from her home tucked at the end of a quaint Mass-achusetts neighborhood full of overgrown trees and electric cars. She had to make do with a set of sensible footwear and combo bus and subway pass as she rushed to the main road just in time to see her coach roll into traffic. "Deep, cleansing breaths, Meg. You're just pre-disas-tering for your day."

She slipped earbuds out of her purse while selecting the deepest, soothing dubstep playlist on her phone. Meg swayed in time with the beat, dancing around the weather shelter at the bus stop—much to the amusement of some local teens. Four songs later and the bus arrived. Meg munched on her sugar-laden breakfast and enjoyed her first bit of luck in a twenty-four-hour period as she found one of the choice seats in the back for her commute into Boston. She kept herself awake by searching for accuracy upgrades for mages in *Lands of Eternaquest*. "Oh man, there were drops in the Verdant Caverns I could have used. Gosh darn it!"

Even a bit of theorycrafting couldn't keep her completely lucid as she nodded off a few times until the bus pulled into South Station. She grabbed a gigantic iced coffee on her way to the subway, trying to ignore the looming clock overhead. As she was about to leave, she remembered to pick up a bottle of water. By the time she reached her stop, it was already 9:15. Still she took a moment to detour off the crowded sidewalk and set her extra drink next to one of the unfortunate landmarks of her daily travel.

"Hey, you," a lady in mismatched Boston sports memorabilia said, picking up one of the multitude of cans that made their way into the alleyways of the city. Her canine companion wagged his bob tail at the sight of Meg as well.

"Got an extra today." Meg handed the beading bottle over.

By the time she got an appropriate amount of head scritches and small talk in, fought past waves of tourists *and* an overloaded elevator—it ended up being closer to half-past-nine when she made the long walk into the familiar row of cubicles. She kept her gaze low and fixated on the looped-pile carpet, avoiding eye contact at all costs.

"*Reynolds!*"

Meg froze. She gulped down her mouthful of coffee, the gulp somehow louder than the clacking of keyboards and the cacophony of voices spewing pleasantries all around her. She lifted her gaze, gulping again as she saw a pissed pair of baby blues staring back at her. "I'm sorry I'm late."

"Sorry?" her pod leader replied, venom dripping from his narrow lips. "Are you prepared to tell Yang and Leibowitz that you are sorry as well? After all, they had to cover your absence for a full half hour."

Meg nodded vehemently. "Yes, sir."

"Well then, you can start the apology by covering the IP relay open line...all day," her team lead said with a wicked smile. "If this happens again, I'll have to take it up the ladder, and you wouldn't want Gina to hear about—"

Meg eyed the office in the corner as her blood ran cold. The mere mention of Gina was enough to send the entire row into a frenzy of earnest busywork, all phones and other distractions vanishing in an instant.

"Reynolds, do you want to be a screw up your entire life?" her boss asked.

She shook her head, then took her walk of shame all the way to the back corner, where the voicemail light and a mountain of sticky notes awaited her on a Monday morning. "Well at least it can't get any worse," she said as she booted up her machine.

Her mild-mannered and bug-eyed cubicle neighbor lifted his notebook up to the glass. "The pranksters are out—sorry," his note read, with a little frowny emoji at the end.

Meg's heart sunk as she signed in to see the queue lining up in her CRM software. "Thanks for the heads up, Dylan," she whispered as she slid on her headset. The headband snagged on her beleaguered bun. "Ready for another day in paradise."

"Paradise" for Meg consisted of being one of the last of a dying breed, a real-life assistance operator at International Accessibility, a company that, on paper, sought to help those with hearing and visual impairments navigate important phone calls, but ended up being eight hours a day of waiting on hold to cancel subscriptions or return big box purchases. Unless, of course, a specific type of caller decided to make an appearance first thing in the morning.

The screen lit up with her first number to call, and message to relay. Meg took a deep breath and prepared to be invisible for another Monday. "I'm the messenger. I am *just* doing a job." The click echoed in her ears followed by her beeps as she typed in the requested extension on her call log.

"*Hello big boy, this is Candy.*"

Meg took a deep, cleansing breath before reading the text filling her window. "Oh, yes, Candy, I would really love to lick you, lick you so hard," she said, in her most monotone voice. To Candy's credit, the operator remained a consummate professional as robotic Meg filled in the voice for one "Big Boy Mike" as he quite anatomically inaccurately described both his genitals and the acts he wanted to do to Candy. Meg finally had to mute and whisper, "that is not even physically possible," at the fifteen-minute mark in her call, but then carried on as the subject devolved into fantasies about strap-ons and calling in a four-legged friend. By the half-hour mark, Meg had turned scarlet from head to toe, and she choked back her gag reflex at uttering the word "bukkake" in a non-anime context. She ended up only being saved when Mike's credits inevitably maxed out, and Candy disconnected from her end.

She scribbled on her own notepad and sent a "you weren't kidding," note back to a pale-faced Dylan. Her unlucky coworker had landed the task of relaying funeral arrangements for his caller's wife, while Mary across the hall had to yell "*REPRESENTATIVE,*" at the top of her lungs while she tried to order bedsheets for the speech impaired.

"Well, now that the prankster is out of the way..." Meg dutifully logged her ticket and pulled up the next caller in queue. Her face fell as she saw the same number pop-up onscreen.

"*Hi, this is Candy. Are you ready for some fun?*"

"I'm in Hell," Meg mouthed to her flushed reflection. "Living, breathing, hell."

Chapter 2

A Demon Named Vocharlian

J ust another bloody day in Hell," Vocharlian said as he buried his face into a mountain of paperwork. He groaned at the incessant beeping from the outdated computer that had been relegated to the Department of Virtual Envy, drool dribbling on his inbox.

"*Variegatus!* Variegatus, are you sleeping on the job again?"

Vocharlian snapped to attention. Unfortunately, in his haste, he failed to notice the memo slip impaled on his right horn. A shadow loomed over his cubicle. Vocharlian noticed the cat-o-nine-tails out of the corner of his vision. "Lord Asafran, it is not what you think, guv—"

The whip landed squarely on the desktop, sending Vocharlian's bowl of paperclips flying. The young demon pushed up the sleeve on his business casual chain mail and showed off his med-alert bracelet to the seething ogre that served as his immediate supervisor. "Medical dispensation, my lord. As you can see here, I have been clearly diagnosed with slothalepsy—"

Lord Asafran huffed and puffed through his hog snout, but even an oversized monstrosity like him paused as Vocharlian pointed toward the portcullis marked "Demon Resources." The porcine ogre narrowed his empty eye sockets at the scrawny little wage slave, then snatched the pink slip of paper off Vocharlian's forehead. "Get back to work!" Asafran bellowed before stomping back to his desk. A pair of scantily clad succubi darted to the boss's side, one fanning him with palm leaves while the other blotted his brow.

"Must be good to be the king," Vocharlian muttered, starting back on his daily grind of looking up the hopes and desires of poor schlubs on social media before selecting the perfect images to send them to make their envious hearts grow stronger. For the first few, he flipped through the recent browsing history, looked at a few tidbits, and customized the advertising to each desperate human. Soon, however, he just clicked penis-enlargement for every male and weight loss for every female and called it a day. As he mindlessly clicked with one hand, his other slid his outdated Scrymaster personal demonic data device out of his drawer so he could slyly spy on the latest gossip from across the seven kingdoms while continuing to earn a living. "Oh, Belial really gets around," Vocharlian mused as he read the headline "Love Child Number Fifteen for Hell's Stallion."

"Dude, are you really playing with your PD3 at work?" a simpering little voice hissed from across the aisle. Vocharlian swirled the vapors pouring out of his eye sockets before leaning back in his chair so he could face the wretch from cubicle 29-A. This particular demon seemed to be of the Aztec variety, with a vibrant feather headdress and golden mask to go along with his tie and briefcase. Vocharlian noted the drinking skull etched with "World's Greatest Dad" on the cheekbones and a picture of him with a pair of little hellions pulling hearts out of victim's chests.

"Mind your own business, Tez," Vocharlian snapped. His coworker lifted his mask just enough so he could poke his blackened tongue out. Vocharlian swirled his eye mist again. "We're all stuck in this sodding assignment."

"Yeah, well not all of us are affirmative-action untouchables, half-breed, so can you tone down the junior rebel routine so Asafran stops busting all our chops?" Tez asked.

"Well, since you asked so nicely," Vocharlian said, putting his PD3 back in the drawer. He smiled as sweetly as he could, his metallic fangs glistening in the fluorescent gothic chandeliers. He then opened a new chat window on his screen and began typing diligently like a busy bee. Tez resigned himself to his own mountain of misery, while a chat icon popped into view for Vocharlian.

"*Remember that favor from last week?*" Vocharlian typed to IT. "*I'd like to cash it in.*"

A few pertinent details later, Vocharlian started humming to himself as he switched it up and sent some overpriced real estate into the inboxes of cash-strapped couples. A few moments later, Tez began cursing violently as he stared at a blue screen of death. To Vocharlian's credit, he hid his shit-eating grin behind his mountain of paperwork. The terrible monotony continued for hours as the demon got sucked into the horrible, banal problems of the humans he was watching, rather than the horrible, banal problems of his demonic existence. By the time the gong struck six and the succubi came to unchain him from his desk, Vocharlian had to wipe more drool from his chin.

"You still have an open ticket," the mistress chided him, cracking her whip.

"I beg your pardon—" His computer flickered ominously and, sure enough his header flashed red despite it refreshing only milliseconds before. "Fine."

Vocharlian rushed through the details on his last file of the day—some pathetic gamer who spent her time searching how to kill bosses in a game called *Lands of Eternaquest*. "Oh, this will leave a mark," he hissed as he popped a server-first kill feed into her recommended videos. "Keep playing and ignoring your life!" For bonus points he tossed in a coupon for a double-stuffed burrito. "I'll send you weight-loss next week, *mwah-hah-hah!*"

"Excellent initiative, Variegatus," the sultry siren said as she saw his twofer setup. She leaned over his desk so that the young demon could get a clear view of her company assets. Vocharlian could see the reflection of his eye sockets against her breastplate, the bright green mist sparkled and shifted to a lusty violet. "I'll be sure to tell your mother when I get back to the brothel." The violet immediately faded back to green.

"*Cheers, luv.*" He took his time easing out of his cubicle, adjusting his codpiece as soon as the succubus had turned her attention to the next cube. Tez muscled in front of the smaller, slimmer Vocharlian, making a point to whack the young demon with his spiked tail on his way out. "Oy, I deserved that."

Vocharlian shuffled along with the throng of wage slaves slogging through the bowels of the Department of Envy. Rows of green glow filled the eye sockets of the dejected hordes. He swiped his PD3 on the turnstile on the way out of the building, and a paltry sum of silver dropped into his account. A message popped up on his device, *"I got the good stuff."*

"Thank you, Dorp!" Vocharlian exclaimed as he picked up the pace. His path took him along a lazy river of Hellfire and into the shadow of the twin towers of Greed and Avarice. The gilded walls blinded him as the sun set along the jagged spires of his homeland. He passed luxury condos, glistening swimming pools, and the most beautiful female demons lounging on deck chairs. While golden-eyed servitors of greed lived the high life, their sluggish minions toiled in the shadows. Just past the gated communities lay a warren of blackened brick buildings, each stuffed with the poor demonic communities. Vocharlian wandered past garbage piles full of filth-eaters and a stream of second-string succubi all begging for his hard-earned coin.

The smell of rot intensified near his end of the alleyway. Vocharlian smiled as an oozy mass of flesh poured out of the first-floor window. "Evening Mrs. Splatowski, so nice to see you."

The blob shuddered and shifted until a pair of spectacles erupted over two beady black holes. She seemed to blink a few times as all her slimy bits flipped around so that she could address Vocharlian. "Why hello there, sonny! How are you holding up at, um, at um—Where are you stationed this time?"

"Envy, social media division. Oh my, did you absorb a new perfume, Mrs. S.?"

The blob quivered. "Oh, I just ate some of the gardenias around Gilded Gardens. Do you li-iiiike?"

Vocharlian leaned over and kissed the blob on what should have been a cheek. She opened her gaping maw and slathered her tongue across his face. "Love you, always."

"Hey, stop hitting on my mom!" a new voice called from the first-floor apartment. A squishy, but opaque face peered out of the window. Vocharlian beamed through a mask of mucus.

"What can I say, she's irresistible, mate. Hey, is that bacon I smell?" He peered inside to see the gourmet kitchen hidden within an otherwise unassuming flat. Piles of bacon, eggs, and pancakes covered the Splatowski table. Vocharlian wasted no time vaulting through the window as he saw three places set for brinner. "You have outdone yourself, Mrs. S.!"

The translucent blob blushed from deep within. "You need to eat more. You've gotten so skinny. You look like you're trying out for Pestilence Pride! Dorp! Boy, your father was nearly four-hundred pounds when he was your age, you need to step it up. For Lucifer's sake, you have solid bones and I still weigh more than you."

"Mom! You know sometimes I don't have time to eat a proper meal at work," Dorp whined. "By the time I got to the canteen, there was only broccoli—"

"Broccoli! I packed you three pizzas and a gallon of sweet tea, and you snacked on broccoli? What has gotten into you, boy?"

Dorp jiggled and broke into a gaping grin. His mother shuddered as she could clearly see bits of incriminating green stuck between his massive teeth. Vocharlian facepalmed as the jelly within Mrs. Splatowski began to boil. "Dorp, *mate*, tell your mum the truth."

Dorp's beady black eyeholes sparked a bit as he sighed. "Mom, it was just a little, and I smothered it with processed cheese, garlic salt, and bacon bits. We have an initiative at the office to corrupt a new health food each day. Next week there is a contest to see who can get the most calories into kale." He squeezed his mother's appendage, nearly causing a fresh puddle on the table. "I know how hard you work for us."

"I *know*, it's just after your brother—"

Vocharlian eyed the picture stuck to the fridge. Two hefty bags of flesh and a corpulent ooze surrounded an emaciated ivory-skinned demon with ribs sticking out of his sunken chest. A slight pall cast over the table, until Dorp gulped down a fistful of deep-fried ham with a butter coffee chaser. Once he belched heartily, his mother let out a flatulence of relief. "I'm so glad *one* of you is making smart choices. Anyway, I want to hear all about your days, you crazy kids."

Dorp, now working for the Bureau of Gluttony, began going on and on about all the recipes he disseminated into the upper realms. Vocharlian munched away on buttery flapjacks and his own bacon while the ever-attentive Mrs. Splatowski poured everyone double-rich cocoas with whipped cream. By the time Dorp got to showing off his new skill of bacon-weaving, a general ease fell over the table. However, just as

Vocharlian had settled back to undo his belt and enjoy his food-baby belly, mama ooze shifted his way.

"And how was your Monday, Vocharlian?"

"Well, it wasn't as exciting as donut burgers and bacon weaving. Envy is more of a slow burn. However, I did show someone who was struggling to keep fit a two-for-one burrito coupon."

Mrs. Splatowski quivered joyously. "I am so proud of you, son. You may be cursed with being skinny, but you are fighting the good fight against restraint. I'm sure your mama would be—"

"On that note," Dorp interjected. "We did have plans tonight, Mom."

Mrs. Splatowski raised a goopy brow. "Oh?"

"My cousin is working a double down in legal, and Dorp didn't want me to be alone, especially considering it would be the one-year anniversary of...you know..." Vocharlian trailed off, the green mist rolling out of his eye sockets so intensely that the end of the table lit up with a sinister glow. "Just need a distraction."

"And what kind of distraction are two handsome young demons going to get into while their responsible friend is away, *hmm*?"

"Oh Mom, it's Monday, there is new porn and we're probably just going to do some drugs and play video games."

"Might even put on one of my mum's films," Vocharlian added with an innocent smile. Mrs. Splatowski jiggled with delight.

"Oh, now that sounds like a fine time. I think I'll eat a gallon of ice cream and watch some pornography myself. Have fun you two!"

Vocharlian started to take his plate to the sink, but then remembered his manners and brushed the crumbs and residual grease onto the table for Mrs. Splatowski to absorb. He led his friend toward the fire escape and had to wait as his rotund companion struggled with each step. "Why did you have to rent the fifth-floor walkup again?" Dorp paused to vomit over the railing, much to the delight of the filth-eaters below. "You're welcome, guys!"

Vocharlian corrected, "You mean fifth-floor flyup."

Dorp laughed and smacked his best buddy on the back. "Yeah, well you don't have any wings—"

"*Yet*," Vocharlian declared as he whipped out his keys. "As soon as I've saved up enough—"

"Dude, you've been saying that for six months."

"It's not my fault they keep driving up the prices for the soul-forge." The pair entered the dark upstairs apartment, tripping and stumbling over the clutter until Vocharlian could stoke up the lights in his eye sockets enough to see the path to the sofa. Dorp chuckled again and plopped on the couch, causing the poor frame to groan in protest. Vocharlian sighed, flipped on the lights, and went diving for brewskies in his fridge. "No one can bloody afford any time in there because the posh bastards on top refuse to retire. That leaves us bumming scraps of silver while they live high and mighty in their towers."

"Hey, what about the fifteen minutes your mom got you for your birthday, hmm? It didn't give you wings and barely made a difference—"

"My horns, mate." Vocharlian pointed to the metallic spikes jutting from his forehead. Dorp crossed his arms over his burgeoning belly. The skinnier demon scoffed.

"They are not really any bigger, man."

"Bloody hell, mate! They're not *bigger*. They got *sharper*. They may not look like much, but these bad boys are prime stabbing machines."

"Take it from me, dude—size matters. Maybe you should have asked the soulforge keepers to enhance—"

"Don't be a wanker."

"I'm just saying. You're technically an incubus, and maybe if you played more to those natural strengths then *she* wouldn't have left you. I'm only saying it because I care."

Vocharlian slumped on the sofa and handed an ice-cold beer to his friend. Dorp clinked the glass in a half-hearted toast. "Cheer up, Charlie."

"I *hate* that nickname," Vocharlian growled.

"I know, that's why I use it. Now come on, there is a family orgy flick on Titillation TV, and I got a free sample of devil's lettuce from work. Let's chill out, and then maybe, just maybe, I've got something special for you." Dorp patted a small bulge along his side. The sparkles in Vocharlian's sockets shifted from green to a greedy gold.

"You don't say?" he asked, his accent suddenly a few classes higher than before.

"Told yah, I got the good stuff, but if we don't wait a little while, that nosy bastard downstairs will report us for a lack of noise violation. Let's crank it up!"

"I say, how about a bit of metal and some ultra-violence then? I'm rather sure that this new family picture—"

"Has actual members of your family? Yeah, *awkward*." Dorp shuffled to get controllers while Vocharlian blasted music to an acceptable ear-destroying volume and set up the TV.

"Time to swear like a peasant and kill without discrimination," Vocharlian added as they began an appropriate evening for two young demons.

After six rounds and a few blunts smoldering in the ashtray, Vocharlian leaned back and started staring hopelessly at the ceiling. Dorp took advantage of the lapse and made sure to gank his friend. He waved his chubby fingers in front of Vocharlian's face.

"Hey, dude, you aren't having another spell, are you?"

Vocharlian grunted and rubbed his face, the gold in his eyes now a festive mix of red and green. "Fuck off, it's not bloody slothalepsy every time I'm knackered!" The red flashed brighter, and his accent shifted again. "Mate, it was so fucking Leviathan snoring today!"

Dorp stared at him blankly. Vocharlian roared, "Boring, you Satan's hunt!"

Dorp stared blankly again.

"CUNT!" Vocharlian bellowed.

"B-but think of all the quality evil you did—"

Vocharlian took a few deep breaths and the fiery sparks faded back to the dim, Christmassy glow. "Yeah, more beer time," he said before escaping to the kitchen. He grabbed a whole six-pack for each of them, and a bag from the crisper. He then tossed a bag of baby carrots onto Dorp's lap. "Oy, I'm sorry, mate. Wrath slipped out for a bit."

The gluttony demon salivated as he flipped them over to see kale pesto dip sitting amid the luscious nuggets of fiber and vitamins. "Oh, baby. I can't believe you found this."

"Make sure to floss this time. If your mum finds another bit of green in your teeth, she is kicking my arse halfway to the Wrathlands, mate."

"Well, that's the closest your sorry ass is going to get to the Bureau of War, isn't it?"

"Wanker," Vocharlian said as he tried to snatch back the crudité. Dorp put on his best apologetic smile and yanked the bag back.

"Asshole," Dorp grumbled. He pointed to the controllers. "Oh, come on, you aren't still all mopey over getting rejected by the rage-bots, are you? Why would you want to be a perpetually pissed-off anger junkie bashing heads with the bros? I mean, those guys get mutilated on a regular basis...or worse."

"Yeah, but they get hazard pay, and let's face it, the birds down here, they go all gooey for the Wrath boys."

"You mean *she* would like a Wrath meathead. Oh man, you are still hung up on her and it's been a year. Damn boy, you're an incubus, just use your mojo and get laid already—"

"I'm not an incubus and you know it. My mum *was* a succubus, and my dad was—"

Dorp waved his hands frantically. He shushed Vocharlian by shoving a beer in his mouth. "Come on man, if you don't, *you know*, talk about it, no one will know. I mean you got lucky. You really favor your mother's side of the family. Don't rock the boat and you'll fit in."

Vocharlian shook his head. He gulped down his beer before explaining, "Dorp, I'm a Cambion and a Variegatus. There is no place in Hell where I really fit in. Ugh, let's just blow some shit up and eat some veggies."

After a few more rounds of battle royale, Dorp managed to chow down half the bag. Vocharlian zoned out to the rampant violence, red sparks beginning to flash deep within his sockets. His reactions sped up until he was able to lay waste to the entire rival squad with a well-timed flurry of virtual grenades. Dorp whistled appreciatively as they collected their sweet victory loot. He gave his buddy a sidelong glance and sighed at his half-eaten carrot. "You know, maybe you've got it all wrong, buddy. I mean, you might suck at most things, but at least you have a choice, and that's more than most of us get."

Vocharlian shrugged. Dorp pulled a vial out of his pocket and set it on the coffee table. "Also, you did a solid for me, and I got one for you. Just don't get caught with this again. Are you *sure* your cuz is out for the night?"

Vocharlian picked up the bottle gingerly. He licked his lips as he read the label. "Fucking Kruger has a chance to arse kiss with the best. No way he's coming back early. Is this—?"

"Pure, grade-A Nostalgia. The chefs distill it for stimulating recipe creation. I managed to swipe a dose while no one was looking. Who's da man?"

"Dorp is da bloody man." Vocharlian pulled up his PD3 and transferred a tidy sum to Dorp's account. "Of course, you're also the reason I'm too skint to afford more than five-minutes in the soulforge."

"We all have our vices." Dorp gobbled down the last bit of pesto on a carrot and then bared his teeth for his friend. Once he got the all-clear signal, he waddled toward the door. "I love you like a brother, dude, but I do *not* wanna be around while you hit that. You might want to wait for the weekend, you know, that is potent emotion, and you have work tomorrow."

"Come on, I made someone envious of a videogame achievement. What could be more pathetic than that? It's not like I've changed anything, and it's not like I made a difference."

Chapter 3

Worlds Collide

No frickin' way," Meg lamented as she stared at the news feed on her phone—a MyTube video of a server first kill of Voldara —The World Slayer. The smug digital faces of the Knights of Valhalla stood over the dragon's corpse. Meg narrowed her eyes at a pale, blue-skinned elf mage standing front and center with the tag "Vanth Mistweaver" over her head. Messages had already started appearing at the bottom. "*At least the Knights of Valhalla mage can land an ultimate.*"

Meg sunk into her seat. A drizzle had started outside, casting the suburban streets in a gray light. Her stomach rumbled as she saw a few fast-food signs on her way home. "No, I'm going to be better. I'm going to be—"

"*I'm giving your slot to Albert for DPS tonight. Go gear up, Zazzy, so maybe next time you won't blow it.*"

She swiped the text away, choking up even more. The rest of her ride faded into a haze. She staggered home from the bus stop and let the drizzle cool off her burning cheeks then groaned as she saw a pizza delivery peeling away. The smell of marinara and sausage overwhelmed her nostrils the moment she slipped into the vestibule. A tall blonde in glasses and a severe bun peered into the hallway. "Oh Meg, good to see you. Figured it was one of your game nights, so Dad and I got pizza."

"I'm not raiding tonight actually." Meg looked away and shuffled off her shoes. She plastered on her best smile. "But don't worry about me. I'll heat something up or pick the cheese off a slice."

"You okay, sweetie?" her mom asked, a trace of worry creeping into her voice. "Bad day?"

"Just a typical Monday. I'm exhausted, so I called out for tonight. I think I'm going to head up to my room and get an early night." Meg leaned and gave her mom a one-armed hug. Her mom raised a brow and reluctantly let her go.

"Well, if you're not gaming with your friends, we could do a movie or something. There's this one from *my* time that just came back to streaming called *Back to the Future*... Crap! I have to grade some papers first, but—"

"I'm fine," Meg protested again. She gave her mom one more hug and tried to make a quick escape to the upstairs. A man with a balding head waved distractedly as he futzed with his tablet on the couch, a golfing program both on his small screen and the TV. "Love you, Dad," she called before retreating to the stairs. She heard a mumbling, "Love you too," once she reached the landing.

Meg flopped on her bed. She watched the full video of the kill one more time, complete with the mage successfully dropping a meteor for the win. Then she blasted some tunes in her earbuds and half-napped, half-moped until her stomach couldn't take it anymore. She eyed the late hour and groaned. A coupon for a Tex-Mex place caught her eye, but as she scanned the website, she found it was already closed. "Worst Monday ever. Can't the universe even give me a taco salad?"

Her day ended how it had begun—with misery and toaster pastries. She tried once or twice to find the energy to log into her computer but ended up toying with her phone until she gave up the ghost and passed out. Sweat dripped from her forehead as the mix of sugar and stress percolated through her bloodstream. Meg limply pawed for her phone and put on the first recommended playlist she could find that had the words soothing tagged for it. In her blurry, glasses-free vision she swiped left on some sort of urgent update text and just let whatever wanted to run, run. Her phone screen flickered ominously then flashed green.

"*Listen to my words, let them fill your soul,*" Meg heard as she drifted off. "*Meg, listen to my words, let them fill your soul.*"

"Whatever," Meg mumbled as the song called "Magic Dance" settled in her subconscious.

Chapter 4

Recreational Emotions

W hatever," Vocharlian grumbled as he saw the content advisory on his PD3 screen. He dove into the privacy locked setting on his Fellnet browser, wading through popups and confirmations to get to his stash of videos so that he could cast them onto the screen on his wall. The projector spell flickered on the bare patch briefly until the words "Warning: Not suitable for demonic viewing" faded. While the content continued to load, Vocharlian spread a plush blanket over his bed of nails and retrieved a box from the hidden compartment in the base. He licked his lips as he pried it open to reveal a water pipe and various dime bags full of all manner of illicit substances. He rooted around until he found a golden powder. He grabbed another handful of shriveled leaves before darting through the living room mess to grab the kettle from the stove and hurried back just in time to pause his video in that perfect millisecond between that last bit of legalese and the title.

He shuddered as he filled both the pipe and a mug with boiling water, then took the vial from Dorp and one of his trusty tea-towels to bring the festivities in full bloom. The demon held his breath and ever so carefully dropped a few drops of the pure Nostalgia into the bubbling water. Silvery distilled emotion bubbled and frothed until the whole pipe filled with iridescent mist. Vocharlian worked quickly—tossing a towel on top of his bong while he measured the leaves into his cup. He let out his breath all at once as the aroma of pure English breakfast filled the air, and made one last run for the pantry, grabbing his hidden stash of boxed milk and sugar cubes from the recesses of a cabinet.

He fixed up his tea reverently. "I can do this," he whispered before shutting his door. A few wisps of the mist began slipping through the cloth on top, so he dove to his now cushy bed. Vocharlian cracked his neck, before tilting his head back as far as the armor-plating on his collar would allow. The bong trembled in his clawed hands and he slowly, ever so slowly, lifted the towel so that he could pour the thick vapors into his empty eye sockets. The towel got slapped over his face before he flopped onto his back and shivered. "Oh, heavens yes."

Moaning and groaning, he fumbled on the bed for his PD3. He managed to tap the screen with his talon, and the projection on his wall lit up once more. Warmth radiated from his face all the way down to his toes, and his silvery skin shifted to a peachy ivory. He licked his lips once more, catching the aroma of tea in the air.

Vocharlian reached toward the plate of dust. "Come back to me." The crumbs swirled as the mist rolled from the demons face all the way down to his fingertips. The vapor coalesced into a disk with the crumbs suspended within it. "I remember you."

The power of the pure Nostalgia transmuted the pinch of crumbs into an oatmeal biscuit slathered in milk chocolate. Vocharlian pulled away his mask to reveal a ghostly set of eyes to take in the glory of tea, a biscuit, and his forbidden programming. The Children's Workshop logo quickly faded to show off sunny days on a certain iconic street. "Now this makes up for a properly shite day."

He gingerly picked up his biscuit, marveling at the nooks and crannies before sniffing deeply. This time his toes curled in his boots. Vocharlian nibbled the edges so he could savor every moment. "Brilliant!"

The contraband TV show continued to happy people and bright-colored puppets living in harmony. The more the gentle music filled the air, the more blue-tinged the mist in Vocharlian's eyes became. "Oh, bollocks!" He bolted, flailing for the caffeine, but the slothalepsy hit before the Count could get to three. The young demon flopped onto his bed, biscuit in hand and a serene smile planted on his face.

"Vocharlian Milton Variegatus!"

Vocharlian lurched upright. His ocular sparks reignited a bright red as he saw the silhouette of bull horns. "Fuck, it's not what it looks like," he blurted out, biscuit crumbs spewing from his lips.

"Not what it looks like?" the bull-horned demon asked, stepping into the light. He pointed an accusatory claw toward the frozen image of a big yellow bird. "Lucifer's kittens, have you been eyeballing emotions...again?"

"Kruger—" Vocharlian trailed off as he knocked over the pipe by his side. He let out a pathetic hee-hee as the bigger, obsidian-skinned monster picked up Dorp's vial from the floor. He only needed a tiny sniff for his golden eye mist to burn bright enough to make Vocharlian cringe. "It's just a little recreational emotion, you Satan's hunt!"

"Recreational? *Recreational?* There is still an ounce in here of pure, unfiltered Melancholy—"

"Nostalgia."

"Excuse me?" Kruger raised one of his spiky brow ridges. Vocharlian shook his head and slowly pushed to his feet. The smaller cambion ended up staring right at his cousin's tie. He rolled his now greenish gaze upward and tried his best pensive look. Kruger remained dreadfully unamused.

"It's Nostalgia, not Melancholy, and if you'd ever felt a single real emotion in your life—"

"Enough! I promised your mother when you came to this city that I would keep you clean, and here you have enough sentiment secretions to be charged with intent to sell." Kruger paused to give a disappointed sneer. Vocharlian looked away. "Damn it, boy. Can't you just make it a single month—?"

"Look, it's been a rough patch, cuz. Come on, I was thinking about Lashma—"

The lights in Kruger's eyes swirled sarcastically. "Please, it's been almost a year. You can't possibly still be holding out hope. Get over her, man. She moved on and so should you. Now as much as it pains me to do, I have to turn you in. You need help."

"I'm a cambion. I have a medical card—"

"That was revoked after you abused it. With another offense—"

Vocharlian cracked his neck and narrowed his eye sockets into slits.

"Oy, Kruger, what do you want?" The larger demon rubbed the points of his prominent chin, until Vocharlian snapped, "You're a bloody lawyer, so let's make a deal."

Kruger smiled. He paced around his cousin's bed, kicking some of the loose armor and empty cans left strewn on the floor. He snapped his fingers, and the image of Big Bird vanished. He tucked the incriminating vial into a pouch before returning to stroke his chin a few more infuriating times. Vocharlian started tapping his feet.

Kruger's eye lights burned mischievously. "Well, I do have a pro bono shift at the Golgotha Bureau tomorrow—"

"But that's a shite assignment, *literally*!"

Kruger leaned in and licked his lips. "It's your choice: the Golgothans...or I call your mother."

Chapter 5

What Goes Around...

A nd another crappy day begins," Meg muttered as she plopped into her seat at work. By now she had memorized the number she was asked to dial. "Maybe I'll get Candy again."

Her Tuesday continued much as her Monday had, complete with saying the words, "Oh, yes, I want you to suck my cock," in a monotonous robot voice. At least today she had managed to make it to the office in time, remember a packed lunch, and otherwise make her dead-end job bearable. She even got the bonus of seeing some messages piled up begging her to come back to the guild raids since the other mages hadn't fared any better in their attempts against Voldara last night. "Yes, it is going to be a good night, Meg," she declared. "In fact, I'm going to treat myself to a burrito."

Meg finished her day by posting in her guild chat that she'd be on for raiding. She squealed with delight as she found the same playlist she had listened to last night, complete with the latest Princess Space tracks mixed with her other favorite dubstep bands. It quickened her pace and kept her company as she walked a few blocks to the nearest Poblano's to redeem her coupon, rather than take her usual T stop to get back home. She loaded up on spicy salsa, beans, and extra meat, complete with guacamole and a side of chips.

"No cheese please."

"Any queso?" the guy at the bar asked in a bored tone. Meg blinked at him incredulously.

"I'm lactose intolerant," she blurted in reply.

"Is that a no?"

Meg sighed. "No." She then grumbled, "Queso *is* cheese," before heading to the register. She smiled as the counter guy was immediately saddled with a group containing two vegans and a gluten intolerant, orders sure to drive him mental as the dinner rush started to pile into the queue. "Sucks to be you," she sang as she pranced her way to the next station over. She soon cringed as she noted her snarky schadenfreude. "Karma won't notice a teensy slip-up, right?"

The aroma of spices and greasy meat made her stomach growl, but she resisted the urge to dive in on the packed subway. Instead, she took a few moments to watch that server first video again and pay extra attention to Vanth and her fantastic mage skills.

By the time she reached her house, she tore into the lukewarm burrito like a starving tiger. Her mom had left a note that she was working late, and her dad texted that he was staying with Grandma to help her install a new garbage disposal. "Aww, yeah!" Meg flopped on the sectional and got the prime spot with both the ottoman and a TV tray for uninterrupted afterwork vegging. She ordered the smarthome speaker to play "Magic Dance" at club-level volume.

It was a traditional synthetic number, with an ethereal female voice mixed with a guy autotuned to sound like a sexy android. The chorus mixed with something that sounded like a harpsichord, and, of course, the beat was dropped at every opportunity. Meg semi-sang, semi-mouthed the ridiculous lyrics about the power of dance bringing magic back to the earth—in between bites of her tasty Tex-Mex. She put the song on repeat as the mix of rhythm and chili fire stimulated something deep within her soul. Unfortunately, it was at that very moment when she felt the first quakes in the depths of her bowels.

"Oh no," she gasped before making a mad dash for the toilet. "Colon karma!"

Chapter 6

Crappy Assignment

Welcome to the Golgothan Division. We are so glad to have you here after last week's attack," a churning blob-style demon made mostly of feces babbled as he extended his hand toward Vocharlian. A large bite had been taken out of its arm. "Filth-eaters, what can you do?"

"Anything to help the greater Fell," Vocharlian said weakly, refusing to shake the shit demon's hand. He clasped his hands in front of him and gave a respectful bow, careful not to breathe in as he dipped forward. "It's the duty of us all to keep the soul fires burning."

The blob's swirling black eyes lit up, and he folded forward as best he could. "Oh, you must be from an eastern tradition. So sorry. Yes, yes, the recent bouts of Listeria and E. Coli on the feeder plane have kept us super busy, but that attracts...you know."

Vocharlian flipped his hands over, allowing ten shiny obsidian claws to pop out of the tips. "I can handle a pack of filth-eaters, don't you worry, guv."

The shit demon seemed to nod. He then scratched his head. "I just worry since Master Kruger is so much bigger than you, and he has wings, and much, *much* bigger horns—"

Vocharlian grit his metallic teeth and snapped a claw against the tip of one of his modest imp horns. "Trust me, it's not the size, it's the sharpness. They can gore your enemies, never fear."

The turd monster made a gurgling "Hmm," scratched his wobbly chins, and pulled out a nugget of corn that seemed to be irritating him. He then motioned toward a stinky cave guarded by two large, red wrath demons—full-blooded Rakshasa judging by their fiery manes and impressive horns.

"Why do they need me?" The massive demons chuckled as they saw Vocharlian approach. They growled to each other in ancient Hindi, but Vocharlian didn't need a translator. He gave them both a snappy salute. "Let me guess, you're both too ginormous to fit into the shite cavern, hmm?"

The guard on the left snorted. He said something else derogatory, this time tossing in the word "cambion" just to get Vocharlian's goat. The shit demon stopped his shuffle and flipped his eye vortexes back toward Vocharlian.

"Oh, you're a...a..."

"Temp?" Vocharlian offered helpfully. He flicked the membranes across his eye sockets mimicking an innocent look. "*Oh,* you mean a cambion. That won't be a problem, will it?"

The shit demon quivered a bit. Vocharlian shrugged. "I get it, you already have a bunch of wrathtards out front, so you really don't need my rubbish—"

"Oh no, we are grateful for the help, and frankly, the greater demons won't deign to come in close enough to guard our back door! Needless to say, that's where we have all our unwelcome invaders as of late. It's simply that we have exposed soul conduits inside, and I had heard that cambions are not...strong enough to be close to such power."

Vocharlian tapped his fist to his breastplate, causing a series of protection runes to light up. "One step ahead of you, guv. My mum gave me a soulforged breastplate as a graduation present. It's resistant for up to three thousand chakras, and I doubt you get anywhere close to that even during a cholera outbreak. Am I right?"

The shit demon nodded. "Still, I would keep a distance from the walls. The conduits run around the entire perimeter."

Vocharlian eyed the sheer layers of filth clinging to every surface as he stepped inside. "Yeah, no worries, I'll avoid touching...*everything.*

Kruger told me I was here on lookout and patrol. Anything else I need to know?"

"Come, come," his guide said, motioning him deeper into the cave system. Vocharlian wrapped a handkerchief around his nose and mouth, crunching on the peppermint candy Kruger had given him in an act of mercy. He tried his best not to listen to the squidgy sounds his boots made, nor the occasional guano bombs that dropped from the ceiling. The corridor opened into a striking, enormous chamber with spiral paths of steppingstones surrounding a cesspool. In the center of this vat of muck, shining puddles of what looked like oil collected on the surface. A grand filter sucked these pockets of soul energy into a central pipe, ready to be carried off for processing into the main soulforge. A few smaller pipes diverted a fraction of the energy to workstations scattered in smaller pools, where festering blobs puttered away on workstations encased in scat-proof shielding. As a few of the inky droplets coalesced on the murk near Vocharlian, cries of pain echoed in his mind. The same cries emanated from the outlets at a nearby cubicle.

"Is this—?" Vocharlian started. His guide quivered excitedly again.

"We are a completely self-sufficient sub-processing station. As of the super spreader food-poisoning outbreak of this spring, we had more than enough energy to power ourselves *and* make our quota to the forge. We even got dispensation by Beelzebub himself to have our own lesser forge installed in the conference room. It is glorious. When it's bonus time, we can enhance ourselves without a line!"

"The shite demons have a soulforge," Vocharlian mouthed under his mask. "Fuck me." He half-tuned out many of the explanations of the glorious work the Golgothan Division created in service to Hell, focusing instead on the warren of rabbit-holes along one of the walls. Any one of them would be large enough to let a pesky, if not slightly suicidal, filth-eater in to interrupt the workday. He tried his best to look excited as he was taken on a tour. No sooner had they rounded the first bend of the central cesspool, when a critter with buck teeth and skeletal ears burst out of one of the openings. Vocharlian's guide gurgled and swooned, while Vocharlian roared as his eye sockets flickered from green to furious red.

The creature hopped onto the nearest desk, sniffing deeply the nutty smell of its favorite prey while the wage slave fainted into a puddle of poop. Vocharlian's claws snapped to the right, slicing the minion's neck so that he could get a clean grab at the spine. One crack later and the filth-eater disintegrated into a pile of sparkling black dust. His guide's eye sockets widened. "You'll do," the shit demon squeaked as fresh methane wafted in the air.

A round of wet, slappy, clapping sounds filled the office cesspool. Vocharlian shoved his filthy fist in the air, and then rampaged against more skittering from the shadows. "Die, you little Lilith tits!" His next few hours consisted of a surprisingly satisfying game of Whack-A-Filth-Eater. He also discovered one of the more feminine displaying blobs rolling her eye sockets his way as he darted about the room. "Bloody shame I'm not a blobby-banger. Could get lucky if I wanted."

After he managed to shatter enough critters to send a strong message, he had a bit of free time to wander around the complex. His guide had been taken to supervise some Listeria outbreak in Boston, so Vocharlian decided to let his aspect shift from the flames of wrath to a decidedly different fire. An alluring violet mist rolled over his cheeks as he sauntered toward the female blob barely hiding her trembling at his approach. "Hello there, care to show a stranger around?"

"Marry me," she sputtered as flecks of violet reflected in her eyeholes. Vocharlian cringed under his mask but tried to increase the smolder in his eyes. The Golgothan bubbled with embarrassment. "I mean, I'm Shishi. I'm a cross-contamination specialist here. Thank you so much for saving us back there. I'm...too young to be eaten."

"And too lovely," Vocharlian said, holding back a gag. "You don't have a break soon, do you? I was hoping to finish my tour...maybe see the conference room."

Shishi couldn't lock her computer and slosh out of her cubicle fast enough. Vocharlian noticed that she had put in the effort to shift her gelatinous body into a classically jiggly feminine form. She even somehow had managed to make her shit not stink as she sashayed ahead. Vocharlian raised one of his brow ridges as he watched the junk in the trunk wiggle wonderfully. "Remember that lust hits both ways, you Muppet."

All his distraction faded as Shishi regurgitated her PD3 out of her midsection. She swiped it over a mini portal, and a mighty portcullis dropped into the floor so they could shuffle through to the back part of the office. A filth-eater streaked toward the helpless Shishi, but Vocharlian dispatched it easily as his eyes turned a fuchsia color before flickering back to violet. His companion gasped.

"You...you're a shifter, aren't you?" Shishi all but drooled. Vocharlian gave her a coy glance and shuffled his feet.

"We call it Variegatus in Succubi-Incubi circles."

"Can you do gluttony too? If you can be gluttonous, I'm gonna talk to my daddy—"

"Sure," Vocharlian said, distracted as he saw a burning glow in the heart of a surprisingly clean conference table. In fact, the entire room remained divorced from the filthy surroundings—cleaned and scrubbed to the point where Vocharlian could see his reflection in the obsidian. At the heart of it all, a mix of chartreuse and black flame crackled, forming a pillar between the arcane runes etched in the ceiling, and the ornate brazier on the floor. Images of the patron archdemon of gluttony, Beelzebub, filled the walls, and four statues of his incarnations danced around the base of the forge. "Lucifer's kittens, it's really here and I've never even heard of it."

The closer he stepped, the more a rumbling started stirring in the depths of his belly. He salivated at the pure Fell energy coursing through the room. He looked down, the runes on his breastplate lit up in his defense, and as he looked up again, black swirls began to overtake his eye sockets. "I'm hungry," he growled in a brand-new voice.

"Never going to eat again," Meg moaned as she held onto the porcelain throne for dear life. She tried her best to vomit, but the tank was empty, and the dry heaves refused to stop. "I'll do anything to make this stop."

"Betrayed by the burrito," she moaned. "Magic Dance" by Princess Space continued to blare on repeat from the living room, Meg's only consolation as her insides twisted. She rolled her eyes heavenward in this momentary respite from projectile puking. "Please just make this stop."

"Make it stop!" Vocharlian roared, clutching his head. Shishi vibrated in time to the terrible clang of synthesizers suddenly filling the conference room in Hell. Vocharlian's eyes flashed an unending rainbow of colors— cycling between red, blue, violet, and green with rare blips of black and gold to change it up. Although the gelatinous lady quivered, she stared blankly at her more solid companion. "Make *what* stop?" she asked.

Vocharlian slammed his fists into his eye sockets, rattling the gray matter in his skull. Shishi slithered toward him, getting slightly closer to the central soulflame. The cambion, however, thrashed violently as the beat dropped. "Dear lord, is this dubstep?" he whined. No sooner had his mouth opened than a rush of lyrics poured out of him.

> I get on with life as a demon,
>> Flames kindle my soul.
>> I like my rage and battle.
>> And magic fills another hole.
>> However, when I start to daydream,
>> My mind turns straight to dance.

"Um, excuse me?" Shishi's eye-blobs swirled with confused black sparkles. Vocharlian hissed and spit like a cat fighting with a hairball. He dropped to one knee as his guide shambled his way. Before she could reach him, a klaxon sounded as a double-reinforced portcullis raised over the conference room door. Shishi gasped. She pointed a dripping digit toward Vocharlian's glowing armor, before the pure Fellfire of the soulforge erupted from the central brazier.

"No!" Vocharlian's eye-lights shifted to red, and he used all his wrath-given speed to snatch one of the conference chairs and scoop the blob up as best he could. Unfortunately, in his gallantry to slide Shishi to safety, he took a step too close to the inferno and black and green flame poured straight into his back. "Oh...bollocks," he managed to spit out before the conflagration consumed him.

"This is not lactose. This isn't even food poisoning. It's an alien, I'm sure of it," Meg moaned, leaning against her bathroom tile. She turned, pressing her cheek into the cold porcelain, all while clutching her favorite pink towel to her heaving chest. The song, still on repeat, reached the point where the female singer in Princess Space started on the chorus for the umpteenth time this evening. Meg hummed softly, half-singing, half-whispering the words she had totally memorized while being stuck in the john.

> *Inspiration becomes a thought,*
> *Thoughts go into motion.*
> *Motion becomes a rhythm.*
> *Rhythm begets emotion,*
> *Emotion turns to song.*
> *The song invokes a spell...*
> *(And then the deed is done.)*

She traced her finger along the grout, muttering her thanks that it'd been recently cleaned and redone. A few magenta sparks flicked off Meg's chipped fingernail. She paused, shaking her head at the phantasm. Still, she couldn't resist tracing her finger in a little circle on the wall. Meg gasped, a circle of fuchsia light forming on the running-bond. "Oh boy, I'm hallucinating. This is not good."

The circle began to spin before the whole bathroom tilted on its axis. Light shot from her portal to the shower enclosure. The bathtub filled with chartreuse flames, and a shadowy hand grabbed her shower curtain. Meg couldn't scream. She couldn't even breathe as claws slapped against plastic. "Oh...my...G—"

"*Oy, is someone asking for help?*" A British-sounding voice echoed in her brain. Meg responded the only way she could—by passing out.

Episode Two

Inner Demons

Chapter 7

Once Upon a Time

"Aren't you lonely, Meg?" her father asked gently as she kicked her feet over the edge of the swing. The sun warmed her skin as the trees swayed around the playground. "I'm never alone, Daddy," tiny Meg replied.

"Okay, bunny. You want a push, or should I go back to my coffee?"

"I'm fi-ne!" The moment her dad walked away, little Meg giggled and looked to the swing next to her. A boy in a patchwork hoodie raised a finger to his lips. No one else at the park seemed to take any notice of him, even with his technicolor dream-coat and neon Doc Martins. "So, Mish-gan, what are we going to play today?"

The boy kept his face covered, but as he scratched his chin thoughtfully, he did reveal equally bright painted nails. "Today, Meggle-Peggle, I'm going to tell you a story about the Land of Onions."

"But I don't like onions." She stuck out her lip in a furious pout.

"I know, kiddo, but onions have layers, and believe me, as you peel them away, you're gonna cry..."

Meg moaned and sniffed as she felt a tickle against the side of her nose. Her lashes fluttered open to reveal nothing more threatening than the tip of her loofa. Meg reached for her glasses that had fallen onto her security towel. "Just a bad dream?"

"*Guess again, luv.*"

Meg's blood ran cold as she saw a blurry, shadowy hand holding the other end of her exfoliator. She pushed her glasses up her nose, but the arm remained fuzzy, even as the rest of the room came into focus. In her scramble to get to her feet, she ended up bonking her head against the towel rack, sending the world spinning once more. A fresh wave of nausea rushed through her. "Oh my God, I'm having a nervous breakdown, or I hit my head when I was sick—"

"*Or you summoned a brilliant servitor from a Hell dimension to do your bidding. That is a possibility.*"

"That's imposs—that's imposs—"

"*Come now, pull yourself together,*" the shadowy monster projected. "*We haven't got much time.*"

"Time?"

"*You are familiar with the concept of time, are you not?*"

Meg stared at the arm, dumbstruck. "Do you mean in a more theoretical sense or a practical one?" she asked, seemingly forgetting for a moment that she was speaking to an extraplanar entity in her bathtub. "Is there some sort of timer I don't realize?"

"*Yes...and no,*" the voice in her head offered unhelpfully. "*More like reality is a bitch, and she likes to slap your arse hard when you fuck with her—*"

"Do you have to use that language?"

"*I thought I was projecting the Queen's English.*"

"No, I mean, do you have to be so vulgar? I don't like it."

The shadow in her shower stall slapped its forehead with a twisted palm. With this shift, Meg could just see a pair of horns jutting from the beast's head. Her hands shook, but she managed to drag her weak body toward the bathroom door.

"*As much as I would love to get out of here and for the love of all things unholy shut off the damned dubstep! I am afraid that reality isn't going to move on this one, darling.*"

Meg rattled the knob, but no matter how hard she tugged against the door, it refused to budge. "Did you do this?" She shook her head rapidly. "No, if that thing did it..."

"*I would soundproof this room or throw your stereo out the bloody window!*" the demon finished for her.

Meg pounded on the paneling a few times. "Mom! Dad! Can anybody hear me?" She banged again, but the only response was a rousing chorus of "Magic Dance." The monster groaned from his hiding hole. "*Not again.*"

"Anybody? I need help." Unfortunately, the exertion reignited the flames of nausea, and Meg barely had enough time to heave a bit of spittle into the toilet. "I've hit my head, or I'm unconscious from dehydration—"

"*Or the beat was dropped one too many times.*"

"What *is* your issue with dubstep, really?" Meg snapped as she rolled back onto her security towel. "Oh God, why can't I stop throwing up?"

"*Food poisoning, perhaps? That might also be the answer to how dubstep came to be, now that I ponder it further.*" He made a retching noise with a distinctly metallic timbre and clang at the end. "*Those synthesizers must have recorded me after a particularly rough evening with Dorp.*" It was Meg's turn to retch this time. "*Like I said, I can help you.*"

"Then help me!"

"*Well, there is a price...demon and all that.*" The hand reached around the curtain once more. This time it contained a rather innocuous-looking binder stuffed full of old-school printouts. A sticker on the front read, "Contracts and Legal—Greed Division." Meg's eyes widened.

"I am seriously messed up in my own mind. I've played too many video games." She grabbed her side again. Fresh pain tore through her guts.

"*This isn't a game. You tore a hole in reality and dragged a poor, helpless creature out of his native environment—*"

"Are you okay?" she asked reflexively, smacking her forehead immediately afterward. "How crazy am I?"

"*Well, if you're already mad, then you might as well go all the way. Sign on the dotted line and I can make all your troubles go poof.*"

Meg paused and rolled the demon's words around in her head. She inched toward the binder splayed on her bathmat, reaching her fingers to poke at the fake leather. She jerked back as she touched a solid edge. "Tactile sensations...in my dreams. How bad did I hit my head?"

The walls to the bathroom shuddered, as if a train passed by. Meg lurched but became distracted from her pain by a yelp from beyond the curtain. The shadows swirling around the talons flickered and she could see that the actual nails were dark yet translucent like obsidian. The flesh surrounding those talons shone against the white tile—a mix of silver and gunmetal stripes. Then as soon as it had disappeared, the haze reformed, turning the demon into a blur in the corner of her vision. Meg poked the paperwork again.

"It's not going to bite, luv. Just look. I know you're curious."

"This is ridiculous."

"If it's a dream, what's the harm in looking?"

"Fair point," Meg muttered as she snatched the contract and dragged it to her haven by the toilet. Despite the strangeness of the creature that provided it, the document would look at home in any office file room, tucked away with old white papers and some procedural manuals drafted by the ghost of employees' past. The paper curled at the corners. Meg furrowed her brow as she noted streaks and fades from the printer. "Well, it's not in blood. I guess that's something." She snagged her glasses off the tile and began studying the mix of Latin and English. The demon snorted behind the curtain.

"'A contract to bind one human soul with a denizen of the Fell,'" Meg read softly, scanning the paragraphs. She squinted to see fine print mixed amid regular text. "'For a term of ten years, the Fell servant swears fealty and grants boons appropriate to his source and station...'" Meg cocked her head. "What does this even mean?"

"The short, short version?"

Meg shook her head. "No, I'm not going to TL; DR a document that makes references to my immortal soul, thank you very much!" She reached a hand into the vanity and pulled out one of her mother's many makeup bags, grabbing a couple of eyeliners to make notes. She began annotating and questioning each paragraph. Her scanning grew faster and more furious as the initial pages devolved into a bodged-together mix of standard legalese and clip-art infographics. She did linger on one that looked rather like the instructions for putting a soul back into an empty vessel, but in the same style as the instructions for her nightstand. "Is there really an IKEA in Hell?" Meg mused.

The bathroom shuddered again. The creature in the bathtub nearly pulled the curtain off the rings. *"Damn it, woman! Reality is about to dish out a pimp slap, and the fucking chorus is on...again. Can we sign first and read later? It's like the terms and conditions on the internet. No one reads those, and everyone is bloody fine."*

Meg shook her head, still reading, and picked up the pace. The more she scanned, the more she became aware of a new light source in the room. She dared to peek in the mirror and gasped as her irises glowed as bright pink as a strip club sign. "Yeah, I've totally lost it." Still, she returned to her reading project with renewed fury. The next page made her cheeks quickly match her eyes. "Demon, why is there porn in a contract?"

"Porn?" The creature rolled to one edge of the tub and twitched a bit, hissing something in an unfamiliar language as he made frantic gesticulations. Meg cocked her head at the explicit images of a creature with horns trying out various positions with a girl on a bed. "Oh, that's not right," as she saw it continued for the next six pages and started involving common household objects. "That is not even humanly possible unless you are double jointed."

"I am going to kill Kruger," echoed in Meg's mind, while the creature hissed something unintelligible and serpent-like.

"Freddy Krueger?" Meg mouthed as she read the caption for all the enticing imagery. "Ways to conceive a new soul to pay the master in lieu of the traditional sacrifice." That was enough of an image to send her diving for the porcelain throne again, and the world began to spin.

"Why am I the only one who can see you, Mish-gan?" Little Meg asked as she put down her bright purple crayon. "Is that because you're imaginary?"

Her companion laughed. His patchwork hood covered most of his face, but his smile still shone through as bright as the sun streaming into the playroom. "Very clever, Meggle-Peggle. Maybe I am." He leaned in and whispered in a conspiratorial tone, "Or *maybe*, you're just the only one who can see me because you're a special little girl."

"Mommy says I'm spe-shul." She wriggled her nose and gnawed on her lip before grabbing a turquoise crayon to add an accent to the arm on her piece of paper. "She thinks I should be working on my reading, but I haven't finished Goop yet."

"Oh, he's coming along nicely. Is he one of your other friends?" Mish-gan asked. Meg nodded emphatically. She added a few more flourishes before turning her sketchbook around to show off a squiggly squid with bright blue spots. Mish-gan gave her two big thumbs-up. "I hope you get to meet him too, and maybe I'll let you meet my puppy."

She shook her head. "No silly, I'm allergic, and Mommy and Daddy wouldn't want a puppy. He'll go poo poos on the floor."

"That he would. Listen, Meggle-Peggle, I want you to remember something for me. Can you do that?"

She nodded, set her crayons down, and folded her hands dutifully in her lap. His voice broke a little and he looked away. "It's funny, we don't usually understand the importance of things when we first experience it. That's what we have memories for, Meggle-Peggle. One day you're going to come back here, to this time and this place, and you are going to remember what I said, because if you don't, you will never understand how wonderful this universe can be."

"Should I write it down?" Meg gulped and picked up a pencil.

"Meggie! Time for lunch," her father called from the hall. Mish-gan flickered in and out of existence. The little girl reached for him, but her hand passed right through his arm.

"You're not really-real!"

"I'm as real as you believe I am, Meggle-Peggle, but I won't be able to stay with you forever. You have to grow up, and the rules don't like it when grown-ups keep their imaginary friends—"

"But you're my best friend!"

"That's what you need to remember."

"Always. You're *always* gonna be here!"

"Meg, did you say something?" Her dad asked from just beyond the door this time. Mish-gan flickered again. He leaned in and waved his hand through hers.

"Friends show up where you least expect them. If you take a chance, then you'll never be alone again. I know it, you know it, but I hope when the time is right, you'll remember what I said." He tilted his head. "Then again, I think if I'm here, you've already remembered someday...not too long from now."

"Huh?" Meg said, raising a brow over her pink glasses. "I remember it...in the future?"

"You already have..."

Chapter 8

Fine Print

Meg rubbed her eyes under her glasses. "Wow, I remember way more Latin than I thought, and to think, I burned out in contract law..." A tremor shook the room again, shaking Meg out of her trance. "How long have I been here...and is this really happening?"

"*Bloody hell, judging by the number of times I've heard this fucking song, it's probably the apocalypse by now.*"

Meg leafed back to the first page of the contract. "You expect me to forfeit my soul, for help with food poisoning and some sort of service for ten whole years? No thank you, my insurance isn't that bad, and frankly, you're a demon and I think I like my soul."

"*Oh, come on, do you really ever use it, luv? You'd be surprised how many people have gotten by just fine without one.*"

"How many then?"

The clawed hand slapped against the curtain. "*Enough that there is a form letter for a contract—*"

"But has anyone ever used it?"

"*Do you always ask so many questions, woman?*"

"This puts my immortal soul at risk. *Of course,* I have questions! Yesterday I wasn't sure the soul was real and today a demon is trying to bargain for it. It's a heck of a lot to take in."

"*How do you think I feel? There I was minding my own business, and you ripped me out of my home. Don't you think the least you can do is help me out by signing on the dotted line, so I can stay a while? Come on, you get to share in my brilliant demonic powers, and I have to be your servant so long as you feed me and shelter me. It's a good deal. It's not like you lose your soul instantly, it's just that the energy of it gets funneled to my homeland when you die, and you aren't even using it anymore. It's recycling at its finest!*"

"Only I would have a nervous breakdown and create a logical, British demon in my toilet. I'm that far gone. All I wanted was a burrito—"

"*You were the burrito?*"

"Wait...what?"

"*Nothing!*" This time the voice in her head had a sing-song tone and she could just hear a little whistle from behind the curtain, followed by some guttural muttering. "*You know you get a magic boost, too. Now, before you say the obvious 'magic isn't real' codswallop, bear in mind that you are having this conversation in your mind with a demon that you've summoned.*"

Meg scanned the contract again. "Why is this happen—?" She stopped as the room shifted violently. One of the corners near the vent shimmered and bent in a way inconsistent with the other molding.

"*Reality check, literally. The universe doesn't like creatures like me in places like this, so you can either tether me to you and to this world or it's going to crush us both for being uppity. Unless you know a better way, you've got a contract to sign.*"

"Can't you just go away?" Meg cried as the world shuddered. "Go back to whatever Hell dimension you came from!"

For a moment there was silence. The shadows swirled a little more. Meg held her breath. She choked back a fresh wave of nausea and continued to pray under her breath, "Just make this nightmare end."

"*Please,*" the voice whispered in her ear.

"What was that?"

"*P-please, please don't send me back...Meg.*"

"You know my name? How do you know my name?"

"*The guy at the junction...the nexus between worlds, he's the one that told me to get a contract and do whatever it takes to come here. He wanted me to help you, and I need this. The journey left me knackered. I don't know if I can make it back. Read the contract, carefully. It's not that you must provide your soul—you have to pay the contract off with a soul. It can be yours, one you create, or one you conquer—*

"Conquer? Really? The closest I come to any conquering is getting all my dailies done in *Eternaquest*! This is insanity, pure and simple. There is nothing you can say or do that could convince me that I should put my soul at risk—"

"If you sign a contract with me, you'll never be alone, and together we can see all the layers of reality. It's like one big old onion—"

"The onion realm?"

"I know...stupid analogy, but it's what the wanker said."

Meg picked up the contract once more, flipping through to the terms and termination clauses. "Okay, demon, does this contract allow redlining?"

"You can put all the red lines you want, I don't care. Just sign the damn thing."

"Let me...let me see you first."

The corner of the room contracted a bit. Meg's heart raced, but she managed to drag herself to her feet and steady against the towel bar. She let the tile chill her cheek once more. A wheezy sigh echoed from beyond the curtain. *"You want it bit by bit, or like ripping off a plaster?"*

Meg took a deep breath. "I'm not sure exactly what you said, but I get the gist." She grabbed the edge of her shower curtain firmly in both hands. The spotted plastic trembled a little. Her belly cramped, sending spasms all the way down her legs. Still, she held fast. "Just do it, Meg," she muttered before ripping the barrier aside. Her jaw dropped.

The gaping-mawed creature hissed, spraying black spittle from his metallic teeth. Without the protection and bulk of swirling shadows, Meg could clearly make out chicken arms and ribs poking out from under a charred breastplate. Soggy flaps of flesh flopped over his bony shoulders. *"Not quite what you expected, hmm?"*

Meg zeroed in on an oozing gash on the side of his stomach. "Oh, you poor thing!" She cast aside her own discomfort and dove for ace bandages and a bottle of hydrogen peroxide under the vanity. "Can demons get infections?"

The creature cocked his head, and a mess of silver and black hair fell over the empty sockets that glowed a mix of blue and purple. *"They don't like you leaving, and if I return emptyhanded, the hellhounds finish the job, luv."*

"Did I...really do this to you?" The song launched into another chorus, and for a moment the demon's sockets flashed red. "And you *really* hate this song, don't you?" The monster nodded. Meg turned to the contract. "So, in theory, could you conquer some sort of really bad soul and use it to pay off this contract, like a serial killer or something like that?"

"Well, not to be stereotypical, but this is Hell and there's definitely a preferred type of soul energy there. I'm fine binding a rampant pedophile or dubstep per—"

"There is nothing wrong with dubstep!" Meg snapped. The force of her words sent a shockwave ricocheting around them. Toothpaste and floss clattered to the floor. Meg whipped around just in time to dry heave over the toilet.

"So...if I lay off the dubstep hate, will you sign the contract and save my life, or am I utterly fucked?"

Episode Three

Literal Demons

Chapter 9

Three Hours and Thirteen Dimensions Prior

F uck me," Vocharlian growled as he landed hard on a pile of bones. Scorch marks covered every exposed inch of flesh, giving him the appearance of tiger stripes along his arms. The runes on his breastplate glowed brilliant Fellfire green.

"Fresh meat, fresh meat comes..." a sinister voice snarled from the shadows. Vocharlian snapped out his claws, red mist rolling out of his eye sockets as he scanned the edges of whatever refuse pit the soulforge had catapulted him into. Glowing red dots greeted him from every pool of darkness.

"Mammon's swell." One of the walls of the pit shuddered and stumbled to life, a towering behemoth of pure stone. Vocharlian snarled and scrambled into the mess of demon remains. Unfortunately, something heavy, limp, and quite attached to his back caught on a rogue femur. "What the...?"

Despite the insanity unfolding around him, he had to reach over his shoulder and feel the new spiky protrusion jutting between his scapula and spine. He felt the scales still covered in slime and the tips of new talons, from which draped a sheet of bloodied skin. A change in the cavern breeze made the demon shudder and brand-new parts of him stiffen. "Now, *really*? Fuck, I have to grow wings *now*!"

The mass of rocks pivoted in the center, rotating to show off a mouth full of craggy teeth—teeth that dripped with half-consumed creatures. A few cried for help as they saw Vocharlian tumbling for his life. This monster oozed an inky fluid from a single socket, revealing to Vocharlian just what sort of gluttonous fiend was after his scorched backside.

"Fressssssh meaaaaaaaaaaaaaaaaaaaaaaaat," echoed throughout the pit.

"I'm a toothpick. Not worth your time." Vocharlian dove over a bony mess so he could land on a relatively cushy puddle of slime. Freshly lubed, he used his saggy starter wings to surf into the shadows, deciding to take his chances with the red-eyed demons lurking there, rather than the granite goliath. Goat-like critters with rabbit hindquarters scattered as he crashed into one of their hidey-holes. Vocharlian flipped the bird to the giant, then squeezed into a cave.

"MEAT!!!" The walls thundered, and detritus poured over Vocharlian. He shimmied and wedged himself deeper, into a space too tight for a titan. A light shone beyond one more bend, so he took a dive for the source. The jagged edge tore into his burned flesh just under his armor. "Bloody hell, shit, fuck, bollocks, Satan's hunt! Yeeeeeeeeeeouch!"

"Wow, that is an impressive grasp of the English language for someone from Hell Prime."

Vocharlian whipped around so his back was to the wall, flipping his claws out on one hand while grabbing his side with the other. The light source bobbled and turned his way, only allowing him to see an amorphous shadow drifting around the center of a perfectly round room. The young demon squinted and could just make out some primitive etchings interspersed with obsidian daggers jutting from all sides. He snarled, but the creature behind the light merely chuckled in return.

"Now, now, Vocharlian Variegatus, there is no need for you to hiss at me. I am here to help you. Come, you've made it out of your home dimension and survived a Fell cyclops, let's not make the day worse."

"Who the Heaven *are* you? How do you know—?"

Vocharlian could barely make out the shadow of a raised hand. "All in good time. Names have power, and you'd be wise to keep yours to yourself."

"But you know—"

"Precisely," the stranger said. "Now I want you to roll that thought around for a moment, take a deep breath, and retract those claws, tiger. You are in no shape to tangle with me right now. Easy...*easy.*"

The light in Vocharlian's eyes faded from red to a gentle, calming blue. Despite his best efforts, he couldn't quite hold back a yawn. "Not now, damn it," he got out just before the haze of his slothalepsy hit him like a ton of bricks. "Well...shit."

"Heya, Vocharlian, my friend, now I don't want to alarm you, but you might want to wake up. You were singing in your sleep, and judging by the language, I don't think it was on the local Top 40."

"Ugh." Vocharlian rolled to his side, wincing as fresh pain stabbed through his ribcage. He gritted his teeth as the membrane peeled back from his sockets and he still found only darkness. A gentle grasp eased him into a sitting position. It was at this moment that he realized not only were his eye sockets bound, but his hands were clamped together in what felt like chains. He struggled for a moment but gave up as he felt the skin quickly rubbing from his wrists.

"Easy, Tiger. I can't heal you if you continue to struggle."

A warm sensation soaked into Vocharlian's side. "What're you doing?" The demon gnashed his teeth a few times in random directions. He stopped as the warmth spread further into his core. His flesh and skin knitted together with a slurping sound. "Okay, keep doing whatever you're doing. I'm all tingly, so tingly."

"I have access to more abilities in a place like this. It's a realm between realms, a garbage depot if you will, where there isn't enough singular consciousness to tell me what I can and cannot do. You could do well here, Vocharlian, if you could find a source of soul energy to sustain you."

With that, Vocharlian's stomach growled. The warmth continued from his side, but a cold, sinking sensation remained in his belly. The stranger helped him lean against stone, now a singularly uncomfortable experience with freshly grown lumps of flesh along his spine. Something soft was wedged under his back, and the straps on his breastplate were loosened so he could breathe better.

"You are far from home, Tiger." Vocharlian cocked his head as the words rolled around. The stranger continued. "Yes, I am speaking English. Don't worry, your secret is safe with me, but it *is* your secret that makes you uniquely able to help me with a cause near and dear to my heart, Vocharlian. Now, you received quite a blast of pure Fellfire when you entered my portal, and that will sustain a demon of your size for one, maybe two days, but the farther you are from the source—"

"The faster I'll weaken. I'm not a complete cockwomble. Wait, did you say, *your* portal? Did you honestly open a portal to Hell *on purpose?* What kind of Muppet are you, outlander?"

Laughter echoed in Vocharlian's ears. "I like you, Tiger. Now the simple answer to your question, is no, I didn't really open a portal to Hell Prime, but then again, I kinda did."

Vocharlian growled, both from his mouth and his aching stomach. "Piss off, I'm in no mood for games."

"*Really?* Says the demon who just gave sass to a cyclops? I don't buy it. Look, I can't *technically* start a conduit myself, but I can ride them, and extend them once they get going. Ripping open a portal is advanced chaos magic, but sometimes if a person is motivated enough and they have that rare ability to generate mana-sparks, then bingo, a tear opens. Now most schmucks have absolutely no idea what to do next, so I just do what any self-respecting warlock would do and borrow that tear."

"*You mean steal it.*"

"Ohh, that sounds far more terrifying in Fell Enochian, my friend. Yes, I speak that, too. I had the Babel Curse cast on me a few years back. Believe me, there is nothing worse than being able to understand everything that is said to you. Hmm, I'm guessing that you've had the same mental manhandling."

Vocharlian remained silent, his face pressed against the wall. The stranger's footsteps ebbed and flowed throughout the room. "Listen, I'm here to help. I stole, as you so colorfully put it, a portal and shot it far past the outer Hells where the nasty savages live on the off chance of going the distance. Your aura tells me that I succeeded in summoning a higher demon and successfully transporting him to the outer rim. If you have the will, Vocharlian Variegatus, I can send you to the place you want to go most of all. I can send you to an Earth."

"There is only one Earth, outlander," Vocharlian muttered. He could practically hear the stranger rolling his eyes as he sighed.

"There are as many possible Earths as there are layers to reality, Tiger. My own dimension is long gone—swept away in an eternal Ice Age with a dying sun. However, there are as many realities as choices exist, and countless versions collapse harmlessly upon one another at any given moment. Indeed, it's only at a moment of observation that any given reality survives. The tragedy is that those within it, they have no idea which path they're on until time passes them by. Of course, then the choices are set, and it is too late."

"You're mad as a box of frogs, mate."

"That I am," the stranger agreed. "But I'm also your only hope. What will it be?"

"I could feast on you, arsehole!" Vocharlian chomped in the direction of the voice, but without his wrathful strength, he could barely pull away from the wall. Laughter echoed around him.

"Tempting. Yes, a warlock like me would sustain you for weeks, but then the hunger would return, and all you'd have are Hell-rats and scraps. It's not a life. It's...desperate distraction. I want you to have more."

"Why?"

"Because it serves me. Because there is still an Earth where something I care about exists and because, frankly, you're desperate enough to do what I need done."

Vocharlian slumped. "That was surprisingly honest...I think. Shall we cut the shite and you tell me *exactly* what you want?"

"I want to send you back to Hell, and then you have two hours and twenty-seven minutes to complete my task. Know anyone who can draft contracts?"

Chapter 10

Two Hours and Sixteen Dimensions Prior

This is so bloody crazy," Vocharlian whispered as he flattened against his entryway wall, constantly alternating eyeing the clock in the kitchen and the smoldering bundle in his hand. "Oh, for fuck's sake, Kruger, please don't be brownnosing tonight."

He jumped at the vibration under his breastplate and immediately smacked his forehead. "You're a bloody Muppet, Vocharlian. You forgot you have a fucking PD3." He whipped the tiny box out of its hiding hole and his eye sockets widened at the flood of notifications. "I really was out of dimension, wasn't I?"

He didn't bother wading through the alerts and instead hit the speed dial for "Legal Arsehole and Guardian." Kruger answered before the first ring finished.

"Vocharlian, is it you? Is it really you?"

"Is that...concern, Kruger? I've only been gone—"

"What the Heaven did you do at the Golgothan Bureau, you little runt? They're currently investigating a workplace obliteration. Do you have any idea how much paperwork that is?"

"For once can you shit...err *shut* your judgmental piehole and listen to me? Where are you?"

Vocharlian was answered by the key turning in the front door. "Almost—" Both Kruger's jaw and his briefcase dropped as he saw a scorched, emaciated form crouched against the wall. Vocharlian lifted one of his limp wings and gave a sheepish smile.

"Surprise!"

"Y-you...you're not dead!"

"And you're the one who got into law school, *really?*" Vocharlian dragged himself to his feet, his eyes empty and barely flickering green. "I've only got two hours left—"

Kruger shook his head and recoiled. "You goddamn, lying little prick! Your mother—" He charged and took a flurry of swings at the smaller demon. "You broke into a soulforge, stole Golgathan energy, and then fucked off and left your whole family..." He trailed off as he saw the dim glow still flashing on his cousin's breastplate. He leaned in and sniffed the smoke still rising off Vocharlian's now striped skin. "You *should* be obliterated."

"The night's still young," the smaller demon deadpanned.

"I need to turn you in to the authorities. Stealing Fell—"

"Damnit Kruger, I didn't nick anything...well, not on bloody purpose. Just hear me out and give me a tiny bit of help."

"Help? Lucifer's kittens! Why in heaven would I help a brat that should be annihilated?"

Vocharlian raised a talon and gave the tiniest of waggles. "Because...if you help me, Kruger, not only will you have enough quid to buy a flat in the Tower, but you'll also get the bonus of getting rid of me...*for-fucking-ever.*"

Kruger took a moment to rub his cleft chin. "I'm...listening."

Vocharlian smiled broadly. Unfortunately, this led to a literal shit-eating grin as he tasted the faint aroma of the Golgotha Bureau on his lips. He eyed the time on his PD3 once more. "Short, *short* version, Cuz, I need a wee little contract drafted in under two hours, then I need to get back to Beelzebub's Fell Forge in time to catch my lift outta here."

Kruger remained locked in place, glaring from under his massive horns. "You want *what?*"

"A soul contract, you know one of the garden-variety ones for an easy mark...nothing fancy—" Vocharlian started for the door, took a sniff, and then ran straight for the shower. Kruger barreled after him, averting his eyes as he saw the smaller demon struggle to pull off the remains of his chain mail. When the breastplate seemed irrevocably stuck, Vocharlian settled for jumping into the shower only naked from the waist down.

"You want a *human* soul contract?"

Vocharlian peeked around the curtain. "What do you think I want, a bloody cocker spaniel? Lucifer's kittens, man! Oh, can you toss me your industrial degreaser? I still smell like shite."

"You always smell like shit, runt," Kruger sighed as he tossed a bottle straight at his cousin's head. "Word of advice, make sure you scrub your wing skin."

A moment later a squeal echoed from behind the curtain. "You cock-sucking, fanny-flinging Muppet-muffin! I'm going to... *OW*—!"

"I never thought I'd get a chance to do that." Kruger indulged in a rare snicker, the grin cracking the skin around his lips. "Now, why are you really here, runt, and why do you have wings? How did you survive? What even happened—?"

Vocharlian wrapped his claws around the curtain once more. "You wouldn't believe me if I told you everything, wanker, so let me get my bits and bobs as clean as I can and do your bureaucratic mumbo-jumbo so we can get me out of here. I'll explain, I swear!"

"You'd better. What the heaven is smoldering on our toilet?"

The curtain moved again. "Oh that? That's a bribe. Lemme just finish up—" He hadn't even slid the plastic all the way across when he heard his enormous cousin make a sound more at home in a tiny filth-eater.

"Where did you get this?" Kruger gasped. His cousin made him wait until he finished his scrub down. "Voch—" Rather than finish the sentence, the larger demon settled for flushing the toilet, sending another round of high-pitched squeals throughout the cramped bathroom.

The smaller demon streaked half-naked to his room rattling off the extremely edited version of his previous few hours, summing up with, "I have a chance to get out of Hell, get a human soul, and be a hero. All I need from you is one teensy contract, something you can do in your sleep, especially with that thingamajig... At least that's what the magic man in the garbage dump between worlds said. We need to get going."

"Are you wearing *her* pants?" Kruger asked as he noticed the laced-up, skintight leather on his cousin's legs.

"Of all the questions you could bloody ask, that's the one you choose? We are in a hurry, and you have some magical thing—"

"It's a Mendacity-Veracity Axis quill, the likes of which I haven't seen since my days studying at Lilith." He raised the dimly glowing feather to the light. One side of the shaft was etched with black runes, the other gold. "It's magnificent."

"Sounds great, the outlander bloke said it could make you write all the words and stuff, so can we get a wriggle on?"

Kruger, distracted by the quill in his hands, just nodded and wandered back toward the foyer. "I could draft anything with this, but it belongs in the archives, not in one lawyer's talons."

"Is that *selflessness* I detect, cuz?" Vocharlian didn't get to finish his teasing this time, as the door rattled with desperate pounding.

Kruger moved to shield his smaller cousin. He tossed the quill on the sofa and straightened his tie before opening the door, but for no real reason. He got immediately mussed up as Dorp Splatowski barreled into the living room and promptly joined the squeaky convention. "Dude, you're alive!"

"Not for very much longer if you get in my way, mate. Oof!" Vocharlian nearly fell over from the tackle hug from his weepy, heavier friend. "There, there... I'm all good, really not dead, just rather desperate and knackered."

"Don't you ever fucking scare me like that again!"

Vocharlian winced as Dorp switched from hugging to pummeling. Kruger finally broke them up. "How much time do you have? It takes an hour to draft and print a contract, even a standard one."

"Dude, are those Lashma's pants?" Dorp pointed at his friend's constrained crotch.

"This is gonna be a bloody long night."

Chapter 11

One Hour and Sixteen Dimensions Prior

S o, when you say you *got out of Hell,* you mean you literally got out of Hell?" Dorp asked between handfuls of cheesy poofs. Kruger eyed the growing pile of orange residue on his otherwise pristine desk while Vocharlian paced. An old-style blood-jet printer spat out pages at a snail's pace from its perch on a bookcase.

"How else could you possibly interpret *got out of Hell?*"

"I dunno, a day trip to the Purgation Fields?" The gluttony demon shrugged. His friend whirled around, his eye sockets blazing red.

"They reported my obliteration tonight. How, the fuck, could that be confused for a spa holiday?"

Dorp held up his cheesy digits in surrender, sending another wave of residue onto the obsidian surfaces. His own sockets darkened a touch. "You didn't even call," he said with a sniff.

"Other...goddamn...dimension! Do I look like an arsehole who can spring for an ED plan with UT&T's rates?"

"To be fair, I never thought you'd ever need one, but your mom—"

"Fuck you, you—!"

Kruger slammed a binder onto his desk. "Both of you shut up!" he roared. Everyone cringed as even the windows shook, prompting the janitor walking his filth-eater crew to pause and look their way. Kruger waved sheepishly while the other two dove behind one of the other desks. In the excitement, Dorp let one rip that made Kruger's desk thorns wilt. Vocharlian stomped his foot on his friend's, prompting another round of chemical warfare.

"Jesus!" Vocharlian blurted out, his eyes on fire.

"The J-word? Really?" Kruger leaned down and glared the most withering glare he could manage as his sockets wept from the stench. "*You* watch your damn language. And *you*, seal that orifice before I burn it shut! We've been noticed."

Vocharlian's wrath rage subsided, and he and Dorp scuttled under the desk before the door opened. Kruger slammed his head against the underside of his station, prompting him to whine, "I chipped a horn."

"Pardon, did something die in here?" the two hidden demons could hear a sweet voice ask. Both curled into tiny balls as they saw a few sets of paws scuttling and sniffing around the desk. Vocharlian bared his fangs as a scraggly mess of spotted fur crept closer and closer. The tamed filth-eater chattered in return, but quickly got distracted by Dorp's leftovers. Breaking and entering proved no match for artificial cheese.

"Bad smell, need help?" the cleaner asked in broken Fell Enochian. He switched to his local dialect and added, "*Fucking greed bastards and their messes. Something probably died up his cloaca.*"

"What was that?" Kruger asked while Vocharlian stifled a giggle.

"Need find smell?" the cleaning demon asked again. The filth-eaters lapped up the last of the floor dust and one hopped on the desk, prompting a shoo from Kruger. "Slay...something in here?"

"No, just doing a little overtime! I'm...lactose intolerant and had too much cheese..." Kruger kept going on and on while Vocharlian held his breath to suppress the laughter. "Family issue... I'm sure you can relate."

"He's still talking," Dorp squeaked as his stomach gurgled again. Vocharlian held his nose, but mercifully the only sound that followed was the door closing.

"What is wrong with you?" Kruger barked. "If I'm caught—"

"Finishing your bloody sentences?" Vocharlian fired back as he clambered out from under the desk. He stopped cold as well as the printer had finally stopped spitting out pages. "Wait, are we done?"

Kruger ignored his cousin and rifled through the latest printouts. The last few curled with streaks along one margin. Vocharlian sneered, but Kruger shoved him aside. "Don't worry, humans never read."

"Why did you need a contract again? Some magic man in the sky said he was gonna send you to Earth?" Dorp emerged from under the desk as well, picking his nose while deep in thought.

Vocharlian raised a brow ridge. "Did you listen to a word I said?"

His friend shrugged. "I did, but...it doesn't seem right. Come on, demons don't just get sucked into Fell forges and sent off into space—"

"Not space, just another dimension."

"Yeah, whatever, dude. But you have to admit, it seems pretty crazy." He cringed as his friend flashed his wrath aspect again. "Dude! I get that your mom went off plane, but that was sanctioned by the home office, like in a proper summoning circle and everything after years and years of outreach with those cultists from Milton Keynes. It was all official and stuff."

"I never thought I'd say this, but I believe Vocharlian," Kruger sighed.

While the cambion gloated, Kruger pulled out the glowing quill and made a few annotations on the last pages. The tip left a trail of sparkles with each precise stroke. Kruger looked up. "Can you sense it? This quill is amazing."

Dorp blinked a few times. "It's a glitter feather. What's the big deal?"

Kruger swirled the glow in his sockets and continued to scribble away. He notated page after page, both the quill and his sockets glowing brighter with each entry. Dorp and Vocharlian watched, entranced for a while before they both pulled out their PD3s. "Um, cuz, not to be that guy, but *I have to get a wriggle on.*"

"Holy crap, Squifeldous Kandar is on the scene at the Golgothan Bureau! He's the biggest shit in town, literally. Judas, man, what did you do?"

"I'm not bloody explaining this again."

Chapter 12

Thirty Minutes and Sixteen Dimensions Prior

"A lright, you weren't kidding about the enormous shite."
Vocharlian crouched behind one of the many, *many* police
chariots surrounding the Golgothan Bureau. The nightmares
had been led to the nearby park to get food and water, so the interlopers
could get a half-decent vantage point to survey the ridiculous response
unit.

"So...huge," Dorp gasped as the guardian wrath demons had to look
up to address the head investigator.

In a scene full of first-class turds of all shapes and sizes, Head Investigator Squifeldous Kandar represented the most hardened and painful
of the breed, a furious coprolite in polished armor with chiseled features
and glowing white eyes. "To think, enough people were proud of their
deposits to the porcelain throne to create that," Vocharlian mused.

"I've heard he actually has a porcelain throne at FPPD headquar-
ters," Dorp whispered. He curled into the tiniest ball possible,
condensing his gelatinous flesh. "We can't get past an archdemon, dude.
Let's go home."

Vocharlian eyed the serrated and thoroughly unsanitary blade on
the arch-turd's hip. His right pauldron also displayed a gaudy trio of
pentagrams, one glowing white, one red, and one Fell green. "Well, at
least he's only first-level certified in disintegrations."

Dorp squinted as he peered over the hood again. "Um, dude all those three rings add together."

"You sure, mate?"

"I watch a *lot* of *FPPD Uncovered*. That guy can belch acid and turn a cambion like you into soup in three seconds." He tugged at his friend's arm. "Let's get out of here."

"And do what, Dorp?" Vocharlian waited for a response, but Dorp could only compress a bit more.

They watched as a few of the Golgothan crew shuffled around the entrance, shuddering as larger demons kept questioning them and taking copious amounts of notes. One particularly quivering form kept oozing from her sockets, trying her best to slip away from the mess. The head investigator made a point to block her way. Vocharlian tensed as he saw Shishi fade from her normal brown to a sickly gray.

"Who is that?" Dorp asked. "She's...beautiful."

"She's my ticket into the soulforge." The young cambion straightened his armor and doublechecked the binder Kruger had unceremoniously dumped on him the moment he finished. Two more officers walked out of the Bureau both holding their noses and looking genuinely miserable. "But how to get past a small army of cops?"

"There's so many, and for a simple obliteration? It doesn't make sense. I know your mom is famous, but why...?"

Vocharlian, however, tuned out Dorp discussing the deviations in police procedure, and instead focused on Inspector Kandar getting distracted by the new folks reporting in. He took a few deep, slow breaths, until his green socket glow flickered and changed to light blue.

"Hey...dude? Dude, are you listening to me?" Dorp paused to yawn. "Wait, what was I even saying?"

"Nobody worry about the cambion in the shadows," Vocharlian said, his voice slow and slurry. "Everyone...just...chill."

Blue vapors poured out of his eyes, mixing with the ambient moisture rampant in this section of Hell Prime's capital. The nearby puddles took on a similar sheen to his sockets, and his gluttonous buddy yawned once more. "Hey... Vochar—?"

"We're chilling," Vocharlian continued. He crawled at a snail's pace from his hiding hole to the next chariot, using his new stripes and dark wings as camouflage against the slick pavement. A few of the nearby cops joined in the yawn fest.

"Am I *boring* you?" Inspector Kandar bellowed as one of his subordinates joined the train. "What is wrong with you demons? We have a supposed obliteration, and not a trace of ash on the scene. Anyone care to explain that?"

Vocharlian kept crawling, while the cops floundered. One even dared to say, "Oh yeah, I forgot about that."

"You forgot? You *forgot!*" The stench of burned poop filled the air as a pillar of fire erupted at the inspector's feet. The previously lackadaisical minions around him all jumped to attention, but the guys on the perimeter merely stared in fascination at the spell.

"Ooh, pretty," one deadpanned as Vocharlian crawled by.

"Nothing to notice down here," the cambion whispered.

His destination ended up being behind a larger chariot marked with the logo for emergency medical services. There, a demon in full plague doctor gear checked out the traumatized waste workers at an arm's length. The clerk who had shown Vocharlian around earlier wrung his hands, squeezing foul liquid onto the ground. The doctor inched away but let the guy continue weeping. "We've never had an incident like this, not with an outsider!" he moaned. "Will this affect my performance review?"

"Oh, who cares about your damn review, Karl? A demon died saving my life and all you care about is your bonus?"

Vocharlian could see another demon slosh into view. Shishi slumped over the edge of the ambulance, prompting the doctor to go diving for cleaner and wipes. "If you wouldn't mind—" the doctor started.

"No one's ever died to save me!" Shishi wailed. "And all these people are poking around like my hero is a criminal. Can you imagine how horrible that is?"

"Well, if you hadn't let him near the forge, we wouldn't have had this incident!"

"I was being hospitable!"

As the two shit demons' argument grew in furor, filthy spittle sprayed over the medical supplies. The doctor tried to intervene, but only ended up streaked with scat as Shishi collapsed against him with a loud squelching sound. Vocharlian rolled under the vehicle, yawning as the slothalepsy threatened to take him over.

Karl rubbed his sockets and yawned as well. "What was I going on about?"

"You were being a total shit," Shishi snapped.

"Why, thank you."

"Please, this is a medical unit. If you could kindly—"

Vocharlian waited as patiently as he could, but the alarm vibrating under his armor warned him that time was running out. "Here goes nothing. Come on Shishi, be my hero tonight." With that, he closed his sockets, took a deep breath, and let go of sloth in exchange for a far more lustful aspect. He rolled to the left and put himself squarely in line of sight of the quivering Golgothan. "Time for the smolder."

Shishi gasped as she saw the ghost emerge from under the ambulance, and he quickly pressed a talon to his lips. "Help me," he mouthed.

Shishi immediately let go of the doctor, inhaled deeply, and then let out the wail of all wails, all while pointing furiously to a section of the bureau wall. While everyone focused on her, Vocharlian slipped into a convenient alcove. She also managed to create such a spray that the doctor pitched a proper fit.

"I need to be alone!" Shishi cried, her histrionics mounting rapidly. Karl and the nearby cops all had the decidedly male bystander reaction of finding anywhere else to direct their attention, and even the previously unflappable Inspector Kandar shifted his briefing to the other side of the entrance just to avoid the overwhelming emotions. Once thoroughly ignored, the blubbering blob slithered to the shadows where Vocharlian could only whistle in appreciation.

"You...you're not dead," she barely choked out.

Vocharlian clamped his usually gaping maw shut, toying with the remains of his lips.

"I saw you disappear in the fire. You...you...vanished. I thought..."

Her PD3 jiggled in her translucent belly, the key to getting back into the forge—the biometrically locked key. Vocharlian gulped, taking note of the vast array of gold and jewels also floating in her corpulent form. The riches sparkled even in the dim evening light.

"I came back...for you," he whispered, his sockets still swirling brilliant violet. Shishi swooned, slapping against the stones. "But..."

"There's always a *but*," she sniffed. "Please, it doesn't matter to me that you're a cambion! I'll explain everything to my grandpa—"

"That's just it, I need to prove to your family that I am worthy," he said quickly. "There's only one way a half breed like me could ever be able to provide for a beautiful demon of station like yourself—"

"You know who I am?" Shishi asked, her sockets wide and quivering. "But I was trying so hard just to fit in at the Bureau like a normal demon."

"You could never hide how special you are, dear Shishi. It's as plain as the slime on your face, but it doesn't matter to me. I felt our connection the moment I stepped into that cesspool, and I have to do whatever it takes to win your favor."

"Well, I can make a few calls, and everything will be fine. You don't have to do stunts to impress me," she gushed. "You know, I felt that connection too."

"Then you know that I have to do this the right way. When I was connected to the forge, I met someone, someone who can get me to Earth—"

"To Earth! Are you kidding me? Our forge isn't powerful enough, and you'd be ripped apart—"

"Yet here I am, just a silly half demon with a contract and a prayer, trying his best to win the..." He stared at her chest and quickly counted. "...hearts of the most amazing demon he has ever seen."

"Oh, Vochi!"

"No one's ever called me that before." He held his breath as Shishi slipped alongside him, even with her best attempt at surface tension stretching, she couldn't quite ooze her way to his face. Vocharlian breathed a sigh of relief. He swept his claws gently through the slime on her cheek. "We shall make it work, I promise, but the only way I will ever have enough soul energy to earn a girl of your station is to go to Earth and..." He pulled out the binder. "I can do this, but I cannot do it without you."

"You saved my life...twice... You came back... You want to... Sweet Judas, you love me!" Shishi's quivers turned to a crushing wave throughout her midsection.

"Is it not obvious?" he asked with the tiniest of laughs. "But I must get back to the forge if we are ever going to have a chance, my darling."

"Follow me." She rolled back her shoulders, standing tall as possible as she pulled out her PD3. Her goopy digits texted remarkably fast. A few moments later, Vocharlian peeked around the corner to see Inspector Kandar now on the phone, looking remarkably pensive. Soon the entourage of cops collapsed around him for an emergency briefing, allowing Shishi to saunter straight to the Rakshasa pair at the door. She whispered to each of them then slipped a couple pieces of bling out of her arm. "Come on, what are you waiting for?"

Vocharlian darted from his hiding place. He stopped short as he took in the two monstrosities, but both turned away as the smaller demon approached. "The Union probably wouldn't approve of this, gentlemen."

Before the guards could retort, Shishi grabbed Vocharlian's arm. "Come on."

"Damn half-breed," one guard muttered. Vocharlian responded with the cheeriest of middle talons before darting into the empty office. Without the jolly glow from terminals or chatter from workers, the main office took on the sinister hue of pure Fell fire. The pair could hear every glug and bubble from the cesspool as well as faint chattering in the walls.

Vocharlian brandished his claws. "I will not let them hurt you. Just open the conference room and then you slither as fast as you can for the entrance." Shishi nodded furiously, but before they could head for the door, they heard a commotion out front.

"*Someone was lurking on the perimeter, sir.*"

"*Appears to be a glutton!*"

Vocharlian slapped his palm with his forehead, the violet glow wavering. "Dorp! He's my friend. I must save him."

Shishi slithered at record speed for the conference room, swiping her card even as the filth-eaters crawled from the shadows. "Go! I'll help your friend."

"You really are amazing," Vocharlian said, blowing her a kiss as he ran. He hopped over the portcullis as it was halfway raised, turning just once to see Shishi returning the affectionate gesture.

"I Shishiananzura, daughter of Anphara, Lady of the Foul Lake, do swear my affection. I'll wait for you to return with a bounty of soul energy and an ascended form!"

"Wait, where have I heard that?" he said, rolling the new information around in his head. Before he could think too much more about it, however, the forge in the conference room flared with unholy light.

"Oh, bollocks..." Music swelled before the flames engulfed the poor cambion. As he was sucked into the forge, he could read the names of all the children of Beelzebub carved into the walls, including his favorite child—Anphara, Lady of the Foul Lake.

His screams faded into a wave of synthesized music, forcing him to grab his ears and thrash wildly within the column of fire. His chest burned as the runes absorbed all that they could, but residual energy continued to singe his already charred fur, darkening the gunmetal stripes to jet black in places.

> *Inspiration becomes a thought,*
> *Thoughts go into motion.*
> *Motion becomes a rhythm.*
> *Rhythm begets emotion,*
> *Emotion turns to song.*
> *The song invokes a spell...*
> *(And then the deed is done.)*

"Make it stop!" he roared, and then everything went dark. Once he could peel open the membrane on his eyes, he found himself staring at a row of colorful poufs hanging from suction cups. He fumbled against a cold, slippery surface, sending him sliding and jamming his already tender wing buds into unforgiving cast iron. He yowled, but his voice crackled and failed him.

"Oh boy, I'm hallucinating. This is not good," a voice moaned from beyond a hazy film of plastic. Energy rushed from the direction of said voice, slamming into the demon's skull and sending him reeling with an overwhelming mix of pain and confusion, followed with a sucker punch of desperation. He slapped the curtain.

"Oy, is someone asking for help?" he asked, grabbing his throbbing head.

Episode Four

Let's Make a Deal

Chapter 13

As Seen on TV

S o...if I lay off the dubstep hate, will you sign the contract and save my life, or am I utterly fucked?"

Meg flipped through the contract as she rolled the demon's words around in her throbbing head. She braced against the wall and immediately recoiled. "*Ow!*" Blisters burst from her palm.

"*Can't you bloody feel that? If it's toasty for me, you must be frying.*"

Meg snagged her towel and tapped the knob, prompting a sizzle. Puffs of steam drifted out of her faucet as well. "Did I set the house on fire?"

"*Come on you daft*—woman! *This isn't a normal fire, it's Fell fire coming to burn away what doesn't belong here on Earth.*"

"You!" Meg stared at the signature page with the tacky "Insert Human Name Here" line left on one side.

"*You mean us,*" the demon growled in her mind. She looked in the mirror and saw her own glowing magenta irises mere moments before the glass cracked. "*You think you get a pass for only* accidentally *summoning a demon, luv?*"

"I've made a few adjustments, will you still initial and sign?" A terrible wrenching sound surrounded the beleaguered bathroom. The toilet bubbled and churned, making Meg wretch again.

"*Initial and sign? What are you, some kind of solicitor?*" Meg didn't

get a chance to answer as the monster in her bathtub yelped and rolled
onto her floor, taking the shower curtain with him. Verdant embers
littered the fiberglass basin while tiny green and black flames sputtered
from her shower.

"Why is the fire green?" Meg moaned even as she tossed the binder
onto the plastic mummy. Her complaints faded to slack-jawed wonder
as the ceiling ripped away not to reveal the tacky carpeting of the master
bedroom, but rather waves of fire rippling over an unfathomable void.
The demon peeked, and his empty sockets changed from red to a dim
and sickly green.

"*I don't want to go to the void, not yet.*" The demon's hand shook as
he grabbed the binder. He promptly poked the pad of his left index
finger and began flipping to the last page. Meg waived her hands frantically.

"You need to read and in—"

The demon snarled and flipped and scribbled, barely scanning the
redlines done in makeup while a mini cyclone started sucking personal
hygiene items into the sky. Meg reached to catch her favorite hairbrush
instinctively, and that simple motion sent a wave of force toward the gap
in her ceiling. "Please give us more time," she whispered, and, with that,
a shimmering forcefield erupted around the pair. Both Meg and the
demon exchanged confused looks before the monster shrugged and kept
scrawling away. Meg almost stopped him around page twenty but bit
her lip and let him keep going. Despite the new mysterious barrier, the
temp continued to rise until sweat dribbled along her rapidly frizzing
hairline. The demon whipped to the final page and swirled his finger
into a messy streak. "*There we go, Vocharlian Variegatus ready to serve
you.*"

He chucked the binder at Meg. She gulped. "If this is just my insanity, nothing will happen, but if it isn't..." The fiberglass enclosure to her
shower exploded in green flames. "Yeah, not much choice."

She picked up her errant eyeliner, but the demon slithered out a
bit more, waggling his talon. "*Gotta be blood.*" He then offered said
talon.

"Eww, I don't know where that finger's been."

"*You're worried about that?*"

She grabbed the hydrogen peroxide from earlier and flung it on the demon's hand. He yowled in protest. She then poked her left index finger into his claw. "*Oy, another lefty.*"

"You're concerned about *that*?" Meg fired back as she ran her finger over the page. For a moment they just stared at each other while the fires continued to rage and the rest of the bathroom crumbled around Meg's bubble.

"Did it not work?" both asked—a heartbeat before reality dissolved into a disco around them. "What the...?"

"...everlasting fuck?" Vocharlian moaned as he awakened surrounded by a rainbow of shag carpeting and blinking incandescent lights. He dug his nails into the plush pile while an array of *beeps* and *boops* assaulted his ears.

"Welcome to *Let's Make a Bargain*! I'm your host, Hamilton Hock."

Vocharlian blinked a few times, as a gangly figure in a plaid suit sauntered into his field of view. He could just see a pencil-thin microphone surrounded by spindly fingers, even as the lights hid the stranger's face. "Welcome, contestant number one, Vocharlian Variegatus!"

The lights flared to blinding levels, sending the demon scuttling against the wall and yelping as his wing buds picked up a nasty case of rug burns. "Staaaaaaaaaaaahp!" The more he clutched the sides of his skull, the more the ringing intensified.

"Contestant number one—" Hamilton started, his voice dripping with as much oil as his stringy ponytail. Vocharlian snarled and snapped with his talons but was rewarded only with a spray of confetti and the roar of a laugh track.

"This some kind of bloody game?"

"Clearly, you got more looks than brains, Fell-baby." The host snapped his manicured fingers and did a little shuffle over the roar of the invisible crowd. "Contestant number one is here from the crowded bowels of Hell Prime. Charlie, can I call you Charlie?"

"No!" He lashed with his claws again, prompting a condescending wave of titters. The demon narrowed his eye sockets but could only make out the silhouettes of heads with relentless lights obscuring all detail. As he raged, more lights flickered to life, binding him in psychedelic colors. The second his talon brushed the light, sparks shot up his arm, prompting another yowl.

"Oh, Charlie, you're gonna love this game, so sit back, relax, and let's introduce contestant number two."

"Why the heaven are you doing this, you fuck-witted knobgobbler?" Vocharlian cocked his head as bleeping sounds echoed over his last few words. He started a fresh tirade, but the noise and titters of the crowd drowned him out. His eye sockets flickered with red flames.

"Meg Reynolds," the host declared even over the din. The curtain parted to reveal a stunned young woman in a stained, oversized t-shirt and no pants. She immediately ducked behind the curtain. Hamilton twirled his mic. Once he sucked up a fresh lung of studio air, he dragged out, "Meg... Reynolds!"

The curtain rippled. After a pregnant pause, Meg stumbled and landed on all fours. Her hair, now free of its scrunchie, expanded into a dark halo with magenta curls snaking from her crown. Vocharlian's eyes slipped downward, eyeing the curve of her thigh and a bit of ink peeking from under her boy shorts.

"Eyes up here, boy." Hamilton leaned toward the demon and gave a wink. "That's a different game show."

"Where am I?" Meg said between gasps. She grabbed her chest with one arm, prompting the other to buckle. "Wake up, please wake up."

Vocharlian sized up the slim host, his pointy ears, and the lightness of his eyes. "You're a bloody Fey. What the everlasting f—" The beeps this time added a bonus shock to shut down the demon's tirade.

"Let's keep it clean, contestants. This is daytime TV after all."

Vocharlian replied by extending his middle finger while Meg curled into the fetal position. "This isn't real. This can't be real," she repeated, still struggling for breath.

"I'm with you for once," Vocharlian muttered. "This is grade-a bull...*stuff*. Listen, pointy, why don't you skip to the part where you tell us why the...*hell* we are here?"

Hamilton clucked his tongue. "This simply will not do. Neither of you are camera ready!" He then snapped his fingers, and the lights blinded Vocharlian. When he could see once more, Meg now wore jeans and a TV-friendly solid top. Looking down, he found his armor back to its pristine and polished metal and his lace-up leather pants replaced with modest trousers.

"Glamour...great. What next, hexes and curses?"

Hamilton smirked. "Let's not spoil round two." Music swelled from the wings of the stage, and in a blink, Vocharlian was standing behind a beige podium with the wall of shadowy figures planted firmly in front of him. Hamilton mugged and prattled to the throng a bit, giving the demon a chance to face the stunned Meg, her lips quivering but her eyes unblinking.

"I've totally lost it," she whispered. She finally returned Vocharlian's gaze and clasped her hands over her mouth. "You're a demon."

"Just figured this out, luv?" He buried his face in his talons. His ears only perked up as he heard, "It's time to *make...a...bargain!*"

"I loved game shows as a kid. Always wanted to be in one, but not like this..." Meg mumbled as she ran her hands over the set pieces. "Is that thing one of the monsters from *Lands of Eternaquest*... Maybe an expansion? No—"

"She's gone daft from the magic," the demon started in his own exterior monologue. "Oy! Pointy, why don't you talk to me for a sec?"

Hamilton gave a "who me?" gesture before leaning in with the mic. "So, Charlie, I hear you're a Leo and you've always dreamed of flying. You like long walks in the rain of fire and have an accent as mutable as your ocular mist—"

"I have cold iron in my armor and salt in my skin, you pissblooded wanker." He flinched as the censorship siren wailed over his colorful colloquialisms. The host grinned from ear to ear. "Why are you here, Fey? Just spit it out...if you even can!"

"*You* look like a high elf from Wintergrove." Meg squinted. A blink later and stylish cat's-eye frames materialized on her nose. "Wow, my hallucinations are so detailed."

"It takes a moment for redbloods to acclimate to this much mana, Charlie. She'll perk up once the magic percolates thoroughly through her skull dumpling." The host twirled his mic a few more times. Meg continued to babble about hit points and side quests until someone muted her. Hamilton leaned in further, seemingly unfazed by the spikes jutting in random directions from Vocharlian. "You know why I'm here, don't you, Charlie?"

"Not a bloody clue."

The host's eyes flashed bright gold. "Allow me to illuminate you." With that, the lights flared, and the crowd gave a collective coo. A screen descended onstage, showing off images of cartoon devils with pitchforks and cheeky grins. One demon poked a hapless schoolgirl while a circle of prissy spinsters and priests pointed and frowned. "Since time immemorial, the Fell of the darkest Hell have sought to entice humanity into bargains, while the righteous Fehr—"

Vocharlian snarled as the screen shifted to show angelic figures looking down from the clouds. "Leave those blighters out of this."

"Precisely the idea. You two tribes have been at odds since the big bang was a teensy-weensy whimper." He winked at Meg this time. "Thus, I present to you, sweet human child, option number three."

The screen shifted to the same girl being surrounded by friendly fairy folk, from goofy-grinning goblins to tapdancing trolls. Comely fairies flanked a figure that bore an uncanny resemblance to Hamilton in golden armor. This version of him spread his arms wide to the gobsmacked human in the image. Meg shook her head a few times. "Did I start the tutorial?"

"As is the custom, so let it be done. If the Fell wish to bargain with humanity without a valid contract, then the Fehr dictate our kind step in to arbitrate."

Vocharlian shook a talon. "Oh no, no-no-no, pointy—"

The host clutched his mic to his chest. "Oh no, no yourself, my ill-begotten buddy."

"I have an iron-clad contract with standard terms!"

"That you let a mortal modify." Hamilton clucked his tongue.

"My redlines!" Meg interjected. The host gave her a big thumbs-up. "I told you to read them, Charlie."

"Hey, human, don't call me that."

"Then don't call me *human*!" The fire in her words made Vocharlian clamp his maw shut, and Hamilton burst into guffaws. Music swelled over the trio, and the stage shifted and split to reveal glittery boxes and curtains as well as something large and draped in rainbow sequins.

"I think our Fell friend is eager to get the party started, but first let me finish laying out the terms. As our mortal Meg here so thoughtfully pointed out, *Charlie*, you allowed her to alter the contract, thereby making it anything but standard, and all non-standard contracts are subject to impartial arbitration."

"But how do we know you're impartial?" Meg asked. The fog had faded from her eyes, and she no longer seemed dazzled by the lights. "You said you're a Fey, but what kind? Are you like the legends I've heard, or something...else?"

"All very good questions, Meg. It's simply a matter of balance. The Fehr act as guardians of order from the heavens above, the Fell are servants of entropy in the pits of Hell, and us Fey, well, we're just stuck in the middle with you, babe." He fluttered his eyelashes ever so sweetly. "Now I know you asked what I am, but it's probably not something we can fully explain before commercial break. I have it on good authority that the humans who did know about my kind called me a Seelie sidhe, and that is all you need to know. But hey, enough about me, tell us about yourself, Meg! I'm sure your soon-to-be servant is just dying to know."

"Actually—" Vocharlian started.

"I'm nobody, really," Meg finished quickly. "And why should I believe a word you say?"

"To be fair, you should have thought of that before signing a contract with a demon. It's probably a little late to be worrying about the process now. You know, your card says you went to Harvard University. That doesn't strike me as a very nobody thing to do, especially considering this fine specimen you dragged out of the void."

Meg recoiled from her podium and looked away. "Can we just—?"

"*The* Harvard? Aw fuck, you mugged me off, Meg!" He cringed from both the beep and the dirty look from the human. "Stop that infernal noise!"

"And you remember, it's a family program, Charlie."

"What are you getting out of this?" Meg interjected again, steering the conversation cruise back on course. "I know he wants my soul—"

"Hey, I just said *a* soul. We discussed this."

"Fair point, fine. So, you want *a* soul, and I wanted not to die in my bathroom. What do you want, Mr. Hock?"

"Please, sweet mortal, call me Ham, everyone here does. To answer your question, which is a valid one, I might add, the standard fees apply, in exchange for arbitrating and finalizing your little deal, you both owe me either a geas or a quest. The choice is entirely up to you."

"I've played enough *Dungeons and Dragons* to know that you never take the geas. It always gets your character killed."

"Nerd," Vocharlian muttered.

"Does that mean I can put you down for a quest?" The host motioned to the screen that started flashing with big blue question marks. "Just say the word and I'll make it so!"

"Can we see what the quest is?" Meg asked.

Hamilton waggled his finger "no" once more. "That takes all the fun out of it."

Vocharlian growled, "Don't bother asking him, luv. No matter what a Fey says, it's nothing but rubbish. They lie more than an elected official, then swing around and smack you with painful truth the moment you let your guard down."

"Aww, flattery will get you everywhere, Charlie. So, have we got a bargain?"

"Whatever," the demon replied while the human hemmed and hawed.

She wiped her brow. "It's so warm here."

"Oh, time is slowed in this realm, but you're still burning back on earth," the host added helpfully. "If you can't make a deal before our time runs out...we have a lovely consolation prize of being burned alive."

"We'll take the quest," Meg and Vocharlian said in unison.

Chapter 14

Commercial Break One

S o, is there a game to this game show?" Meg asked the moment the music died, and Hamilton stopped gladhanding the faceless crowd. She glanced once more at the demon at Podium One: the scrawny, spiked, and striped monstrosity with a gaping maw and dripping sparkles where eyes should have been. The creature shrugged, and the lights in his eye sockets slowly shifted from red to a pale blue. Meg yawned immediately.

"Sorry, stress is...yeah..." He blinked, and the sparks transformed to green.

"You're like a living mood ring," Meg whispered just before Hamilton whirled around. The host snapped his fingers, and a busty bombshell in a tiny dress walked over to the sequined lump in the middle of the stage. The host let out a wolf whistle, prompting an involuntary "Ugh" from Meg.

"Get on with it!" the demon bellowed. With his cries, the two limp swaths of skin draping from his shoulders stiffened slightly, and the tips of his claws seemed just a bit longer.

"He's right," she chimed in. "We don't have time to mess around. I'm guessing there aren't any portions of this program being edited for broadcast, huh?"

That certainly put a gleam in the host's eye. The screen lit up with the word "quest," and an envelope appeared in the host's hand after a flick of the wrist. "Well, should you two survive to our special bonus round, then I'll let you crazy kids know just what arduous task you've won in addition to our grand prize of continued existence on the mortal plane."

A disembodied voice echoed from above: "*Not to mention a collection of prizes from our sponsors: the Seelie Court of Midhaven, the bards of Aquatica, and Clucker's Interdimensional Fried Chicken, if you need to feed an army of fuckers, look no further than your neighborhood Clucker's—*"

"How come he can bloody swear?" Anything else the demon tried to spit out ended up covered in a barrage of censorship beeps. His oversized mouth made it tough but not impossible to read his lips.

"Because Clucker's pays for these fine designer suits, my good man. Now if you're done making the booth earn its keep, let's explain how the game works." Vocharlian let out a deep sigh, crossed his arms, and put on the airs of a scolded teen, but he kept his mouth shut. The host continued, "To be certain that your bargain is fair in the eyes of the esteemed Fehr—"

"*Not that those blighters have eyes,*" the demon hissed.

"...is the glorious equalizer, random chance!"

Meg stood up a bit straighter. "Wait, what? You're making us gamble on games of chance to finish up a contract? How is that fair?"

"Actually, pure chaos is the only thing that is fair, my dear. No interference, no influence from one party of the other. Your contract will be leveled out according to the wheel...of...*chance*..." He pointed his mic toward the center stage, and his assistant whipped off the curtain. The sheer amount of new glitter made Meg blink. An enormous wheel now filled the stage—one covered with so many slots, the naked eye couldn't read them. A magnifying glass descended from the ceiling to amplify the current selection: "immediate death." Next to it read "a brand-new car."

"You've got to be kidding me," Meg said. "My life has boiled down to one spin on a cheesy game show?"

Hamilton whipped another card out of thin air. "Now let's get a few ground rules laid out. Since you altered the contract, Meg, you get to spin the wheel once. Wherever you land, that's your fate. We clear?"

Meg nodded. The host made a "go on" motion. After a few awkward seconds he pointed to his mouth and Meg mumbled, "Okay?"

"Sucks to be you, luv," the demon said, laying on the snark.

"As for you, *Charlie*, since you were careless enough to sign a contract without reading, you have to spin twice. You also gave up all rights to control your logic glamour. So, for round two, Meg here gets to design your new disguise all by herself."

"What's a logic glamour?" Meg asked at the same time Vocharlian cried out, "No fair!"

"If you don't want to play, I can always throw you right back in that immolating lavatory. The choice is yours, my Fell friend."

"Bring it on, Pointy. Which one of us spins first?" The red returned to the demon's eye sockets. Meg recoiled. More droplets of sweat welled up, but she held steady all while trying to read as many potential outcomes as possible.

"Why don't you take your first spin, my good demon? Let's see what the universe thinks can possibly balance out your idiocy."

Meg covered her ears as the bleeps took over while Vocharlian stomped toward the wheel. He ripped the gameboard with enough force to make it wobble. The crowd oohed as the lights flared. The demon kept his back to his fate, unfazed by the horrible deaths passing him by. The human gulped as "Implosion" loomed as the wheel decelerated.

"Please don't implode in front of me," she prayed as the plastic doohickey slowed over the grizzly fate, prompting more gasps. Only at the final second did it flip past the demon folding in on himself and instead read, "Tether of Temerity."

The screen flashed another healthy infographic, this one showing the schoolgirl and a cranky demon chained to each other. Every time the monster tried to fly away, the pair would crash back into one another and end up bouncing from corner to corner. "I have a bad feeling about this," Meg mouthed mere moments before a ring of light surrounded her and Vocharlian.

Hamilton, meanwhile, mugged for the audience while the pair hammered at the walls of their new prisons of light. Meg squealed as the floor lifted and glided across the studio, plopping her cage next to the snarling, thrashing Vocharlian. "Let us out, you—!" The rest of the demon's diatribe consisted of so many bleeps, the operator just held the button down.

"Now, now, Charlie," Hamilton tried to interject.

Nothing but bleeps filled the air. Meg made a kill gesture and pointed to the screen filling with more rapid-fire images of chains. "Please, I can't hear!"

Any chance of quiet disappeared instantly as shackles erupted from the floor beneath both contestants. Meg screamed as red-hot iron wrapped around her right wrist. She heard the sizzle as the stink of burning skin filled the air. In the other cage, black blood splattered from the barbed chain digging into Vocharlian's right arm. He yanked the offending iron, and Meg went sprawling to the ground. The chains fused into her flesh drawing another scream.

"Johnny, tell these contestants what they've won!"

"Since you've shown such trust in this human's judgement, Vochar-lian Variegatus, the universe has decided to reward you with the Tether of Temerity! This ten-foot length of eldritch chain connects you both body and soul to your human companion. You'll live together, eat together, sleep together—"

"What?" Meg tuned out her frying wrist and jumped to her feet. That motion sent Vocharlian toppling, roaring as the barbs lodged deep into bone. "What do you mean sleep together?"

The host turned to the couple and beamed. "Oh, this is rich, dear friends. It looks like you're going to be spending a lot of time together. After all, the bond between summoner and minion is paramount to your continued survival. This tether should help you strengthen that bond immensely. Who knows, it may even expand with enough time."

The cages dropped and only a glowing chain remained, locking the pair wrist to wrist. As Meg stared, the metal transformed, shifting to translucent energy while her skin bubbled up and healed over in an obvious scar. Across the way, the demon stared in awe at the new black band on his wrist, the opposite to her faded skin.

"A tether? You have got to be kidding me." Vocharlian immediately tried to bolt for stage left. The moment he ran ten feet away, he smacked into an invisible wall like a drunken mime. "Bloody...*bleep!*"

Meg rubbed her arm. "We're stuck together?" Meg then attempted the same maneuver in the opposite direction. Instead of hitting a wall, she grabbed her head and winced. "*Ow!*"

"Maybe you got more looks than brains too, Meg," the host sighed, prompting another titter from the crowd. "There you go, the universe has spoken! Welcome to your new bond. Oh, did we mention the whole emotional/physical connections as well? It's probably best you figure that out on your own. Meg, it's time for you to make... a... bargain! Spin the wheel and face your fate."

"Hey, Charlie, can you move over a bit?" They both shuffled awkwardly until she could grab hold of the beastly wheel. She gulped and lifted it up and down a few times until it synched with her trembling breath. Finally, she closed her eyes and whispered, "Okay, universe, do your worst."

"Never say that," the demon warned.

Too late, the wheel stopped at the ominous "Bridge to the Nowever."

Chapter 15

Commercial Break Two

"What the heaven is the Nowever?" Vocharlian asked, echoing the confused murmurs of the crowd and the stunned faces of Meg and Hamilton. Even the previously helpful screen of exposition remained damnably blank.

"Is that bad?" Meg asked.

The ceiling flooded with light, bathing the human in a golden glow. Vocharlian tried to duck away but slammed into his wall again. The glow scorched the edge of his wing, prompting a tirade of bleeps.

"What's happening?" Meg's feet lifted a few feet off the ground, blinding light bursting from her midsection. The demon blinked, then found himself in a vastly different scene than the stage.

"Fuck me. Oh, I can swear again. That's brill." A muddy field stretched as far as he could see, full of decaying vines and broken trees. An equally decrepit cottage sat on a tiny hill, rotting ivy draping from its sagging roof. "What a shitehole."

"I see she unlocked the Nowever, good for her."

"Not you, anyone but you," Vocharlian growled at the disembodied voice. "Is this nonsense your doing? Tell me, you bloody space wizard! *Tell me!*"

Before anyone could reply, Vocharlian blinked and landed in the land of sequins and censorship. He dropped to his knees, head in hands. "Bollocks."

"It seems that the universe has a sense of humor. I'm getting word from the booth that the Nowever is a legendary pocket dimension removed from the reality of time and space. It seems that you've unlocked the ability to send your minion there to rest and recover," Hamilton read off a new card. "I've never actually heard of this before, but yeah, I guess that's a thing. You've also won an Enochian text courtesy of our sponsors at Clucker's to help you figure out how to use this ability. One note, abusing the bridge may result in a permanent tear in the fabric of the universe, so I would do your research."

"I'll keep that in mind," Meg said, distracted by her smoldering demon. "Charlie, are you Okay? What ha—?"

"What did you..." He trailed off as he glared at the booth. "...do to me?"

"I don't know!"

"As endearing as this banter might be, you have one final spin before the bonus round, assuming you survive. Charlie, my boy, it's time you face your fate once more."

"This is ridiculous, mate."

Hamilton leaned in and whispered, "Life is ridiculous. Now take your licks and get this over with so I can claim my prize."

"Your...?" Vocharlian followed the Fey's hungry gaze toward the dazed human. As the light surrounded her, he could just see another glow emanating from her burnished skin. The phantom chain dripped from her hand, but an occasional pulse of energy flowed from her. A moment later, a wave rushed into Vocharlian's arm, sending shivers down his spine.

"*She didn't need a ritual to summon you, boy, and now she has the keys to a realm where there is no time or space to annoy creatures like us. Think about it.*" The words echoed in the demon's skull without any movement from the Fey's lips.

"*You stay away from her.*" He could see the bright green of his eyes reflecting off his breastplate. With a rumbling growl, he crawled over, dragged himself to his feet, and spun the wheel. "What now?"

Sure enough, the doohickey stopped in a blank space.

Episode Five

The Odd Couple

Chapter 16

Back to Reality

F ive more minutes," Meg whined as the bass dropped on her alarm. She smacked her lips and opened her eyes to take in nothing more exciting than her popcorn ceiling. She groaned and looked at her bare chest and the stains on the edge of her comforter. "So...sick... Such messed up dreams."

"You're telling me, luv. I had a nightmare that I moonlighted as security then ended up trapped on Earth with a barmy bird named Meg."

She scrambled and clutched her comforter to her shoulders, shaking as she saw a flicker of movement coming from the bathroom door. "Who...who are you?"

A slim figure stepped into her view, unassuming in height or breadth. Floppy waves of chestnut hair fell across his face, while he stared at fingers coated in pasty flesh and trimmed nails. Meg, however, focused on the strange man wearing nothing more than her unicorn boy shorts and Union Jack crop top. "Who... no... it was just a dream. It *had to* be a dream."

The stranger slapped his palms on her bed, shaking the frame and knocking her glasses from their precarious perch on the nightstand. Meg fumbled for them, doing her best to roll into a protective cocoon. Unfortunately, momentum decided not to be on her side. "*Ow,*" she proclaimed after a monumental thud. Still, she managed to slip on her glasses and inch up the wall just enough to peer over the bed. The new angle locked her gaze smack dab in line with a bulging unicorn snout. "Wow."

Owner of said package crouched and flipped the hair out of his eyes, revealing blurry, dark eyes tucked behind hipster glasses. "We have got to talk. Why the heaven would you give me a cheeky mug like this, but still make me fit as fuck everywhere else? How am I gonna pull looking like the boy next door? It's not like I can walk around like this."

He yanked up his crop top to show off baby smooth pecs and a six-pack. Meg squeaked, but the stranger only kept going. "Also, while we're at it, can we talk about the meat and two veg you saddled me with? I get that it might be a main for you mortal folk, but for a demon, these would barely be a starter."

"W-What?" Meg blinked a few times, letting his words roll around in her head. The stranger hopped on the bed, raised his arms to the sky before swinging down and wide to frame his technicolor crotch in all its splendor.

"I mean my boy and his bollocks! Don't you think you could've dreamed a little bigger, my dear?"

"You're that scrawny demon from my bathtub." The lightbulb finally lit behind Meg's eyes. "What do I have to do with your...your...you know?"

"Dick? Willy? One-eyed-trouser-snake? Satan's silly string? Ding-Dong? Knobzilla? Pen—"

"Enough! I get it, we are discussing your penis, okay!" Try as she might, she snuck a peek at the impressive bulge. It might not have quite been David Bowie in *Labyrinth*, but any ballet dancer would be proud to shove that beast in a leotard. "What I don't know is...what it has to do with me."

"You gave me this form—"

"I did?"

Her guest smacked his forehead with his palm. "Bloody human brains, always going to mush with the slightest touch of mayhem. What's the last thing you remember?"

"Cheesy game show music and the smell of polyester."

"Well, there is that." He flopped on the bed and patted the mattress beside him. "So, do you want to just get the old rumpy-bumpy out of the way now so you can bake me up a soul or what?"

"*Excuse me?*"

"I don't know about you, but I've had a heaven of a night and I'm ready to blow—"

"Just who do you think you are?"

"Vocharlian Variegatus, we've met, signed a contract in blood, bing-bang, Bob's your uncle—"

"I get that you're a demon..." Meg stared at his new face. The demon growled, but in his new guise, his voice cracked. "But you look so...so..."

"Ridiculous?"

"Adorable," Meg finished under her breath. Her alarm going off again managed to distract her from the demon in the room. She fumbled for her phone and her eyes widened at the time. "Crap, I have to get to work."

"You have a demon in your bed, ready and raring to go, and you're worried about the nine-to-five grind? What is *wrong* with you?"

Meg, however, rushed to the comfort of her routine scramble. She made a point to inch across the carpet in her comforter, keeping modest even as Charlie seemed determined to flash as much pasty skin as possible. "Can you leave the room, please? I need to change."

"Your priorities are so out of whack, luv. Still, I live to serve." He rolled to the other side, stretched to show the crack of his almost nonexistent bottom, then sauntered into the attached bathroom. "Oh, this is certainly familiar."

Meg sat, unblinking for nearly a minute, until she let out a deep breath and made a run for her closet. She grabbed her head a good foot from the door and heard a bang and "*Ow!*" echoing from the bath. Still, she tried forging ahead, wincing as the pain increased. She collapsed on her shoes and begged, "Charlie, can you come out here? No peeking!"

"You rammed me into a towel rack!" he complained as he stumbled into the bedroom. "But nice bum."

Meg resisted the urge to whirl around and give him a piece of her mind. Instead, she dove into her closet. "Oh my gosh, where is my bra?"

A torn mess of elastic and underwires landed on her feet. "Sorry, still getting used to human hands and I gave up when I saw how much vomit soaked into your knickers. Trust me, you'll thank me later."

"You...you..." She fought to catch her breath. She noticed her different underwear. As her mind raced to all the potential violations she may have suffered at the hands of a renegade demon in the night, she started shaking.

"Lucifer's kittens, your virtue is still intact, woman."

She peered around her closet door. "Stop calling me woman, *Charlie*."

They remained at an impasse until Meg's third alarm warned her of the impending doom of her workday commute. That stressor overrode her current indignation and she grabbed clothes before bolting for the shower.

"Stop bloody running off, you're gonna yank me again and I'm not in the mood!"

She blasted the water and remembered to shove on her shower cap in time. Her eyes widened as she saw brilliant magenta curls intertwined with her normal dark brown. "I hope that's in the dress code... Oh crap, I'm tethered to a demon, and I have to work!"

Now Meg's inner demons chose to strike. The tightness in her chest surged to suffocating levels as she curled into a ball and let the steamy water pound on her back. Over and over, she fought to control her breathing, blocking one nostril then the other, trying to count to five. She tuned in to the pattering of droplets on plastic, the smooth tile under the tips of her fingers and the herbaceous aroma of her bar of soap. "I can do this. I know I can."

Alas, anxiety had different plans. Meg's legs trembled until she landed on the shower floor. Once more she tried to find focus—a scent, a touch... She even licked her lips to taste the minerally water.

The door burst open. "*Jesus*, woman, are you alright?"

Meg slipped and would have banged her head if a hand hadn't shot into the shower just in time. Every inch of her turned pink as the demon invaded her private sanctum, but before she could go apoplectic, she noticed his glasses were steamed over. "Were you *worried* about me?"

She twisted around onto all fours and scuttled into the far corner to use a pair of poufs as modesty shields. The demon sighed deeply before retreating beyond the curtain. "I felt like I'd been stabbed while being chased by a hellhound. Did something maul you?"

"You felt...my panic attack?"

"Was awful, luv. I'm a demon, not a monster. I had to see if you were all right."

"I have to go to work. I have a life. I...can't handle this!"

"Well, you should finish your fucking shower first, then we'll deal with the rest," he called before slamming the bathroom door.

"Stop swearing!" However, in her irked state, she found the strength to blast through the rest of her shower and get herself ready for one hell of a day.

"Go on, ask," Vocharlian offered as he lounged in the back of the bus with his newfound human. He kept tugging on the waist of his borrowed trousers, trying to keep the khakis from slipping down. Meg, meanwhile, stared at his face, until the demon started studying his alien reflection as well. "*Well?*"

"You're really coming to work with me?" Meg squeaked out.

"Not the question I was expecting, but considering we can't be more than three meters apart and you won't bloody call out—"

"I only get five sick days a year, and I already blew three of them. I'm going to have to sneak you in...somehow."

Her demon sighed. "Well, I certainly look boring enough. I suppose you want me to do some hand-wavy Jedi mind trick thing."

"You can do that?!?"

"This is going to be a long-ass day, isn't it?" He eyed her sour face. "Should I say long-bum day so as not to offend your delicate sensibilities?"

She furrowed her brows. "That somehow sounds even worse." *What is with this thing? Is he really a demon? Does he even have magic at all or am I hallucinating?*

He pinched her arm, prompting a yelp. "Ever so real, hate to break it to you."

He can hear me?

The demon rolled his eyes. "Yes, I can hear you." *Lucifer's kittens, why did I get stuck with the densest bird on this planet?*

"I am not a dense bird!"

Shite, she can hear me.

They stared at each other a good, long moment until they thought in unison—*so how does this work?* Though a few colorful turns of phrase enhanced Vocharlian's query.

Am I thinking at you, Charlie?

Don't fucking call me Charlie!

Yup, that works.

"This is bloody exhausting. Can't we just speak like—?"

Normal people? "I'm so not normal."

"I'm getting that loud and clear, luv." Vocharlian tapped his noggin. *Are you thinking sentences in your head, or what?*

I've always had a running commentary in my mind, but I've never had anyone listen in before. Is there a way to turn it off? Will he read my mind forever? Oh my God, how can I control my thoughts?

"Clearly, not like that. Let's just try to use our outside voices for a while and maybe we'll stop overlapping."

Meg nodded furiously. *Seems like a solid plan.* "Um, sorry, yeah let's keep it to talking."

They stared at each other for the next two stops. "Why isn't it working anymore?" the demon asked.

"Why are you asking me? Twenty-four hours ago, magic only existed in video games to me. You're the..." She lowered her voice and eyed for any potential eavesdroppers amid the fellow commuters. "...demon here, so you need to tell me!"

Vocharlian shrugged and leaned farther into his seat, spreading his legs so wide he made Meg shift uncomfortably. He seemed oblivious to her dagger eyes, and to the nearby women ogling his egregious manspreading. Instead, he stroked the nonexistent hairs on his chin and took a wander into a labyrinth of thought. Before Meg could get an answer out of him, their bus rolled into South Station.

"This is our stop, Charlie," Meg said with a sigh.

"I hate—"

"Human world, human name!" she hissed, dragging him to the front. She paused to give a fresh glare to a woman staring with contempt from the front row. The old lady didn't say a word but pursed her lips as she took in Meg's wild streaks, curves, and darker skin next to the pasty, bespectacled, skinny white boy. *Aren't we in the 21ˢᵗ century? Ugh!*

The demon snapped out of his reverie, gave a cheeky wink, and made a point to wrap his arm around Meg's waist as they exited the vehicle. He licked his lips. "Casual racism tastes like strawberries and flat lager. I rather enjoy it. Or is that fat shaming I detect?"

"Are you...empathic?"

"I'm a demon, negative emotions energize me, and as a Variegatus, I can taste the rainbow, not just feed on one type. A little bit of mild wrath really energizes me, while your morning laziness soothes my soul. Admit it, it's rather brilliant."

Meg blinked at him a few times. His cheeks took on a rosier hue, and she could see a rusty undertone to his dark eyes. He peered in so she could get a closer look, oblivious to blocking pedestrian traffic. The more Meg stared, the more that same flush crossed her cheeks. A dude lost in his phone grazed her shoulder.

"Fuck off, you twat!" she blurted out, prompting a middle finger from the rando and an appreciative grin from her demon.

"*Hoh-oh*, she does know all of the Queen's English!"

Meg gasped and started running for the station. *What came over me?!?* She didn't look at her companion, instead focusing on getting to the Dunkin' Donuts line, getting her coffee, and getting to work before she could get reamed for being late. As she ruminated upon the last moments of her commute, she nearly got jumped in line while zoning out instead of ordering her iced extra light.

"Hey lady, what you want?"

"Sorry, um..." She stared at the menu, despite ordering the same drink for four years straight.

"Well, I doubt you have bacon and sadness on the menu, so let's just stick to one of those egg sandwich things and two of the biggest damn iced coffees your gluttonous heart could possibly desire, and donuts...all the bloody donuts."

"Wait, what?" She did her best to clarify the order while Vocharlian wiggled his fingers in glee. Before she could protest the dozen glazed, her demon pressed a finger to her lips.

"No one can be too pissy with donuts, it's universal office currency. Think of it as a distraction from bringing an otherworldly terror into your cubicle today."

How on earth could I argue with that? "And a bottle of water too!"

Chapter 17

Bring your Demon to Work Day

I used to think Hell went overboard on the torture levels of modern office spaces, but now I see, they were just imitating Earth." Vocharlian gawked at a carpet straight out of the eighties and sniffed the stale, musty air. Before he could get too comfortable in his contempt, he turned his attention to the matter at hand, namely Pam at the front desk with her steely eyes yet messy bun.

"I can't do this," Meg whispered, her hands trembling, shaking the precious cargo in the pink and white box. "You're right, should have taken that sick day."

"Bit late now." *Besides, she looks fun. Damn it, stop the internal monologue, you Muppet!* "Sorry about that."

He's not sorry.

Vocharlian clutched the coffees to his heart. "You wound me to the core, woman." *Even if you are bloody right.*

Rather than dwell on his rogue thoughts, the demon took a deep breath and let any anger go. Instead, he focused on the top button this Pam had conveniently forgotten to button, and the little wisp of hair toying around her glasses. As the pièce de résistance, he glanced back toward the other gal with specs in the room—Meg in her just too tight slacks with thighs for days. That image shifted his phantom irises from ruddy brown to deep violet in a heartbeat.

"Why hello there," he said leaning on the ledge around the admin's desk. "I was wondering if you could help me this glorious morning."

"Anything you want." Her longing gaze, however, didn't land on the smoldering monster in front of her, but rather to the shaking box. "Dear lord, do I smell chocolate?"

As she rose to eye the pastries, Vocharlian could just spy the bump hidden behind the furniture. "Of course."

One box of pastries and a hastily concocted backstory later, and the demon became the proud owner of a visitor's badge while Meg followed in a daze, shaking her head, and tapping on her phone. "How?"

"Lust is a capricious master, my darling. Still, it drives people to focus on what will give them the most pleasure at any given moment..."

Meg kept tapping and tapping. "If I run Shadow's Deep tonight, I could get a slight improvement to my offhand weapon."

"I received a badge to invade your office with a single box of donuts, and you are completely ignoring my spectacular charms." He waited a moment more, even waving a coffee under her nose couldn't break the spell as she now slipped in headphones and watched an online video. She licked her lips hungrily as little cartoon characters hurled digital magic and stabbed at a hideous two-headed dragon.

"Mmm, a new wand is a drop," she all but moaned.

"Fucking humans." His eyes faded back to brown, and Meg immediately frowned.

"Watch your language. Oh, crap we're here. I don't know—"

Really, woman, you lust over a game when I'm right here?

Don't call me woman, Charlie!

"Reynolds, who is that?" a new voice called.

"He calls you Reynolds? What is this, the bloody army?" Vocharlian straightened his collars and cuffs and put on his cheesiest corporate smile. He ended up eye to forehead with a potbellied, balding little man with pallid eyes and a terrible combover. "I'm..." He took another deep breath and steeled himself to say the words. "I'm Charlie, um, De—"

"*Damon*, from corporate. He's a consultant, and I brought him in from the lobby," Meg interjected.

"I wasn't told about any consultants," Baldy said suspiciously.

"Well, it wouldn't be a surprise inspection if they told you about it, now, would it?" The demon stood up to his full height, and while not that impressive, it certainly was enough to cow this welterweight wonder. The demon's face softened a little, and he leaned in to give a conspiratorial whisper. He eyed the nameplate in the corner office. "Now, don't repeat a word of this, my good man, but I have it on good authority that little miss Gina over there is having a few issues with the home office, if you get what I mean. However, anyone who plays nice-nice with this little inspection would be looked on pretty favorably by the big guy, am I right?"

"Steve sent you?" the guy whispered in the same hush-hush tone.

"Oh yeah, and you know all about that guy, right?"

Meg rolled her eyes at all this wink-wink, nudge-nudge action happening, especially as her demon gave her a quick thumbs-up. Meanwhile, Vocharlian endured a thirty second handshake from Captain Clammy Hands who introduced himself as the appropriately ridiculously named Bob Roberts.

"Reynolds, can you show our guest from corporate around and get him anything he needs? I'm going to log that you're in. Oh and no need to bother Gina yet, she's got meetings all morning."

"Um...sure?" She escorted her demon to her corner cubicle, prompting rounds of curious stares from everyone not stuck typing or reading off random dialogue. Once tucked behind semi-sound damp-ening glass, she turned to her companion and scowled. "This is never going to work. You have no idea how terrifying Gina is. Bob-Squared is gonna cave and then it'll only take one call and—"

Vocharlian raised a finger to his lips, prompting Meg to raise a brow. "Firstly, you underestimate the power of greed and envy. Bob-Squared —*ooh how I like that, luv*—is a small man with small ambitions. I could feel his desire for that corner office and Gina is in his way."

"But she's going to come out at some point—"

"And I'll tell her all about Bob, and her insecurity will lead her to watch him instead of me. Now, I need you to log me into the network, and as long as there is a connection to Hell Prime, I'll do a wee bit of razzle-dazzle, bingo-boingo, and *poof*! I'll be in like Flynn."

"Why would our call center be connected to Hell?" Meg squeaked. She then eyed the sea of soul-draining putty and terrible patterns combined with the banal chatter of dead-eyed wage-slaves. "I guess it's not *completely* unreasonable."

She slumped in her chair and typed in her password with a heavy sigh. *Why am I doing this? It's insane, but I can't seem to stop myself. Maybe it's just a terrible nightmare and I can't wake up.*

Vocharlian pinched her again. "You're bloody awake, woman." He ignored her glowering and pulled his phone out of his pocket. After a brief marvel at its glossy surface and plastic case, he waved his hand over the screen. Nothing happened. "What did this dimension do to my PD3? Fu—"

Meg slapped his arm. "Watch your mouth, we're at my work!" she hissed, a glint of red in her eyes for a change. Vocharlian gulped a little. He kept rolling the device over and over in his hands until he felt the raised buttons on the side and the divot in the back. The moment his index finger crossed the sensor, the screen lit up with a picture of a smiling young woman with a nose ring and ornately decorated horns.

Meg stared at the girl's red eye sockets and wicked smirk. Vocharlian cringed. *Lashma.* He tapped and swiped as furiously as he could until it switched into an interface both familiar and slightly jagged compared to a normal Earth phone.

"What are you...?" She trailed off as he tapped an app and her work computer flickered with the image of a pentagram. "The internet connects to Hell?"

"Where do you think all the lag comes from?"

"Too much streaming of porn?"

"Not the worst guess. Sadly, more people seem to desire cat videos. What that says about humanity, I don't know. Now give me a moment and keep a lookout for prying eyes." He logged into a browser and smiled as the screen flickered again. "Please let this place have the same time zone as Prime. Dorp, I need you buddy."

"What's a Dorp?"

The screen flickered green for a moment, then popped up with a chat window for BlobinatorS69. The demon slapped the desk with glee, prompting a round of dirty stares. Both Vocharlian and Meg tried their best to hide in the dinky cube.

"*Hey Dorp, I need you right now. My PD3 is twitchy, can't access the Bureau of Envy...*" He grinned as he saw three little dots immediately pop up next to Dorp's smiling avatar.

"You're...typing to another dimension."

"I am, and before you start all that rubbish in your head, you *are* still awake. We will catch up as soon as my best mate hooks me into Envy Central."

"Fuck me, you're ALIVE. Sweet baby Satan, you're alive!!!" appeared in bold text next to BlobinatorS69.

"Between you thinking you're dreaming and Dorp blabbering I'm dead, I feel like I'm stuck on repeat."

"Come on, man, can we skip the recap and get to the part where you get off your fat ass and help me?"

"You call your friend a fat...ass?" She scowled as the word left her lips.

"He's a gluttony demon. It's a compliment."

"So he's chonky?"

"Oh, I shall now nickname him Chonky Boy. The universe has spoken." True to his word, he changed the avatar's nickname while he waited for the three dots to materialize into words.

"I guess there is a little interdimensional lag, that or IT is blocking you. You can't even get to MyTube—"

"My...what? No, this chonky boy likes to go on and on and he always forgets to hit enter." Vocharlian sighed before the wall of text appeared, scrolling so fast that Meg could only catch the tail end since she blinked.

"...that mega shit, Kandar, is going mental, says you stole Fell energy from the Golgothans, and now—"

"Demons speak English?" was all Meg could blurt out as the texting stopped and an old-school ringer announced an incoming call on the demon's phone. He let out a deep sigh as Meg's screen popped with an incoming video chat as well, like something straight out of the movies.

"Don't—" Vocharlian started, but Meg tapped the mouse just a split second faster. Both stared slack jawed as the same ivory-skinned demoness from his lock screen shoved into view, this time wearing a studded bustier and shoulder armor straight out of any classic role-playing game. Another shadowy form kept hopping and trying to get into frame, but this stranger shoved him away, showing off impressive, spiked gauntlets.

"Oh Pookie, what have you gotten yourself into this time?" she asked, sounding more like a California girl than a hell-beast.

"L-Lashma?" the demon gulped. "Why—?"

"*Pookie?*" Meg asked, raising a brow.

The female demon briefly disappeared from view as a bulbous figure shoved his way in front of the camera. He froze as he stared at the screen, then his dripping black eye sockets widened into veritable saucers. Meg, meanwhile, focused on his pointy black teeth and veiny mounds of flesh. "It's a... *It's a...*" they both stammered.

"*Human,*" Dorp gasped, pointing a chubby finger. He squeaked as Vocharlian nudged Meg to one side as well.

"Bloody heaven, mate, it's just a mortal suit," he sighed. Any facade of calm crumbled as the female demon grabbed the camera.

"*Oh Pookie, what has that sorceress done to you? You look so...so... dreadfully adorable! Ooh, that flesh cover is a good look for you.*"

He slumped so low in his chair the slightest breeze could send him to the carpet. *This is the worst, the literal worst.*

Meg meanwhile continued to gawk at Lashma's perfectly smooth skin and the ample curves in her sexy armor. She gulped as even the demoness's horns were sculpted to be enticing rather than terrifying. "I didn't mean to make him so adorable. I'm kinda new at all this."

Lashma cocked her head onscreen. The red of her eyes softened just a bit. "*Not what I was expecting from a summoner, not what I was expecting at all. Pookie, we really need to talk. Come back to me.*"

That at least perked him up. His eyes flickered violet and he quickly tousled his hair before leaning next to Meg. "I...I... Wait, what are you doing with Dorp?"

The red returned full force in her eyes. "*What am I doing? WHAT AM I DOING? You stole Fell energy from motherfucking Beelzebub, you arrogant little shit.* Pun intended. *Now I knew you'd get Splatowski here involved, but Kruger...really? And what is this about you seducing a member of the royal family? Should I be jealous?*"

"What?" Meg asked, now as slack-jawed as Dorp.

"I thought she was a bloody intern, and she was cute, so sue me! Like you have any room to tell me what to do after—"

"*After what?*" She seemed genuinely hurt, prompting Vocharlian to scratch his head. A flicker of motion from a nearby cubicle and a surge of stress from Meg pulled his priorities back into focus.

"Lucifer's kittens, Lash, I don't have time to get in a strop with you. I need my mate to patch me into the B of E for one teensy little favor and I'll be out of your hair. I can't do my job without a little more help—"

"*Help? If you think for one second, I'm going to let you get into any more trouble up there—*" Flames now flickered along the curve of her ever so shapely horns.

"I can't believe you still care, babe, but I've got a contract to collect." He waggled his finger as he saw Lashma's nostrils flare. "Don't do it. Do not bring up my mum."

"*Oh, your mother is going to rip you into pieces and feed you to her cats at this point. The only reason she isn't riding the next portal to Earth is that greedy little fuck-fart, Kandar, has a DOS order on your sorry scrawny ass.*"

"DOS?" Meg continued to stare blankly at her hijacked machine.

This time the blobby guy pushed his way back in. "*Disintegration on sight, dude! What did you do?*"

Vocharlian could only rub his temples. "You *were there*, mate." After a few more moments of awkward silence, he leaned in and whispered, "Damn, if I go back, I'm dusted on sight."

"*Dude, what were you thinking? How the heaven did you hook up with an actual human? Did the witch force you into a contract?*"

"No! It was a total accident—" Meg tried to interject.

"*Humans can't be trusted! They just want to use you for power and magic and she's going to eat your soul like an enormous filth-eater…even if she has a beautiful second chin starting.*" Dorp gushed. Meg immediately covered her neck. Before she could spiral into full body image meltdown, she got distracted by movement from the corner office.

"Oh crap, Gina." *I'm so gonna get fired for talking to demons on company computers.*

"Enough!" Vocharlian started typing furiously. "One crisis at a time. I can't bloody worry about getting blasted, cause I'm in another fucking dimension. I have one job right now and a human with less PTO than we get in Hell. I didn't think *that* was possible. Now, I need a quickie into the Envy Bureau, so I can get to the business of collecting a soul and will deal with everything else later. Just hook me up, mate, and stop frigging thinking. It's not your strong suit."

"*I—I—*"

"Do it, you Muppets!" Vocharlian barked.

"You seem so different, Pookie..."

Meg inched up to see a woman with a dyed blond chignon slipping out her door. *Please no, not now, anything but her.* She started to stand up, but the demon grabbed her hand. That simplest of motions caused a flicker of green to mix into Lashma's flaming sockets on the screen. Dorp shoved back into view, his lip quivering. *"Alright, I'll do it for you, dude, but promise me you won't fall prey to her substantial feminine charms and be her slave. It's just what your mother would want, and you made me promise—"*

"Charlie, what is he talking about?"

The demon growled and raised his hand as if to shush Meg. "Just give me a min."

Meg, meanwhile, felt her blood run cold as the one and only Gina made eye contact in turn with each of the cubicle monkeys flying under her command. *Don't notice me, notice anyone but me.*

As if on cue, a bird smashed into the windows. The office collectively jumped as a smear of blood and feathers slid down the glass. No one noticed Meg as she clutched her chest and tried to slow her breathing. "Did I— D-did—?"

Never forget, Meggle-Peggle, that the will of the one can sometimes overtake the will of the many. You should be careful what you wish for.

Meg struggled to breathe, and as she trembled, Vocharlian had to look up from his furious typing. "I need to focus here, you da—" He trailed off as he had to clutch his chest as well. "Just breathe, *breathe*, luv, or else we are right and proper fu...*fudged.*"

Now why the heaven aren't my credentials working?

They took a few slow breaths together, while everyone else stared at the gory mess. Vocharlian was able to click through and close the chat window as the tall, skinny bottle blonde in a pantsuit finally looked away. She raised an overplucked brow at the young man sharing Meg's cube. "Do we have a visitor, hmm?"

Meg gulped, words failing her as the boss lady sauntered over. She tried to nudge her demon, but missed terribly, knocking her monitor. Then Meg had to scramble to stop the cascade failure of her pens and paperclips pouring off the desk. Her shaking hands failed to prevent the catastrophe and managed to tip Vocharlian's coffee over the edge and onto his lap.

"Gina! I was just going to introduce myself, but I heard you were in meetings. Charlie Damon, I'm here from corporate."

Meg blinked a few times as she saw the demon holding the condensation-covered cup with only two fingers. Before she could say a word, he set it down with nary a drop on his khakis. Though he kept a cheesy smile plastered on his face, Meg could clearly see a bead of sweat dripping from his temple.

"You came from the fifth floor?" Gina asked with a raised brow. "Are you new?"

"He's a consultant," Meg added, a little too quickly.

"I didn't hear anything about any consultants in the weekly conference call—"

Meg hustled to fix her desk, knocking her sticky notes over in her furious desperation to avoid eye contact with the boss. No amount of box breathing could stop her shaking.

"My good woman, this is about the all-mighty dollar," Meg tuned in to hear Vocharlian saying, a flash of gold reflected in the black plastic that filled her cube.

"I should ask for a raise..." Meg whispered, before giving the side-eye to her demon companion. Now Meg noticed the same golden glimmer in her boss's eyes.

"Are you saying if your cuts take effect, there's more out there for the survivors?" Gina asked, her lipstick cracking from her smile. "I think we should talk in my office."

Meg sunk in her chair, once more comfortably invisible as her demon sauntered off, babbling glibly in corporate speak as if he'd been born on Wall Street rather than Hell. In fact, she had just gotten into her Zen state and logged in for her first call when an unseen force jerked her clean from her chair and sent her sprawling into the aisle. "Oh crap, three meters."

As she pulled herself to her feet, she ended up looking down at a familiar comb-over. "Are you going to actually start work for the day, Reynolds, or are you trying to get yourself downsized?" Bob-squared asked.

She took a couple steps to the left. "I...I..." Unfortunately, Vocharlian must have chosen that second to move, as Meg jerked to the left again. *Stop it!* Vocharlian responded the only way a contrary demon would, and Meg went sprawling.

"Reynolds, are you on drugs?" Bob asked. She jumped to her feet and stepped right, eliciting a yelp from Gina's office. Red crept into her peripheral vision.

You need to stop this or I'm going to get fired, Charlie!

Oh, you can just—

Unfortunately, the "Fuck off!" blurted from Meg's lips.

Oops.

Episode Six

It's All Fun and Games Until Someone Crosses Dimensions

Chapter 18

For Every Action...

I can't believe you got me fired," Meg said, clutching her box of personal belongings as she waited outside for the bus.

I can't believe Lashma was there. Maybe there is hope...

Hey, can you focus on me for a second? I lost my job!

"I did you a favor. That place was rubbish. Bonus points for drama though. I've never told my boss to fuck off and I'm a bloody demon." He looked around the gray-tinged streets full of gray, bland people and switched gears. "Come on, let's do something fun."

"Fun? *Fun!* I got fired—"

"Which means, *luv*, you have nothing better to do. Am I right?" Meg tried shaking her head, but the demon kept circling her and giving her puppy eyes from behind his coke-bottle glasses. "I'm right, aren't I?"

"You're horrible."

Charlie snatched the box with Meg's cup and plant inside then chucked it in the nearest trash bin. Before Meg could squeal in protest, he grabbed her arm and began prancing her toward the nearby Boston Common.

"That's my—" she started.

"More rubbish! You can do so much better, and I'll show you."

"B-but my plant!" she protested weakly.

Vocharlian eyed the single leaf left on an otherwise shriveled succulent in the chipped planter. "It's dead."

"B-but, it might come back..." He dragged her toward actual live greenery. "And my mug? My nice staple remover?"

"Let it go. You are literally standing at the crossroads of endless opportunity!"

"Tremont and Park?" she asked, noting the nearby signs. "How far did I wander without thinking?"

Vocharlian raised a brow. "Earth to Meg, are you there?"

"Wait," she whispered, rubbing her pounding temples, before rushing to the trash can to steal back her office stash. Vocharlian scratched his head as he watched her take it into an alley. She made a point to tuck the box away from the dumpster and among the cleaner recycling. "Maybe someone can use it."

"Right...that'll be the day, luv. *Anyway*—"

"I've totally screwed up and I have no idea what to do right now."

The demon in disguise cocked his head. "We should have lemonade then."

"W-What?" she stammered even as she followed. She did manage to stop the demon before he jaywalked. "I don't get—"

"Life has just given you a big old tart as fuck lemon, so let's do the thing and get lemonade to make it all better. That's how it works, right?"

"I don't think that's quite how it works." *Why is everything so confusing and fuzzy?*

Wee human brain plus magic equals land of confusion.

The light changed to the walk sign and Charlie all but dragged her to the cart in the corner of the Common. She raised a brow as he slipped cash out of his pocket. "Nicked it from your mum's dresser," he explained. Before she could protest, he shoved a tall, frosty cup of sweetness into her hand. She stiffened as he wrapped his arm around her shoulders and motioned her to a rare empty bench. *Enjoy the freedom, you silly bird.*

"Call me that again and I'll dump this on your lap." She then raised the lemony goodness to her lips and scowled as she couldn't find the strength to take a sip. "Now what?"

She tried again. The demon cocked his head. "Is the straw all pinchy?"

"I can't do it," she said, trying again.

"Don't be daft." The demon took the cup and tried to sip, stopping at the same place. "Well, this has never happened to me before."

Meg stared at the single cup. "I'll share this with you," she said softly. Instantly the liquid sputtered up the straw and into her companion's mouth. He then handed it back to her and she could take a sip as well. "They weren't kidding about the eat together part, were they?"

It was Vocharlian's turn to look confused. Then he looked at his and Meg's matching scarred wrists and gulped. "Eat together..."

"*Sleep* together," Meg added in horror. "Live together."

"Well, the sleeping together doesn't sound all too bad, now does it?" He did his best to smolder, and his eyes shifted ever so lightly toward violet. "Come on, darling..." He trailed off as Meg pulled out her phone to start looking up *Lands of Eternaquest* drops. "Really, woman? This usually ends up in swooning."

"Every time you call me woman, I'm calling you Charlie," she grumbled, though not looking up from her phone. "Dang it, why am I looking up this when I need to figure out what is happening in my life? Maybe I need to set up an appointment with Dr. Nair—"

"You don't need a bloody shrink, Meg. You need to just take a chill pill, *preferably of the fun and illegal variety*, and tell me exactly what sort of shenanigans you want to get into with your happy-go-lucky guardian demon."

I just want things to go back to normal.

Vocharlian rolled his eyes. "Why? Normal is pathetic."

"Go away!" Her eyes widened in horror as her companion blinked out of existence, leaving her alone on a bench with a lemonade she suddenly couldn't finish.

"What the unholy fuck?" Vocharlian cried as he sank into a mound of mud. As he slapped his hand against the goo, he marveled at the talons and tiger-striped fur. "Oh, I'm back. Thank Lucifer, I'm back!"

He rolled onto his back and cringed as muck covered his delicate new bones and membranes. "*Joy.*"

"Still getting used to the wings, eh, Tiger?"

"Not this wanker again." He rolled up, creating a tremendous squelching sound as he popped free. He flicked more mud from his breastplate and sneered at the endless swath of earth tones. His sockets narrowed and flashed red as he saw a hooded figure leaning against a gnarled tree nearby. The stranger snapped his fingers, and a breeze whipped from him to the demon. The zephyr kicked into a cyclone, not only lifting Vocharlian to his feet, but whipping away all traces of filth in seconds.

"It's the least I could do after you've done so much for me, *Charlie*."

"That's not my name!" Vocharlian rushed the stranger. Even with all his wrath-begotten speed, he couldn't reach the tree before the hooded figure snapped his fingers. The demon stopped mid pounce, flailing in the air while his intended victim chuckled.

"But it is your name now. That's what she calls you, and we both know who calls the shots in your latest relationship, don't we?"

"Who...are...you?" Vocharlian snarled while thrashing against the unseen hand holding him aloft. The guy in the hood tilted his head slightly to show off a scraggly goatee.

"I am the one saving your pathetic excuse for a life, *Charlie*." His smile only widened as the demon gnashed his teeth. "Listen to me, and listen to me well, you need to stop faffing about and help Meg learn how to use her powers."

"But she's hopeless," he sighed, slumping over the invisible grip. "She doesn't know the slightest thing about magic."

"Why yes, and without the slightest idea, she managed to rip a hole in the fabric of the universe and drag a demon out of the farthest reaches of the Hells, now didn't she?" The stranger cocked his head the other way. "Imagine what she could do, what you *both* could do, if only someone believed in her and gave her the tiniest nudge."

Somehow, the demon found the means to slump further, almost melting in the unseen hand until the stranger dropped him unceremoni-ously into a heap. He picked up a nearby stick and poked the demon's shoulder. "Cheer up, Charlie, you can do this...that is if you get off your ass and put in some effort. Hey, *Charlie*?"

"*Don't* call me Charlie," he growled, looking up with fiery red eye sockets. The stranger shrugged off the intimidating display. The inferno dialed back to little more than candlelight. "What the fuck do you want me to do, arsehole?"

"I want you to take this whole situation seriously and help her."

The demon snorted. "Hah, if there's one thing I've learned in this life, it's never take things too seriously, so I guess you, outlander, are shit out of luck."

"I have faith that you'll come around—"

The demon snorted again. "Don't give a fuck."

"But—"

Vocharlian spread his arms wide and surveyed the vast countryside full of mud, dead branches, and filthy rocks. "Behold all around you, for you have seen the field in which I grow my fucks. Note that it be barren and devoid of any toil that might one day make it bear fruit. Ye—" He grabbed his throat as the words caught in his mouth. A sinister red glow emanated from under the stranger's hood while the demon gagged.

"I've tried being nice, friendly even, but it seems that you need a firmer hand to get things done," he explained, stretching out his fingers. As he coiled them back in, the demon's gasps turned to wretched silence. Vocharlian clawed at his throat, struggling for air. The stranger flicked his wrist and Vocharlian crashed face-first into the ground. His silvery skin faded to an ashy white. "Never forget that demons exist to serve their masters. *Never forget* that your life, your *very soul* now rests in the hands of those mad enough to summon you. We gave you a life beyond torment, and we can just as easily snuff...you...out. Have I made myself clear, *Charlie?*"

Vocharlian nodded, sinking into a puddle. The stranger released his phantom grip, and all at once, a torrent of bubbles percolated through the mud. The demon burst free, snarling for a moment, but one twitch from the warlock sent Vocharlian genuflecting. "I get it! Just let me fucking breathe!"

"Are you ready to listen?"

He nodded.

"Good, now you need to help Meg learn about this new world she's discovered, one full of arcane mysteries and wonderous power." The stranger paused as the demon burst into pathetic laughter. "Do we need to go back to choking?"

Vocharlian raised his hands in surrender. "No mate, I'm laughing...

because you picked the wrong demon to work on your little project. I'm rubbish at arcane mysteries as you so colorfully put it. No matter how hard I revised for my exams at Pandemonium, I always fucking failed. I am, as my dear, sweet proctor said, an utter dimwit when it comes to spellcraft. Even having a tutor with double-D...assets at her disposal couldn't get me to cast a cantrip. Now, I'm not really into choking, but you can throttle me till we both get off... I still can't do what you ask. I'm only here because I was in the fucking wrong place at the fucking wrong time."

The stranger groaned. "You think I don't know about your arcane deficient hyperactive disorder, Mr. Swearypants? I'm not asking you to *teach* her anything, I'm asking you to protect her from those who want to teach her the wrong things."

"Me? Protect—?" He narrowed his gaze as his tormentor began pacing again. Vocharlian reached for his neck. "Oy, I already have a vested interest in keeping the barmy bird alive for the next ten years or until I get my damn soul."

"That would be five, actually."

"I beg your pardon."

"You really should have read those redlines, Tiger. Anyway, it's my experience that the universe tends to provide in moments of great need, especially when the universe gets a little nudge from someone in tune with it."

"Someone like you?"

"Why, yes, someone exactly like me! Get to work encouraging her to learn about her abilities, and if anyone tries to hurt her, do what demons do best."

"My main talents are using fuck like a comma and slacking off," the demon confessed.

"I think you need to diversify; you are a Variegatus after all."

Chapter 19

...The Universe Provides a Reaction

Where did he go?" Meg whispered as she looked around their little corner of the Common. She gave a conspiratorial look at the lemonade still on the bench, and, sure enough, as she lifted the straw to her lips, she could easily take a sip. "Am I free?"

"Nothing in life is free, I'm afraid."

"Excuse me?" She tried to figure out just who was talking, but other than a snoozing homeless guy and a passel of squirrels, no one seemed to be within conversational distance.

"Look down."

Meg began to study the bench, the well-maintained grass and a lone candy wrapper fluttering under her seat. As she watched the orange plastic wiggle, her pocket began to vibrate. *"Not that far down."*

Meg raised her brow at the incoming call message, and immediately swiped the reject button. Instead of a voicemail popping up a moment later, the call notification lit up again this time with an ID of "Don't You Dare Reject Me."

Meg swiped the little red phone icon even faster this time. "Not gonna do this," she whispered as her heart raced and sweat broke out of her palms. She heard buzzing again, this time from above instead of below. She could only sit there, gobsmacked, as a brightly painted drone buzzed over her head. "What the—?"

Once the synthetic dragonfly settled into a holding pattern about a foot from Meg's face, a beam of light projected from its nose, creating a flickering cone of light straight out of a sci-fi classic. The light solidified into a four-winged fairy with a perturbed expression on her tiny face. "Don't you screw with me, Meg Ryan Reynolds, you're my only hope."

Meg responded by fainting, right onto the remains of her lemonade.

———

"Hey, listen! You, normal-sized person, would you, like, please wake up and listen to me?"

"Am I allowed to swat this gnat? She's been flitting around my head for a bloody half hour, and I can't be arsed to deal with her anymore."

"Charlie?" Meg moaned. Her eyes fluttered open to see more mani-cured greenery. However, this lawn seemed contained within boxwood hedges trimmed into perfect walls. Tiny titters of laughter filled the air.

"Oh, my gah! You named your demon Charlie? Totes adorable! And just look at you with a human suit covering up teensy little horns and petite claws. You're so precious, you sweet lil' Hellspawn!"

Meg blinked a few times at a solid fairy flitting about this garden as if it was the most natural thing in the world. The winged creature darted about in thigh-high patent leather boots and a Lolita dress, prompting Meg to ask, "What's happening?"

The human form of her demon crouched next to her, allowing her to get some of her bearings. She took in a wrought iron door and a barbecue reflected in his thick lenses. She then ran her hands along the wicker arms of the chair she'd been plopped into. "How did I even get here?"

"I carried you from the park, luv. You should have seen the looks a string bean like me got hauling your—" The fairy flitted in front of him and zapped his nose with a bolt of miniature lightning. He swatted wide and snarled, "I fucking hate you, you tiny-winged twat-waffle!"

She put her hands on her hips, but he only shrugged. "What? Would you prefer bitch-biscuit? Cun—"

"Charlie!"

"I know, I know...language," he said with a sigh. "Why are you more worried about my colorful expressions than a wee woman with a stun gun and emo fashion sense?"

"To be fair, your language isn't colorful so much as pejorative and derivative. I'm guessing you're compensating," the fairy said as she looked him up and down. Her gaze landed squarely below the belt. "Compensating...a lot."

"Why, you—"

Meg pushed to her feet and managed to maneuver between the flitting princess and her angry demon. The moment she stepped between them, the red faded from his eyes, and he only pointed to their new companion. "She started it, I swear."

"Says the sweet little demon," the fairy replied exactly as singsong like as one would expect from a being of her ilk.

"Are you one of those creatures like I saw in the game show?" Meg asked, cocking her head to stare at the tiny woman's luminous azure eyes. "A...Fey?"

The little woman burst into laughter. "Oh, so you've met those golden-blooded bastards."

"Finally, something we agree on," the demon muttered before taking over the empty seat. "They are indeed bastards."

The diminutive lady smirked. "I'm a projection. Meeting in real life is *so* last century, don't you think? Like, it's easier to fake something on the small side, so you'll have to deal with my fairy form until the time is right."

"Who are you?" Meg asked, still cocking her head.

"My friends call me Vanth." She nodded over to the sulking demon. "*He* can call me Lady Mistweaver."

"I know that name." Meg pulled out her phone. "It's—"

"I'm not gonna apologize for the server first, *Zazzy*. We were prepared, you weren't, but that's not to say I don't hold your guild in high regard. Dreamskull is a tough server, and being second place there is way better than leading in the land of scrubs."

"You *are* the mage from the Knights of Valhalla?" The fairy nodded. "How did you get max accuracy for the fight?"

"Oh, I didn't. I rolled the dice, and I won," Vanth replied with a smug grin. "Sorry you had to be the loser this time around."

"You mind speaking English? My High Nerd is a little rusty. This is a game you're talking about, right?"

Vanth flew to a nearby bird feeder and perched on the crook of the hanging post. "Your minion always this lippy, Zazz?"

"Minion!" Vocharlian jumped to his feet.

Meg verbally kneecapped him by conceding, "Yeah, I guess he is."

"I guess it's kind of a grab bag when you go poking around in other dimensions. So, now that we've got all the boring introductions out of the way, are you gonna tell a girl how you managed to pull off the magical coup of the century?"

"Um, I might know *of* you in *Lands of Eternaquest,* but I don't know you at all. I'm still trying to figure out how I got here—"

"Carried you," Vocharlian chimed in.

"I saw a drone, didn't I? Is that what is projecting the image?" Meg continued. The fairy flickered for a moment, and the same peacock painted drone from earlier buzzed into view.

"If you need it to be, then it is, or you can simply accept that I can both be tucked in my bed, and here, projecting my consciousness as a pixie avatar. The choice is yours, but the resolution is so much better if you'd just believe me when I say I can do this," Vanth explained.

"Let me guess, basic projection spell, but because this is the land of the lunkheads and not an outer realm, you need to dress it up with that toy?" The demon then rolled his gaze over to Meg. "What I mean—"

"She doesn't need to be magicsplained, *minion,*" Vanth snapped. "You don't, right?"

"Reality doesn't like it when you break the rules, so it snaps back?" Meg offered. "You're using a drone with a projector to explain the fairy in case other people notice it. I guess that works, but I didn't think holographic technology was good enough to create an image like this." Meg then walked over and waved her hand between the drone and the sprite, making the fairy wink out of view.

Once she reappeared, Vanth straightened her dress. "Thank goodness for the ridiculousness of television. Enough people have seen the crap spewed on procedurals regarding computers that I can get away with murder. It's even better when I whip out my tablet and it interfaces with everything, *and I do mean everything.* I am one-hundred percent sure it will work with alien technology thanks to a certain classic blockbuster—"

"I got that reference," the demon chimed in.

"But it's not real," Meg interrupted.

Vanth smiled. "You do realize that your average schmuck believes what they see on the boob tube, right? Throw in the ubiquitous nature of conspiracy theories, and I guarantee you that any Joe Schmoe in Boston that bothered to look up from their phone thought it was some military experiment or Nile finally figured out the whole package delivery thing."

Doesn't she mean Amazon? Meg stared at her demon in utter confusion. "She's talking about an online superstore, not a river," she hissed at her friend.

"Yeah...*Amazon*," Vocharlian said aloud this time, as if somehow his emphasis would make Meg instantly understand. Vanth stared at him quizzically as well. "Never mind, let's just get to the point, Pixie Sticks. Who are you and what do you want?"

She stared at him, dumbfounded. "Oh hon, I'm Vanth Mistweaver, longtime rival, short-time buddy of my good friend Zazzy here—"

"Her name is Meg," he corrected.

"I am also a mage," she finished. Before Meg could open her mouth, Vanth added, "IRL, not just in game."

"Oh," was Meg's stirring reply as it started to sink in. "Magic is real... Wow."

"Says the girl with the honest to goodness demon groveling at her feet. Hang on a minute, you've got just enough of a deer in the headlights look in your eyes for this not to be next-level sarcasm. You...really don't know much about magic, do you, Zazz?"

Okay, I know I'm probably not one to lecture about coincidences, but don't you think it's bloody convenient that your nerd sister shows up right here, right now?

Meg eyed the door, as well as a quaint gate to her left. Through the gap she could just see a dumpster and a few boxes. The breeze shifted and she had to wrinkle her nose. "Where am I?"

"Beacon Hill, but that's not important right now," Vanth said, now flitting in front of Meg's face. Her tiny countenance grew surprisingly pensive and reserved. "Where you really are is at the crossroads of the mundane and the magical, and you need to decide quickly which road you want to take, because indecision may cost you your sanity."

"And Meg thinks I'm dramatic." The demon didn't help his case by swooning onto the grass with a flourish. "We all know that ship has sailed, so let's get on to the lessons about how to be a good little witch, unless you want to be bad. That...I can certainly help with."

"What makes you think I'm here to teach anything?" Vanth asked with a huff. "I want to learn how she did the unspeakable deed."

"I don't know," Meg said, taking her seat back. "I'm sorry, but I don't know."

"Whoa." The fairy managed a miniature face palm. "Let me get this straight, you cast a major summoning ritual, brought forth and successfully bound a greater demon—"

"She called me greater, you hear that?"

"Ahem, a *possibly* greater demon, and you have no idea how you did it? Why don't you start at the beginning? I get a feeling this tale is gonna be a doozy."

"Wow, that has to be the most ridiculous story I've ever heard," a miniature woman in pigtails deadpanned without the least trace of irony. "He appeared...in your bathroom? Jesus, what was in that burrito?"

And you complain about my language.

"Nothing divine, that I can assure you," Vocharlian added out loud. "Believe me, it was as ridiculous for us as it sounds to you. Now that we've shared with the class, tell us about yourself, Pixie Sticks."

"I suppose it's a fair enough question. Like I said, I'm a mage all the time, it's a thing, and I felt a disturbance in the Force, if you will, when reality was torn. Naturally I cyberstalked every address on your block until I found a person of interest. Once I saw that an IP address went back to none other than Zazzy here, I put two and two together."

Vanth continued, "It's a statistical fact that eighty-two percent of modern magi are also gamers. We don't tend to do social interaction much and the same proclivities toward anxiety and addictive personalities also equate to arcane adeptness. We drain our dopamine hardcore doing what we do, and a little instant gratification online goes a long way to help. That or we medicate with a shit-ton of pharmaceuticals...or both. I don't really judge. Anyway, once I pinpointed the residual energy signature, I hacked into your front PC camera, Zazz. Low and behold I see a 'human' with an infernal aura. It didn't take long to figure it out, at least it didn't take long...for me."

Meg sat back and took it all in. After a moment, her eyes widened. "Wait, you hacked my camera and *spied* on me?"

"This is what you take out of the conversation," the demon deadpanned. "She's a bloody witch, and she just happened to show up—"

"When I was required most," Vanth finished. "The universe is funny like that. It tends to answer you at your time of greatest need."

Bollocks, I've heard that before. Meg shot him a dirty look but managed to regain her composure as the sprite drifted into view again. "I'm not sure a pixie is what I need. I'm kinda trying to...maybe take things slow."

"*Yeah*, I have a feeling that the universe doesn't agree with you, but hey, who am I to judge? You do you. I'll be here if you need me, tending my little fairy garden, totally not getting into trouble." She raised her tiny hands and flittered toward the gate, which opened on its own. "Maybe I'm wrong and you'll get a pass."

"Whatever," Vocharlian muttered before hopping to his feet and making a beeline for the exit. "You coming, luv?"

"Yeah, I think I am. No offense, Vanth, but I'm not ready for anything new right now, except maybe a job. I'm...um...still trying to absorb the fact that magic came out of my bathtub before I get involved with anything else. Thank you, though. Maybe when I figure me out, I'll start working on everything else." Meg then took up a flanking position on the demon. "Let's go, Charlie."

I'm...not...Charlie!

"The universe is laughing at us. You know that, right?" Vocharlian said as he clutched his side and stared at the streaks of blood oozing over his fingers. "It's a goddamn laugh riot. Meg? *Meg?!?*"

Meg's eyes glazed over as she collapsed against the wall of the alleyway they'd ended up in after wandering away from Vanth's fairy hideaway. Her breathing grew shallow and weak as she kept staring at the other figure slumped against the dirty brick. "He tried... He tried..."

The knife slipped from her would-be assailant's fingers and clattered to the asphalt.

"He tried to kill us!" the demon snapped. "*Fuck*, why aren't I healing? That was mundane shit that stabbed me, wasn't it?"

Meg shook her head, sinking closer to the ground. "Never...never happened. This isn't happening."

"Fuck," was all Vocharlian could spit out before the same iridescent shimmer that had surrounded Meg's downstairs bathroom now descended over the alley.

Episode Seven

Don't Forget Your Consolation Prize

Chapter 20

All Inclusive Insanity

I t was all just a dream—a terrible, nonsensical dream," Meg sighed as she woke. The grungy alleyway had faded to glorious sunlight, and the aroma of trash metamorphosized into briny freshness. The gentle roar of water soothed her frayed nerves. "Wait a second..."

Meg's contented moment transformed as she flopped one hand over and felt a shoulder next to her—a rather lumpy, leathery joint with a texture more at home on a wallet rather than a human. "Five more minutes, luv," he groaned before rolling over and taking the duvet with him.

"Yup...insane." Meg then pushed herself up on her elbows and blinked a few more times as she took in a four-poster bed with one of those gauzy canopies straight out of a photo shoot, tons of wicker, and all manner of shells mounted artfully on the azure walls. "And I ended up on vacation." She then noticed the matched luggage set on one of those fancy racks from hotels.

Her companion yawned and flopped the other way, splaying his torso across her chest and nearly putting out an eye with one of his polished horns. From this angle, she could see patchy scales mixed with his tufts of limp, streaky hair, as well as a secondary set of lumps just behind his unimpressive current protrusions. *Do demons get baby horns?*

"Now what kind of rubbish is that?" Vocharlian smacked his lips a few times and tried to settle even more comfortably within the peaks and valleys of Meg's assets before he was rudely shoved away. He went toppling off the other side of the mattress. "Oy! I was... Why am I on shag carpet? Wasn't I supposed to be stabbed?"

"You noticed the carpet before the lack of stabbing? Really?"

"What can I say, it's rather fucking luxurious," he grumbled.

Meg looked down and saw she was dressed in her very own highly modest unicorn pajamas, covering her safely from collar to rainbow-toed feet. She even found her glasses on the nightstand, with her phone fully charged and her purse resting in a nearby chair. "Apparently I packed too."

"You weren't the only one." The demon curled to his feet and stared at his sweatpants with a series of pentagram logos running down one side. "My favorite tracksuit bottoms! I thought Kruger had ruined these in the laundry." He then turned to reveal a chest covered in dented and etched metal where the edges fused with his tiger-striped skin.

"Is that comfortable to sleep in?" Meg asked, pointing to the armor.

It was the demon's turn to dial up the snark. "Here we are, in some mysterious seaside hotel—*and not stabbed, I might add*—yet you want to question my choice in sleepwear. Tisk-tisk."

"I might have deserved that," she said softly as she rolled to her feet. "Is this a dream?"

"*A dream is not as far off as you might expect, Miss Reynolds.*"

"Who—?" She trailed off as a cloud of mist rolled in through the window and instantly solidified into a stately male figure, resplendent in a white linen suit and executive ponytail. "You...were the host of that game show?"

"Hamilton Hock, in the flesh, well what constitutes flesh for a creature like me," the stranger purred as he sashayed around the suite. "How are you settling into your winnings?"

"What are you doing here, you Fey bas—" The demon's voice warped into a comically loud buzzer.

"Now, now, this is still a family show," Hamilton warned as titters echoed from an unseen audience. Both Meg and Vocharlian searched frantically around the room but saw nothing more sinister than a TV cabinet and minibar. The Fey smirked and winked to the confused Fell creature. "Plus, I love ruffling your feathers there, Charlie. You don't mind if I call you Charlie, do you?"

"Yes, I bloody do!"

"Good to know, Chaz. Now I know you crazy kids must have a million questions, but I doubt you want to face the legendary breakfast buffet here at Paradise Junction in those duds, so why don't I let you freshen up and I'll meet you at the waffle volcano." And with that, the well-dressed stranger *poofed* into a shower of golden sparkles.

"Did he say waffle volcano?" both asked immediately. Sure enough, the laugh track followed.

The demon did rub his side a few times, and even poked as best he could around the edge of his armored plating. "I was stabbed, wasn't I?"

Meg nodded and retreated into her thoughts. *We left the garden with the weird techno-pixie and were headed to the T...*

"Can we speak with words and stuff? This place stinks of Fey magic and that gives me a pounder something fierce." He then switched to rubbing his head and broke into a smile as he felt the horns jutting over his empty eye sockets. "So good to be back in my old skin."

"You *are* a demon!" Meg blurted out.

"Oh, not this again..." Vocharlian groaned. "Yes, I'm a bloody demon!"

Meg took a few slow, controlled breaths and began tapping at her temples until she could peek over her fingers and stare at her companion again. "I...know what you are, but this is the first time really seeing you—"

"Bollocks, I've been in your loo, not a meter away so try again."

"But you were all shadowy and I felt too terrible to see anything. Then when we were in the game show, I felt overwhelmed, and the lights were in my eyes, so yeah, this is my first chance to get a good, long look at you!"

The demon smirked, showing off his pointed, metallic teeth. "Well then, why don't you take a good...long...look."

As instructed, the trembling girl did stop to study her companion. Her eyes cleared as she studied his sunken belly and gaping jaw that looked like it could swallow her any second. Then she looked at his chicken arms and sagging sweatpants. "Are you some sort of hungry spirit? Is that why you arrived when I was sick?"

His once cavernous maw collapsed into an all too human pout as Meg's question hit him. "*Moi*, a hunger spirit?" he asked between sputters. "Next thing you know you're gonna call me a filth-eater because I ate a little ass in college!"

"I have no idea what that means."

Vocharlian's eye sockets lit up a fiery red. "No, you don't know what anything means. Somehow a bitch without the slightest clue about how *anything* works *somehow* rips a hole in reality and drags my arse here. At first, I thought it was cute, but no one can be that dumb without an angle. So tell me, *woman*, what is your game?"

"Game!" Meg snapped, a crimson tinge in her own irises. "There is no game! Either I'm insane or someone is playing a cosmic joke, because before you appeared, my life consisted of work and video games and the occasional takeout that I could afford when I was done paying my bills—"

"Spare me, princess. You got a fucking house—"

"That I pay rent to my parents for! Oh God... How am I gonna pay rent since I lost my damn job? I'm so screwed and it's all your fault! Why did I listen to a desperate demon in my bathtub? You're controlling my mind, aren't you?"

Now the jaw dropped, slapping against his chest. "Fuck no! I'm not a sodding mind master—"

"Oh yeah? Well, why do I feel angry when your eyes go red, huh? I'm insane and I'm stressed and I'm totally over my head, but I... am...*not*...stupid!" Now the red energy surged from her eyes and crackled off the tips of her left-hand fingers with a sinister glow. The demon raised his claws in surrender and took a few tentative steps back, the red fading.

"I can't control minds... Emotions...maybe. I'm an empathy demon who can also project, but it's not what you think. I don't control people; I can only nudge, and it doesn't seem to work on you like it does on others, I swear." As he tried to smile, the floppy wings on his back chose that moment to twitch and expand, prompting a nervous "ooh" from the unseen audience.

Meg stormed to her luggage and turned her back to him so he couldn't see the tears welling in her eyes. "So, you have tried to control me," she said with a sniff.

"Wait!" He stopped as she stiffened at his shout. His eye glow softened to a light blue. "*Please* wait."

She ran her hands over the faux leather of her battered rolling case. Meg took her time undoing the zipper, making a point to feel each tooth with the tips of her fingers. She then closed her eyes and focused on touching the soft fabrics and zeroed in on the scent of her favorite soap that she'd somehow packed as well. She opened her eyes and looked at something fluffy and yellow. "Apparently, I have the hoodie I've kept eyeing for months but never bought. I'm going insane with style."

She looked around the room again. "This room is like a real-life version of the Daydream Coast. It's...it's a holiday area in the game I play. You do...you do the Midsummer Festival event... Midsummer...like *A Midsummer Night's Dream*...which had fairies in it..."

"Hey, your brain is off doing its thing, so I'll just get dressed... Yeah... Let's just do our thing..." He trailed off and winced as his side twitched.

"*Yes, you are still bleeding, so you might want to hurry things along,* Charlie."

Vocharlian paled, the bleaching amplifying the dark stripes on his arms. "I think you're right. This is a nightmare."

She whirled around just in time to see him stumble and drop to his knees as a bit of black ichor dribbled from the corner of his mouth. *If you refuse to play the game, the referee will throw out a red card.* Meg then coughed, and a few sputters of blood landed on her hand.

"Did someone just hijack our inner dialogue?" the demon moaned as he struggled to push to his feet. "It's bad enough with just you."

"I don't know...but I think, I think we should go to the breakfast buffet. I mean, if your dream is trying to tell you something—"

"You follow your dream," Vocharlian finished. "Time for waffles it is."

Chapter 21

Waffling with Benefits

I like this dream. I won't lie." Vocharlian gawked at the restaurant full to the brim with every delicacy a hungry traveler could imagine, including one from the outer circles of the cosmos. He salivated at fresh chops of filth-eater being breaded and deep fried so they could be topped by Hell's gravy. Meanwhile his companion focused on the centerpiece of the spread—a stunning tower of golden pastries with a torrent of maple syrup erupting intermittently from the top while butter lava oozed from cracks at the base.

"Oh, they have a full English station!"

"Yeah, it's pretty amazing," Meg acquiesced. "Those home fries look like the ones I had at Old Orchard Beach every time we visited."

"You can even get them topped with lobster, which I highly recommend," a cheerful voice chimed in. A well-manicured hand grabbed both Vocharlian and Meg's shoulder. They jumped, but his grip remained frighteningly strong. "Dig in and meet me in the corner. We have much to discuss."

"I hate the bloody Fey," Vocharlian grumbled as he shuffled toward the plates and silverware. He then nudged his human. "Hey, could you grab at least a snack? I'd like to eat."

Meg surveyed the glorious spread one more time before shaking her head. "Isn't there something about not eating food provided by fairies? It's in the back of my head, but I can't remember the details."

"Oh, *now* you know something, that's a first," he groused before reluctantly putting down his own plate. "However, my mum did warn me that anything that seems too good to be true, probably is. You got any gut feelings about fairy coffee?" He pointed to the takeaway bar with flimsy cups and instant packets.

"No, I don't remember any fairy tales warning against the dangers of cheap coffee, but I should probably cut back for my anxiety's sake."

"Suit yourself." The demon's sockets lit up to find sachets of English breakfast tea next to the hot water spigot on the old-fashioned coffee machine. "Time for a bit of builder's brew." He proceeded to horrify his companion by dunking three bags in his mug as well as milk and sugar, squeezing and stirring till the whole mix turned a dark, creamy brown. The tannin-enriched steam wafted into his nostrils, and for a moment, shadows of eyeballs flickered in his empty gaze.

Before he could take a tiny sip and burn his tongue, Meg slapped his hand, sending the precious liquid tumbling to the tasteful tile floor. "Oy! What the—?" He trailed off as he saw strange golden vapors drifting from the fresh spill.

Meg pointed to some little pink and orange packets to the side. "Why would a fairy buffet specifically stock Dunkin's coffee? I think it's food *and* drink. My gut's warning me that this is a trap. It's meant to lure us in—"

"Clever girl, as always," a deeper, silkier version of the game show host's voice called from a nearby booth. The demon's eyes shifted instantly to red as he turned to see "Hamilton" lounging in a full set of golden armor. A black-tipped spear leaned next to the Fey. The mere sight of the weapon made Vocharlian clutch his side. "Oh, allow me to elucidate to you, little Charlie." He flipped his weapon around and the backside of the spearhead glowed a divine white. "Yes, this little pigsticker was made for critters *just like you.*"

Meg, however, trained her gaze on the golden crown hovering over his equally shiny blond hair. "Who *are* you?"

"A very dangerous question to ask, especially considering that neither of you seem to know who *you* are. Ahh, the innocence of youth." He waved his hand, and in a blink of an eye, he returned to his sleezy glory, clad in linen and silk with a golf bag now perched by his seat. "It's rather simple, really. You two kept faffing about, to borrow one of Chaz's favorite colloquialisms, and I got bored."

The demon snarled, "You got *bored*? What's that supposed to mean?"

"It means that I didn't feel like watching you two crazy kids redis-cover all your powers by running around Boston and reenacting some horrific slice of life rom-com. *Blah, blah blah*, Meg has magic, Charlie's a demon, let the hijinks ensue!" He rolled his eyes and let out a tremen-dous "*Ugh*, it's enough to make me want to lie on a bed of cold iron nails if I have to sit through that one...more...time."

Meg stayed a healthy distance away, shaking her head furiously. "Rediscover? I've only known—"

"You know more than you give yourself credit for, Meg. You just keep clinging to that outdated notion that time is linear. Humans, so simple, yet so charming. Why, I bet you two crazy kids think you're from the same universe!"

Vocharlian and Meg stood there dumbstruck until their gracious host leaned on his elbows and grinned. "The first thing you two need to let go of is an overwhelming need for things to make sense. You're still clinging to the old, and you've wandered into a whole new world. Big bang...big crunch and everything in between—it's all happened and it's all gonna happen and it's all happening right at this very moment. However, your consciousness is stuck experiencing one tiny moment at a time, so I thought, why not make things a little more interesting?"

"You—" Vocharlian snarled.

"Now, if you really like, I can boot you back into that stinky alleyway and you can limp off to an urgent care where some schmuck will be traumatized for life when she realizes that Charlie there ain't quite human. You'll then have a merry chase through New England, have some boring conversations where you two realize you have more similarities than differences, before you finally take up that charming pixie's offer for training in a smelly bookstore in Salem. Total snooze-fest."

Hamilton yawned before continuing, "It'll get the job done. Yes, you'll learn how to utilize a focus for your magic, so the pesky energy stops draining your life force, Meg, but it's been done before. Rather than relive those charming escapades, I thought, let's spice it up. After all, you owe me a quest, don't you?"

"I owe you some claws to the face!" With that, the demon lunged, but rather than seem the slightest bit alarmed, Hamilton waved and sent Vocharlian flying into a pile of bagels.

"Don't worry, he'll learn," the Fey sighed, leaning toward Meg. "After all, the outbursts are part of their charm. Sit down, take a load off, and we'll have a chat."

"No!" the demon snarled and pounced straight from the pastries to the tabletop, fire blazing in his sockets. The muscles on his arms expanded as his hair filled out into more like a lion's mane. His voice dropped to a guttural roar. "*Leave her alone.*"

Hamilton looked past the beast and beamed at Meg. "He doesn't even know, does he? Precious!"

"*I don't know what you're talking about.*" Meg rushed to Vocharlian's side and immediately the red from her demon's eyes expanded around his whole body. She stared in horror as the red glow began to creep up her hand as well, her right hand this time. "How am I doing this? Give me a straight answer!"

"Mind calling off your pet first?" he asked, pointing to the flames now licking the tip of his nose.

"*Charlie, stop!*"

The inferno winked out in a heartbeat. Vocharlian transformed into a soft, weaponless body wearing a tracksuit, his human form now perched on Formica. "Bollocks."

"How did I—?" Meg stammered even as her legs gave out and her companion had to help her to a seat. Two steaming hot beverages materialized before them.

"They say that instinct is our unfettered connection to the will of the universe, a fleeting moment of understanding that our stuck-in-place consciousnesses cannot quite comprehend," Hamilton explained. "That's why you humans put such emphasis on trusting your gut. Those colonies of mindless organisms writhing within you have no such preconceived limits. Tap into them and magic happens."

"Are you saying I need a probiotic to cast spells?" Meg replied flatly, prompting a snicker from her demon. The Fey took a moment to collect himself as well.

"I like you a lot, Meg, I really do," he said, resting his chin on his neatly folded hands. "We'll get to the point where we can talk, *really* talk, but for now you need...a tutorial. Isn't that more in your vernacular, gamer girl? Oh, and feel free to have a drink. I give you my word that these are completely mundane."

"Why should we trust you?" the demon growled before sniffing both beverages. "You pointy-eared pi—"

Hamilton waved his hand, slamming Vocharlian's mouth shut with a puff of air. "Trust is a gift, I understand that, but if we are going to work together this once, we need to start with a small gesture. What does your gut tell you right now, Meg?"

Meg picked up the sturdy brown mug. "My gut and I haven't always agreed," she confessed.

"I did use soy milk, if that helps." Hamilton then leaned back and crossed his hands behind his head, showing off a chunky medallion straight out of the disco era. The moment Meg noticed the onion embossed on the front, she tipped the rim to her lips. The Fey grinned wickedly. "Oh well, now you're trapped in this realm forever."

Meg sprayed her drink across the table while Hamilton rolled with laughter. The demon tried to pounce, but once more went flying into baked goods. "I'm kidding, I swear. By Titania's tits, the look on your face was priceless. Now, where were we? Oh yeah, skipping to the good parts!"

Chapter 22

The Good Parts

How did we end up on the beach?" Meg asked as she stared at the expanse of ivory sand while her demon gawked at his droopy Hawaiian print swim trunks. His breastplate remained fused to his chest, but a kind soul had embossed the edges with puka shells to fit the tropical theme.

"Bloody Fey...you never can trust them," he muttered as he brushed off his shoulders. While he shuffled and instantly shredded through his flip flops, Meg adjusted the floral coverup she now wore. Her eyes widened in terror as she lifted the collar to find a bikini waiting underneath. She tugged at the creeping back hem and gave quiet thanks that whatever magic had changed her outfit, thought to pack a magic razor as well.

"*Welcome to the Daydream Islands...of Aquatica!*" Hamilton's voice called from an invisible speaker. The now-expected phantom *oohs* and *ahhs* followed from every direction. As if on cue, a perfect tropical breeze fluttered around them, sending Meg's curls into a humidity-buffed halo.

She found herself surrounded by a dense jungle of palm trees. The water sparkled and frothed, a gemstone blue more at home in animation than any reality Meg had seen before, and every trace of their luxury hotel had faded into the horizon. She turned to her equally awkward companion. "So, you know about Fey... What they can do?"

Vocharlian grinned sheepishly, the sunlight glinting off his fangs. "Well, most of it comes from telly, but so far it's all checked out."

"Wait...what?" she snapped, but any further questions had to wait as the water nearby churned to reveal a multitude of humanoid shapes.

The world around Meg shimmered and shifted. The bells and whistles of *Let's Make a Bargain* pounded in her temples.

"*Our lucky winners have selected an all-expense paid luxury quest at one of our fine friends in Aquatica's eastern kingdoms! While staying at a four-star hotel and enjoying such amenities as pools, tennis courts, and not getting eaten by local wildlife, Meg and Charlie can save a kingdom from certain disaster while learning how to create a focus and harness the arcane. Travel includes two coach dream navigations from Boston to the adjacent realms as well as luggage and wardrobe furnished by Subconscious...*"

"Oh my God, we're still on the show," she whispered.

She blinked and found herself back on the beach as the watery shapes solidified into all manner of fish men and women, complete with scaly tails and seashell bras. Meg mused, "That's something I never understood. Are mermaids fish or mammals? I mean, most mammals don't have feathers, fins, or scales, but why on earth would a fish need a bra?"

Vocharlian turned to face her. "I hate to break it to you, luv, but we aren't on Earth." He then pointed to the double moons hovering in the otherwise clear teal sky. "Also, that's what you think about right now? That fucker has a trident!"

The head merman rolled his bright silvery eyes and looked to his two-forked spear in his hands. "It's a bident, you Fell moron. Learn to count." He then flipped the polearm around to show off glowing white metal, like the spear Hamilton brandished in the hotel. Vocharlian recoiled and hissed.

A smaller, slimmer fish man with lavender scales and a frill of pink fins slithered forward and bowed. "Please, you must excuse my brood mate. He's from the north where the monks teach sarcasm as the highest form of art. I am Piceus Decimus Meridius Pike of the Eastern Front, and I welcome you, kind witch, to our shores. It's been far too long since a mortal has graced us with their presence." He then gave a dismissive wave to her left. "Your minion is welcome as well, of course."

"Not a bloody minion!" Vocharlian sputtered, but he quieted as another wave of merfolk crested onto the beach. He sidled up to Meg and tried to look intimidating, but his claws had little reach in comparison to all the pointy sticks.

"This has to be a dream," Meg kept whispering as her breath sped up and went shallow.

"You gonna freak out on me, luv? Cause dream or not, the Divine energy radiating off that demonsticker, feels quite real—"

Meg steadied her feet. "If it is a dream, I'm in control," she reminded herself. "Also, mermaids are cool, so let's do this thing." She did her best curtsey to the fish man in front. "I'm Meg, Meg Reynolds, and I'm happy to meet you too Sir...um Lord... Um..."

His oversized eyes lit up as she fumbled for the honorific. "Piceus Pike if you are being formal, my dear Lady Reynolds," he offered gently. "But friends of these lands know me simply as Pike. I do hope that a witch mighty enough to venture this far from her home plane chooses to be my friend."

"Pike it is then."

The friendly fish leader then waved over the vast expanse of water in the cove. "Shall we be off? We can discuss our needs further once we are on our way."

"On our way?" Meg asked.

"Well, there is not much that can be done on land in Aquatica, am I right? Don't worry, Meera here has all the necessary spells if you didn't come prepared."

"We didn't come prepared," Meg and Vocharlian replied flatly in unison.

"That's new," the demon said as Meg glowed purple. A wizened lady with a goldfish head made some clicking noises, but Meg remained frozen in place. "Oy, you all right?"

Meg rubbed her neck, and the glow faded "I'm fine, I think," she said before turning toward the fish woman. "Thank you for um..."

"Such a splendid water breathing spell, yes?" Pike interjected before swooping toward Meg again, prompting a flash of green from the demon's sockets. This scaly bastard had a face that looked like it had been animated in Japan, complete with saucer-sized eyes and a perky little pout. His fuchsia ticked tail slithered next to Meg's bare leg, so the demon cleared his throat and took another step closer.

"Mind if we have a moment, Bubbles?"

Meg let Vocharlian drag her away from the fish-folk chattering amongst themselves. "You seem frightfully calm, luv." He sniffed the residue of magic. "This is weird for you."

"Oh, it's hinky, but I'm not feeling panic. A sane person would probably be panicking right now, but I think it's just so weird that my brain is too excited to be terrified. You know, my visualization meditation...*when I actually do it*...is a beach just like this one, and I totally maxed out my Merfolk reputation in *Eternaquest*—"

He made a rapid-fire time out gesture. "Back to the point, we're in a Fey realm, in case you didn't get that—"

"Okay, but it feels like a dream, and if it's a dream, then, I'm in control, right? Don't you get it? For the first time ever, I feel like I'm in control!" Her entire face lit up, forcing even the grumpy demon to smile a little. "I wish I could explain it better, but ever since I got here, I don't feel like everything is spinning and I can't do a thing about it. I feel... I feel..."

The demon inhaled deeply. "It's called happiness. You should try it out more often." He then whipped around to face the curious contingent. "You gonna zap me too so we can get this show on the road?"

A few clicks and glows later and the demon felt a strange rippling sensation along the edges of his collar. "Um, fish people... I don't..." His words devolved into sputtering gags.

"Charlie!" He didn't have the ability to correct his name as he gasped for air. The side of his neck flared and expanded, and he could feel something unknown and squishy under ridges of skin.

"He can't seem to split his focus like the human can!" Pike squawked. Vocharlian had no strength to fight the burly mermen dragging him into the water. Once dunked under a wave, the world cleared, and oxygen rushed to his brain.

"What the fuck?" he cried, his voice working even under water. "What did you bastards do to me?!?"

"This should not have happened, Great Witch, please do not punish us. Although we do not often perform magic upon the Fell, he should have kept both his lungs and his gills and been easily able to switch between the two..." Pike explained, his voice shaking.

The demon, however, chose to focus on a different figure, one of his human diving after him and whipping around to stare at his neck. After a double take to feel the slits along her own throat and a few confused blinks, she said, "You can breathe underwater, phew. Wait, I can speak underwater, that's new."

She then crested out of the ocean, cocked her head, and declared, "I can still breathe air too. Why is it working for me and not for him?"

"Perhaps if we get to our citadel, our sages will know more." Pike then pointed off on the horizon. "I promise, Lady Reynolds, we will do everything in our power to correct this. If you would prefer us to reverse the hex and leave him here while we convene with the elders—"

"No!" she snapped. "I mean, he has to stay with me. It's just the way it is."

Please don't send me to that other place. I don't think there's any convenient water there.

What other place?

Just don't send me away.

That thought echoing through both their heads made each of them pause, as if for a moment Vocharlian didn't feel any water rushing into his eye sockets, as if something for the briefest of moments blocked the flow. However, he immediately became distracted by Meg still standing in the shallows next to him, her coverup loosened to show off more glorious skin than he'd seen on her before. He gulped as the water around him shifted to all shades of violet in a heartbeat. "Simmer down, lad," he chastised himself. "You got five years to enjoy before you have to make a move."

"What was that?"

Vocharlian made a point to swim away from Meg's valid question. "I said, the fish boy is right, and we should get a wriggle on. My side is starting to twinge and that probably means the Fey pulling the strings is getting antsy."

"O-okay."

They began to swim in a tight convoy into the bay. Meg had managed to wrap herself back in her coverup, despite the difficulty of wrangling it underwater, and the demon learned that his limp wings on land made for excellent fins. As they expanded, even the dour-faced guards paused to take in the translucent panes and the faint patterns of stripes developing toward the edges.

"They're bigger than I thought they'd be," Meg said, wide eyed.

"I get that a lot."

Meg shifted her wonder to the swarm of scaled creatures flitting around them, their own fins a rainbow of glorious shades. Vocharlian pouted as she continued to ignore him, but as they descended and greater swarms of glittering fish danced around the group, even the jaded demon had to take a moment to gawk. "All right, I admit...it's—"

"It's all my *Little Mermaid* fantasies come to life!" Meg exclaimed, taking another moment to gently press her own gills. She twirled a few times, then pointed to a sea turtle with a giggle of delight. "Is this magic? Is this really magic?"

Vocharlian shook his head in disbelief but then shifted the gesture to a nod as her beaming smile infected him too. "Of course, it's magic. You're just picking up on this now, you barmy bird?"

She let his mild insult slip as she stared at his face, now softened by the water. Pike swirled around her too, his own saucer eyes sparkling as he took in her delight as well. "It is a wonder, what we find in the vastness of the universe, when only we let go and accept its will," he said mysteriously. "Lord Hamilton, for once, undersold his treasure."

"What was that?" Meg asked.

His face settled back into a more placid countenance. "I was merely remarking that our Fey lord failed to describe you well. I cannot wait to see what happens once you reach my palace—"

"*Your* palace? How posh are you?" the demon asked.

"All will be revealed in time, of course. For now, let me simply be your guide." He then punctuated his point by lifting Meg's hand to his lips. The water shifted to green, and Vocharlian flared a wing to block Meg's view.

Charlie?

This magic is messing with me.

His internal over-explanation seemed to do the trick, and they soon returned to gawking at oceanic life and the wonderous clarity of the water of this realm. Pike pointed to each reef and grotto and dropped informational tidbits that made Meg's eyes wobble while her demon stewed.

The sarcastic fish from earlier swam alongside a wingtip and raised what passed for a brow on his hairless face. "You are the guard for the witch, Fell?" he asked, sizing up the scrawny demon.

"What's it to you?"

"If we go to war, I think the witch is going to need more protection," the soldier fish said with a dismissive gill snort.

"Wait a bloody second, *war*? Who said anything about a—?"

"Welcome to the Eastern Front of Aquatica!"

Vocharlian whipped around to hear Pike declare, "Please, don't mind the kraken."

Episode Eight

Requisite Two-Parter

Chapter 23

Part One, Read the Room

H oly Mary, mother of cephalopods!" Meg's eyes widened as a creature straight out of 20,000 *Leagues Under the Sea* slapped one of its appendages down on a castle carved out of ancient corals. The suckers recoiled once they struck a shimmering barrier, shooting waves of sparks into the giant.

"Oh, fu—" Vocharlian didn't get to finish the thought, as their entourage swept them into an open gate before the sea beast could notice their approach.

"Please don't mind the mess," Pike implored as they darted past some scattered barrels and weapon racks. The demon did cast a longing eye to a giant serrated fishhook just lying there on the floor. "While our force field does an admirable job repelling those vile creatures, it cannot stop all the kinetic energy."

The walls vibrated, as if to punctuate his point, then came a crash off to the left. Pike motioned to a pair of guards to check that out before he took Meg's hand in his own. "Please excuse us, but our defensive magic by its very nature must be more permeable than most. The waters, they simply must flow."

"Of course," Meg said, her face lighting up. "You need the oxygen moving through the water so you don't drown."

"Did you really just worry that a fish could drown?" Vocharlian muttered in her ear.

"Fish *can* drown," she hissed. But that conversation needed to be tabled as she swam out of the narrow entrance hall and became overwhelmed by the colors and motion of a coral reef molded into a magnificent great hall. Meg toppled backward to follow a squadron of manta rays as they patrolled the glittering ceiling. Vocharlian, meanwhile, had to keep flicking to stop the army of sea life swarming to investigate his wings. Pike laughed as the demon swatted away a tiny blue and black striped fish. The offended creature rushed to the merman's frills.

"He means to clean you, my Fell friend. Creatures from land are treasure troves of errant crustacea and insect larvae."

Meg squealed as another cleaner snaked its way through her curls. She then froze as something scampered along the edge of her ear. Vocharlian snapped his claws, startling the curious crab and sending it skittering back into one of the thousands of crevices lining the walls. He started to chuckle but stopped short as he saw Meg still frozen in place, her eyes wobbling and betraying that if they hadn't been surrounded by liquid, tears would be pouring out of her eyes.

"Are you alright?" Pike asked, frantically scanning the waters around her. "Is our spell—?"

"I'm fine," she snapped. "Can we move on?"

Crabs creep me out.

Better than spiders, luv.

Before they could continue their inner monologue, a flurry of helpful fish folk surrounded Meg, escorting her into another corridor. Vocharlian didn't need to swim after her, as the moment she got at the edge of their tether, the unseen string dragged him along the current. He banged his shoulder and got his wing snagged on the coral wall, prompting a wave of expletives. "Fell brute," one guard in a seashell bra huffed before slapping him with her tail fins.

"Nice pearl necklace," he replied before yanking himself free. "Damn these blighters sting."

"The walls are worth more than you, demon," the prissy fish lady explained as her fins flared a brighter shade of pink. "Your mistress may be a guest of my brother, but you swim these halls as a barely tolerated interloper."

"I'll keep that in mind, Princess Pinky. Now if you'll pardon me, I need to keep up with the witch, so I don't—" He never finished his sentence as the entourage went into a room. Unfortunately, the angle dragged the demon face first along a jagged patch of reef. The pink lady-fish giggled as the stingers of a nearby anemone swayed over and slapped the demon on the cheek for her. "Bloody tether," he grumbled before rolling around the rocks to find himself in an entirely different sort of underwater room.

"Wow," Meg exclaimed, so enamored of her surroundings that she didn't notice the welts covering her companion's cheek. The pendulum of her moods had already swung from paralyzing terror to paralyzing wonderment as even the demon ended up gobsmacked. "So many books!"

Bioluminescent sconces pulsed with variated lights, making the pearlescent shelves shimmer a rainbow of colors. Pike beamed and proudly produced a leathery tome that would look more at home on land. "For you, my lady."

Meg stared at him blankly.

"It's the history of witches in Aquatica," Vocharlian said as he scanned the text.

"*You* can read this?" Pike's sister asked as she swam next to her brother. Their eyes both widened. "A *demon*?"

Meg confessed, "It's Greek to me."

"Closer to Enochian actually," Pike corrected. "But we have some Greek texts from when Arsenios first visited our fair citadel."

Vocharlian scanned the walls of titles. "I've picked up a bit here and there," he said innocently. Pike made an appreciative "*ahh*" and turned his attention back to Meg, while his sister kept her gaze firmly locked on the demon. She sneered, showing off needle teeth that would look at home in Vocharlian's maw.

"Are you feeling less overwhelmed, Lady Reynolds? I had hoped that the comfort of a magical sanctum would bring you back to ease. We spend so much time under the sea that we forget that the pressure can overcome the land-bound so easily at first. There is even a reading nook that can be placed in an air bubble, should you wish."

"You're very nice, and you're right, it's a lot to take in. Could I just have a second...a little space please?" Meg asked as she tried to smile at each of the seemingly endless school of merfolk that kept flitting about. "I don't even know all of you."

Pike clicked a few times, and the pack of fish folk swarmed out the door, leaving only him, the big sarcastic guard, and his sister undulating in the alcove with the land lubbers. Before he could get another word in edgewise, the smaller pink mermaid swished in the fish equivalent of a curtsey and then took Meg's hands in her own delicate webbed ones. "Please excuse my tactless big brother. I am Picea Linnea Hesperia Brinehilda, and this library is my domain, a domain that I open freely to you in the spirit of friendship."

Vocharlian didn't stop his guffaw in time, the infernal belly laughs echoing through the chamber. "*Brinehilda!*"

Everyone turned to glare at the demon, but instead of shutting up and doing anything to further land-sea relations, he doubled down on the ridiculousness bursting into a rousing chorus of "Oh, *Brinehilda*, you're so lovely!" to the tune of the *Tannhäuser Overture* with a ridiculous lisp and emphasis on her name.

"Are you propositioning my sister, *demon?*" Pike's normally calm demeanor shifted, and this time as his frill expanded, a pair of gnarly spikes emerged from his temples, a far more impressive sight than Vocharlian's nubs.

Vocharlian turned to his gobsmacked human. He hummed a bit more of the tune and made some expectant jazz hands. "Only the greatest cartoon of all time," he prompted. "*Spear and magic helmet?*"

The big guy jerked his bident away from the demon. "You are *never* touching my spear, wretch!"

Meg shook her head. "What on earth are you talking about?" She then addressed the agitated fish-folk. "The pressure must have gotten to him. Maybe the spell is still acting all wonky. I'm sure he didn't mean to insult your sister, Captain Pike." Now it was Meg's turn to giggle. "I mean *Piceus* Pike. Sorry, it's just a name from a show where I come from, and yeah...that's not really important right now."

Everyone exchanged a round of awkward glances, until Pike lowered his spines. "Perhaps we have all been overcome with the giddiness of introductions. Sister, why don't you have the chefs bring in the special seaweed tea and take Garfield with you."

This time both Meg and her demon had to turn away quickly.

He doesn't look like a cat!

Charlie, we can't keep giggling at their names...no matter how silly they may sound!

He's a...he's a—

Don't, please don't...

He's a bloody catfish!

They both quickly faked an underwater coughing fit until Meg managed to choke even with her magical gills. She waved away Pike and pointed to the book. "So, you wanted to show me something...before we got all distracted?"

"Why yes, I know it's a lot considering the short notice, but Lord Hamilton assured me that you were quite capable and looking for a challenge," Pike explained. "That's why I assumed the library would be a good place to start. It contains the collected works of all our prior visitors and our own arcane weavers."

"Oh, the wanker said we were eager," the demon grumbled, earning him an elbow from Meg. He coughed, and a streak of blood slithered out of the corner of his mouth. The second the sanguine stain dissipated into the water, the guard—now all the way at the door—leered and showed off his sharklike teeth. Vocharlian rubbed his phantom wound again. "What do you need us to do, damn it?"

Pike focused solely on Meg. "I do realize that our Fey overlords are sometimes...less than forthcoming. Did Lord Hamilton actually tell you what was required on this mission of mercy?"

"Well...you know those pesky Fey," she said with a weak little laugh. "You could say he just picked us up off the street and dropped us here."

The merman's face fell. "I see. You are a witch, correct?"

If someone asks if you are a witch, say yes!

"Yes! Yes, I think so. I'm just...overwhelmed," she said, shooting her demon a glare. "Maybe if I had the quest text...err I mean, you tell me what you need, and we'll figure out how to help. It's not like we have any choice, right? I mean, I have to complete...this quest...or else...or else..." Her eyes glazed over.

Hey? You fading out on me? Meg? Meg?

"This is the quest we had to do," she whispered. "I...remember."

While in the luxurious Aquatica Citadel, our contestants will enjoy gourmet meals, legendary oceanside spa treatments, and even experience the resurrection of a cosmic horror from the briny deep!

"Do you still hear the laugh track too?" the demon hissed.

Meg nodded, but kept her attention trained on Pike. "There's a giant octopus attacking your castle. Is that what you need help with?"

It was the fish man's turn to chuckle. "One kraken? Oh, heavens no, nothing so simple for us to entreat the Fey overlords for help... We can handle our own fight there. No, our issue stems from a deep-sea mining expedition last month. We opened a new gold vein in the Everlast Gorge—"

"You mined something in the deepest part of the ocean, and you're surprised when something bad happened?" Vocharlian asked incredulously. "There is clearly no Hollywood in this dimension to teach you the folly of your ways."

Meg elbowed her demon again. "Please, go on."

"Yes, normally our expeditions encounter nothing more dangerous than a methane deposit or a cantankerous sperm whale's territory. However, this time, the leader informed us that his scouts went missing, then a few days later, we get reports that the mineshaft walls seemed to 'come alive.' Then the final message—"

"Screaming, gurgling then an abrupt cut off?" the demon offered.

"No, actually, something far more troubling." Pike leaned in and furrowed his fins. "He reported that suddenly *everything was fine.*"

"We're here because 'everything is...fine'? The fu—"

"I beg you silence your lippy companion." Pike flared his gills. "Although the message initially seemed like a relief, the expedition never returned. Indeed, the two follow-up envoys we sent never even checked in. I fear sending another team."

He swam to a nearby shelf, tracing his fins along the books. "Our most talented scrymasters see activity flitting in and out of the tunnels. They detect lights in all our gorge settlements...yet no messages are returned. To make matters worse, last night, our town on the edge of the frontier, Virlandia, sent us but one reply—*we are all fine.*"

"Body snatchers," the demon sang under his breath. Meg didn't bother elbowing him this time.

"I am quite concerned because my sister's intended is the reeve of Virlandia. If this strangeness continues, she may impulsively run off to see what the matter is herself, and while she is a glorious warrior on our senate floor, I do not fancy her chances out on the frontier, especially with the kraken on the move for the season."

"That's a lot to think about. Um, do you think I could have a little while alone in the library to think this all over, maybe...um—"

"Formulate a brilliant land-based magical strategy?" Pike finished for her. "Of course. We were instructed to have all our arcane means at your disposal. Garfield will guard the door, and should you need anything, anything at all, I shall be in my office in this very same wing."

"Formulating brilliant land-based strategies is what we do, guv. Don't you worry."

"We'll be right on it!" Meg exclaimed. Pike beamed and gave her the deepest of bows. The moment he slipped out the door, Meg's eyes flashed red, and she glared at Vocharlian. "What are you doing? We must be a hundred feet underwater and are only breathing because we have spells cast on us—spells cast on us by *the merpeople you insist on insulting!*"

"Now you're right and proper freaking out—good! For a moment there I thought you'd been taken over by the pod people too. I mean it's obvious some *Invasion of the Body Snatchers*-level shite is going down."

"How can you possibly know that from a five-minute conversation?"

"Easy, laws of Hollywood state that no one is ever fine when they say so. Now considering that we are clearly in either a fantasy or horror framework judging by all the magic and the mer—"

"You can't use movie logic right now! That's...ridiculous!"

"More ridiculous than being *poofed* out of an alley in Boston and tasked with saving a bunch of anthropomorphic fish with nothing more than our wits and my stunning good looks?"

"You...have a point."

With that, they drifted through a room full of books only one of them could read. Meg twirled over to a shelf and ran her fingers along the spines, imitating Pike's earlier maneuver. "Is this sharkskin?" she mused as she traced over a gray section.

"Earth to Meg," Vocharlian called. He used his now effective wings to rush next to her in the blink of an eye. "You still with me?"

He swished left as to avoid Meg flopping against the divider between the bookcases. As she landed, the sconce in her section flared and dislodged, revealing its true nature as a jellyfish. Said jellyfish retaliated by zapping one of Vocharlian's ears. When he hissed and missed his return swipe, Meg laughed until she doubled over. "This is insane... *I'm* insane!"

"Oh bollocks, I've lost her again."

"Lost me? How did you even *find me?*" Her laughter stopped abruptly as she once more studied the strange creature hovering next to her. From this angle and shaded by his wings, he cut quite an infernal figure. His elongated shadow accentuated both his horns and claws. "Is it wrong that I hope I'm crazy? Because...right now it's all hitting me that you are indeed a demon, and I somehow...I *brought* you here. Wouldn't it be better if I was just nuts?"

Vocharlian stared at his shadow, then took in the random mix of fur, scales, spikes, and leathery bumps that covered his arms. His eyes flickered from red, to green, before finally settling into a blue deeper and more serene than any of the ocean around them. "Hey, I'm not that... Well, I'm not as demon-y as you could've gotten. Just...relax."

Meg grabbed her temples, shaking off his soothing sloth aura. "Relax? I have too many questions! *Why* am I here now with you? Of all the things that could happen, *how* did I summon you?"

"Meg—"

"I don't believe in magic. I didn't try! There is no reason this should happen, and the more I stop and think about the past few days, the more I realize that I'm *not* getting a chance to stop and think. It's as if something or someone is keeping me from asking...these...questions. Why?!?"

"Come on." Vocharlian stifled his own yawn and stoked the blue vapors. "What we need—"

"*What* I need are answers. I don't understand anything! For all I know, you're like some twisted part of my id I brought out because I'm having a breakdown and I'm really drowning in my bathtub right now. I—I—"

"Stop!" the demon begged. "You're trying to look too much for a reason. The first thing I ever learned about the universe is that there *is no reason*. There can't be a reason for everything or that would mean that every single one of us every single day got *exactly* what they deserved, and I, for one, call that as bullshit! Yeah...you are right, someone *is* trying to jerk us around—there is a bloody Fey who's gotten his sticky fingers on us, so *of course* you aren't getting any time to think because the moment you take a breath, you'll feel that anger and try to stop the yellow-blooded bastard! Lastly, and most importantly, I don't care how insane you might be, what human would dream of a creature as ridiculous as me to be stuck with? If I *was* your id, would I be so pathetic?"

Meg rubbed her head and slumped along the tomes. "What if I'm dreaming?" she whispered as her eyelids grew heavy and closed.

Vocharlian's eyes sparkled and shifted quickly back to their default green. "Oh, bloody hell, slothalepsy is hitting!" He started shaking her, until she snorted and gave him a sleepy, "Five more minutes."

He made the executive decision to swing her over his shoulder and sink to the sandy floor. The longer she remained out, the more the blue tried to creep back into his sockets, until he yawned. "Stupid sloth. Meg, wake up!"

She yawned and opened her eyes at last. This time she pressed a finger idly against his cheek. "You *do* have fur on your face. Do you have to shave?"

"That's my barmy bird," he said with a gaping smile. "If I shaved this off, I'd look like one of those creepy baby demons they keep in the Pride Citadel." He shuddered. "Trust me."

"You are so weird."

"Says the lady who summoned me into her bathroom. Like you're one to talk."

She took a moment to sit up and fidget with her coverup. While she fussed with making herself slightly more presentable, she also stared at the mountain of books surrounding her. Her face fell. "I have no idea what I'm doing, Charlie."

The demon growled under his breath but didn't correct her this time. They watched the jellyfish settle back into its empty rest, casting a magical glow on the wall. As the bioluminescence shifted to magenta, she rubbed her head. "I don't know how I even summoned you, so how can I cast any more magic? Is this like my game where I have mana and can read spells in these books and just cast them, or is it something mental? Physical? Is it part of my soul? Oh God, do I even have a soul if I summoned a demon and put it in a contract? Wait, I must because it's on the contract...right?"

The demon booped her nose. "Now you're getting something. Look, I flunked magical theory at the academy—"

"There's demon school?" Her eyes lit up even brighter than the jellyfish sconce.

"Six years, six months, and six days of it to be exact. They are big on numerology down below. Dreadfully boring, and before you ask, when I say I flunked my magical theory, I mean I slept through it, so I can't help you."

"How could you sleep through learning magic?"

"Quite comfortably. That class had the best desks for putting your head down. There weren't even spikes on them."

Meg buried her face in her hands. "I summoned the *one* demon who knows nothing about magic."

"Hey now, lots of demons are rubbish at magic. Sure, it's more common down there than on Earth, but it's not like you got the one defective fucker in the lot."

She balled her hands into fists at her temples. "This is not helping. Nothing is helping! I don't even know where to begin—*arghhh*!!! Why can't this be like *Eternaquest*?"

"I don't know, why can't it?"

She stared at him. "Because that is a video game." She then stopped, cocked her head, and let those words sink in. "A video game that makes more sense than what I'm doing now. Maybe I'm overthinking." She shot the demon a glare before he could quip. "I've done it before, so there is no reason why I couldn't cast a spell again. Weird things have happened since you appeared, right?"

He made a go-on motion.

"Is it gut instinct? No, that's too unpredictable and there are all these fish people, and that Hamilton guy...and...and..."

"You're doing the thing again, where your brain is running a marathon but we're still sitting here, luv. Maybe we start at the beginning—"

Meg swam to her feet, taking a moment to appreciate how easily she could maneuver in this foreign environment. "The beginning... It all started when I got the burrito, didn't it?"

Her demon shrugged.

"No, I've gotten sick from Poblano's before, but I've never ripped a hole in the universe...just my plumbing." Vocharlian gave her an enthusiastic thumbs-up at her confession. She rolled her eyes before tapping her fingers as she replayed the insanity. The tapping became a beat. Meg hummed a familiar tune.

"Not that bloody song again," her demon moaned.

"The song! I just got that song. Come to think of it, I don't remember who shared it with me. I heard it on my playlist, and I loved it immediately."

It was Vocharlian's turn to swirl the lights in his eye sockets. "Fucking dubstep."

"What *is* your problem with dubstep?"

"Nothing if it's being used to torture a damned soul! However, as far as music goes, it's derivative claptrap that makes the same three noises. It's like you're stuck watching an action movie trailer on repeat, not to mention the lyrics—"

"The lyrics! That's it." Meg began swirling her arms, finding her way into the rhythm of the song. "Come on, help me. You heard it as many times as I did. How did it go? Inspiration! *Inspiration becomes a thought...*"

He stared, unmoved. She twirled away, nodded a few beats, then spat out the next line. "*Thoughts go into motion. Dum...dum...dah...dah...* what is it next?" She sang those two lines over and over again until her demon swam up to join her.

"*Motion becomes a rhythm,*" he growled through his teeth.

"*Rhythm begets emotion,*" she continued, her eyes lighting up. "*Emotion turns to song.*"

"*The song invokes a spell...*" Vocharlian sang softly, eying the room for any changes. He turned back to Meg and motioned for her to finish.

"And then...and then the deed is done," she whispered, also looking around frantically.

Nothing happened.

"Thank Hells, it wasn't the damn song," Vocharlian said, showing off a smug grin. "I told you..." He trailed off as his companion's eyes glazed over and she started swaying in the current. "Meg?"

"Inspiration becomes a thought,
    Thoughts go into motion.

Motion becomes a rhythm.
Rhythm begets emotion,
Emotion turns to song.
The song invokes a spell...
(And then the deed is done.)"

This time as she sang, she moved her arms in time with the bass pounding in her head. Magenta sparks danced from tip to tip of the demon's claws, and his body began to undulate in time with a song he claimed to despise more than anything. "Hey, Meg...um—"

She didn't acknowledge his protests. Instead, she stared at the same lights hopping along her fingers and then traced a smooth, steady circle in the water in front of her. "I need help," she pleaded.

The circle erupted with magenta light. Then came a whoosh and a tiny, winged form coalesced hundreds of feet underwater. "Oh, crap!" Meg cried as she heard the gurgle.

Chapter 24

Part Two, Focus on the Present

A re you kidding me? What were you thinking?"

"Oh great, the punk pixie is back," Vocharlian dead-panned as he floated around the room.

Meg shrank away in horror as she stared at the newly formed bubble bounding around the room. The fairy inside muttered some sort of incantation, her sodden pigtails stuck to the makeup running down her cheeks. "You're lucky I have contingency spells for everything, up to and including being yanked out of my chair mid-raid. Do you have any idea how long it took me to get a solid Archelm group going and now I've just up and AFKed right at the last boss!"

"And she's still a nerd," the demon sighed.

"I kinda forgot about the underwater thing. This spell or whatever makes it seem so...so normal," Meg confessed. "I needed a little help, and you were the first person I could think of, and I didn't realize you had a daytime raid group."

Vanth whizzed around so she could stare the larger woman in the eye. Meg gulped. "I'm sorry," she mouthed again. The pixie then noticed the vast number of books surrounding them. "Holy shit, where are we, Zazzy?"

"Aquatica," the demon called from his new perch on a sconce-free section of shelving. "Eastern citadel or something like that. Don't mind the occasional banging. They seem to have a kraken infestation, but it's under control."

The pixie alternated staring incredulously between the mortified Meg and the glib demon. She stopped for an extra moment to take in Vocharlian in his true form, particularly eyeing the runes on his breast-plate. "Those are some leet Fell protection runes, aren't they? Now why would a rough and tumble critter from the bowels of Hell need protection from the very energy that gives him his powers? Also, do you have an eating disorder? Seriously, dude, munch on a sandwich or something."

"I beg your pardon—" he started, but soon got drowned out by the girls both oohing and ahhing over a magnificent Portuguese Man-O-War-looking creature drifting around the upper levels. He curled under his wings and rubbed his sunken belly. "Some ladies like a Twiglet, you know," he protested. In his moment of insecurity, Vocharlian missed most of Meg recanting the short, short version of their story so far.

"So, you ended up on the Fey version of *Wheel of Fortune*, and now you're *so* lost you summoned me—the girl that you told not two hours ago to bugger off—because you need help. Normally I'd be like *fuck you very much*, but I must admit this is too awesomely weird to pass up. However, going forward we really need to establish some ground rules, mm-kay, Zazz?"

"Sure...anything."

Vanth whipped around to look at the demon. "She really thinks she summoned you from the bowels of Hell via dubstep. What aren't you telling me, Spike?"

Vocharlian toyed with one of the nubs jutting off his cheekbone. "To be fair, the song is hellaciously bad. The moment I heard it, it locked up my whole brain."

That made the pixie pause. "You heard the same song...in Hell? Was it on the radio or what?"

"That would be cruel," he deadpanned. "No, it came from the soul-forge in the Golgothan Bureau. I couldn't help myself. Once it started playing, I sang along."

She snapped her fingers. "Well, that leaves only one possible explanation. I'm thinking quantum entanglement."

"Quantum...what?" the demon started to ask.

"Of course, spooky action at a distance!" Meg cried out. "At one point even though we were worlds apart, Charlie and I were singing the same song at the same time—"

"Allowing for an arcane string!" Vanth finished. "It's like the string theory they taught you in college, sort of, but an arcane string is a special connection forged by the right mystical energy spontaneously affecting two beings at a single moment regardless of distance. It's still mostly theoretical since most of the experts were killed off a century ago—"

"K-killed?" Meg's face collapsed.

"The mundos have never liked us. Please say you've read *The Crucible*. Anyway, yes, it's theoretical, but I think Spike here is proof-positive that you managed to reach out and touch someone. Let me get a good look at you both. Guh, I wish Thor was here. Then again, he's a total asshole."

"Do you know a god or an Avenger?" Vocharlian asked from his perch.

"Neither. He's a guildie, both of the virtual and the magical kind. We've had a bit of a falling out as of late, so I think it's best if we keep all this summoning business on the down low. I'm pissed at him too for nixing my idea to have a paranormal podcast to reach out and find lost lambs like... Nah, that's not important right now. Hell, I don't even know what to make of you two crazy kids. Does he get your soul, or what, Zazzy?"

"I...I'm still figuring that all out. I owe him *a* soul, whether it's mine or someone else's, I guess that's still up for grabs," Meg confessed. "You must think I'm terrible."

Vanth rolled that around for a moment then zipped over to a nearby bookshelf. "Nah, for a chance to try out infernal power, I'd offer up my stepdad in a heartbeat. You'll eventually find some idiot who is both really bad and really desperate for power. They're a dime a dozen, so that's a non-issue. What we need to focus on *now* is the fundamentals before you yank another poor schmuck into Ariel's dungeon."

She raised up a finger, as if to press pause, then flitted around the library, chanting something that sounded like, "DaH jIHvaD choqe-Squ'mo', puqloDwI'," while her fists spewed out violet sparkles.

"Is that some magical language?" Meg asked looking over to her demon.

"Sounded like 'find me what I'm looking for, you bastard' to me," he replied.

"Oh, you speak Klingon? Truly the most elegant of languages for spellcasting." A moment later, a translucent lavender spider appeared on the top of the shelves and then scuttled over the books. Vocharlian recoiled and hissed at the glowing critter while flaring his limp wings. "Oh, how cute, he's scared of spiders too!"

"I'm not scared! My bloody cousin had one as a pet for years. That overgrown furry cockroach couldn't stand me, and believe me, the feeling was completely mutual."

"Methinks the demon doth protest too much. *Anyway*, I've got Skippy here crawling for any basic treatises on magic to get you started. If we're in luck, it will be in one of the languages I can translate, if not—"

"Don't worry about it, Tiny," Vocharlian interjected.

"*You're* a cunning linguist?" Vanth taunted as she sized him up. He grinned and rolled out a tongue that could flick the collar of his breastplate. Both women found themselves at a loss for words for a moment.

The demon then blew the pixie an exaggerated kiss. "Nothing so fun. I happen to be the unlucky recipient of a Babel Curse after I slagged off the wrong headmaster. You heard of it, short-stuff?"

"I thought it was a myth, but hey, the day is young and full of surprises. Since we've got you, Universal Translator, why don't we get cracking on finding Zazz here the perfect help guide?"

"So yeah, apparently the basis of magical theory is using a disciplined mind to suppress all emotions and gather the strength of will to bend Mother Nature to your command, blah, blah, blah, *study*, blah, blah, *boring shit*, blah blah *patriarchy*... NEXT!"

"How is it that the dude who cares about nothing, understands everything?" Vanth asked while lounging in her bubble. In the time it took her arcane spiders to find every Intro to Magic text in the library, she'd managed to repurpose a mushroom coral skeleton into a seat, as well as mix the world's smallest margarita out of thin air.

"Maybe if you found something a little more interesting, I'd get more enthused. This is clearly a crock of shit, because look at our Meg—she can't control her emotions and yet, here I am."

"Hey!"

"No offense, luv, but I can't put you and all this boring nonsense together, even if you did go to Harvard."

"Nice," Vanth added. "Still, mundane education doesn't always work once you get the old magic involved. There are tons of nerds in our line of work, don't get me wrong, but the demon has a point—from what I've gathered, the classical approach isn't quite your jam. Hey, Spike, try the one with the pretty seashells on the cover next."

Vocharlian stared at the table full of tomes inlayed with various seashells and raised a brow. The pixie pointed to one with a pink sheen. The demon scanned the first few pages then chucked it into the failed pile. "Can't your creepie-crawly find something short and useful? We have a bunch of fish to save."

The pixie tapped her chin and took a few long, slow sips of her magical beverage. "There *is* the school of thought that the best way to learn is through practice. As good as all this theory is—*and I'm totally going to steal as much of it as I can*—it's not going to get us through the next day, now is it?"

"So, what you're saying is she should just put on her big girl Nike's?" the demon asked. His smirk faded as the girls stared blankly at him. He flexed and boomed out with, "*Just do it?*"

"Oh, like the Victoria slogan?" Meg asked.

"You mean Nike," the demon corrected.

"As fascinating as this is, guys, the clock is ticking," Vanth interrupted. "Let's start with *really basic* basics. You've got your magical creature all summoned and stuff, so let's whip out your focus and pump out a few drills."

"What focus?" both Meg and Charlie asked.

"Rewind, hit the pause button, and listen closely to what I'm about to say, you crazy kids," Vanth said as she pulled down a screen in front of the bookcases.

"Was that always there?" Meg asked.

In lieu of a marker, the pixie produced a pointer shaped like a cuttle-fish, and as she lined up the tentacle end with the screen, an animated image popped into life. "Yes, I use magic to do presentations, sue me," Vanth said with a little side eye to the unseen audience. "I've also always wanted to break the fourth wall."

A chorus of oohs and ahhs surrounded the confused pair in the sand. Vanth swirled her pointer with a flourish to show some derivative super-heroes punching each other complete with sound bubbles. This trig-gered an unseen cheer and the pixie to lean in conspiratorially. "So that Fey dude and his posse are watching your progress after all...or this is a reactionary cantrip meant to confuse you." That got a round of boos. "Yup, definitely scrying on us."

"Fish people are waiting, Tiny. Can we hurry this up?"

"Just like to know all I'm dealing with," she explained. "Whatever magic this game show host has, it's not wise to fuck with if he's watching us all the way in Aquatica. This is an outer realm, isn't it, Spike? Like at least three removed off the old Terra Firma?"

"Something like that." He then whispered to Meg. "I slept a lot in cosmic geography too."

Vanth ignored his confession and kept setting the clip art scene. On one side she showed the punch, on the other the masked villain sliding into a cracked wall. "You did physics in the Ivy League, right Zazz?"

"Pre-law actually," Meg corrected. "My mom is a physics professor though, and that looks like Newton's Third Law."

"Roger-roger, Zazzy. There's some magic that totally screws Newtonian Physics, but there is a big principle we all gotta consider when we cast—the whole conservation of energy thing. You *cannot* truly create or destroy anything, merely transform it. That means if you bring a big, bad source of Fell energy into this world and intend to keep it going, then you gotta feed it. Oh, and if you want to cast, well, you pull that energy from somewhere too. The big question is, what energy are you feeding into your magic Meg, *especially* if you don't have a damn focus to regulate it?"

"I...I don't know."

The images shifted to an imp sitting on a girl's shoulder with all sorts of squiggly lines radiating from it. Vanth then drew a boy with horns next to her. "I see that you made a human form for him, one that you can recharge with food and sleep and shit, but do you have any idea what happens if he transforms into his real form? *Casts a spell?* If he blows too many special abilities in the real world, he's gonna go straight for the traditional source of Fell energy."

Meg stared blankly.

"Human souls! Demons feed off souls."

Vocharlian jumped to his feet. "Now that's just racist. We absorb discarded soul energy and negative emotions. I'm not some soul-stealing bogeyman! Meg, you have to believe me—"

"I'm calling it like I see it, Spike. I can feel the energy flowing out of Meg and into you. Hey, are you feeling confused, lightheaded, like you can't string two thoughts together, Zazzy?"

Meg nodded.

"That's your friendly neighborhood demon-man leeching off you. If you don't figure out a focus soon, then he's going to drain you dry. Hey, are we even sure that's not what Spike here is really after?"

Vocharlian snarled, "If she dies before our contract is complete, I die too! What do we need to do to sort this shite out?"

"Good to know that little clause is in your contract." She gave a bit of side eye to Meg. "Pre-law, *right*. Well, it's a good thing we aren't on Earth anymore 'cause let me tell you, a focus that can handle a...well I'm assuming you're a greater infernal despite being so janky...those, um, are really hard to come by. This being an Outer Realm gives us a snowball's chance, so I'll have my spider keep snooping, and hopefully these fish people will do us a solid. Otherwise, every time you cast magic, or your demon even exerts himself—tick-tock, down winds the clock if you know what I mean."

She facepalmed as she took in their blank stares. "It's a miracle you've lasted twenty-four hours," Vanth muttered. "Oh, and when you say fish people, are we talking *Little Mermaid* or *Creature from the Black Lagoon?*"

"Kinda in the middle," Meg replied. "Seashell bras but no hair. Their fins are super pretty and Pike, he's their leader, he's really nice."

"To you," her demon added.

"Like nice enough to part with a magic item capable of translating ambient energy into something a Fell can consume?"

"Maybe," Meg said with a shrug.

"I guess that'll do, Zazz."

"Let's get the fish bloke then. I'm not in the mood to die on a Tuesday."

Meg only needed to knock once for the door to burst open. "How close is his office?" her demon asked as Pike swam straight to Meg.

"Meet, Vanth, she's a...pixie friend of mine," Meg offered weakly. "She had some ideas—"

Vanth bounced right over and waved. "My good friend Meg here messed up her focus and is unable to help unless your gracious—"

"Oh no, your focus was damaged? Why did you not say so? Our resources are at your disposal, just say what you need, and by my gills will, it shall be done."

Meg pointed weakly at Vanth. "Um, I need—"

"Just point me to the toys, I'll take care of the rest."

And with that, the pixie sped into the hall with a confused merman in tow.

I didn't know, luv, I swear. You have to believe—

I don't know what to believe anymore. Just give me some space.

Vocharlian couldn't formulate a response, so instead he escaped to the darkest alcove in the undersea repository. Here most of the spines were wrapped in cracked black leather, with rusty red writing that looked far more familiar to him than the nautical themes in the main room. He could hear phantom gasping as he reached toward a solid black tome. "*Of Variegatus and other Aberrations* by Dolion Hartwick," the demon read. "Oh *hello*."

As he pulled the book from the shelf, he heard another gasp, this time from under his hands. As he stared at the cover, a face pushed out from under the leather, moaning as its empty eye sockets squinted in the dim light. "Fuck me!" the demon cried as he dropped it to the ground. His horror only amplified as the book landed open to a page with a seven-faced fiend standing on top of a pile of skulls.

"Charlie? Why is my anxiety suddenly spiking?" he could hear Meg call, just over the thundering of his heart in his chest. *Charlie, is that you?*

"The most feared of all infernal creatures, a shifting aspect, is called upon when a summoner wishes to inflict the most possible damage with a single spell. However, the caster must be cautious. Because of their capricious and violent nature, demons of this kind should only be summoned by the most cunning and experienced magicians..." he read, trying not to look at the monster in the picture.

"Charlie?"

He didn't get a chance to close the book in time. Meg immediately dropped next to it and stared at the demon shaped more like the mythical hydra than a human. Her eyes scanned over to a passel of succubi crowding around the front legs of the behemoth. "Is that a demonic dinosaur?" she asked. "With a harem?"

"They're his daughters," Vocharlian whispered. "I, um, read the caption. It's Typhon, the demonic version, not the mythology one, but I think the stories are based on him. He's one big, bad motherfu—"

"I get the idea. I also feel...upset looking at this picture, and I think that feeling is coming from you. What is it, Charlie?"

"It's a big joke, that's all. This book is having a laugh at us saying how dangerous Variegatus demons can be, so they're showing the grandaddy of them all. Apparently only *experienced* summoners should mess with demons like me."

"You're...*that*?" She pointed at the tail as long as a bus and the many gaping maws.

"No, I'm the shite version of that. We have the same aspect, nothing more. Instead of being one flavor of demon, I'm the rainbow." He flipped through a few pages and stopped at another image, one of a smaller demon holding a flaming sword in front of a hooded figure. "But hey, according to this, I can use any sort of focus to serve my masters, so that's good, right? I mean, I wouldn't want..." He flipped the next page to show an imp with an abacus. "To be your demonic bean counter like this greed fellow here, but I could do it in a pinch." The next page showed a succubus with a whip and nothing else on her over-endowed form. He flipped one more to show something that looked like a sinister angel with a shield and pitchfork. "Pride, now that's the one aspect that'll never happen."

"This is a guide to summoning demons! Does it say how I did it?"

He flipped through a bit more. "You didn't sacrifice a goat, did you?"

Meg blanched at some of the gruesome illustrations, so Vocharlian closed the tome. "I don't think you did any of this, so let's tuck it away and call it a day."

"What aren't you telling me?" Meg asked slowly. "I may be confused, but I'm not dumb."

He opened the book back to the original picture of Typhon and his daughters, then pointed to a gray-skinned succubus wearing a tiger pelt on her back. "Meg Reynolds, meet my dear old mum, Argaebast, chosen daughter of Typhon."

"That's *your* grandpa!" she blurted out, taking a few steps away from the sheepish demon. "For real?"

"He would be...if he hadn't disowned me. Trust me, I take more after my father's side of the family, and I'm never going to end up like that."

She let out a sigh of relief and started perusing the other books on the shelf. Vocharlian joined her and made the mistake of flipping to the last chapter of a work titled *On Cambions and Other Hybrids*. His green eye-lights darkened into inky swirls as he saw majestic wings and horns casting a fearsome shadow over a battlefield on one page. On the next, the same demon's gaping mouth clamped around the throat of another robed figure, this one a woman.

The caption read, "The fate of the foolish summoner."

He slammed the book shut.

"All right, you crazy kids, pick your poison," Vanth said as she splayed a collection of random objects over one of the library's many coral tables. Pike fluttered his fins as Meg surveyed the confusing collection. "Though I'm not sure the hairbrush is going to be the best bang for your buck."

Said hairbrush lay nestled in a pile of silky fabric that seemed mysteriously undamaged despite being sodden to the core. Meg stared at everything from a frying pan to a frayed old fountain pen, each object intricately decorated—and while well-worn—not swollen, rusted, cracked, or even salt damaged from the briny deep. While she studied each one in turn, the demon focused entirely on a single object, a gutting knife with a curved tip. "Can I keep it?" he asked as he studied the serration.

"Typical Fell brute," Pike grumbled. He then smiled apologetically toward Meg. "Please, select whatever you like. Each of these objects have been well loved and well used, as requested by your tiny companion."

"Give us a minute would ya, Piceus," Vanth said. "Magic is about to happen."

The fish man nodded and started his swim for the door. Vanth watched him closely, noting how his gaze lingered on the same end of the table as the demon, but instead of staring at the knife, he focused on the lone broken object sitting among the corals. The pixie flittered over once the door shut. "That's the most valuable object, right there."

Meg picked up the strange item, nothing more than string wrapped around a handle. She turned it around to stare at the sheared metal at one end that was surrounded by an ornate ring. At the other she found a pair of beautiful fish intertwined, with one of them missing the rubies inset as eyes, while the other seemed to stare right at her. "Is this...a handle?"

"It's rubbish, that's what it is," the demon snarled as he picked up the knife and gave her another hopeful look. "See this? I can stab the bad guys with this. Let's focus on that."

"Focus," Meg said closing her eyes. "I need to focus." She ran her fingertips along the various textures, taking in the rough and the smooth. As she ran her palm over the handle, the two remaining rubies in the hilt began to glow. The corners of her mouth turned up and she closed her eyes. "What are you?" she asked.

Vocharlian started to open his mouth, but Vanth whipped her hands around and slapped an errant starfish right across his lips. While he struggled with the sucker feet, Meg swayed gently to a silent beat until the strange hilt lifted on a torrent of crimson sparkles and then danced around her upper body as if it knew the same song.

Meg, what are you doing?

Hush little demon, don't say a word, Hamilton's gonna snare him a summoning bird...

The red now flashed from Vocharlian as well, as he thrashed and sent the echinoderm flying. Vanth raised a glimmering barrier around the entranced human, but the demon swiped it away as if it'd been little more than a soap bubble. "Meg! The bloody Fey is— He's in our heads!"

"*SILENCE, FELL!*" This time the voice echoed through the entire library, stunning both Vanth and Vocharlian. Even the phantom audience gasped.

The demon whirled around and snagged the hairbrush in his claws. "Use this instead! Whatever you do, don't—" He stopped cold as the room flooded with magenta light. His eyes blazed red, but his body fell limp. A new current lifted him helplessly over his summoner, and he tried to cry out as steam sizzled off his wrist. Vanth, meanwhile, dove for cover in among the shelves, her barrier squeezing around the tomes until it nearly burst.

"D-don't—" he choked out as the chain between his wrist and Meg's became visible, the tether pulsing with burning energy. Meg ignored the blisters rising around her wrist, instead swirling more forcefully until their tether wrapped around her entire midsection. The hilt now lined up perfectly along her center axis, and the demon tried not to stare at her chest barely contained within a bikini. The summoner opened her eyes to reveal nothing but magenta light.

"For a thousand generations, in a thousand worlds, we have slumbered, waiting for the moment of our reunion," Meg said, not with her own voice, but with a legion combined. The hilt then flickered and shifted, changing into a different pommel or cross guard with each shift of the light.

"You're hurting me, you..." he snarled as his own eye lights began cycling from red to blue to gold and every color in between. "Meg, *please!*" The other half of the chain wrapped around his throat, shutting him up by squeezing his new gills.

"The endling meets the foundling once more. The first and the last rejoin. All is as it is meant to be," Meg continued, the lightshow now reaching every corner of the library.

Vanth cowered as her barrier flickered in time with Meg's mysterious chant. The summoner soared to become level with her writhing demon. She raised her chained hand and touched the back of it to his quivering cheek. "There are no accidents, Vocharlian Variegatus, Lost Heir of Typhon, Destroyer of Worlds. You would be wise to remember this. What has come before, will come again. The circle is still closed. She will perish once more. Try hard, and try again, little one."

What do you mean? Who are you? What have you done to Meg? Meg, answer me. Come on, you barmy bird, answer me!

The glowing girl cocked her head, then slowly rolled her hand around to boop the demon on the nose. "Remember, there are no accidents, once you accept that, you can finally move forward."

And with that, the hilt stabbed straight into her chest.

"Feeling better, Zazz?"

Meg's eyes fluttered open as she found herself floating in the middle of a magnificent library. She blinked a few times to take in the leathery shadow drifting just overhead, then flexed her left hand a few times. She ran her other fingers over her skin and began to palpitate a new and mysterious lump in her palm. "What happened?" she asked.

"You ran your hands over the table, reached out with your feelings like I told you to, and then you were drawn to the old broken sword. Everything went hazy then it...merged with you for lack of a better word," Vanth said quickly. "Big flash, your demon passed out, and the focus disappeared into your chest and wandered down your arm."

"They...do that?" Meg kept rubbing her hand.

"Well yeah, all magicians bind their foci to them in some way. Most of us just have them on our person, but it's not unheard of for the paranoid to actually meld the item into their body. It's called the dungeon smuggler, from the old days when the inquisition tried to murder us all. I can't believe you did it. You *sure* you've never had any training?"

"Positive." She cracked her neck then stared once more in wonder at the bump on her left palm. "You're right though, I feel...less confused. I can remember being on the game show so clearly now. We had to amend our contract because it wasn't standard. I redlined the pages and Charlie didn't read and initial them all properly, *like I told him to.* Anyway, as penance, we ended up tethered to each other, and I got access to this place where I can store him if I'm sick of him, like a little pocket..."

"You have a pocket demon! I have got to start writing this shit down," Vanth exclaimed as they both swam up to the snoozing demon with tiny azure sparkles floating from his closed sockets. "I *will* have that podcast one day."

Meg frowned. "This is not right. We were cursed. We can't eat, drink, or sleep unless the other one is doing it as well. It's part of our tether, so how is he...?" She waved a hand over his face and ended up brushing away an errant snot bubble floating from his gills.

"I don't think this is normal sleep," Vanth said as she studied him closer. She pointed to the pulsating lumps emerging behind his tiny horns. "I'm not an expert on infernals, but I do remember they go dormant and mutate if exposed to certain forms of energy. Maybe that doesn't count to your curse?"

"His armor is glowing too," Meg noted as she looked at the creature as if studying him for the first time. "You said it was some sort of protection magic? If so, why is it active now? Did I...do something to hurt him?"

"Of course not, you just bound a focus, like you should have done before you started bending reality," Vanth said with a little laugh. "Anywho, what's going on in that crazy brain of yours? You remember how you did the summoning thing yet?"

Meg alternated nodding, then shaking her head. "I'm still not sure about that. I know there was the song, and I was sick, and then it just sorta happened. It was an accident, but is that possible?"

Vanth chewed at her lip. "Spontaneous generation may be a myth in the mundane world, but there are cases...rare, *rare* cases where thaumogenesis can occur via trauma. Thaumogenesis is basically the arcane equivalent of your first period."

"Oh..."

Vanth kept staring at the unconscious demon still floating so blissfully. "I've never heard of *this* being anyone's mystical cherry-popping, I won't lie. Usually, it's pure force that comes out—either a bolt or a barrier. To do this, you needed some serious mojo. I know your house is pretty close to a ley line, but...woof. You got some magic in your family by any chance?"

"I'm adopted," Meg whispered as she pushed some of Vocharlian's streaky hair off his neck to reveal another new addition, that of a sword tattooed into his skin, just behind the gills. The moment her nail brushed against the ink, a shiver ran up her arm. "There is so much I need to learn. Can you help me?"

The pixie seemed to consider it carefully for a spell. "I don't know, to be honest, but it's too fucking cool not to find out. I mean, we are surrounded by flipping mermaids, aren't we?"

Meg smiled, the lights fully on behind her eyes once more. "Yeah, we *are* surrounded by flipping mermaids. Maybe we should save them, since I now remember, that's what I have to do to avoid being a slave to a fairy lord named Hamilton Hock."

Episode Nine

Off the Deep End

Chapter 25

We Interrupt Your Regularly Scheduled Program

W hy would anyone want to know my story? It's ridiculous and completely unbelievable. Yeah, I'm the girl who got so sick they summoned a demon in their bathroom, and ever since that fateful moment it's like my brain has fractured into a thousand pieces, each forming their own channel, and I'm stuck with the remote, flipping endlessly and only catching fragments of my own life. Can you imagine what that's like? That every moment you think you know exactly what is going on, the program changes. It's like some fricking episodic TV show and you can pick up at any time and sorta follow along, but in the end it doesn't really matter. I hate shows like that... They jump around and only give you a tiny bite at a time. The only thing worse is that they have the main character explaining things like there is some impartial observer, but in reality, they are talking to the viewers. *You ever feel like your life has turned into that?"* Meg asked as she looked straight across a stark metal table. She cocked her head at the shadows obscuring her interrogator. "What I really want to know, is why am I talking to you here, right now?"

A light flickered on, the screen of a phone, and barely illuminated a tense jawline and red painted lips. Another streak of red framed a ghostly face, but a pair of sunglasses obscured the interrogator's eyes even though the room remained dimly lit. Meg tried to squint and read the message in the reflection, but the notification faded too quickly.

"You're talking to me, right here, right now, because I happen to be the only person stopping a well-armed man with good aim and questionable morality from eliminating a threat to the order of the universe as we know it," the interrogator replied with a voice as smooth and even as her makeup. "As for the cognitive dissonance, I am not qualified to comment, but if you'd like, I could send a specialist in once we're through, Miss Reynolds."

Meg looked down, not at the handcuffs holding her to a steel chair, but to faint burn scars around her right wrist. "Charlie," she whispered as she turned her hands over to see a similar scar in the middle of her left palm. "Where...where is my friend?"

"A friend? Is that what you call it?" The interrogator's manicured hand slipped out of the shadows and pointed to the wall behind Meg. A moment later and a section lit up with industrial fluorescents, flooding the room with harsh light. Meg had to awkwardly bunny hop her chair around, banging her knees on the table leg in the process.

Meg gasped as she saw an ashen figure splayed across an exam table not ten feet away. Rows of blackened chains strapped him down from his oversized clawed feet to the spikes on his shoulders while two curtains of translucent striped leather draped to the floor.

Meg raised a brow as she saw pale blue spines jutting from his back, forming a ridge curling over his shoulders and constructing the tops of his enlarged wingspan. "That's new."

A pair of men in clean suits decorated with ornate crosses prowled around the creature, occasionally poking the unconscious demon with silvery sticks while a third figure wearing chainmail approached Vocharlian's head with what looked like Hell's version of wraparound sunglasses.

"Wait, what are you doing?" Meg asked. "Don't hurt him!"

Thick black liquid oozed from his otherwise empty eye sockets. As the dude in chainmail drew closer, the demon hissed through interlocking black fangs as opposed to his former silver needle teeth.

"*Hurry, the subject is waking up!*" Meg could hear through an intercom. The band of metal sizzled as chainmail guy placed it over Vocharlian's eyes and quickly clamped it around the back of the demon's head.

As it locked in place, the monster yowled and thrashed against his bonds and a new light source erupted from his ever-present breastplate. "Ready sedatives, the demon is armed! Ready—"

Meg clamped her eyes shut. *Charlie, can you hear me? Charlie!*

"Go home, go home, go home, go home..." she whispered frantically. "Go back to your little pocket and don't let them hurt you anymore."

"Doctor, we have a situation," echoed over the intercom. "The demon has..."

She whispered one more breathless prayer before daring to crack open her eyelids. Her face fell as instead of seeing an empty table, she saw a naked human laying there, covered only by some now loose chains and a blindfold over his eyes.

She flinched as a hand wrapped around her shoulder, perfect crimson nails digging into her t-shirt. She could now see more red hair coiling like a snake in the impossibly tidy braid wrapped around the stranger's face like a crown. The painted lips curled into a smirk as she surveyed the subject now. "Well, I must say, that golem you created for your demon is...impressive, or is it some sort of oversized homunculus that you created for him to shift into? Believe me, I don't care however you chose to do it. So...inanimate or fully alive?"

"I have no idea what you're talking about. I was told I had to decide on a human form so he could walk around and not disturb reality. I don't know how I did it!" She craned her neck even further to see the same cross in pin form on her interrogator's lapel. "Who *are* you?"

The stranger whipped Meg around in her chair with surprising ease. She held her breath as she fought to stem the fresh tide of anxiety. The interrogator leaned in ever so close. "Now, you honestly didn't think you could rip a hole in the fabric of reality and there not be...consequences?" she asked, a sinister sweetness creeping into her voice.

Meg stared into the darkness across the table. "Am I even supposed to be here? I don't remember..." A tiny green light flickered in the heart of the darkness. Meg turned her gaze that way. "I don't remember what happened, but I'm scared, and I need help. I don't want to hurt anyone. Please, if you're listening, help me."

"Who are you talking to, Miss Reynolds?"

"I have no idea, maybe it's just the audience."

"Can you tell us your name?"

"Piss off," Vocharlian grumbled as he fumbled and fought to get up. He flexed his hands and felt the restraints against his delicate human skin. He'd been bound, stripped naked, and covered with a scratchy bit of fabric. He smirked at the unseen voice. "Now, as much as I'm into a bit of bondage, I usually wait till after breakfast."

His stomach growled loudly to punctuate his point. He cracked his neck side to side. "How long has it been since I ate?"

"We found you bleeding in an alleyway near Beacon Hill, Mr.... Mr....?"

"Call me whatever you like, guv, but I'm not talking until I can see what's going on," the demon replied. "Think I can have a sip of water, maybe a pudding cup? This is a hospital, isn't it?"

After a moment there came a whirring of gears and Vocharlian's body shifted from straight horizontal to his upper body being at a forty-five-degree angle. He noticed the lack of shooting pain in his side. He also noticed a slight looseness in his left handcuff with the shift in positions but kept his face as bland as possible. He rubbed his head against the bed and sneered at the elastic holding fast to his messed-up hair.

"You are very lucky to be alive, Mr....?"

"Yeah, I barely remember the asshole who stabbed me. The coppers ever catch the guy? I think he might have been a nutjob, one of those Jesus Krispies who mistook me for someone else," Vocharlian said as he kept fidgeting. "Any reason for all the S&M?"

"You were gravely injured, stabbed as you recall. We need to keep you still so you can heal," the stranger said, his voice as bland and calm as ever.

"Oh yeah, that old chestnut. So, tell me, Mr. Smarty Pants, was I stabbed in my fucking face, or is that just another of your bloody kinks?" the demon growled as he tried again to slip his head free of the blindfold. "Or are we gonna stop faffing about and you tell me what is really going on?"

"We need to confirm your identity so we can contact any next of kin, Mr....?"

"Call me Mister Fuck Off, cause that's all your getting out of me until I can bloody see."

Oy, I need your eyes right now. What the hell is going on? Where are we? What the holy fuck is going on? Meg? You better not be ignoring me, Meg!

He stiffened as he heard the creak of hinges followed by the clicking of heels on the floor. The tippy-tap of the feet stopped right behind his head and he breathed deeply to take in traces of perfume over all the cleaning product aromas filling the air. "I am already tied up if you want your way with me, lass."

"His name is Charlie, I believe," a perfectly even voice said. "At least it's something we can go with for now."

The demon sneered. "You the one in charge?"

"I'm merely an advocate for now. You have limited options at this moment, and we have both the knowledge and the firepower to send you straight back to Hell, *Charlie*. I would strongly suggest that you cooperate with the good doctors here so that I don't need to use other methods to persuade you to give me the information that I want."

Vocharlian nodded slowly. "Well, I am not normally one to disappoint a lady, so I guess there is only one thing left to do, isn't there?"

He waited, but the mysterious lady didn't respond. "Oh, I see, I got myself a patient little jailer," he said. "Should I ask for a lawyer, or does that only work on the telly?"

"I'm not as patient as you might think, but I am in control of the situation," she replied. "I suppose I'll return to questioning your companion."

"You do that. She's as mad as a box of frogs and won't tell you a bloody thing," he bluffed.

"What if I told you that she's already told me everything I need to know, Charlie?"

"Then you don't need to waste your time with me. The fact that you're resorting to threats only means one of two things."

"Oh?"

"Either you're lying, or you like what you see."

He heard the click of heels and a tiny chuckle. "Piss off," she sang pleasantly before slamming the door.

Chapter 26

The Descent into Madness

Y ou know what I hate, luv, when I tell a bloody brilliant anecdote and all you do is stare at me like I have two heads. Why do I even bother?"

Meg turned a few times to take in the wall of reef on one side and her friends lounging around the sea anemone installation on the other. She tapped her neck for good measure, feeling her gills and finding nary an interrogation room in sight.

"Excuse me?" She focused on the school of clownfish darting in and out of an anemone the size of a dinner table. She rubbed her hand, feeling the strange nub once more. She shivered, as this time something wiggled under her skin.

"Let's face it, Spike, your delivery sucks. Only you could ruin a punchline about Belial's yogurt stash," Vanth added. She then pulled a puny pocket watch from her bodice. "Damn it, I hope they think my internet dropped or some shit like that. I'm missing the whole raid."

"Nerd," Vocharlian grumbled.

"Scrub," Vanth said with the deepest of sighs.

"Guys...*what were we doing again?*" Meg asked.

"Besides being bored to death by amateur hour here?" Vanth toured around the clown fish paradise. "Just making sure you'd recovered enough to make the trek down to the deep and check out the—"

"Obvious body snatchers plot?" the demon offered. "Or perhaps getting crushed to death by a billion gallons of water? That's assuming that we don't freeze or get pimp slapped by a frisky kraken first."

"You really have a negative attitude, Demon Boy."

"Does magic ever make you have visions...stuff like that, or is that only in movies?" Meg asked suddenly. "Just asking."

Vanth paused her pixie version of pacing. "*Just asking*, hmm? There is a bunch of magic designed to give you visions—everything from boring-ass scrying to conjuring up the trip of the ages with nothing more than some finger waving." Vocharlian tried to interject but got slapped by another random starfish. "I know what you're thinking, even without magic, Spike. *Anywho!* Yeah, if you need a little clairvoyance, I have tons of enhanced tech that will get the job done. If it's more the rave experience you're after, that's another buddy of mine I'll have to introduce you too once we're done saving the fish peeps." She narrowed her eyes at Meg. "Wait, what am I missing here?"

Meg shrugged. "It's probably nothing."

"Lady, you got the shits and opened the gates to Hell. Let's not be too dismissive here."

Vocharlian grinned at the pint-sized princess. "I'm starting to like her, luv."

"Does casting magic have side effects I should know about?" Meg blurted out. "Yes, like seeing things, or losing focus and imagining you are somewhere else?"

"Like twenty thousand leagues under the little mermaid sea?" her demon offered. "Because we've already established that I'm sharing this hallucination too so it's probably—"

"No, I was in an alley—"

"And then that Fey bastard punted us here. We've been over this."

"Yes, I get that, and now that my head is clearing—"

"Well, *actually*, that is a side effect of doing magic without a proper energy source," Vanth offered. "You may have fried a few circuits casting such a big kahuna of a spell sans focus, Zazz. I wouldn't worry too much. You're probably having flashbacks as your gray matter settles down. But—"

"No!" Meg interrupted. "I'm sick of being talked to like I don't know anything...even if I don't know much about magic. Ugh, I know how it

sounds, but I'm not stupid. I'm having these...moments where I'm somewhere else, and I think I was captured by someone...someone scary, so
part of me is wondering if I really am in some dream, or I'm drugged,
or..."

"Please don't say crazy, luv," Vocharlian said, his voice surprisingly
soft. "Just...don't."

"I..." She trailed off lost in the dance of the tiny fish surrounding her.
"I loved going to the aquarium ever since I was a little kid, and *The Little
Mermaid* was one of my favorite movies. If I was gonna crack and build
some amazing alternate reality in my dreams, it would probably be
something like this," she confessed. She then stared at her mismatched,
sodden, demonic companion. "But you're right, I wouldn't imagine
something like you. I guess we need to make a plan or something..."

Vanth nodded. "Yeah, a plan. Use that supremely logical gamer side
of you, Zazzy. What would we do in *Eternaquest?*"

"We'd look at our map, make sure we're geared up, get any consum-
ables we might need, and above all else, double check the quest text,"
Meg said, her eyes lighting up nearly as bright as when she held the
focus. "We should find out everything we can about this Everlast Gorge,
its people, et cetera."

Vanth whipped her hands frantically around and soon projected a
map within the shimmering walls of her barrier. "I'll start on recon,
never fear. My spiders are supercharged in this realm, and I'm sure if
I'm missing anything, those sexy AF flounders out there will have our
back."

"Do I at least get something...stabby?" the demon asked.

Meg nodded. "Yes, I think we need to get you something stabby."

"Right, just take a magical lift down to the bottom of the bloody sea.
What could possibly go wrong?" Vocharlian whispered at a shimmering
column of bubbles on the edges of Pike's citadel grounds. His mood
soured further as he saw the soldiers surrounding the newly formed
aperture in the center of the floor, each of them brandishing impressive
polearms, whereas he had only been gifted the gutting knife from the
library.

The head guard, Garfield, swished by, showing off his shiny full armor as he barked orders to his men. "You'd be best served battered with a side of mushy peas," the demon grumbled rather than listening to anything remotely important.

"...so remember, whatever you do, once we descend past the red marker on your depth bracelet, do not cross the ring of light."

The demon whipped around to see Pike, slithering dangerously close to Meg. The fish man took her hand, showing off new jewelry. Meg toyed with her fancy golden bangle and smiled sweetly at him. "That's this one, right?"

"Depth, oxygen, temperature," he said, his webby paws brushing Meg's wrist. "So, you know what is happening beyond the barrier. Never fear, we have a pressure suit for you that can also contain your diminutive companion quite easily waiting once you reach Virlandia. That will allow you to transverse the bubbles safely."

"Yeah, bubbles of death. That'll be the day," Vocharlian scoffed. Still, as he stood on the edge of the glowing wall, he did make a point to stare at his own bracelet and the comforting green stone set on the back of it. "Oy, why does mine only have one bloody stone in it?"

Garfield turned to face the demon. "Oh, is a mighty Fell afraid of a little cold?"

"Temp's not the problem. I still need to bloody breathe. Even with these things on my neck, they aren't worth shit if there's no O in the water, right?"

"Never fear, the water will crush you long before you would suffocate," Garfield explained with a grin. "Shall we be off?"

Vocharlian straightened his breastplate and triple checked his dagger was still on his belt before making a little beckoning gesture. "We gonna get this show on the road before the pod people spread, luv?"

Captain Pike bowed his head and took Meg's hand completely within his own. As the water in the lower chamber shifted to envious green, neither Pike nor Meg seemed to care about the subtle shift in the surroundings. Instead, the fish man leaned in and said, "Oh, in answer to your previous question, we're about half and half."

"Excuse me?" Meg asked, cocking her head.

"While we came from the depths of the seas, our ancestors made a bargain with the great Fey of the light to gain some aspects of the land

walkers, specifically what you call mammals," he explained. "We transform ourselves as the situation requires."

"You're shapeshifters?" Meg asked.

"Merely...adaptable, as I'm sure you shall see one day. Now, please
stay safe and close to your guardian—"

"I'm not gonna let anything happen to her, guv." Vocharlian gently
tugged her other hand. He then followed Pike's obvious sight line to
the buff, armored captain of the guard. "Oh, you meant Sylvester
here."

And with that, they began their descent to the briny deep.

"It's like my best dream and worst nightmare rolled into one," Meg
whispered as she continued her plunge into the darkness. Her borrowed
gills seized up as she saw her companion silhouetted in the last remains
of the light, his wings spread to their full span to slow his fall down the
column of bubbles.

"You getting Batman vibes too?" Vanth's barrier wobbled slightly as
they entered the twilight zone, carried gently deeper by a current that
felt far too warm to be from the abyss.

"I hope that's magic and not Moby Dick pissing on my head."

"Maybe not the caped crusader..." Meg muttered as she kept scanning the shadows beyond the bubble wall. The central gem on her
bracelet faded from green into yellow as well, prompting their head
guard to corral the ladies more toward the center of their protective
channel.

"It's perfectly safe, milady," Garfield added even as he waved Vanth
a bit closer. "A team of five sea hags maintain the Descent at any given
time."

"Five is a powerful number in thaumaturgy," Vanth added. "It forms
a full pentagram to balance any energy fluctuations and makes for
smooth spellcasting, especially when you need concentration to maintain... Oh, hey Garfield, my man, this barrier keeping like a million PSI
off our heads isn't maintained only by will alone, is it?"

Meg tensed until the captain shook his head. "Of course not. We
have thirteen independent runes powering the barriers, the hags are

merely for moderating and adjusting the flow. We would never be so careless."

Vanth flittered close to Meg's ear. "That's grade-A shit in case you didn't guess. If you have the time and power to etch a spell into a solid object and imbue it with your power, then you don't have to concentrate. We'll get there with you...eventually."

If Meg heard the reassurances from the pixie, they certainly got drowned out by the cacophony of distractions as they continued their descent. Garfield and the rest of their merman escort all pulled out glowing orbs that sparkled in the twilight zone. The new illumination allowed Meg to take in an eerie array of shadows drifting through the murk. Any important information got missed as a whale buzzed the bubble wall, making her heart skip a beat.

"So, it's just a glorified bubble between us and getting pancaked by a ton of water, isn't it?" Vocharlian asked as he drifted next to her.

"Oh, we won't die from this pressure," Meg mumbled, still watching the shadows. "The nitrogen dissolving into our tissues will kill us far faster as our lungs collapse."

"I bet you're fun at parties." His smirk dimmed a little as his empty sockets took in an eight-limbed shadow. "That's quite the cuttlefish out there."

"The kraken cannot breach the Descent. We've triple warded it against their kind," Garfield explained.

They sunk into true darkness, the shadows replaced with occasional sparkles in the abyss. Even the magic radiating from the walls couldn't dull the oppressive chill and the infinite expanse of blackness. Meg strayed closer to the demon, taking comfort in the glow emanating from his chest.

Vanth huddled in too. "With those gills, your lungs are probably full of water and will equalize the pressure. I'm, however, researching every gas conversion spell in my database...in case it's not just my conscious-ness transferred to this dimension, but rather my full soul." She gave a bit of side-eye to Vocharlian. "Can you tell, Spiky? Am I all here?"

"Why are you asking me? I'm a demon, not a cocker spaniel. It's not like I can sniff out a soul."

"You can't? Are you an average specimen of your species or like the worst demon ever?"

"Guys," Meg interrupted. "We're not alone."

Meg's feet touched the bottom first, sending plumes of dust into the water column and amplifying the otherworldly haze. At least a dozen lights bobbed in the distance, some brilliant while others faint and twinkling, but each moved in a distinct rhythm. This formed a wave that parted the bubble wall to reveal not only a tunnel, but a cohort of fish people unlike any she had seen before. Some featured eyes like dinner plates, others no eyes at all. Meg's jaw dropped as the leader of the new delegation swam forward. With her enlarged scales and distinctive spots, she looked right at home in the Devonian Period. "A coelacanth mermaid, I must be dreaming," Meg choked out.

"This is the coolest thing I think I've ever seen," Vanth added, flittering in front of Meg.

"*Nerds.*"

Said coelacanth mermaid drifted toward them, her eyes luminous in the eternal night. The closer she got, the more freckle-like white scales could be seen covering her beefy arms. She tilted her head and stared unblinking at Meg. Captain Garfield swam front and center, making the denizen of the deep immediately hiss and pull away. "Where are the reeve and the elders of Virlandia? Answer me, worker!" he barked.

"Swim Bladder," she hissed, her words thickly accented as if this section of the deep had been transplanted from Wales—the country, rather than the giant locals.

"Now that's an insult even I haven't heard," the demon noted.

If Garfield was insulted, he didn't let it crumble his stoic façade. Instead, he puffed out his breastplate and extended his fins fully. "Where is the reeve?"

"You...only care when the shipments stop, or when...your invaders are all quiet. They're...in the mine, go see for yourself...Swim Bladder."

"I command—" Garfield started again. This time Meg slipped around his dorsal spines and gave a wave followed by a curtsey.

"Hey, what's your name?" she asked softly.

The coelacanth repeated her head tilt and sized up Meg's scaleless skin, unwebbed fingers, and the slight glow to her borrowed gills. "You... you are very far from home. Why does the land come to the deep...with the invaders? Do...you mean to invade us too?"

"What's with the Welsh Shatner speech?" the demon asked.

Meg and Vanth exchanged a quizzical glance. "We're nerds but you don't have to go that obscure, Spike-o." Vanth then flittered next to Meg's head, prompting the strange mermaid to gawk anew.

"So...tiny...from the land as well?" the stranger asked. She then pressed one of her stubby fins across her chest. "Joan...is my name, if must you know."

"I'm Meg and this is Vanth. The winged guy is Charlie...err, Vocharlian."

With his hollow cheeks, sunken belly, and silvery highlights, the demon fit in far more with this group of deep-sea merfolk than with any other company Meg had seen him in before. Only when his wings flapped around his shoulders, did Joan and her crew seem taken aback. "From further away...from the skies, yes?" she asked softly. "This is... not...your...place."

"Why do you sound like a stoned sheep-shagger, lady?" he blurted out. However, Joan seemed to miss the reference entirely and simply stared at him in confusion, even as Vanth and Meg remained mortified. "Sorry, I'm starting to get that you're damp not daft. What's really going on down here, Freckles? Don't mind the swim bladders over there, they do want to help, at least they told us they wanted to."

"Do you have *any* ability to shut him up?" Vanth hissed.

"Freckles? What...is freckles?" Joan asked, blinking again. The demon waggled his talons over all her spots. She smiled, showing off needle-like teeth. As the demon returned the sinister grin, she snorted and motioned toward a nearby cave. "I...like you Charlie err Vocharlian. Come...not safe to here talk."

"Not safe?" Garfield asked, attempting to remain relevant in the conversation. "What—?"

As if on cue, the water above shimmered. The deep-sea workers instantly scattered, and a moment later the sea floor trembled and a flood of freezing water splashed against the group. One of Garfield's cohorts didn't quite move fast enough, and everyone watched in horror as he gagged and gasped as his midsection instantly crushed.

"What the holy fuck!?!" This time Meg didn't blanch at her demon's colorful expressions. "He got pancaked. You bloody told me you couldn't get—"

"Inside...now!"

No one argued with Joan as the water above shimmered again. Meg, however, stared, transfixed at the light as another cold torrent threatened to crush her. The scream caught in her throat while time lurched to a standstill.

A pair of scrawny, striped arms snatched her midsection. She slammed hard against glowing metal, as Vocharlian swept her out of harm's way.

Icy water crashed again. She heard the yowl, then a sickening snap. Still, the demon snarled and lurched, using every bit of his weight to shove Meg into the arms of the coelacanth girl. As she was pulled away, Meg watched a wing shear off his back, and a font of blood poured into the water. To make matters worse, most of the throng looked part shark.

"Oh bollocks," the demon sighed as he stared down so many teeth.

Episode Ten

Tentacles are your Friends

Chapter 27

Welcome to the Abyss

I don't think they make a 'sorry you've been attacked by sharks' Hallmark card yet, but when they do, I'll snag you one, Tiger."

Vocharlian grabbed at his throat, a mix of blood and seawater gurgling from his mouth as he gasped for air. He thrashed in the mud, flailing and unbalanced, with only a single sodden wing flopping next to him, while the broken stub of the other drove into the ground. He opened his mouth again but only another gush of water poured out with some unintelligible hissing.

"What was that?" the stranger in patchwork asked, cupping his hand around where an ear should be under his hood. "I swear, you end up gasping so much, I think you're into choke play."

The demon reached a hand toward the shadow looming over him. Never one to waste an opportunity, Vocharlian took his last moments to slowly extend his middle talon before passing out face first into the mud.

Wanker.

Meg paddled furiously away from the feeding frenzy. "Where did he go?" Vanth asked as she too rode the current away from the fracas and dove into the cave. "And why the hell is the barrier collapsing? I thought you said we were safe, Garfield!"

"It cannot be..." Garfield hadn't quite caught up with the plot as another section shimmered and failed while they rushed into the cavern. This time it ended up being one of the blood-crazed deep mermaids that got crushed, though being better-suited to the pressures at those depths than the shallow water guard, he ended up merely stunned, his eyes bulging and him struggling for a moment before he could be dragged to safety by some of his lucid buddies. Meanwhile the blood-crazed brigade continued to gnash and lash at the wing remnants left on the seafloor until only a few leathery shreds remained.

Vanth landed her bubble on Meg's trembling shoulder. "You did like *bamf* him away, right? They didn't...eat him, right? *Right?*"

Charlie, Charlie can you hear me?

———

Somewhere, far across time and space, a pair of salt-streaked talons tore into the mud as a fresh inferno of scarlet erupted out of once lifeless eye sockets. Vocharlian ripped through the earth, clawing out enough muck to create a puddle deep enough for him to dunk his head into. As the murky bubbles filled his makeshift pond, his tormentor in the patchwork hoodie stood over him and laughed.

"I like your determination, Tiger, but wouldn't it have been easier to ask me for help?" he asked.

The demon wrenched his arm around to give the stranger a brand-spanking new middle finger. *I don't want anything from you.* The whole pool turned crimson as his sockets flared again.

The patchwork stranger kneeled next to the puddle, seemingly unfazed by the proximity of the nasty talons. "You know what your problem is?"

I'm choking to death, you Satan's hunt!

"I suppose, right now at this very moment that might be a concern but—"

I'm gonna rip out your throat, Blizzard.

"You have anger issues," the stranger finished. The demon flailed a bit more, but the patchwork man leaned in and patted his shoulder under the torn off wing. "I mean that literally, you know. Every time you get in the least amount of trouble, you jump straight to wrath, forgetting that you aren't a rakshasa or their ilk."

Vocharlian gurgled in frustration. *So what? Should I have killed the sharks with fucking kindness?*

"They say sarcasm is a sign of intelligence," the patchwork man continued. "But right now, it's not really helping. Come on, Tiger, it's time you realize that you're never going to be the strongest, or the fastest, or the smartest demon out there. What you have going for you is that you can be...the most adaptable."

The puddle gurgled again. *Tosser.*

The stranger erupted with laughter. "If I had a dollar for every time you said that...oh, anyway, our time is growing short. She needs you, probably more than you both yet realize. Listen to me, little demon, and listen close." He leaned his shadowy face right next to the surface. "It's not your anger that will save you right now, but your hunger."

The bubbling and flailing paused for a moment as Vocharlian let those words roll around in his skull. After a few agonizing seconds, the red completely faded from the puddle. A smile appeared under the hood, as the patchwork man flicked his fingers until magenta light danced from tip to tip. "Go get 'em, Tiger."

A column of light erupted around the demon, cutting Vocharlian's next tirade short.

"I don't know what I did. I sometimes send him away. I don't know *how that works!*" Meg cried as she tried to get her bearings inside a glowing cave full of panicked merfolk. She then saw a pair of the half-sharks swimming in the opening, each one picking bits of her demon out of their jagged teeth. "Maybe they did eat him. Why did your people eat my demon?" She whirled to face Joan. "You attacked us!"

The coelacanth did her best to smile apologetically with her grue-some needle teeth. "Accidents...happen. The blood-thirsty are not...used to guests. Food is...scarce in the deep."

"Did you really just 'too bad, so sad, we ate your demon' us, Joan?" Vanth challenged. "Because that is not cool." She then flitted around to face Meg. "And why did you *finally* send him away? You told me you had a Digi-ball for your demon and yet you're not using it when he's being annoying. Now what, is he dead? Alive? Start talking, Summoner Girl."

Before she could even open her mouth, an unseen hand lifted Meg and dragged her straight up to the roof of the cave. She squeaked out an "Ieeeeeee!" as that same force dragged her helplessly toward the entrance while all the confused mer-people watched.

"Are all...surface folks so...strange?" Meg could just hear as a flash blinded her.

"Donkey-fucking wanker!" echoed in the abyss.

Charlie!

Vocharlian spat out a mixture of mud and foul language as he once more found himself dropped underwater. He could hear someone calling his name, feel the pull of the tether, yet his empty sockets remained focused on the sea floor. A fading orb barely illuminated a warped figure crushed against the sediment. The demon then eyed the barrier overhead, seemingly stable after the previous lapse, before diving next to the twisted pancake of a fish man. The moment his talons stirred the sea floor, the pathetic creature twitched. His eyes bulged almost comically as his jaw quivered and choked out a mix of gurgles and clicks, but the demon with his Babel Curse heard the meaning all too clearly: "*Kill me.*"

For a moment time stood still, as the demon loomed over the pitiful soul. Vocharlian's talons and teeth lengthened while his nose widened into a porcine snout. Finally, his sockets shifted into a blackened void somehow darker than the depths of the ocean.

His stomach growled. He pounced.

Vocharlian felt the pull, trying to drag him away from his prey, but the gluttonous urges overtook his soul. His jaw snapped open to its full freakish width, ample enough to snap around the dying soldier's head and clamp cleanly through the neck and spine.

"Ch-Charlie? Is that...you?" the voice called behind him, but the demon remained locked around the body, viscous black goo pouring out of his sockets, enveloping the corpse until nothing more could be seen—darkness upon utter darkness.

Then as quickly as it had emerged, the slime retreated into the demon, leaving a trail of sickening chartreuse sparks. A shriveled husk, little more than a headless skeleton drifted back to the sea floor, and for a moment, calm descended across the deep.

Then the trail of sparkles landed on the edge of his breastplate, starting a chain reaction of runes burning across his chest. Vocharlian lurched, throwing his hands back and yowling in pain. The picked-clean skull of the guard plopped from his mouth and rolled right to the feet of Meg. She didn't scream, she didn't move, she didn't even swish her borrowed gills as she watched in horrendous wonder while a replacement wing unfurled from her demon's back in slow motion. Once the wings fully expanded, she could see a new ridge of spines jutting from his shoulders, just like the fins of the guard.

"Oh my God," Meg choked out. Her demon turned, and she could see the ink swirling in his eyes as the rest of him glowed with Fell fire. "Maybe...not the right thing to say. Charlie, is that...really...?" She stared at the growing lumps behind his existing horns, and could only keep watching, dumbstruck as his face shifted from its gluttonous guise back to his normal mishmash of human and feline features. His neck then stretched and expanded, with brand-new armored plates protecting his larger gills.

He reached his hand toward her, showing off that his fingers now sported convenient webbing. Vocharlian's face fell as Meg inched as far away as the tether allowed. "He...he asked me to do it," the demon choked out, his voice as flat and American as Meg's. "Meg, please, I'm not a...mon..." He didn't finish that thought as he noticed the infernal light emanating from his chest and the extensions to his freakish hands.

"What have you done?" Garfield asked, surrounded by the staring merfolk now trickling out of the cave.

Only Joan seemed completely nonchalant about the demonic display as she swam next to Meg and pointed to the bubbling ceiling. "We...should head back to the cave before again the weakness hits. Come...yes?"

Garfield swam across the entrance. "That thing ate one of my men!"

The shark-like merfolk looked at each other sheepishly, but it was

Joan who responded. "Eat we all...must. Rules...of the deep... Feed... when you can."

"I guess that's how it goes down here," Vanth added. She wiggled her fingers within her barrier creating a pattern of light that expanded and strengthened her walls. "I'm starting to not care how cool this is. I wanna go home, Zazzy. Hey, you even listening?"

Meg turned and started swimming for the cave. This time it was the demon who helplessly drifted after her, still staring in horror at the changes to his body. The disgust only amplified as he reached back to feel a new lump growing from the base of his spine. "Not a tail, anything but a tail," he moaned before following them inside.

Meg did her best to slow the flow of water in and out of her gills, as if somehow her breathing exercises would work underwater...on another plane of existence...while surrounded by sharks and a demon and an angry fish man. She did stop mid-panic attack to watch Joan swimming around her demon with a strange glint in her oversized eyes. The fish lady then invaded his personal space and pressed her scaly forehead to his. "The rules...of the deep are harsh...harsh but fair." She then pulled away and winked. "And...if you want to devour any more swim bladders, go...ahead."

"These fish are weird. We should probably get the hell out of here now," Vanth said quickly. She then looked at her palm as if checking her phone. "Though I first want to finish this detection spell to figure out where that barrier is failing...before we run off."

"Your demon—" Garfield sputtered again.

Meg spun around and glared at him. "Your guard got crushed when the barrier you said was perfectly safe, *failed*," she snapped. Her face then softened. "I'm sorry that my demon bit off his head, but I don't think he was going to make it, not after suffering a pressure shift like that. Now we can apologize all we want for what Charlie did, but that isn't going to help us figure out what is wrong here in the trench, is it?"

The captain shut up and took a defensive position by the door. As he looked out and saw the shimmer move from place to place, he finally murmured, "This isn't right."

"That's because...energy is...drained," Joan offered. "The prison... takes too much power."

"Prison?" Meg asked. "What exactly do you have captured down here?"

"Well, that's a metric fuckton of calamari."

Only Vocharlian seemed to have retained the powers of speech as Joan led the shallow water crew to take in the prisoner housed within the bowels of the cave. Even motor-mouth Vanth remained gobsmacked as she swam eye-level with a pupil bigger than her entire pixie body by a factor of three. Meg gawked at the mass of tentacles undulating back and forth beyond another style of barrier—this one solid energy rather than made of bubbles. Each time one of the enormous suckers struck the walls of the prison, a line of runes would light up along its arms, filling the room with aquamarine light.

"It's a lot bigger up close," Meg said. She immediately facepalmed at her obvious observation. Vocharlian tried to give her a reassuring smile, but with his jaw still slightly distended, the effect read more soul devouring nightmare rather than genial support.

"You captured a kraken," Garfield said, extending the chain of unnecessary exclamations. "How?"

"Swim bladders...let us be...bait," Joan explained. Her expression hardened as she turned to face Garfield. "Then used...their precious barrier to...make these walls. Only...diverting from our side of camp."

"But there was no sea hag assigned to this mine!" Garfield sputtered. "How could anyone do what you claim? Also, the Descent is triple warded against kraken—"

"This one...*different!*" Joan said, pointing to the symbols carved into the cephalopod's many arms. "Pressure...does not hurt him. Magic.... So much strange...magic."

Meg and Vanth studied the imprisoned creature again. While Vanth seemed intent on mapping the symbols on the inside of her bubble, Meg instead extended a finger to the barrier.

"Hey, are you daft? Don't ever touch—" But the demon's warning came a split second too late.

Chapter 28

Never Touch a Tentacle

W hat have I done?" Meg whispered as she opened her eyes to find herself back on land yet still soaked from head to toe. Monsoon rains pounded against her body as she did her best to flip the mess of limp curls out of her face.

She swiped her fogged-up glasses, and could just make out a building, one of the old brick mills that filled her home state, standing along the banks of an overflowing creek. Lightning streaked the sky as the rains rushed faster, blinding Meg to everything but a single, overwhelming shadow. Pain constricted her ribs as she fought for breath. She reached to her side and yelped in agony as she saw a chunky titanium chain coiling from just under her chest to her waist, forcing her to gulp for each breath. "What...have...I...?"

Something crashed to her left, not thunder, but rather a more immediate, meaty thud. She could only watch in horror as the tentacle swept through the storm, crashing into the walls of the mill, and exposing a glowing winged figure chained in a circle of Fell flames.

"Charlie!" Meg cried. Her eyes snapped open, and she collapsed in a pair of tiger-striped arms. Rather than focus on any fainting, she stared squarely into the monster truck tire-sized eyes of the caged kraken.

"Why? Why Goop here?"

The words made Meg vibrate from head to toe as everyone else seemed intent on arguing over magical barrier rights. Only Vocharlian leaned in and poked Meg on the forehead. "Oy!" he said. "You in there, luv?"

"Did you say something?" Meg asked the prisoner.

"You...you hear Goop?"

"Goop, is that your name...Goop?" Meg asked softly. "Why is that so familiar?"

"Who are you...?" the demon trailed off as he watched the runes on the kraken pulse in time with the aquamarine sparks now dancing in his summoner's eyes. "Hey, Squid, leave Meg alone!"

A tentacle slammed against the barrier, drawing everyone's attention. Vocharlian's eye sockets flashed red as he totally dropped the stunned summoner and lashed out at the wall. As Joan and Garfield pulled him away, Meg crawled a little closer to the prisoner. "Do I know you?" she whispered as the tentacles flashed even brighter.

"Goop confused."

"You're not the only one. Why are you attacking these people? What happened to you?"

"Goop...told. Goop fight. It is war."

"It's obvious, this tentacled fiend is responsible for the disappearances. We need to tell Piceus Pike at once and send an eradication squad —" Meg could hear Garfield telling the others.

"Others attack when Goop attacked. Goop scared of others. Don't go to the mines," the monster warned. *"Goop warn you because you understand. You understand Goop."*

Vocharlian hissed again. "Leave Meg alone, you fucking supersized sushi!" As he lashed out, Meg could feel the burning around her wrist. As she looked down, she could see the dark iron chain linking her to the creature she summoned.

"Oh dear," she said with a pathetic little laugh.

"So, let me sum this all up," Vanth said as she studied the notes scrawled on the inside of her protective bubble. "Kraken and merfolk are ancient enemies, and this super kraken was sent to destroy your whole deep sea mining operation, but you outsmarted it and got him wedged in a ravine until one of your village elders—"

"Invader...elders," Joan corrected.

"*Invader* elders picked up an old book of deep-sea magic and imprisoned the big squid by using energy from the Descent. Then she ran off with the reeve and all the shallow water folks to quote-unquote, 'unearth more powerful voodoo to defeat the giant mollusks for good,' but you don't know anything else because they took all the communication pearls with them?" the pixie continued.

"That...is all we know...for now," Joan confirmed with a little nod. "My people...were not welcome to follow...left to die here...not that the swim bladders care."

"And Spike can eat people and suck up some of their power, good to know," Vanth added as she scratched a few more notes. Before Vocharlian could interject, "And Zazzy speaks Kraken, also good to note for the future. Can you understand him too, Captain Curse?"

"I didn't hear a thing from the octopus, and I didn't mean to eat your soldier. It just sort of happened," Vocharlian apologized. He clamped his maw shut to give Garfield and Joan a chance to glower at each other again. "I'm so sick of seafood."

Meg, however, remained lost in her own little world as the discussions continued. She kept rubbing her sides, but no trace of the chunky chain from her dream remained. "What am I missing? *What did I do?*"

For the first time in ages, the disembodied audience made an *ooh* sound. Meg looked around the room but could only see the merfolk, Vanth, and the despondent demon. In her search for Fey answers, she completely missed the question directed at her, only picking up the tail end of Vanth saying, "Earth to Meg? Your thoughts?"

Meg blinked a few times, taking in the crushing weight of all the alien stares. "I...I think we should—"

"Yeah, I was totally zoning out over here, could you repeat that?" Vocharlian asked, blue sparkles flowing down his face. He then yawned, nearly dropping his jaw to his chest. "I have slothalepsy, it's a demon thing."

Vanth rolled her tiny eyes. "The only decision we can possibly make is *play it smart* and go back to get a *small army* to take out the super kraken..." She slumped in her bubble. "*Or* be every idiot in every horror movie since the dawn of mankind and go into the mine to see what the fuck is up."

"And why my people are risking the mine instead of the abyssal workers," Garfield added.

"Wait, are you slaves?" Meg asked Joan. Garfield seemed at a loss for words.

Joan thought for a moment, then gave some side-eye to the surface fish. "Slaves...no, but we are...*lesser* in their eyes. We...work in the dark places...places the swim bladders...dare not go."

"Your leaders say you prefer to work in the trenches and mines," Garfield responded, his voice measured. "But isn't that beside the point? It's clear that the kraken are up to something, and the sooner we take care of the prisoner, the sooner we can restore full power to the Descent, which will make things far safer for our land-based visitors."

"I don't think that the kraken is the problem though," Meg said, staring past everyone. "I know it sounds crazy, but Goop said he was scared of some other creatures."

"Goop, that overgrown cuttlefish is named Goop?" Vocharlian snorted. "Anyway, you've all seen how ginormous that thing is, right?"

"There's nothing subtle about an eight-legged kaiju," Vanth noted.

"So why all the hush-hush mixed messages?" the demon asked. "If the squid really went on a rampage, your people would have gone squawky-squawky for backup, or am I missing something?"

"This Charlie...err, Vocharlian, makes sense," Joan said with another nod.

"First time for everything," the demon muttered.

The coelacanth sidled next to him and gestured to all the others. "Kraken...are not a sly enemy, even with...this new kind. They...must have masters or there is...another villain. Perhaps this...Goop is...a distraction?"

"A distraction!" Meg said. "If anyone from the surface came here, what would be the first thing they'd suspect and worry about?"

"A kraken," Garfield acquiesced.

"That settles it, we need to investigate the mine," Meg said, mirroring Joan's nod. "Is there anything else that could be invading down here? Anyone else who hates merfolk?"

"Of course not," Garfield said, a little too quickly. "We have defeated and destroyed all our other foes since the dawn of time."

"Oh, that sounds like a recipe for winning the goodwill of others," the demon mumbled under his breath. *Something's a wee bit fishy here, luv.*

Meg stifled her giggle. *I know something is wrong, but what else can we do? Hamilton is still watching. I can feel it.*

And with that, the unseen audience gave out an "ooh" of warning.

"Is there anything you're not telling me?" Vanth asked as she drifted dead center in the expedition containing Garfield, Joan, Meg, the demon, along with a mixed handful of guards. The remainder stayed safely tucked in the cave guarding the kraken, with Garfield's second ready at a moment's notice to go swimming for help.

"I'll let you know as soon as I figure that out," Meg said softly. "Any hints to help me cast magic in case everything goes wrong down here?"

"What could possibly go wrong as we go into a mysterious mine where there are some spell-casting rogue mermaids? You are so right, Tiny, we are being the plonkers from every horror movie as we speak. You lot might last a while, but I sure as heaven aren't a virgin."

"How do you put the demon away again, Zazz?" Vanth deadpanned.

"They...do not sacrifice virgins for rituals...anymore," Joan added, apparently keen to both stay close to the demon and be involved in the conversation. "Nor...do the hags consort...with *outsiders*."

"Pretty sure she means the ascended beings—Fey, Fehr, and Fell," the pixie magicsplained.

Meg gave Vanth a thumbs-up. No guards rushed to greet the party as they snaked their way into an area of the mine where the walls sparkled with a pleasant mix of gold and copper.

"If I wasn't certain that there are countless hordes waiting to kill me down here, it'd actually be rather lovely," Vocharlian noted, prompting a sigh from Joan as she remained glued to his side. His eye sockets flashed violet. "The locals are rather lovely as well."

Do you have to do that? Meg punctuated her loud thought with a glare.

The demon's eyes sparkled even brighter. *I'm half incubus, darling. Just doing my job. I'm not perchance broadcasting envy by mistake, am I?*

"No, not envy," Meg whispered, looking away. "I don't know what this feeling is."

She held onto that confusion, as the cavern grew murkier and murkier, to the point where even the glowing orbs from Garfield couldn't show them more than a few feet in front of them.

"Stay calm, remember you have a focus, and if anything attacks, concentrate all your energy on deflecting the bad guys. You've totally got the natural casting thing going on, so if you see a bad guy, throw up your hands and imagine a big old shield coming out of your fingertips. Spike and I can handle any attacks, trust us."

"Big old shield, got it."

Vanth gave a reassuring smile and added, "I know you play DPS, but act like support down here."

"I can do this," Meg repeated to herself. The group reached the first signs of civilization—piles of equipment left leaned next to carts overflowing with ore. Joan picked up one of the rocks and frowned.

"Why...would they leave such...quality ore unattended? This is...a full shipment...for the surface." She clicked a few times as she turned it over. "Strange...cleaved not by an axe... Look."

Even Meg's untrained eye could see four narrow slash marks running along the back. Vocharlian held his hand over the stone and his talons lined up perfectly with the gashes. "I'm guessing that isn't normal, is it?"

And then the glowing eyes appeared from every possible direction.

Episode Eleven

When in Doubt, Vampire Mermaids

Chapter 29

Of Course, It's an Ambush

Is this about to be a big fight, darlings? Confession, I'm rather tired from the gluttony episode and woefully unprepared."

"I hope not, because I'm woefully unprepared as well," Meg whispered as shadowy figures undulated out of the mists both in front and behind their hapless crew. A sudden overwhelming itching took over her left palm. Try as she might, she got caught mid-furious scratch as the first figure emerged—a magnificent silvery fish with a crest of rainbow spines and eyes so blue they'd put a movie star to shame.

"Captain Garfield," the stranger said, with a voice far sweeter and more delicate than the spines would imply. "Whatever are you doing here? Did you not get my reports? Everything...is fine."

"My most esteemed reeve—" Garfield started, but he was distracted immediately by the snickers coming from Vocharlian.

The demon gave a wink and a nudge to Joan, who managed to capture a raised brow look despite her fundamental lack of eyebrows. The demon then tried passing his chuckles on to Meg, who alternated between scratching and glaring at him until she blurted out, "*What?*"

"I do believe that's the reeve, the one 'slapping fins' with Brinehilda," he said in his defense. "I'm a demon, you can't expect me *not* to giggle at lesbian mermaid action."

All tension regarding an epic showdown dissolved as the reeve joined in the laughter, followed quickly by a chorus of other fish people. Garfield looked confusedly at this new crew, all clearly the same phenotype as him, while Joan remained silent and on guard next to Vocharlian.

"Back to the matter at hand," Garfield stammered, attempting to bring a bit of gravitas back to the situation, but the reeve had already swum past him to get a closer look at Vocharlian.

She crossed one arm in front of her chest and bowed, showing off the armored scales on her arms. From this angle, everyone could see barbells draping from the sides of the reeve's mouth.

"So Brinehilda's getting catfished," slipped out of Vanth's lips, forcing Meg to now stifle giggles. "Sorry!"

"I am Katarina, Reeve of Virlandia and the Everlast Gorge, and it has been ages since I set my sights upon a creature not of the sea. You also know of my dearest Brinehilda. Tell me, is she well?" the catfish lady asked, staring unflinchingly at the demon's empty eye sockets. The longer she looked, the more intense the violet light burned in his eye-sockets.

Joan bristled and flared, even if her fins lacked the reeve's size and spines. "Oh... I see the swim bladder in charge...is all hearty and hale. How...nice."

While the strange posturing continued, Meg became drawn to watching the other fish in this pack. Like Katarina and Garfield, they had the longer fins, brighter colors, and streamlined forms more at home at the surface levels of the ocean. But they also all had strange scarring around the gills. The longer Meg stared, the more a terrible sinking feeling filled her guts.

"We are all doing well," Katarina was saying. "As I'm sure you have seen, we captured a kraken—"

"At the cost...of our pressure shield!"

"It's not like your kind can't deal with a bit of compression. You are benthic after all—" Katarina said with a dismissive fin wave.

Joan's oversized eyes flashed as bright as anything Vocharlian could muster. "I'm benthopelagic...you swim bladder...twat!"

If Katarina took any offense, she certainly didn't show it. "The good of the many have to outweigh the good of the few. If that super-kraken had escaped, who knows what havoc it would wreak across the gorge and even up to the coastal plains. A little discomfort for the deep-dwellers now, means safety for all later."

As she spoke, everyone but Joan and Meg nodded as if she'd preached the holy gospel and followed it with a promise of free money. The summoner and the coelacanth shared a quick look of confusion as even Vocharlian nodded. Tiny Vanth made a few notes and added, "Hey, I'm sold."

Katarina continued, "Nothing is wrong, and you should go tell Piceus Pike and my beloved that we will be joining them soon with our new weapon against the kraken. You should all *simply go home.*"

"No...we demand—" Joan stopped short as Vocharlian yanked her by the dorsal fin and hurled her against the walls of the mine.

"Charlie!" Meg cried. The demon, however, shifted to his wrathful red aspect and took up a defensive position next to Katarina. *Charlie, stop!*

Meg could see the murky vapors interweaving from the reeve's gills, across a small current and right into the demon's eye sockets. The faster the stranger breathed, the more enflamed Vocharlian became. "That's not right," she whispered. She then looked to see similar gunk filling the water around them, infiltrating everyone—even Vanth's bubble seemed cloudy inside.

"Goop warned you about the others. Goop tried."

"Why can I hear a kraken in my head?" That question had to wait as the once-genial surface folk surrounded the confused and frightened coelacanth. Much like Vocharlian, their jaws distended to show off elongated teeth, including fangs that would put Bela Lugosi to shame. "Oh no, no, no...it can't be."

"If you cannot serve, at least you can be food!" Katarina hissed as she lunged for Joan's throat.

"Vampire mermaids, oh hell no!" Meg then thrust her hands forward, focusing all her will on protecting herself and Joan. "Come on shield!"

The force of her gesticulation made all the strange merfolk pause, but no magic barrier emerged on command. Meg flailed and screamed, "SHIELD!"

She dropped her hands in defeat. A moment later and the ornate handle, her so-called focus, emerged from her palm and then plopped to the ground, creating a poot of sediment.

"Eat her too!" the reeve commanded.

Meg tried her best to escape, but her land-loving limbs were no match for a horde of enraged vampire mermaids. She thrashed and squealed as clawed hand-fin hybrid limbs snatched her and dragged her to the wall beside the equally terrified Joan while the others watched in apathetic silence.

"Charlie, help me," Meg begged. *"Please."*

The focus rolled along a strange current until it tapped Vocharlian's clawed feet. The moment the hilt touched his talon, the metal trans-formed from bronze to blackened steel and it glowed bright enough to stop Katarina a split-second before tearing into Joan's neck. "What is this?"

"Charlie, *snap out of it!*" This time Meg's plea came with a side of glowing magenta irises. The demon extended his wings and claws, knocking away the stunned Katarina as well as the merfolk holding Meg. The second he had a little breathing room, he reached down and picked up the focus. As he wrapped his hands around it, an obsidian blade extended until it nearly stabbed him in the face.

"Oh, me likey," he declared before using it to lop off a confused vampire mermaid's arm. As he snarled and turned to face Katarina, the sheriff let out a high-pitched squeal. Her coterie then turned their atten-tions to Garfield, swarming him with greater fury than sharks. Meg tried to flail in his general direction, but her demon grabbed her. "Time to leave!"

A cloud of blood erupted from where Garfield and the guards used to be. Joan quickly swam along the wake of Vocharlian, whacking Vanth's bubble toward the exit as well. The moment the pixie burst free of whatever miasma the vampire merfolk produced, her eyes cleared, and she chanted rapid-fire Klingon. A bolt of energy streaked from her bubble and slammed into the ceiling, starting a chain reaction that esca-lated into a full cave-in. "Fucking vampire mermaids!" she yowled as the party barely escaped to the relative safety of the open abyss.

Their moment of victory couldn't last, however, as the bubble wall overhead began to shimmer. This time Joan took point, grabbing the demon by the hand and using her improved aquadynamic form to swim them faster than any of the land lubbers could even dream of. The demon took the hint and angled his wings to avoid drag, and soon the chain of unlikely heroes zipped and zoomed through an alarming increase in barrier instability.

"To your left," Vanth cried. She managed to use some sort of magic to grapple onto Meg's foot—bouncing and bobbing and doing her best not to vomit at the bumpy ride. "Your other left this time!"

Joan dodged and weaved even more furiously as they all heard a terrible crack erupting from behind them. Meg looked back but could only see inky blackness. "Get us to the kraken!" she cried as another eruption sounded from the direction of the mine.

"Are you mad?" Joan asked, her voice sounding hurried for a change.

"Yes, but I'd rather deal with the fucking octopus!" Vocharlian snapped.

They sprinted back into the original cave. As they landed at the entrance, the demon snarled, "There should be guards."

Joan pointed to the nearest wall, and a massive spray of blood.

"Bring it on," the demon taunted, loosening his hold on Meg and tightening the death grip on his sword.

"I would like it on record that this is a terrible idea, even by demonic standards," Vocharlian said as he watched his human companion swim gingerly toward the prison barrier.

"I'm not a weeb, but I've seen enough Japanese animation to know that nothing good has ever come from a girl approaching so many tentacles," Vanth added.

"Duly noted." Meg still reached a trembling hand toward the wall of force. She squared her shoulders, took a deep breath, then positioned herself to reach out and touch the kraken. "Goop, can you hear me?"

The barrier vibrated. The mass of tentacles whirled within the prison until a giant eye rolled into view. Joan slipped behind the wings of the demon, using his spines for cover. Vanth seemed to decide that discretion was the better part of valor as well and drifted to the doorway in her now double-reinforced bubble.

"*Goop listens.*"

As the words rolled around her head, Meg watched the runes carved into his tentacles shift between shades of blue and green. "I wish I knew what to say right now, but I've never had a conversation with a kraken before."

"*Goop...never spoken to a human before. How can you move with so few arms?*"

Meg smiled. "I wouldn't know what to do if I had eight."

"What the bloody hell are you two going on about?" Vocharlian piped in.

"Is the Calamari kaiju going to help us with the vampire mermaids or what?" Vanth called from across the room.

"That's right," Meg whispered. "I know this is going to sound weird but...but do you think you can find it in your hearts to help us and a bunch of merfolk out?"

Every rune flashed brilliant azure at once. "*You need...Goop to help?*" The giant eye peered past Meg to the demon and the fins peeking out behind him. "*Fin folk hurt Goop! Lock Goop away!*"

Goop slammed against the wall. The cave shuddered, and bits of ceiling crashed down.

"I don't think the kraken is keen on our proposal, luv," Vocharlian said as he tried to drag Meg away from the monster. However, the moment he touched her, the same azure energy rippled through Meg and sent the demon flying. As he landed, his fur puffed out to a ridiculous volume, giving him the appearance of a cartoon cat, complete with the exaggerated hissing and spitting.

The cavern shook again, this time with laughter. "*Silly fluffy!*"

Meg steadied herself again. "Please, I know you don't have any reason—"

The eye fixated on her. "*If Goop help...will Meg help Goop?*"

"You know my name." She tried to pull away but could only watch in horror as her fingers sank into the barrier. "How do you know my name?"

Her whole world dissolved into magenta light.

Chapter 30

Production Interruption

Our lucky winners have selected an all-expense paid luxury quest at one of our fine friends in Aquatica's eastern kingdoms! While staying at a four-star hotel and enjoying such amenities as pools, tennis courts, and not getting eaten by local wildlife, Meg and Charlie can save a kingdom from certain disaster while learning how to create a focus and harness the arcane. Travel includes two coach dream navigations from Boston to the adjacent realms as well as luggage and wardrobe furnished by Subconscious..."

Meg groaned as she heard the theme song for *Let's Make a Bargain* once more ringing in her ears. This time she found herself standing not on a beach, but in an empty studio with the rainbow dreamscape of the gameshow flickering with light. A few disposable coffee cups littered the area around the cameras, but the cast and crew seemed to have all taken a simultaneous break.

"Hello?" she called to the cavernous set. "Mister...Mister Hock?"

She took a few tenuous steps toward her original podium. The moment her toes sunk into the ridiculous polka dot shag carpet, one of the monitors sprung to life.

"*We'll take the quest!*" she heard herself and her demon say onscreen. This time however, she didn't see any convenient break for commercial, and a pointy-eared young lady with a clipboard and one of those same generic coffee cups approached the Meg in the TV.

"But I don't remember—"

"So, at some point we're gonna take some follow-up footage when you get to Aquatica, mmk," the girl onscreen said. *"The big guy wants maximum bang for his buck. It's a great place, totally manageable from a logistics and filming perspective—friendly locals, low paradox taxes, and above all else favorable incentives for shooting there. If you really pull this off, we are talking major corporate sponsors for any future forays into learning your powers, babe."*

"But this didn't happen..." Meg looked all around to see if anyone would respond, but even the phantom studio audience deserted her here. "I never met any crew." She squinted at all the shadows in the studio. "Charlie? Hey, are you here?"

"...The good news is your tether only affects you in normal space," the PA on screen answered, as if reading Meg's mind. *"So, you can totally stash the fuzzball in the Nowever when you need a break, or we need some pickups with just you. We put all the deets on your phone. You read Enochian, right? Kay, yeah. Moving on—"*

"No! No, don't move on," Meg cried to the screen. "Do you know what I'm supposed to be doing? How can I stop the vampire mermaids? Why can I talk to a kraken? Why—?"

"Why...why...*why?* You sound like a child, you know that, right?" Meg whirled around to see a pair of snakeskin boots kicked up on the back of the front row seats. She didn't need to see his face to recognize the oily tones of Hamilton Hock. "Tell me, would you prefer crackers or cheese with your whine?"

A single spotlight snapped on, showing off the Fey lord in all his tacky outback-inspired glory. He puffed a few times on a ridiculous stogie before waving the sweet-smelling smoke Meg's way. She coughed. He laughed. "You know I'm just messing with you, right? I love you, babe, but you really ask all the wrong questions at all the wrong moments."

Meg watched the smoke coalesce into a bubble before drifting toward the lighting rig. "I'm missing something, aren't I?"

"To be fair, we're all missing something at any given point. That's just part of existence." He kicked down his heels and leaned in to give her a good, long stare. "But in this case, you may be onto something a little more pertinent to your current situation. Like I said before, you could have some perfectly adequate, boring little montage where you and your squad of lovable misfits slowly figure out your powers in a bunch of ridiculously cute slice-of-life moments, but I want a little more...*pizazz*, if you know what I mean?"

Meg shook her head. She groaned as she could hear stereotypical flashback music before another monitor flickered to life. "Here. Have a freebie, Meggle-Peggle."

"How—?" Her jaw dropped as she saw a small version of herself sitting at the art table in her room, surrounded by all her beloved crayons and toys. The longer she stared at the diminutive figure in pigtails, the more she became drawn into the scene, literally.

Tiny Meg looked right past the bigger version of herself, and instead stared at a teddy bear dressed in a patchwork coat and one of her father's fishing hats. "Mish-gan, who should we play with today?" she asked the bear. "I know!"

The little girl then rolled out of her seat and dove under her bed. She emerged with a plushie octopus held together by messy stitches. The raggedy toy had been enhanced with magic marker circles down each of his limp tentacles. "Meet Goop, Mish-gan. He loves to help!"

"I had a toy kraken?" She blinked a few times as she tried to remember any details. In that moment she noticed the box of Twister on her shelf, next to multicolored bottles of cheap bubbles. She studied the books, the art supplies, and the multitude of drawings plastered across the walls. So many mermaids filled the space over her bed, intermixed with unicorns, and a lonely purple spotted dragon holding hands with a stick figure girl. "This is definitely my room, but why don't I remember this moment?"

She flinched as a hand rested on her shoulder. "Memory...is a funny thing, isn't it?" Hamilton whispered in her ear. She shuddered. "People think it's an indelible record, set in stone, but it's a soup of chemicals drifting in the savory pudding that is the brain. Indeed, every time you revisit and observe a memory, the act of observation flavors the recollection."

Meg gasped as she watched her lavender walls deepen to a brilliant magenta. Hamilton snickered. "See what I mean, jellybean?"

Meg pulled away from the Fey, instead focusing on the piles upon piles of toys she'd placed in seemingly random places, yet these monuments of poly-fill served as daises to raise her favorites to eye level. In her reverie she nearly missed her younger self explain, "...Goop is the bravest and strongest of all the cuddlefish. Did you know that, Mish-gan?"

"I, for one, always vastly preferred *cuddlefish* to other cephalopods. They give the best hugs," Hamilton quipped, right as little Meg cheerfully added, "Goop hugs are for free! He told me."

Meg stumbled into a pile of plushies, now noticing a red light coming from under her childhood bed. Little Meg noticed it as well and put her stuffed octopus firmly between herself and the scariest place in any child's room. "Oh no, he's back, isn't he, Mish-gan? The monster is back!"

A tremble entered adult Meg's voice as the memories rushed into her fast and furious. "I had a monster under my bed. His name...his name was—"

"Bad Charlie! You no come out!" Little Meg yowled as this world shifted and disintegrated in the blink of an eye.

"Charlie!" Adult Meg gasped, once more finding herself standing in the cavernous studio. "Why didn't I remember?"

"Time and space are funny things. On one hand, they are the basis for our reality, on the other, completely arbitrary. Once you realize that, however, it's pretty much a one-way ticket to crazy town, so I don't recommend it, Tiger."

"I fucking hate this place," Vocharlian wheezed before he once more plunged his head into a puddle to breathe. The stranger had the decency to twirl his hands a few times until the water formed a globe around the demon's head, allowing the exasperated creature a chance to stand back up without gasping. *Why am I here?*

That's an excellent question, but probably not one I can answer in the time we have right now.

Oh no, one barmy human is enough! I don't want you rolling around in my skull, you—

Beggars can't be choosers, now can they, Charlie?

The demon snarled, the effect dampened by the blob of water sloshing around his face. Even his fiery eyes looked more like glitter bombs in his current state. As the arcane energy kept swirling around the stranger's fists, Vocharlian hung his head and plopped unceremoniously back into the mud for a proper gurgle of defeat. *I'm not a beggar, and even if I was, you'd be the last person I'd choose to spend my time with,* he thought as his sockets shifted to normal green.

Don't be so sure, Tiger. The time may come where you come to see the value of a little madness in your life.

Like hell.

I couldn't have said it better myself.

Wait, what—? Before the demon could get further into his telepathic discourse, however, the skies over the Nowever crackled and exploded with thunder and lightning. A second later and the heavens opened fully, pounding them with enough force to send even a demon scrambling for shelter. He leapt at the gnarled tree among the sea of mud. The moment he dug his claws into the jagged bark, he noticed a doorway recessed in one of the larger mud hills.

"Oh, did you want to go to my place already?" the stranger asked, not bothering either with the mind meld or suppressing the snark in his voice. Vocharlian snarled and dug his claws a bit deeper, watching the cloaked man run ahead in the rain. A moment later and windows burst to life with flickering light, promising warmth as well as relief from the storm.

"Nah, not giving him the satisfaction," Vocharlian grumbled to himself as he curled under the thickest of the windswept branches. Within seconds, his fur soaked through to the skin, and he shivered as the wind whipped around from the north. Soon the smell of snow managed to seep through his soggy helmet, and feathers of frost formed in his peripheral vision.

Did I mention the weather can be temperamental in the Nowever?

"Bloody hell." He curled up and shivered for a few minutes more, until the rime accumulated on his wings. Snow swept over the landscape. Vocharlian's eye sockets flashed red as he saw that despite the now blizzard conditions, a darkened path still wound its way clearly to the stranger's welcoming abode. "I hate random wizards and their fucking spells!"

And with that, he crawled his way toward the hut.

"Don't you just hate *ham*-handed flashbacks?" the Fey asked as Meg bathed in the studio spotlight. "I mean, it's as subtle as your average freight train, but I've never been one for restraint, especially when a pun can be made."

Meg studied her surroundings again, this time taking note that the coffee cups had been squirreled away, replaced by a mix of sparkling water and diet sodas. One of the background displays lit up with a shower of magenta light followed by curtains of bubbles in each of the panels. "That's new, but I still don't get it. It's on the tip of my tongue but...but..."

"I could help your tongue," Hamilton purred. "In fact, I can help with *everything* if you want to play another round."

With that, the spotlight moved to podium one and the sign dropped from the ceiling, blinking with the words "Let's Make a Bargain!" Meg turned to see the Fey lord once more in a plaid suit and skinny tie, his hair slicked into an oily ponytail. He reached out his hand. "Why do things the hard way, when you can have a little help from your friends?"

"Wait...what?" Meg took a few tentative steps back. "When did you become my friend?"

"I've always been your friend, Meggle-Peggle. Don't you want to hear about the onion realm? Or maybe a little more about the monster that's *really* under your bed?"

Meg looked over to the monitor, but no convenient images flickered to life. Instead, she turned to podium two. "Where's Charlie?" The wheel of misfortune once more drifted onto the stage and she could see the clicker still stuck on the blank square, the only blank square on the entire game board.

"You don't need him when you have me," Hamilton continued. "I can cut years off your training, show you the wonders that a human like you is capable of, without having to worry about some foul-mouthed cambion from the east side of Hell. Put all this mess behind you and let's get the cheat sheet going for your thaumaturgical finals. That's what you really want, isn't it? For it to be easy this time? Maybe what you really want most…is someone to tell you what to do for a change."

"Excuse me?" She stared the Fey right in the eyes. "Oh, you did not just pull out the 'gee, Meg burned out of college right before finals' insecurity card, did you? Why not throw in a side 'oh I know you have mental illness, so I'll wave a magic wand and make it all better'? I've got it, wanna toss in a jab about my weight too to throw me off while I'm already confused? Hmm? Is that what you want? Do you think that I went to five years of therapy and three different types of meds just to get manipulated by discount Bob Barker? *Did you?*" Her eyes flashed crimson as she stood her ground, while Hamilton stood there gobsmacked.

"Meg…babe…I think there's been a misunderstanding—"

"I think finally *am* understanding."

"What the ever-loving fuck?" Vocharlian roared as a hot poker rammed into his eye socket the second he entered the stranger's hut. His eyes flashed pure red as he smacked away the pointy stick, but any counterattack was thwarted as the wizard snapped his fingers and instantly dropped the water bubble surrounding Vocharlian's head.

As the demon gurgled and gasped, the stranger could only muster a sheepish smile. "Sorry, Tiger, but our girl needed a little help."

The demon turned his undamaged eye socket toward an old black and white TV in the heart of the stranger's living room. On the screen he could see none other than Meg swept into the arms of a Fey. As he saw her swoon and their lips about to touch, both his eye sockets erupted into flames and the gill plates on his neck fused, allowing him to leap to his feet and charge over the sofa. "That slimy, piss-blooded wanker!"

As he roared and charged, pure red energy surged from the tip of his horns, focusing into a beam that grounded through the rabbit ears and instantly changed the station to brilliant technicolor. This program may have still featured Meg Reynolds as its star, but now her eyes shone scarlet as well. The demon dropped to one knee, his eye-lights already fading to a pale blue in response to the exertion.

The stranger knelt next to him and waved a hand across the

damaged socket, instantly repairing the scratches and burns. "Dude...did you jab me with cold iron?" the demon groaned before face-planting into the sofa.

"Normally a tether would be negated by your being in a pocket dimension, *but* as I hope you've realized by now, your connection to Meg is anything but normal. Bet you that... What did you call him again?"

"Piss...blooded...wank...er..."

"Ahh, yes. Betcha he didn't expect us to counter his little razzle-dazzle glamour attack. It's the strength of emotions, you see. If you rev those up to eleven and bypass the logic centers of the cerebral cortex, you can snap anyone out of Fey manipulation. I mean assuming you know the right buttons to hit. I am *so* glad you aren't turned on by pain like most demons."

"I hate...you..." the demon said before the slothalepsy took hold.

Chapter 31

Bubbling Over

I'm not supposed to be—" Meg whispered as she opened her eyes and found herself once more surrounded by water. She pressed her hands against something soft and leathery, squinting at the light pouring in from overhead.

"You're not supposed to pass out in a kraken-infested cave either, but both you and the world's worst demon decided to take a nap at the worst possible time. I didn't know what to do, and the giant squid refused to talk to anyone else, so Joan and I made the executive decision to run the fuck away," Vanth snapped.

Meg pushed onto her elbows, tucked into a bed of the softest kelp a land-based girl could imagine. A few feet away she could hear hellish snoring as Vocharlian snoozed in a ball, his gills now larger and covered with armored plates. A few snot bubbles drifted from him as he gurgled in his sleep. Meg then looked over to the perturbed pixie bouncing around in a bubble and rubbed her temples. "Vanth, um, I don't know anything about magic—"

"Yeah, I got that memo," the tiny witch scoffed.

"But you do," she followed up quickly. "And I need to know, is there any special type of magic that has to do..." Meg scanned the room again, the bright, frothy oasis of a room. "Is there any sort of magic with...bubbles?"

Vanth pointed to the glow around her. "Like barriers? I mean these fish folks have barriers literally made of bubbles so yeah, it's elementary magic, like the simplest of the simple...the first shit we teach..." She trailed off and started tapping her chin. "Oh, I wonder if it could... nahh... I mean everything about you is a little extra, but it couldn't possibly... Sit tight, I'll look up a few things, while Spike keeps sawing logs. Oh yeah, did you cast the spell to change his gills or was that all like his nefarious magic or what?"

"I—" Meg trailed off as she observed that the scales and spines along his wings had grown out, looking exactly as they did when she'd seen him chained on the table. She gingerly traced a finger along the tip of the longest one. "Did I see the future?"

"Hey, if you're gonna feel me up while I'm out, you should totally go for the..." Vocharlian mumbled as his eye sockets slowly flickered open to reveal lazy azure swirls.

Meg yawned, and gently shoved him away. "Blue...is...*yawn*...sloth, got it."

Vocharlian patted the sides of his armor and looked frantically around his wings and the coralline floor, his sockets flashing green. "We did *not* lose the bloody magic sword after only one fight. That was my favorite thing ever!"

"Oh, the sword...the focus!" Meg too started lifting kelp and looking frantically. "How could I lose it already?"

Vanth's barrier drifted over while Meg stared dolefully out from under a seaweed duvet and a demon tied himself in knots. She raised a miniscule brow. "I'm babysitting the village idiots. What are you two doing? You are nowhere near the point where arcane Kundalini will do you a lick of good."

"Did you see the sword? The f-focus?" Meg asked before diving under her covers.

"You mean the magically bound item that literally melded with your own flesh and bone to become a part of you?" Vanth asked flatly. "Haven't seen it."

Meg's hand began to itch. She then pointed her palm toward the demon and, sure enough, the hilt started to emerge. "I guess I finally have one thing in my life that I can't lose."

"Where does that even go in?" Vocharlian asked cocking his head. "I mean—"

Vanth swam between them and waved her hands. "As *fascinating* as this conversation might be, I think we should focus more on the army of vampire mermaids. No matter how hard Joan tried to explain it, our fishy hosts don't want to believe in an army of undead in their mining colony, so she's off sulking or something. Maybe you'll have better luck getting Pike to listen to you, Zazz. He wouldn't even look at me while you were out." She let out a deep breath. "On the bright side, I've managed to get a stable Wi-Fi connection by running my modified port sniffer over this whole enchanted castle and bounced—"

"Ooh, you got a signal?" the demon interrupted, pulling out his demonic data device from under his breastplate. As he noticed Meg's look of alarm, he added, "What? It has pockets."

"That's not..." She paused. "How the heck do you guys have cell phones that work underwater...*in another dimension?* And why does your armor have pockets when I can't even get pants that hold a credit card? And what does any of this have to do with all the damn bubbles I keep seeing everywhere?"

"The short answer?" Vanth asked.

Meg nodded.

"Motherfucking magic," the demon added ever so helpfully despite the perturbed look from his summoner companion. "Sorry, mother-*flipping* magic."

Meg did her best to sink into her seabed, including pulling the kelp over her eyes. "I'm losing it. Nope, I can't even be losing it, this whole situation is too insane for me to be crazy."

"Is she always like this?" Vanth asked.

"It's one of her charms. Now give me the bloody password so I can call in a little unholy cavalry...and check if someone texted."

Vanth flitted over and stared at the ornately carved machine in the palm of the demon's hand. For a moment the barrier around her extended and she hopped onto his wrist to get a better look at the PD3. A few finger waves later and the Wi-Fi icon lit up. "It's rated for Hellfire storms. Seawater is a doddle," Vocharlian explained.

Once he became fully entranced with scrolling through his infernal apps, Vanth bounced her way to the bed and looked expectantly at Meg. "Is your phone enchanted too?"

Meg surveyed her pocketless swim ensemble. "I don't even know where it is." She then pointed at Vanth's pint-sized device. "I'm guessing that you have all the bells and whistles on that thing."

"Tech is my specialty, specifically research and reconnaissance. It may not be the sexiest of spellcraft, but it's certainly the most useful nowadays. It's the only reason the titans of testosterone tolerate me. Well, that and I'm the best DPS they have for raid night. Now, since the brat is entertained, shall we get on to answering your rather interesting question about magic?"

Meg nodded.

"We've been through the *basic* basics, but I can't stress enough that magic depends entirely on the will of the caster overcoming the will of the surrounding area. Certain situations make it easier or harder to do the extraordinary. The more you can hide your magic as something plausible, then the less likely reality will pimp slap you. Earth is full of billions of boring little people who are all taught from a very early age the rules—whether it be physics or manners or simply the 'way things are'. This creates a fundamental cost in terms of mental energy that must be expended to enact your will—"

"A...paradox tax?" Meg asked.

"*Yeah*, that's one of the terms for it. We mostly call it a pain in the ass. From my point of view, I see it as hacking the simulation we know as reality, but the classic mage boys call it tuning or overwriting, depending on who trained them. It's something we all deal with daily and it's the single biggest limit we have on how much crazy shit we can do. This registering, Zazz?"

"The more you mess with reality, the more it messes back," Meg replied, greatly paraphrasing her demon. "I'm totally onboard with this now."

"Cool. Well, what if I told you there was a way to bypass a large chunk of that mundane inertia and create a zone where suddenly your will rewrites reality? Pretty sweet, right?"

Meg nodded, then shook her head. Vanth facepalmed in her bubble, until Meg finally sputtered out, "If reality itself is fighting you already, the amount of effort it would take to completely overcome that would be huge, like *Star Trek* transporter levels of impossibly huge, right?"

Vanth let out a sigh. "You would think, but the trick is creating a thin membrane of energy to isolate one portion of reality. It's mostly theoretical, but if you generate a field like that, then everything within that space would suddenly be disconnected from the greater universal will, making it easier to change things within that zone—just like a bubble of air trapped under all this water. It's the single most advanced concept in theoretical magic—"

Meg scratched her chin. "So...when Charlie first appeared in my bathtub...I thought the house was gonna burn down but then this... bubble appeared around us so we could finish signing the contract."

"Wait...what?" Vanth said, her tiny jaw nearly flopping to her chest.

"Oh, that sparkly barrier thing," Vocharlian added, not looking up from his demonic device. "It was pretty brill at the time, think you can do it again?"

"Hold the phone here, guys. I need more info because if you can actually create reality bubbles, Zazzy, then you might have bigger concerns than vampire mermaids."

"Whoa. Why didn't you mention the whole barrier thing before?" Vanth asked as she produced a hip flask and took a swig. "Like that's a pretty big omission!"

"I was distracted by the demon in my shower and the intense pain of puking my guts out."

"She has a fair point. I am ridiculously distracting."

Vanth started crunching numbers on the glowing keyboard she summoned within her barrier. After a few nods mixed with *hmm* noises, she produced a projection that looked like every pseudoscientific movie presentation ever. A whole bunch of numbers and letters ran along dotted lines with a pulsing arrow indicating a generic human figure drawn in the middle of the algebraic nightmare bubble. "I think I have a way to explain it, so you'll get it...let's think about it in terms of...Archelm."

"*Lands of Eternaquest* Archelm?" Meg asked softly. "You mean the dungeon?"

"I mean the *instanced* dungeon."

Both girls stared intently at each other for a moment. As the summoner started to smile, the demon looked over his phone with bored confusion. "It's about to be another nerdgasm moment, isn't it?" He then returned to scrolling.

"An instance," Meg mused. "Once you enter, whatever happens only affects you—"

"Once you complete it," Vanth finished. "The scenario is set when you enter and all you have to do is finish it to get out. If you do it successfully, you reap the rewards, and if you fail—"

"You can run it again," Meg whispered. "Why am I so anxious about this?"

"It's a day ending in y, maybe?" the demon offered with a grin.

"You're not helping!" Meg snapped, making both their eyes flash red for a moment. "Sorry! Just let me talk this out. What you're saying is that I can create this zone and set it up like a dungeon scenario? So...when it appeared, I was asking for more time to sign the contract with Charlie, so when I actually signed it, everything went back to normal. Is that oversimplifying it?"

Vanth shook her head. "Nope, that's about it. I mean there's probably a few lifetimes' worth of magical theory and practice you managed to bypass to get to that point... *But* it could be that you pulled it off, especially considering it was a small space...*and* the sympathetic forces and emotions in play." The pixie sighed at the confused pair then pointed at Vocharlian. "You had a greater infernal in your shitter who wanted to survive as well. His survival instincts beefed up your willpower. Get it now?"

"*Ohh,*" they replied in unison, and the demon added a cheesy taloned thumbs-up.

"I'm guessing in that *extreme* circumstance you managed to succeed, but Spike-tastic is right. We have to see if you can do it again...definitely in a controlled environment. I'd hate to see what happened if you accidentally instanced in a place like this with so much ambient magic about. I mean you could..." Vanth trailed off and started plugging in some numbers on her screen. She then looked over to Meg as all her monitors flashed red. "Well...*shit*."

Meg grabbed her head, as bells rattled in her skull.

"Our lucky winners have selected an all-expense paid luxury quest at one of our fine friends in Aquatica's eastern kingdoms! While staying at a four-star hotel and enjoying such amenities as pools, tennis courts, and not getting eaten by local wildlife, Meg and Charlie can save a kingdom from certain disaster while learning how to create a focus and harness the arcane. Travel includes two coach dream navigations from Boston to the adjacent realms as well as luggage and wardrobe furnished by Subconscious. Now, let's see what happens when our intrepid contestant Meg taps into her full potential and realizes that if first she doesn't succeed..."

Now the warning bells echoed through the entire citadel. The trio swam to the nearest window and gawked as a horde of bloodthirsty vampire mermaids poured around the castle, tinting the horizon pink as they ripped through guards. Meg barely managed to scream as the door burst open to reveal Katarina the Reeve tossing the limp body of Piceus Pike into their room.

"No, this can't be happening!" Meg cried. "No!!!"

And with that, the pink haze darkened to deepest magenta. Meg could hear the cruel laughter echo in her ears as the edges of her vision began to shimmer.

Tell me, Meggle-Peggle, would you like to start again?

Episode Twelve

Getting it Right the First Time...Again

Chapter 32

Setting the Scene

L ucifer's kittens, you are totally pulling a Marty McFly!"

Meg, however, didn't have the time or focus to pay attention to her demon's pop culture knowledge as she stared through her arm flickering in and out of existence. She doubled over next to her bed of kelp. "Oh...God...hurts!" she spat out before dropping hard into the covers, blood seeping from her nose.

"You can't say I didn't warn you." The omnipresent smarm of Hamilton Hock offered little comfort as the summoner choked for breath and gurgled even more streaks of red into the already chummy water. Fresh waves of magenta light rippled through the chamber, all coalescing on her trembling form. *"Maybe it's time to accept your limits and give up. After all, your previous takes didn't go much better, did they, babe?"*

Meg gritted her teeth and whipped onto her back so she could get a clear look at her confused demon. "Hamilton...he's...he's in my head—"

She didn't even have to finish the sentence for a fresh wave of crimson energy to surge through her companion. As her own irises flashed red, the phantom audience let out a collective gasp.

"I'm...not...done...yet!" Meg howled.

Chapter 33

Take Two

I'm not supposed to be—" Meg whispered as she opened her eyes and found herself once more surrounded by water. She pressed her hands against something soft and leathery, squinting at the light pouring in from overhead.

"You're not supposed to pass out in a kraken-infested cave either, but both you and the world's worst demon decided to take a nap at the *worst* possible time. I didn't know what to do, and the giant squid refused to talk to anyone else, so Joan and I made the executive decision to run the fuck away," Vanth snapped.

Meg pushed onto her elbows, tucked into a bed of the softest kelp a land-based girl could ever imagine. A few feet away she could hear hellish snoring as Vocharlian snoozed in a ball, his gills now larger and covered with armored plates. A few snot bubbles drifted from him as he gurgled in his sleep. "It's déjà vu all over again."

"What was that?" Vanth asked as she floated a bit closer. "You look like hell."

Vocharlian yawned and rubbed his eye sockets. "Nah, she doesn't look that good. What did that blighter hit you with anyway? I haven't had a slothalepsy attack like this since A-levels."

Meg flipped her laver duvet away with no small amount of panic. "They're going to attack!"

"Which one—kraken or vampire mermaids? I won't lie, I'm kinda hoping to test out the slicer on a ginormous squid, luv."

"Vampire mermaids," Meg said, now stumbling out of her bed. "We need to..." Apparently her thoughts had to take a backseat to a rising tide of nausea, and Meg quickly learned the horrors of vomiting underwater.

"Eww, that's not right." Vanth moaned before switching to a bit of Klingon and forming a barrier around the growing wave of sick. "What's wrong with you, Zazz?"

"I didn't eat carrots..." was all the poor summoner could mutter before sinking back to her bed. "I don't know why I'm sick, but we need to focus. We have to stop Katarina before she and her forces can invade."

Vocharlian, however, seemed too entranced by the swirling mass of sick to listen to his summoner. "Can you magic this shit, Tiny?"

"I got this, Spike," Vanth said before winking the vomit ball out of existence. "I really hope I didn't teleport that somewhere super populated. Anyway, take a chill pill, Summoner Girl. We are currently sealed in, thanks to our fine friends under Piceus Pike. There is a barrier around this citadel that would make the old masters weep—"

Meg shook her head violently, even as green as she still was. After a gulp to make sure no more eruptions were imminent, she pointed to the door and choked out, "Nope, they are still gonna get in, and we have to stop them."

As she retched again, her demon cringed. "Oy, if we're stuck in a fishbowl for a bit, could you stop fouling the tank, luv?"

That made Meg's eyes light up. "Wait, are we really sealed in completely, with all these fish um...*pooping*? Fish poop in the ocean, right?"

"You may have a fetish," the demon muttered.

Meg shook her head again. "I don't have a fetish, I have an idea. Cities...cities all run on how they are fueled and how they deal with waste. Maybe this barrier isn't perfect, and water is let in...or let out some places?"

Both Vanth and Vocharlian paused. While Vanth pulled up schematics inside her bubble, the demon scratched behind his horns and generally looked confused. She whipped through section after section of the castle plans before muttering, "Hmm, Zazz might be onto something."

Meg tried to crawl-stroke her way to the door, until her demon took pity on her and whirled to her side. "Come on, have a bit of a lie-in while the micro-mage does her thing."

She weakly pushed him away. "No, I need to...I need to..." She gurgled and covered her mouth.

"At least the waste portals are still running," Vanth said as a few more toxic tendrils slipped between Meg's fingers. "Oh! Yeah, we should probably ask the Piceus about that..."

"Does anyone finish a bloody sentence? What am I missing?"

Vanth paid the demon no mind and instead buzzed out the door. A few moments later three concerned fish people burst into the room. Meg could only watch in slow motion nausea as Joan barreled past her and wrapped her stubby fins around Vocharlian's midsection. "Thank...goodness that you are well."

Meg paused her seasickness to notice that her demon had a case of the lusty violet eyes as soon as Joan touched him. *Why does this even bother me?* Her jaw tightened as she saw Vocharlian look her way and give her a smirk.

Hey, I'm always game if you want the easy way out of the whole soul—

"Thank the elder gods you are awake!" It became Meg's turn to be on the receiving end of underwater affection, as Piceus Pike bowed before her and gently took her hand into his shaking fins. "When they told me that you encountered a kraken in the deep, I feared the worst."

"The kraken isn't the issue," she gushed. "As crazy as this sounds, your real problem is vampires and they're already on their way to attack."

"No one can attack the citadel, I assure you. Our barrier is stronger than ever—" the fish man said, his eyes still wobbling as he took in Meg's pale face.

She pulled away and waved frantically toward the door. "But they get in! Don't ask me how I know, it's a magic thing, but I know they can get in. The barrier has gaps, right Vanth? Am I right?"

"There are intake ports to let water in, but they have this magical mesh over them to filter out anything bigger than a pea," Vanth started to explain.

"What about exhaust?" Meg asked, wild eyed.

Fetish, sang in her skull.

She managed to push aside the snark and looked to Pike for support. The final member of the triumvirate, Brinehilda, however, scoffed. "Please, the waste ports? That's the most disgusting idea I've ever heard. Not only are the currents there unswimmable, but whomever invaded would be forcing their way through torrents of our filth!"

"But are they big enough for something person-sized to get through?" Meg pressed. "Please, I have to know."

"Oh, you're thinking reverse *Shawshank* action, aren't you, luv?"

"What the heck is that?" Meg asked.

"Do you not watch any movies, you barmy bird? It's a classic, man maybe kills his wife, ends up in the nick, falls for Morgan Freeman—"

"*Charlie!*"

"Escapes by swimming through a sewer!" he finished. "Hollywood rules—this is a reverse *Shawshank* now."

She whirled back to Pike. "I know it sounds crazy, but can you think of any other way for angry vampire mermaids to get in here?"

"What you are proposing is impossible. Let me show you."

Soon the whole coterie entered a dark corridor in the underbelly of the citadel. In the dimmer lights, the colorful coral walls became replaced with splotchy soft sponges, fluffy tube worms, and jagged rows of bivalves. "Filter feeders," Meg whispered as all her marine biology trivia rushed back to her as they reached the end of the hall.

Everyone cocked a head as they took in two doors, one marked with an embossed finned figure and the other with three seashells. Pike cleared his gills and pointed to the finned door. "For those, like us," he said waving to all the humanoids. He then pointed to the other door and explained, "Invertebrates only, the current is baffled there."

"Merfolk have bathrooms," was all Meg could reply at first.

"And they're unisex. Progressive, mate. I knew every other plane was ahead of the humans. So, should I pop in the old loo and look for monsters?"

"Please...be safe," Joan said, still clinging to him like a suckerfish.

"Believe me, no mortal shitter can scare me now," the demon reassured everyone. "But I would feel a heaven of a lot better if I had Mr. Stabby-Stabby at my side. Shit on a biscuit, did we lose the magic sword?"

He turned to Meg in panic, but this time she remembered to stick out her hand. "No, it's a focus and bound to me, like *literally* into my body so I don't think I can lose it."

"I couldn't have said it better myself," Vanth added appreciatively. "Ooh, does that hurt coming out?"

Meg stared in awe at the hilt exiting her palm. "No, not really. It gets easier each time I guess."

That's what she said.

Meg took a deep breath and handed over the focus. This time the blade extended into a smooth, green-tinted saber. Vocharlian gave a wink to the nervous denizens of the deep then proudly kicked open the door to reveal the exact layout of an underwater lavatory.

"Not what I was expecting," Meg said softly as she took in a rushing stream of water ripping through the back of three open stalls with oversized handholds. All the land-dwellers involuntarily clenched as they saw the torrent lying in wait to strip away any waste and whip it off to parts unknown. Inquisitiveness eventually overwhelmed Meg as she saw a distinct lack of anything resembling toilet paper, only an array of holes tucked into the reef-like dividers. As Vocharlian approached, an array of slug-like critters poked their feelers timidly out of the hidey-holes. "Um, how...?" she finally asked.

Pike picked up on their curiosity. "Don't worry, they are just the cleaners."

While Vanth nodded and mumbled something about "Coprophagia," the demon's eye sockets lit up. "Wait...you let filth-eaters polish your knobs? I mean do you lot even have proper bait and tackle down there? Do they have to like, you know, get all rumpy-bumpy in the gudgeon growler...?"

CHARLIE!

The sheer force of her mental command made Meg swoon. "Focus!" But it remained entirely unclear if she was yelling at her demon or merely herself. "Don't you remember we have—?"

Vocharlian pointed at the unyielding rush of seawater. "Are you shitting me? The fish-people are right, nothing could—"

He was interrupted by a spear ripping through his windpipe.

Chapter 34

Take Three

I 'm not supposed to be—" Meg whispered as she opened her eyes and found herself once more surrounded by water. She pressed her hands against something soft and leathery, squinting at the light pouring in from overhead.

"You're not supposed to pass out in a kraken-infested cave either, but both you and the world's worst demon decided to take a nap at the shittiest possible time. I didn't know what to do, and the giant squid refused to talk to anyone else, so Joan and I made the executive decision to run the fuck away," Vanth snapped.

Meg pushed onto her elbows, tucked into a bed of the softest kelp a land-based girl could ever imagine. A few feet away she could hear hellish snoring as Vocharlian snoozed in a ball, his gills now larger and covered with armored plates. A few snot bubbles drifted from him as he gurgled in his sleep. "Oh...crap."

"What was that?" Vanth asked as she floated a bit closer. "You look like hell."

Vocharlian yawned and rubbed his eye sockets. "Nah, she doesn't look that good. What did that blighter hit you with anyway? I haven't had a slothalepsy attack like this since A-levels."

Meg flipped her laver duvet away with no small amount of panic. "I need you all to stop and listen to me, the vampire mermaids are going to attack, and before you tell me that is impossible, they are going to find a way to swim up the nightmare toilet with all the poop-eating slugs."

"But—" Vanth started.

"Magic!" Meg blurted out before doubling over. "It's a magic thing and I don't have time to explain it. We have to seal...to seal—"

"Sealing the shitters, check!" the demon said. "If you had any idea where I came from before we ended up here—"

"Save it! We must find Pike and warn him before it's too late," Meg said, surprisingly commanding in her retching state. As she curled further into a ball, she watched as her little toe shimmered and winked in and out of existence a few times. "Something's wrong...something is so wrong."

Did you honestly think you could overwrite reality and there not be consequences? Come now, Meggle-Peggle, you know better than that.

"What am I doing? What am I doing? What...am...I...?"

She had to interrupt her nervous breakdown to hear a repeat of the incredulous conversation between Pike, Brinehilda, Joan, and Vanth. Once more Joan all but tackled the smirking demon who seemed totally into her affections, but Meg pushed aside any jealousy. Instead, she crawl-stroked to Pike's feet, choked back the rising tide of nausea, and looked him right in the oversized eyes. "Please, you have to believe me, we...have to close off any possible entrances, even the waste ports. The creatures from the deep are going to attack."

Pike nodded. "You were sent here under the highest of recommendations, and I have seen nothing to make me doubt you yet." He waved a fin to his sister. "Make it so."

"But if we stop the currents, our waters will befoul within hours, brother."

"A valid point, but a few hours may buy us time to deal with this new threat from the trenches. You have my orders, now enact them, *little* sister!" He gently took Meg's hand in his fins, slapping her in the face with fresh déjà vu. "When they told me that you encountered a kraken in the deep, I feared the worst."

"I...know." As she said those words in her trembling little voice, a strange expression passed over the fishman.

"I feel like you are so wise and know so much, Meg," he whispered.

"Maybe I've just had a little practice," she said, pulling away. "Please, I know I sound crazy."

"It shall be done." And with that, Pike and Brinehilda sailed out the door, clicking and hissing furiously in their foreign tongue.

Vocharlian raised a spiked brow as he followed along. "The pink boy is convinced, but his little sister needs a bit of work. Mind cluing the rest of us in on the secret? How do you know that the bloodsucking bastards...?"

"Will pull a reverse *Shawshank*?" she asked hotly. "You wouldn't believe me if I told you."

I'm twenty-thousand leagues under the sea with a fit fish goddess feeling me up and a pixie princess shouting Qapla' *all the time. What do you qualify as weird, luv?*

Unfortunately, anxiety chose this exact moment to overwhelm the poor girl, who couldn't stop staring at her pinkie toe as it faded again. The water swished around her gently as Vocharlian forsook the afore-mentioned "fit fish goddess" and curled around to tip up Meg's chin and get a good look at her wobbly eyes. "Well?" he asked out loud.

"I've already seen it happen...twice."

"Come again?"

"Exactly."

They stared at each other in silence for a good long while until the atmosphere became unbearably still. Vanth buzzed over their way and asked, "Do you mean you've had like visions, Summoner Girl, or does it feel like time has looped and you actually went there? It *does* make a difference."

"Been there, done that, and I keep throwing up on my t-shirt," she responded weakly. "I think...I think I'm in a bubble, like a bubble-loop thing. I think...I keep living the same few hours over and over and *over again*."

"Oh...shit," Vanth replied as the information washed over her. "Well, that's something you don't hear every day, now is it?"

"We'll worry about the impossibility of this...*later*. For now, we need to find a solution before we all suffocate," the pint-sized pixie said as she stared at the projections within her barrier. "As it stands, we have four, maybe five hours at most before the ammonia starts burning your gills. In happier news, I can last for days with this amount of mana, assuming I want to float among a fuck-ton of dead sea life."

"Remind me to book you for weddings, Tiny," Vocharlian commented. "You've really mastered speeches."

"You're not helping." Meg flexed her nine corporeal toes into the sand. The pinkie flickered a few times for good measure. "What can we do? If we open the barrier, there'll be a strike team of furious vampire mermaids waiting to kill us all."

The symbols in Vanth's bubble started to flash an ominous red. "Um, about that, Zazz—"

Screeches and wails echoed through the halls as their confused foursome rushed from Meg's room to find guards blitzing through the halls at torpedo speeds. Vocharlian barely managed to snag a fin and yanked a panicked fish out of its fleeing. "Unhand me, wretch! We have an invasion," he snapped.

"Invasion," Meg whispered. They managed to slip through the chaos and find their way to one of the windows of the citadel. Her eyes widened as she stared past the shimmering barrier and locked eyes on the horde erupting out of the opening to the Descent. The forms coalesced like a swarm of underwater bees, with the mass of writhing figures pouring over the edges of the reef and then crashing into the citadel barrier in an explosion of red. Meg screamed as the swarm reared and smashed into the side again with a hideous splatter.

"They...are sacrificing themselves." Joan's voice quavered with a mix of equal parts shock and awe. "And they have...brought something...bigger."

"Oh God, they are—" Meg stammered.

"Lucifer's Kittens, they are chumming the water."

And then the sharks poured out of the abyss.

Chapter 35

Take Six

W e'll worry about the impossibility of this...*later*. For now, we need to find a solution before we all suffocate," the pint-sized pixie said as she stared at the projections within her barrier. "As it stands, we have four, maybe five hours at most before the ammonia starts burning your gills. In happier news, I can last for days with this amount of mana, assuming I want to float among a fuck-ton of dead sea life."

"We've been through this before," Meg said. "We're definitely in a bubble and so far, there is no way out." She then raised her right hand and showed off how her pinky finger had turned translucent. Her demon couldn't so much as open his mouth before she glared at him. "Yes, I know you are strangely obsessed with the cult classic, *Back to the Future*, but I am not Eric Stoltz, okay?!?"

Vocharlian raised a finger in protest, but one more glance at his trembling companion made him clamp his trap shut. Vanth scratched her teeny chin. "If we're truly in a loop—"

"Then we should use each instance as an opportunity to improve our tactics, and figure out a way to solve this instance?" Meg offered.

"I couldn't have said it better myself. I also take it that you're the only person that remembers each attempt?"

Meg nodded. Joan meanwhile snuggled up against the gobsmacked demon. "Are...we truly trapped within ancient...land magic?"

Meg banged her head against the wall of her bedroom. "I can't keep doing this. Each time I loop, I feel weaker and weaker." The unseen audience moaned in sympathy. "Oh, and Joan, he likes you too, so just have your interspecies romance and leave me out of it. He's my minion, not my boyfriend."

Vocharlian's eye sockets flickered a sickening mix of red and green for a moment before he snorted and turned his full attention to the deep-sea mermaid beside him. Meg's grin tightened somewhat as he wrapped his talons around her waist. "You know what, *fuck this*," she said, her sudden use of profanity triggering raised brows all around. "We're gonna be dead either from suffocation or invasion by nightfall so why don't we all just live a little? I'm taking this cycle off!"

Vanth shrugged and whipped out a Mexican cocktail. "Well, if we're giving up early, I'm gonna plow into that library and read the darkest fucking rituals and drink margaritas... Oh, I guess we should all leave the room too," she said as she watched Joan and Vocharlian interlocking their needle teeth in a creepily sexy fashion. "*Oof*, they aren't waiting!"

Meg didn't wait either as she hurried from her room and barreled down the hall...for exactly three meters. An unseen force yanked her back against the wall and she ended up slumped in the hallway, gritting her teeth as she heard crashing and moaning from her very own bedroom.

Fuck yeah, I've been missing this.

Charlie, if you give me a play by play in our heads, I swear to God, I'll banish you to the Nowever right as you're about to—

Sorry, shutting up!

After a few lonely, sniffling moments for Meg, Vanth whizzed back into the hallway. "Oh yeah, that tether is a bitch. Hopefully it's just a quickie." She cringed a little. "I was about to go off and research for myself, but hey, my party member is in trouble, so I thought I'd share something with you while Spike is occupied."

Meg blushed uncontrollably and shifted in her seat. Vanth fluttered to eye level before landing on Meg's shoulder in a weak show of sympathy. "There's emotional bleeding isn't there? I'm not an expert on summoning by a long shot, but that's a well-known side effect. It's not getting all shared health bars with you two experiencing each other's pain, is it?"

"Not yet. Maybe I have something to look forward to if I ever get out of this loop."

"Did I suggest in a previous loop, that perhaps this is a blessing in disguise?"

Meg nodded.

Vanth gave her a thumbs-up. "So, you can take this time to learn some new magic, since we're in a realm where the laws of reality don't slap so hard. We'll get through this, Zazz. What all do we *know* is going to happen?"

"Either the advance force sneaks into the castle and kills us, we die of suffocation, or we die because of the invasion of the vampire mermaids and their killer sharks. At one point we lived long enough to see an undead sperm whale. That was...really *something*. They're like a zombie horde, infecting everyone they can and eventually turning the all the guards against us."

"Do we ever get a zombie kraken? Cause I won't lie, that'd be hella awesome."

"No, it's just fish...mammals..." Meg's eyes lit up. "Red-blooded creatures. Holy—"

Then the whole citadel shook as alarms blared. Vanth let out a pathetic laugh. "Lemme guess, the sperm whale?"

Chapter 36

Take Ten

W e'll worry about the impossibility of this...later. For now, we need to find a solution before we all suffocate," the pint-sized pixie said as she stared at the projections within her bubble.

"We've got four, maybe five hours," Meg interrupted. She then whirled around to face her demon and brandished her missing fingers proudly. "I don't know why you say I'm pulling a Michael J. Fox, but I'm heading you off at the pass here!"

"I'm missing something, aren't I, luv?"

"Just get on your damn demon phone and find me a song. In the next hour, a horde of vampires from the deep are gonna pour out of the abyss, but they can only affect red-blooded creatures as far as I can see. Why do I know this? Because they only acted after they got the super-kraken out of the way. We have to get to Goop, free him, and try to get him to help us to stop the invasion, but I'm not strong enough to do that right now."

"Maybe we're going about this the wrong way," Vocharlian offered. "Maybe we shouldn't be turtling up here and hiding. Maybe I should go stabby-stabby and kill the invasion force?"

Joan finally pulled herself out of her stunned reverie. "It seems...wise."

"We did that *last time,* and not only did the army still come, but Brinehilda was so distraught at seeing Katarina die that she dropped the shield and we died that much faster. We've also tried fighting the army in a last-ditch attempt, but Charlie here is our best fighter, and he can't swim out to face them."

Vocharlian for once, didn't have a quip on his lips. Instead, he stared down at his wrist and the band of scars.

"I...would not want...Charlie...err, Vocharlian to risk his life," Joan said, her eyes wobbling. The demon seemed taken aback for a second until his summoner sighed.

"You two will end up together, I get it. No, I'm *not* jealous, I'm just sick of being stuck outside my own damn room when you two get it on!"

Joan and the demon shared a curious look, until Vocharlian offered, "I'm a demon, I'm easy. If we really *are* about to die, then I'm all for—"

"Charlie, shut up! *Vanth,* is there a way we can use magic to teleport down to the abyss, free Goop, and summon the cavalry?"

That got Vanth bouncing about and thinking. After a few moments, she started drawing furiously inside her barrier. "Oh yeah, that's fascinating."

Meg's eyes lit up. "You got something?"

"Yeah, you're asking me if I can teleport somewhere *I can't see,* with pressure *I can't predict,* through a barrier that's gone *haywire.* That's a one-way ticket to being squished or materializing inside a rock. Not to mention, if we bypass the Descent, does our pressure equalize? *Does anybody know?*"

"That's a rather long way of saying hell no, Pixie Stix. Fine, I'll grab the barmy bird and we'll swim down, try to be all stealthy, and, if that fails, kill everything along the way. Come on, let me do what demons *do.* You know—chaos, death, and destruction."

"I never should have summoned a demon." Meg slumped against the wall and tried her best not to look at her missing digits. "This is a nightmare."

Come on. We can't give up now.

She raised a brow at the comforting words echoing inside her head. "Spare me," she muttered before swimming out into the hall and taking her now familiar slump spot right outside her door. "I'm not good enough, or smart enough, or powerful enough to escape this loop. I'm gonna fade away, so maybe I should just give up."

The door slid open, and she could see an exaggerated shadow looming over her. "Hey now, that's crazy talk, even for you."

"I didn't know I was that loud."

She stiffened as the demon crouched beside her, his wings now curling over them both like a sinister umbrella. He tapped his bumpy forehead. "I think you sent it to here too without thinking, luv. Look, I'm not one for motivational speeches or horseshit like that, but I do know a good pity party when I see one. I'm an expert in self-doubt and loathing. I did two tours in the Ministry of Mediocrity when no one else would hire me."

She cracked the tiniest of smiles. "Ministry of Mediocrity? That's a thing?"

"Oh yeah, you can harvest buckets of negative emotions for making people feel insignificant and worthless. Heavens, I did so well the last time I got promoted to Envy."

"Really?"

Vocharlian shook his head. "Nah, my mom slept with the entire management staff, *at once I might add.* It's tradition down below...and I am a traditional bloke. *Anyway,* enough about little ole me." He picked up her hand and stared at her flickering fingers. "That hurt?"

Meg shook her head. "More...numb than anything," she said, careful not to look right at her demon.

"Well, that's something. Now I don't understand all this magic shit, but disappearing body parts is a universal bad, so we need to get out of this. Remember, if you go, I die too, and I really don't want that."

Meg looked up and studied the strange softness in his monstrous features. His eye sockets sparkled the softest green. The longer they stared at each other, the more violet-tinged his alien stare became. "Do you really think we could fight our way past an army of vampire mermaids?"

"Nah, but I'd rather try than mope here. Who knows, maybe we'll get lucky."

"I'd feel better if I could do something other than cower behind you."

The demon reached into his armor and pulled out his demonic

phone. Unlike human models, this one had a compartment in the back where it could pop out two gnarly-looking spikes. "You ever use earthorns?" he asked with a sly grin. "You said find a song, right? You're still banking on that theory that it was a song that summoned me?"

She nodded. "Maybe. We could try something a little different this time? See if I can summon up a superweapon, or something?"

He jammed one of the pins right into his ear canal. Meg winced. She stared in horror as he raised the other toward her ear. "Trust me, they mold to whatever shape you need."

"Trust a *demon*?" she asked, even as she tensed up and tilted her head.

"Hey now, don't be racist." He then pushed the spike straight in. Meg continued to strain, waiting for the strike, until she gingerly pressed at the plug now nestled safely in her ear canal. "Now I think I have the perfect song to get us going down here."

The first synth clangs made Meg's eyes light up. She instantly soured as the lyrics started. "'Smack my Bitch Up'...*really?*"

Chapter 37

Take Thirteen

You ever use earthorns?" he asked with a sly grin. "Cause, I remember your theory that it was a song that summoned me before. Now, why are you looking at me like that? I get we're in some crazy loop, but you don't have to be so surprised when I come up with a good idea."

Meg instead stared at the location. She felt the kelp, that super soft kelp under her seven remaining fingers, and searched frantically for either Vanth or Joan. "Hey, they're warning Captain Fish-Fingers that there is about to be an invasion."

"H-How?"

"You talk in your sleep, and you were very loud and convincing in my head, luv. I don't know how to explain it, but it's like I could see us having this very same conversation, but it was out in a nasty hallway, and you were so tired, and so sad. I thought it might be better to skip past a bunch of crap for a change. And, hey, the birds listened. I'm sure if they tell Pike this came from you—"

Meg silenced him with a ferocious hug, one powerful enough to smash his breastplate firmly into her chest. She paused as she felt the solid metal soften and warp like fabric. "So that's how he can sleep in it," she whispered in a moment of distraction. She also paused at the warmth radiating from the scraggly demon and the surprising grip strength he could muster as he hugged her back. "I guess I can also get what Joan sees in you."

"What's that? Me...and the fish? Oh, do we?" He slowly pulled away and gulped as he saw Meg nodding. "We *do*?"

"You do, and I'm really happy for you."

Vocharlian cocked his head. "Does that mean you and that posh mackerel...?"

"I'm not into fish, even if the flattery is nice. Um, can we get back to important things? Maybe we can find a song? Something inspiring and not so angry. I'm not as violent as you, Charlie, so before you suggest it again, we are *not* using The Prodigy, no matter how much you like that song."

He cringed before quickly flipping the selection. His talons swept through menus in both English and demonic runes until he finally gave up and put their fate up to chance.

"Is that a random playlist?"

"Well, if you're already right and properly fucked, why not leave it all up to chance?" he asked softly. That got Meg staring at him again and for a moment his human form overlaid the demonic visage. "It's gonna take an eternity to find some song that works."

"*The Nowever is a legendary pocket dimension removed from the reality of time and space,*" Meg whispered before slapping her forehead. "I'm such an idiot. Why didn't I think of that before?"

"Think of wh—?" he almost got out before vanishing.

"What the fuck, Meg!" Vocharlian snarled as he rematerialized in the middle of a muddy field. Rain hammered his face. He immediately grabbed his throat, but this time the scaled plates clamped over his gills, and he was able to reroute his breathing through his flaring nostrils. "Thank Judas, I can bloody breathe."

"She's starting to get it, isn't she, Tiger?"

"Anyone but you," Vocharlian growled before stomping in the opposite direction of this voice. His petulance proved to be pointless as the shadowy form of the warlock materialized directly in front of the demon. The sarcastic wizard gave a little wave but remained hidden under a hooded patchwork coat. "Why won't you leave me alone, wanker?!?"

"Maybe I like you," the stranger replied. The demon plopped his hands on his hips and just stared. "You got me there. Maybe I'm bored. After all there aren't many instances of cross-dimensional summoning to follow nowadays, so you're my entertainment for this fine evening."

"You're no better than the fucking pig Fey," Vocharlian snarled. He couldn't dodge the wave of force that sent him flying into the gnarled tree that served as the heart of this murky void. The demon groaned as his wing spines splayed painfully into the bark and splinters slashed his delicate membranes. "*Ow.* Did I hit a nerve, wanker? That it? You hate hearing the truth? Is *that* it!?!"

The rain increased to a blinding torrent, harsh enough to force the demon to cover his face. For a split second, however, he could see a similar outline to his own flowing behind the mysterious stranger. "It can't be," he choked out as he saw the flash of pure white light. "Oh, go ahead and fuck me sideways with a chainsaw. I know what you are."

In a flash, a gloved hand grabbed the demon by his chin and instantly all the rain suspended in midair—a terrifying silence falling across the Nowever. The stranger jerked the demon's head, so he was forced to stare right at the face of his tormentor. The stranger then whipped back his hood to reveal one brown eye and a pirate-worthy eyepatch.

"You *are* human," Vocharlian gasped.

The stranger then smirked and lifted the cover over his other eye to reveal a swirling vortex of pure silver. "As human as you, *Charlie.*"

Vocharlian reached deep into every reserve his battered body could summon, tearing away from the bark and scrambling across the mud, flaring his wings as menacingly as he could. He raised his talons and snarled, "What does a fucking Fehr want with me?"

"Your fear and your anger *do* make you stronger. Take a look."

The demon gawked as his feet hovered a few inches off the mud. Any joy at his sudden gift of flight became squashed as the stranger whipped out his own set of feathery wings and hovered in front of him. "Hi, I'm Mitch, and I happen to be a little girl's guardian angel...well, Nephilim if we must be pedantic. Nice to formally meet you, Charlie."

"The fuck?"

"Are you really ignoring me to look at your phone?"

"Piss off," Vocharlian growled. He'd wedged himself into a hollow in the gnarly tree, using his wings as both his umbrella and blinders, keeping his gaze focused on a playlist of synth-heavy potential fight songs and not on the flickering movement dancing around his little cocoon.

"You know I can snap my fingers and drag you out of your sulking any time I want, right?"

"Aye, and I really don't care, so see my previous comment and piss off!"

The stranger now known as Mitch chuckled, "You're lucky I like you, Tiger."

"It's Vocharlian," the demon grumbled. "Not Tiger and certainly *not* Charlie!"

He managed a few moments of blissful silence as he kept flicking any tune with mention of death and destruction into a new playlist he named "For Meg." The glow on the screen crept into the red end of the spectrum as he saw a few punk classics in his recommendations even though he'd stayed within the electronica spectrum for his summoner's benefit.

We know that's not true though, don't we?

"Sod off and keep out of my head."

The screen flipped to a playlist titled "Discover The Rage." Instead of it containing merely angry music, the demon snarled as he saw the list featured a one hit wonder, post-punk trio from the eighties. He snapped his wings open and roared. Mitch, meanwhile, sat cross-legged on a nearby rock, somehow dry and in a spotlight of sunshine despite the monsoon surging across the plain.

"I thought you were looking for angry music. Does that not inspire... rage?" He smirked, once more protected by the shadows of his patch-work hood. "I think 'My Love, My Demon' is probably my favorite song of theirs, even if it was 'London Crash' that made them famous."

STOP!

The ground quaked and surged from Vocharlian's mental scream, sending a wave of muck crashing over the half-breed on the rock. Rather than get angry, however, Mitch laughed as he flicked the mud off his face. "Hopefully you can take a bit of that energy with you when you get back to reality. She's gonna need it. I bet she's real tired now."

"You're the bloody guardian angel, why aren't you saving her ass? Oh, right, cause the fucking Fehr don't give a damn about people, do they? You just want her to feel all joyous and triumphant so you can siphon off all that's best in her soul, right? Isn't that your game? You want her—"

STOP!

The return command hurled the demon right back where he started —dizzy and covered in splinters. Mitch whipped his hand back, lassoing Vocharlian with unseen force, so he could slam the demon over and over again into the trunk. Blood dribbled from the monster's eye sockets until all traces of red faded to a pathetic blue. The broken Fell was then dropped into the mud.

Mitch stood over his outmatched foe, pure light radiating from under his hood. "Never accuse me of that again, are we clear, *demon?* Your human side may have died long ago, but I've still got a mortal heart beating inside this chest, and it will not tolerate such slander." He pressed his boot to Vocharlian's throat. "How would you like it if I said you're just here to reap Meg's soul and leave her burning for eternity?"

"At...least...I'm...honest."

"Are you?" Mitch asked, leaning over his victim. "I know better. After all, it's the only reason you're still alive." He finally lifted off his foot. "Get your act together and start thinking like the weak little cambion that you are. Do you really think you can destroy an entire army in your current state? You don't need more weapons; you need better armor. There, that one's for free!"

Vocharlian gulped and clawed his way back up to his feet. Even with his labored breath and slumped shoulders, he did his best to glower at the angelic creature. "What's so special about Meg? What's the... fucking deal?" he choked out, his eye sockets still weak and azure. He stifled a yawn.

"You need your rest, Tiger," Mitch said, his smile returned.

Vocharlian began to sway, the yawn fighting to break through again. "God...damned...Fehr..." He dropped into the mud, barely able to force himself up on his knees so at least he could give Mitch one more middle finger.

The patchwork man crouched to be eye socket level with the demon. "Not long now. You should find a good song when you wake up."

Vocharlian flopped face-first onto the ground, keeping his offensive talon raised defiantly to the sky. Mitch let out another chuckle as the demon struggled to keep his sockets open.

She was kind to me too. That's all she's ever needed to be.

"Piss...o..."

"Piss off!" Meg heard loud and clear as her demon popped into reality on top of her undersea vanity table. His spiky hair flared more than normal, and he grabbed his neck. He then noticed the three confused women in his immediate vicinity. "Sorry, had a..." He struggled for words. "Had a..."

"Did you figure out anything that would help?" Meg asked.

"I...I *can't* talk about it," Vocharlian muttered. He then chucked his phone on the bed next to Meg. "I made a list of some songs. The symbol that looks like an angry pound sign is play. Never mind, lemme just switch it to English. Sorry for any horrible translation."

"Can a human even use a demon phone?" she wondered as she held the ornate metal device in her hand. "And why do you have a torture booking app?"

"That's just a coupon popping up, sorry." He whizzed over and tapped a few buttons until she got to something that looked like many of the music apps available on Earth. "What can I say, streaming is universal now," the demon responded to the question she hadn't asked yet.

"Is it for booking torture for yourself or others?"

"Focus, luv. How much time have we got before all hell breaks loose?"

"We've got four, maybe five hours before we suffocate," Meg could hear as she did her best to find something that would inspire the magic in her soul. She even remembered to pop the button on the back to make the earthorns appear. While the time loop rolled on as normal, she pressed the random button on the playlist. "Well, if you're already right and properly *fudged*, why not leave it all up to chance?" she whispered in her terrible impression of Vocharlian's over the top accent.

She closed her eyes, leaned back, and let the synth line draw her in, as if she was prepping for a raid and not sitting in the middle of the ocean readying herself to battle an army of vampire mermaids.

"Let me take the fall... Let me take the blame..." she sang along as the lyrics finally started. She tapped on the info button. "I've never listened to Assemblage 23 before, but I think it may work." Her eyes lit up as she read the name of the song: "Let Me Be Your Armor."

Before she could get completely sucked in by the chorus, a terrible array of alarms echoed through the citadel. "No, not yet. This is too early! Why are they going off so early?"

She could hear gasps in between the cacophony of alarms. "Stop it!" she screamed.

"Are you sure you don't want a little help, Meg?" she heard as the world stopped spinning. She sat in an old school director's chair. Across a spotlight she could see Hamilton leaning back in his own chair, dressed as a silent film director, complete with jaunty scarf and hat.

"Did you change things? Did you move up the invasion, so I'm destined to fail?"

He rolled his golden eyes and gave her a golf clap. "Oh well spotted, the magnificent lord Hamilton can surely move all of time and space just for you, Meggle-Peggle. Ugh, mortals have such inflated senses of importance. If only I could, then we'd be done by now and I wouldn't be as simultaneously entertained and exhausted."

"Then, what am I missing?"

He leaned forward. "You want the hint?" His leer made Meg shudder, but she slowly nodded her head anyway. "Very well, I'll let you in on a secret, but in turn you owe me a little something. In one year's time, you must return to Aquatica and complete whatever task is first asked of you by the first denizen of the realm you might meet, no matter how small or how mighty the request may be. Do we have a deal?"

"I don't even know how to leave Aquatica, and you want me to go back?" She tried to push from her chair but found her legs heavy and unmoving. She then looked down and witnessed her left calf now flickering in and out of existence. "Damn it, just give me the clue and I'll burn the next bridge when we get to it."

"It's so nice that we have a bargain, isn't it, Miss Reynolds?" The glint of the lights off his ridiculously bright teeth made his smile anything but nice. "Very well, as you have promised me a favor, so shall I give you one in return. Firstly, you should realize that despite what your little loops may lead you to believe, the universe does *not* revolve around you. You are not the only one making different choices each time the circle comes back around. Some loops will always be easier to untangle than others, and there will be a few where you are as your colorful minion might say, *right and properly fucked*. The key is to save your energy for a golden opportunity, and before you ask—stop, listen, and feel the energy around you. The greatest power of a witch is not what they can control, but rather what they can *perceive*."

"So it's just chance? I'm going to keep looping over and over until..."

"You either burn out or fade away?" the Fey offered. "Not really, you can give up at any time. You simply must accept the losses you may acquire along the way. Oh, and since I'm in a generous mood, let me give you one last tip. You know all that energy that your demon siphons off of you to survive, I hope you realize that the energy flows both ways. You can take as well as give, and that might just be the edge to get you to that golden cycle."

"I can...drain Charlie?" she asked, staring at her missing digits in horror.

"Sure, you can, after all, he's just your minion, isn't he? Now I can't wait to see what you get up to next time."

The audience cheered as the world shifted again for Meg.

"This sucks," she muttered as the chorus to her new battle song was interrupted by a vampire bursting through her bedroom door.

Chapter 38

Take Twenty-Two

Lucifer's kittens, you are totally pulling a Marty McFly!"
Vocharlian stared in horror while Meg's arm flickered in and out of existence. She doubled over next to her bed of kelp. "Oh...God...hurts!" she spat out before dropping hard into the covers, blood seeping from her nose.

"You can't say I didn't warn you." The omnipresent smarm of Hamilton Hock offered little comfort as the summoner choked for breath and gurgled even more streaks of red into the already chummy water. Fresh waves of magenta light rippled through the chamber, all coalescing on her trembling form. *"Maybe it's time to accept your limits and just give up. After all, your previous takes didn't go much better, did they, babe?"*

Meg gritted her teeth and whipped onto her back so she could get a clear look at her confused demon. "Hamilton...he's...he's in my head—"

I hear him too, luv. Fuck off, you pissblooded wanker!

A fresh wave of furious crimson energy surged through both demon and companion. As Meg's irises flashed red, the phantom audience let out a collective gasp. "I'm...not...done...yet!"

Meg reached for the breastplate of her confused companion while Vanth and Joan both rushed to find help. "There's no more time. I can't take it anymore, Charlie, but I can't give up. I swear I can't give up. I'm sorry, but I need help."

For a moment, time stood still as Vocharlian watched his striped skin fade from view, replaced by a human guy in glasses and some terrible plaid swim trunks. "What's going on, luv? It's like we've been here before, but I don't know how."

"I know it sounds crazy, but I'm living the same few hours over and over again and I can't get it right. No matter what I do, I can't get it right! I'm not strong enough, or smart enough, and all I'm ever going to do is fail. What's gonna happen if I keep failing?" she begged, her bloodshot eyes searching for any hope in the blank stare of Vocharlian.

"Well, that's a lot, but you didn't ask the best question yet, you barmy bird."

She flopped into her bed, fighting back the sobs that would gunk up her quivering gills. "What?" she dared to ask.

"What if you get it right this time?" He picked her up gently and let her lean against his chest.

"*What?*"

"What if..." He slowed to his best children's program presenter voice. "You get it right for a change?"

"And you just believe me?" she asked suspiciously.

"I'm twenty-thousand leagues under the deep blue sea with a semi every time I look at a fit, freckled fish lady. Also, I've got this hunch we're about to be attacked by lesbian vampire mermaids, so really, who am I to doubt anything at this point? For fuck's sake, you are totally giving me the full Michael J. Fox experience so let's get your parents to kiss or whatever we have to do and save the day!"

Meg didn't argue. Instead, she pointed to the door. "I need to go to the bathroom, now!"

"Really?"

Don't argue!

He scooped her into his arms and swam straight out the door and nearly crashed into the concerned party of Pike, Brinehilda, Vanth, and Joan. "She needs the shitter, mates, and you don't want to mess with this girl when bodily functions are involved."

"I both love and hate you right now," Meg moaned.

Her ears perked up as she heard Vanth muse, "Wait, if there is a chance that there is still an opening to the outside, even a waste one, then maybe we should close it off—"

"No, you *have* to leave it open! Trust me. Take us to the Invertebrates Only bathroom and ask for guards. Stalling this won't work. Just trust me, damn it!"

Vocharlian did his most intimidating snarl to the fish men leader. "You heard the witch. We gotta get her to the loo and stop an invasion!" He looked slightly confused at his last phrase but shook it off and began swimming furiously after Pike motioned toward a darkened hallway. "Why do I have déjà vu all over again, luv?"

"Vanth, Joan, I need to tell you something," Meg said, fighting back what seemed like puke. "Gimme a moment...Vocharlian."

He paused at her using his correct name and let her go so she could swim over to the other gals. Pike chose this moment to swim directly in front of Vocharlian and narrowed his eyes. "I don't know what you've done to her, *infernal*, but I swear—"

The demon clutched his talons to his chest. "*Moi?* You have it all wrong, *Pike*. Don't you get it, I have a rather vested interest in keeping Meg alive, because if she pegs it before our contract is up, well, it won't be pretty for me either. So, don't get your scales in a ruffle, and let us do whatever we need to do to save your fishbowl here."

"But...but...have you seen her hands?"

He cast a sidelong glance at the gaggle of ladies, quickly shifting from default ogle mode to watching Meg's hand fade in and out of view. "She said it didn't hurt, but she lied," he whispered, magenta flickering in his eye sockets. "We need to get this done and get it done fast."

He bristled as the fish man laid hands on him but didn't retaliate. "It's not only the citadel I care about," Pike started to say, prompting the hallway to shift to an ominous shade of green as Vocharlian noticed the fish looking straight at Meg.

Jealousy would have to wait, as every hair on Vocharlian's body stood on end. "She's not into fish," he hissed while shoving Pike to the side. A cold current rippled from the recesses of the darkened hallway, followed by a sinister trail of vapor. "Meg, we've got company!"

Instinctively, he reached out his left hand. A heartbeat later and he heard a strange slurping sound followed by a little toot. "Sorry about that!" Meg exclaimed before flicking her one good hand a few times so that the focus could float free. This time when Vocharlian grabbed the hilt, the sickening green saber shone with Fellfire light. He resisted the urge to make lightsaber noises as he held a glowing sword in his hands and instead swirled his weapon to drive back the miasma that had nearly thwarted them in the mine. He could see the first flickers of skittering movement and readied to strike.

"No! You can't kill her! We must deescalate this situation before it starts."

"*Really?*" Still, he lowered his blade, took a deep breath, and let the green of his eye-sockets fade from ferocious green to a lazy shade of blue. The sword shimmered and shifted as well, rounding its edges, and growing thicker at the tip until Vocharlian held a bright blue billy club.

"You shall serve!" the distorted voice of Vampire Katarina hissed. She clawed her way out of the hall with a billowing cloud of fog enveloping her lower half.

"Nope...not today." He slowly swung the club around and bonked her squarely on the forehead. She stared, dumbstruck for a moment, before the blue sparkles overtook her gaze and she went out not with a bang, but with a bubbly whimper.

"My love!" He could hear Brinehilda crying from the back of the pack.

"Don't worry—*yawn*—she's only sleeping...which sounds really good...right about now." He slumped against the wall alongside the snoring reeve, fighting tooth and nail to keep his eye sockets open.

"Charlie! There's more!"

"Oh man," he groaned before playing his new favorite game of whack-a-fish. Three knockouts later and he gave a lazy thumbs-up to the awestruck crowd. "Can I...stop now?"

Meg swam right in his face, grabbing him and shaking his shoulders. "Charlie, I need you to stay—*yawn*—with me now. That was...only...the advance force here to get Pike and Brinehilda. There's still an army coming. Joan! Joan, I need help!" Meg cried.

"What...happened?" Joan asked as she swam to the demon's side. The blue light shimmered in her gaze as well, and the coelacanth yawned.

"We need to—yawn—stop sloth." With that, Meg plunged Vocharlian's face straight into Joan's seashell bra.

"Lucifer's kittens! I am prepared to do wonderous things to a stunning piece of seafood," Vocharlian cried as he came up for air, violet sparks flaring from his eyes. He looked down in wonder at the purple cat-o-nine-tails now dripping from his hand. He noticed Meg by his side as well and stammered, "Is now really the time for this, because if—?"

"Sorry, really, *really* sorry, but we can't sleep now, and I couldn't risk you getting wrathful either," Meg explained, her gills flaring. "Sorry to you too, Joan."

She then looked in panic at the unconscious vampires, but all four still glowed faint blue and did the fish equivalent of snoring. "Good to know that lasts, in case we need it again. Now come on, we don't have much time."

"Lady Reynolds, do you see the future?" Pike asked completely unironically.

Meg's jaw quivered. "I guess, I kinda do. Now you must let us out of the citadel right now, Piceus."

"But there could be great danger out there. The kraken may return."

Vocharlian watched in awe as his summoner smiled and said, "That's kinda what I'm counting on. Let's get going, Charlie. I think it's time we let you go all stabbity-stabbity for a change."

"You mean it? You want me to go all out?" Vocharlian asked as they approached the Descent. The current had picked up around them, swirling through their hair and wings as if they'd landed in an underwater samurai film. Meg held out her hand.

"There's a very good chance that this won't work, and I don't know how much of me I'm going to lose if I fail this time—"

The demon closed his talons gently around her remaining fingers. "Hey now, I know you're great at thinking the worst, but maybe, just maybe, this is the time it'll go right."

She looked toward the horizon, a sad glimmer in her eyes. Vocharlian raised a brow. "What, have I said this a dozen times before?" he asked.

"Just twice," she confessed. She surveyed the sheer expanse of ocean surrounding them. The eerie current seemed to have driven all the ambient life into hiding, with nary a crab scuttling in sight.

"Not to be a negative Nancy here, but if there's an army coming, don't you think we should have a wee bit of backup?" He then motioned to the swarm of guards hovering behind the safety of the citadel barrier.

"They'd just get bitten and turned against us."

"But what about the blasty-pants half pint?"

"She and Joan have something to do. We're here to buy them a little time."

"Ahh, so you have a cunning little plan. Are you going to tell me about it?"

Meg shook her head. "Nope, it's too late for that. I just need you to get angry and hand me your phone."

"Angry? Why do you...?" He trailed off as the first wave of shadows crested the lip of the Descent. "Oh, fuck me."

"I need your phone now!"

Vocharlian reached into his breastplate, but the moment he yanked out his PD3, the current surged, sending the device flying out of his hands. "I'll get it, deal with them!" Meg cried.

The demon whirled to see a swarm of slavering fish folk barreling down on their present location. He quickly shifted to a wrathful red and the sword somehow managed to burst into flames despite being underwater. Before he could surge into the fray, however, a familiar tug yanked him back. "Damn it, Meg!" He gritted his fangs and tried once more to swim into the swarm.

"Damn it, Charlie!" He could see Meg flailing to get the elusive device. "We have to work together."

He roared and swept away from the battle so he could scoop up his frustrating phone and jam it into Meg's remaining hand. "Murder time, now?" he snarled.

"Kinda. I need you to get everyone focused on you, and we need to survive."

He studied the tsunami of death fast approaching. "Fuck me, anything else? Cuppa tea perhaps, Mistress?"

"Just do it!"

He spread out his wings to intimidate the swarm of vampire merfolk. With the torrents of steam pouring from his blade and his burning eyes, he finally cut a fully demonic figure, ready to slaughter any and all. Indeed, the swarm slowed as they took in the shimmering wall of boiling seawater.

"Are we going out in a blaze of glory because you are sick of this damn loop? I'm all for ripping these Satan's hunts apart."

A larger form slithered to the front of the army. The demon snarled as he saw a familiar bident shimmering in the deep. "Infernal," Vampire Garfield growled, lowering his spear. "How I've waited for this."

Before Vocharlian could return fire with a quip, he became distracted by Meg humming and dancing behind him, rather than focusing on the battle ahead. Even Garfield cocked his head and peered around the demon's wing. "What *is* the land witch doing?"

Vocharlian switched to a two-handed grip on his katana-like blade and pointed it right at the confused captain. "No fucking clue. So, are we going to kill each other here or are you scared? Maybe you'll cheat and use your little army to—?"

"Cheat?" Garfield scoffed. "I need no army to...really, what *is* she doing back there?"

"Not falling for it," he said, a bit of impish green creeping into his glare. "You'll tell me to turn around and then I'll point on the horizon and go 'oh me evilness, what is that thing?' and one of us will be dumb enough to fall for it and get stabbed in the back. It's Hollywood rules."

"Hol... What is Hollywood?"

Vocharlian, however, did indeed find his gaze suddenly drawn to the huge shadows looming beyond the army. "Lucifer's kittens, what is that?" he yelped, pointing his sword toward the horizon.

Garfield laughed. "You fool! You just told me your strategy. Why would I...?"

A terrible pall crept over the battlefield as even the merfolk hidden behind the barrier blanched and recoiled. In this moment of calm, a low voice began to sing.

> *Let me be your armor,*
> > *Let me be your shield,*
> > *Let me take away the pain you feel...*

"Your armor," Vocharlian finished as pure magenta light enveloped him. The moment the light subsided he found his breastplate replaced by a full set of spiked armor straight off the cover of *Vogue Hell*. As he felt the last plates warp around his wings and back, he snuck a quick peek over his shoulder where he saw his summoner safely tucked inside a bright fuchsia barrier, Vanth style. It was her turn to give the cheesy thumbs-up, so that her demon could whirl around and proclaim, "So where were we? Oh yeah, time to go wrath and—"

He did not however get to finish that sentence, as all hell broke loose from the very same point on the horizon that had once brought an army of vampires into the shallows. The plane rumbled and shook as a torrent of bubbles burst from the deep. One more crash and the magical elevator imploded, vanishing in a flash of light. "Jesus," the demon deadpanned, making himself blush a little at his foul words.

"The Descent!" some in the crowd cried. Others lamented, "Our reinforcements!"

Then they all switched to incoherent screaming as an enormous, suckered appendage slammed through the center of the vampire throng. Vocharlian and Garfield could only watch, gobsmacked, as the army scattered. Giant beaks chomped upon the unfortunate merfolk who got separated from the pack.

"Damn girl, you did release the krakens!" Vocharlian exclaimed. His gloating became short-lived as Garfield had enough and jammed his bident straight into the neck of the arrogant infernal. A spray of blood chummed the water. Meg screamed.

"Oh no, you don't!" Vocharlian snarled as he revealed that the armor had indeed deflected most of the blow, leaving the spear lodged in a decidedly non-lethal spot at the base of the demon's wing. Vocharlian managed a satisfying slash to Garfield's side and for a while they traded blow for blow as chaos reigned around them. "Call your blighters off, you bastard. We're gonna win!"

"Never!" Garfield easily outswam the landlubber and sank his fangs into the wound on Vocharlian's wing. As the Fell blood surged into the vampire, Garfield's eyes shifted to a solid inky void. The demon roared and barely managed to wrench free. "I am the Beast from the depths of Hell," Garfield said calmly in a voice clearly not his own. "I shall devour you all and grow from your—"

"What was that? You got interrupted by a tentacle to the face,"

Vocharlian declared as an aquamarine appendage slammed the cocky fish man all the way into the sea floor.

"*Goop help!*" This time even the demon heard the triumphant echo in his head as the largest and most ferocious of the kraken did a number on the remaining bloodsuckers.

Vocharlian swam down to inspect the body and stared at a pulsating bloody mass slithering through the flattened remains of Captain Garfield. The undead fishman gurgled a few times as his barely intact face begged the demon for mercy.

"Yeah, I'll end this for you, mate." Vocharlian raised the flaming sword for the final strike. He froze as the blade shifted to an inky serrated cleaver. "No!" the demon screamed as his stomach growled and his aspect shifted from wrath to gluttony. His arms moved on their own accord. His jaw widened and his eye sockets darkened to soulless voids.

———

"Charlie!" Meg screamed as her barrier crashed into the seabed next to the emaciated husk of Garfield. She froze as slimy black ichor flowed from the corpse into the greedy maw and gaping sockets of her demonic companion. As the gruesome liquid filled him, his new armor burst into Fell flame, his canine teeth elongated, and his second set of horns burst from the nubs, stretching out to razor sharp points. He licked his lips and zeroed in on the faint traces of blood oozing from the summoner's nose. She gasped, "Charlie, what have you done?"

He snarled and dove at her barrier, tearing at her sanctuary with blood red talons. Meg curled into the tiniest ball she could, bouncing and flinching until she found the strength to whisper in her mind, *Charlie, it's me.*

The monster jerked away from her barricade as the kraken destroyed the remaining vampire mermaids. Vocharlian stared at a glowing ball on the horizon, followed by an undulating spotted form. A tinge of blue crept into his empty stare. He heard a yawn from Meg as well.

"Yeah, Charlie, I think we finally got it right. Let's get some sleep."

Episode Thirteen

Truth and Consequences

Chapter 39

Here We Go Again

Meg pushed onto her elbows and found herself tucked into a bed of the softest kelp a land-based girl could imagine. Her eyes welled with tears even though they were soaked with water. "No, not again."

"Again? We haven't had a first time." She stiffened as she felt an arm flopped over her midsection and became painfully aware of a warm current by her ear. She rolled to the side and saw smooth skin and brown hair drifting in the gentle currents of her room. "Now snuggle up and let's have five more minutes, okay? The sunlight is making me all sleepy."

She studied his human form and noticed that his pasty complexion seemed a trifle lighter than last time she'd noticed. "Maybe it's a trick of the light." She lifted her right hand and took a moment to gawk as it was once more completely corporeal. She then nudged her companion's upper lip. Any hope of subtlety dropped the moment she squealed, "You have fangs!"

Vocharlian yawned and opened his eyes. His lids fluttered open, and his human guise disappeared in a flash of green. Meg now studied the spiky, striped, gray and black mishmash of features that made up her demon. He cricked his neck a few times and let his gaping jaw drop to show off his impressive teeth. "Of course, I have fangs, luv." He ran his black tongue over every point. "You think they got toothpaste in this fish-bowl? I'm all slimy in there."

Meg grabbed the kelp blanket and wrapped it around herself as tightly as she could. As she yanked it off him, she saw the demon's chest for the first time ever. "Where is your breastplate?"

"What do you mean, it's right...?" He raised a brow as he rubbed his chest and felt muscles covered in downy silver fur. He then reached ever so daintily to one of his nipples and gave it a pinch. "Ow! They've gotten all sensitive."

Meg yanked the covers, whispering a prayer that her demon's pants hadn't vanished along with his chest piece. In her twirl, she ended up tangled and bound, but the buoyancy of the water kept her from splaying on the floor. "Wait a minute, why didn't I float in my sleep?"

"Because the covers were tucked in, you barmy bird!" her demon snarled as he thrashed in the remains of the bedding. "What the hell is this sticking out of my arse?"

"Whoa! There is a buck-ass naked demon in the room!" Meg heard Vanth declare as the door swung open. Both she and Joan swam into the middle of the room and beheld the wonder of all of Vocharlian.

"What...a sight." Joan exclaimed, wide-eyed. Meg, meanwhile, looked down her duvet, breathed a sigh of relief that she'd slept in her bikini. She then chucked the kelp blanket to create a modesty screen for her naked demon. Once free, she found his breastplate and pants tucked carefully under some shells on the floor.

Meg took her time staring at the sandy bottom, rather than any other one that may have been on display. She counted out her ten fingers and toes. "It's definitely a different day. Oh my God, it's a different day!"

Joan swam over to greet Meg. "I...see...now," the mermaid said, her voice breaking. The coelacanth's jaw quivered as she pointed to both Meg and Vocharlian's state of undress.

Meg waved her hands frantically. "This is not what it looks like! He's just my minion...and he's really into freckles and fins."

"I beg your pardon?" Vocharlian stopped making a seaweed sarong to notice a blushing Meg and sad-eyed fish girl. "Did I miss something?"

"Didn't you two...?" Meg stared at both Vocharlian and Joan. "I mean, didn't you two, have a...a *thing*?"

The mermaid and demon continued to stare blankly at Meg.

"Never mind," Meg whispered. "You know what, we just had a big battle. We *did* have a big battle with the vampire mermaids and the kraken, didn't we?"

"Yeah, about that," Vanth said, floating to eye-level with Meg. "There's kinda a kraken outside and a really nervous Piceus Pike to deal with. So, do you think we can all put on some pants and deal with this shit sooner rather than later?"

"Does...there have to be pants?" Vocharlian asked. His eye sockets flashed violet before he gave all the ladies a wink.

"You do realize that the kraken have been our enemies since the dawn of time, do you not?" Brinehilda snapped as Meg floated over the citadel with her demon at her side. "Brother, witness the destruction that has been brought upon us!"

She waved her fins past the sheepish lineup of Meg, Vanth, and Vocharlian, making sure to linger on the smoking ruins of the Descent before pointing once more to her brother.

"If the Descent had not been collapsed, those monsters—" Pike trailed off as an eight-limbed shadow loomed across the bloodied coastal plain.

Goop drifted over the battlefield, occasionally munching on leftover vampire bits. The distant crunching made Piceus Pike blanche, but he still found the strength to address his land-dwelling heroes. "Lady Reynolds and her companions—"

"We cannot parlay with the cephalopodan menace!"

"Sister, *please*," Pike cajoled. "You have witnessed firsthand what those strange, new horrors from the depths did to your beloved Katerina. What did you three call them?"

"Vampires," Meg, Vanth, and Vocharlian replied.

"Yes, vampires," he continued. "These vampires from the deep are now known to us, and only the kraken seem immune to their foul magic. That means that we must find a way to make some sort of peace, if only for a while." Pike turned back toward Meg. "I promise that I shall speak with this—"

"Goop?" Meg offered.

"Yes, Lord Goop seems to be far more amenable than the rest of his kind, and my sea hags have promised they will have a way for us to communicate freely within days." Pike leaned in and whispered, "Are you certain of his peaceful intentions, great witch? We are putting an awful lot of faith in your recommendation."

Meg looked over at the bobbing kraken. "Don't ask me how exactly, but I'm sure that he wants to help. It's in his nature."

"Perhaps, but there is a long history of conflict between our peoples."

"Maybe so, but times change, right?" Meg offered. "Hey, how did the war with the kraken even *start*? Does anyone remember?"

The merfolk looked at each other sheepishly. "We may have started the conflict," Pike confessed.

"Then *maybe* it's time to finish it, because you have bigger things to worry about now." As the words left Meg's lips, she heard a drawn out "*Aww*" from her unseen studio audience. "I think it's about time for us to go. Just need a moment."

She then swam out to the battlefield, demon in tow. Meg positioned herself in front of an enormous pupil and waved to her new kraken friend. Goop reached the tip of an arm toward the summoner. "*Goop will keep friends safe, not attack fishy folk if fishy folk do not attack friends. Goop...will talk but if this is a trap, Goop will fight again.*"

"I guess that's all we can ask for," she replied softly.

"Hey, are you really gonna bury the hatchet and make nice-nice with the scaly folk just because we asked?" The demon winced as Meg elbowed his ribs. "I don't know about you, but it all seems a wee bit convenient for a suspicious lil' demon boy like me."

The runes on Goop flared angrily. *Demon insult Goop, like silly fish-folk do! Goop knows the truth because Goop dreamed that Meg would come and save him. Seers of the deep foretold this day.*

"So, we're doing this based on squid dreams. That tracks," the demon said. "Not even the weirdest thing I've heard in the past twenty-four hours."

"Vocharlian, give us a minute." And with that, the demon *poofed* out of existence with a flash of sparkles. "The sparkles are new. I wonder if that's because he's part vampire now."

Meg leaned slightly forward, and a sucker touched her forehead as delicately as possible for a ten-ton cephalopod. The moment their skins met, light enveloped the summoner.

She blinked and now floated among dozens of translucent pods, each one filled with an adorable baby octopus. A tentacle occasionally wafted overhead, sending a rush of fresh, cool seawater over the array of eggs. The egg just below Meg showed off a baby with the biggest eyes and a blue tinge on its teeny arms.

This chamber began to glow with a silvery light now, and the ceiling transformed into a familiar image of a child's bedroom. Most of the infants curled into balls, averting their eyes from the alien scene, but the baby blue octopus watched intently for the vision to come.

"Goop is the bravest and strongest of all the cuddlefish. Did you know that, Mish-gan?" little Meg explained overhead.

"Yes, he is," a new yet terrifyingly familiar voice explained from the shadows of the cavern. Meg whirled to see a glowing white bubble hovering over the nursery grotto as time slowed to a crawl. While the glow obscured most of the stranger's features, Meg could see a familiar patchwork hood, if only for a moment.

"Mish-gan?" But the moment the words left her lips, she was jerked back onto the battlefield, with the full-grown Goop patting her on the head.

"Goop never really wanted to fight the fishy-people. Goop would rather be kind and make talky-talk."

"Of course, you didn't. After all, you're a cuddlefish."

"I hate this bloody place," Vocharlian muttered. "But at least it's not *fuckin raining* for a change!"

He tromped across the barren field and took up his favorite perch under the twisty tree. His eye sparkles brightened as he examined the trunk, taking in the faint remnants of claw marks on the bark. "I've been here before."

He shook his head violently. "I've been through so much before..." he said, images of battles and mayhem flooding back into his brain. "Meg wasn't kidding about living life on repeat in the fishbowl, was she?"

This time no voice answered him, so he took the moment of calm to explore his surroundings. Soon he wandered to Mitch's cozy little hut tucked into the hillside, but no cheerful lights greeted him as he approached the door. "Looks like it's wanker's day out," he mused as he let himself into the darkened hideaway.

He poked at the sofa, tried to fiddle with the TV dials, but nothing burst to life. Eventually the demon wandered into the kitchenette area where he found nothing more sinister than some eggs in a basket and a half-eaten loaf of bread. "Guess the bastard *is* part human..."

Once he finished exploring the living areas, Vocharlian pushed through a cheesy beaded curtain to find himself in a miniscule bedroom. Here the ceilings had been set slightly higher than average, with clearance for wings. The demon noted the two extra depressions in the lumpy bed along one wall. "*But* he's definitely part self-righteous asshole as well."

Vocharlian poked and prodded a trifle more, eventually lifting the mattress to reveal a storage box. "Well, well, what are we hiding? An Enochian weapon? Some secret holy magic?" He raised a brow as he opened the box. "Nope, you have a ratty old stuffy that looks like one of the Queen's puppers gone Toxic Avenger."

He picked up the marker-enhanced corgi plush to reveal a childish rendition of a little girl holding hands with a taller boy in a patchy coat. "Meg and Mish-gan," the caption explained. As the demon turned it over, a gruesome, fanged creature with red eyes stared back at him from under a poorly drawn bed. "This can't be," he whispered as he read the second caption.

Charlie can't get me anymore.

The demon dropped the drawing and fought to catch his breath. He reached for his gills, but the armored plates still did their job. A few beams of sunlight drifted over the edges of the paper. The demon spotted a white-on-white marking, some sort of hidden pattern enhancing the artwork. When he touched the area with the etched symbol, his skin sizzled and white lightning shot up his arm. He howled and tried to shake off the pain. Once he stopped, he saw a mark on his palm, a mark that his Babel curse translated for him.

"Drain," he whispered. He threw caution to the wind and rolled the paper around his arm, burning in all the sigils until the full Enochian incantation seared itself into his flesh.

"To drain a soul of kindness, to restore an angel's spark."

The demon roared. "You lying Fehr bastard!"

The runes on the demon's arm flared to life, the holy energy driving Vocharlian to his knees. The door burst open. Vocharlian wrenched around in time to see the patchwork man, his wings once more stretching into view. "Oh dear, I wasn't ready for you to see that, Tiger."

Then came another phantom fist to Vocharlian's face.

Meg grabbed her head as red flashed in the periphery of her vision. *Charlie?*

She shook it off, as for the first time in what seemed like forever, she took her first steps onto dry land. For a moment she just let her toes dig into the soft damp sand and took a few, slow breaths of sea air.

Meanwhile Vanth let out a sigh of relief as she could drop her barrier and take in fresh air as well. She flitted over to the leaders of the fish folk brigade who were all gathered along the shore. "So, what happens now?" the pixie asked.

Pike and Brinehilda stared off at the vastness of the sea. "We change, we adapt, and we move on. If there is one thing this insanity has taught us, it's that we should not be too proud to ask for help from others," Pike said before slithering slightly to the left to show off a new figure, one donning a shiny suit of armor. Her wider, stumpier tail floundered a bit as she adjusted to land, but her beefier arms held onto the magical bident with an iron grip.

"I...can't believe how...bright it is," Joan said, keeping her visor down to shield her eyes. She panted between every word and twitched as the slightest breeze touched her deep blue skin. "Never...did I think...I'd see the shore, nor consort...with...*swim*...err...surface folk."

Meg walked right up to Joan. "Wow, I never realized you were so tall," the witch blurted out. "And I can't believe I'm seeing a coelacanth walking on land either."

Joan wobbled a bit, but her tail, unlike the others, had leg-like support fins on each side to grip into the sand. "It's strange...but my fins...seem to be sturdier than theirs. Perhaps...the deep truly makes us stronger."

Vanth zipped over to Meg and whispered, "Way to see evolution in action. Give her a few million years, and I'm pretty sure it's *her* kind that gets the legs and lungs."

"Where...is Charlie...err Vocharlian?" Joan asked.

"It's just Vocharlian," Meg corrected. She stuck out her tongue as she concentrated as hard as she could. "I'm...working on it. I'm still not one hundred percent sure how to bring him back when he goes poof. But I know he'll want to see you before we leave!"

That made Joan smile, a terrifying sight with her jagged teeth glimmering in the sun. Before she could get another word in, the wind changed, and Meg clutched her chest. The palm trees rustled, and the dry edges of the dunes whipped into a series of miniature cyclones. *Charlie, I need you now!*

Just as she saw a humanoid form coalescing among the whirlwinds, a shadow loomed over the merfolk coterie. Meg gasped as she saw the outline of gigantic wings and sinister horns, but any illusion of demonic grandeur faded the instant a flailing ball of gray and black fur plopped unceremoniously into the sand in front of Meg.

"Crap," Vocharlian sighed as he splayed in front of the merfolk in a decidedly cartoonish position. His wings fluttered a few times before slumping over his back. "Why won't you damn things work?"

"Vo...Vocharlian?" Joan asked softly before awkwardly lumbering his way.

The membranes flicked a few times over his blue eye-lights. "Oh, hey there, dudette." As Vocharlian twisted to right himself, he pressed his forearm to his face and hissed, "Jesus, it's bright!" Flickers of red tried to fight their way back into the demon's sockets, but he still had to stifle a yawn.

"Um, guys, we have company," Vanth said, pointing toward the dunes. A striking figure floated over the sand despite its lack of wings.

Meg spotted pointed ears poking out of a golden helmet. "Not him, anyone but him." Her anxiety overwhelmed any hormones that might have been triggered by the sight of an elfin man in bikini armor, showing off his glorious six pack to the world. "Not him, *anyone but him.*"

Piceus Pike and his sister undulated out front and bowed deeply to the Fey. "Lord Hamilton, you truly honor us with your presence. We did not expect you to respond so quickly to our call."

"Yes," Brinehilda added. "You honor us deeply, my lord."

Hamilton did a dismissive wave and lowered his golden sandals into the sand. He then whipped off his helmet to reveal a mane of golden locks, the strands a perfect complement to his sun-kissed complexion. "I am never too busy for the loyal subjects of Aquatica. I take it that my emissary was well received." He then winked at Meg. "*And* I look forward to us working together in the near future," he said, once more looking right past the fish men and staring at the summoner.

"Was this all just a set up?" she whispered.

As if to answer her, the beach faded from view, and she stood alone in an empty soundstage. "Hey!" she shouted to the empty audience. "Was this all just some set up?!?"

"What do you think, Meggle-Peggle?"

She took a deep breath, centered her gravity, and rolled back her shoulders before facing him. "I think I'm finally getting a second to stop and think," she replied, her voice even. "And I think you didn't want me to catch a break."

She turned to see Hamilton leaning against one of the main cameras. He clapped a few times before taking a bow. "Guilty as charged, little witch. I may have underestimated the force of will your little half breed minion could exert over your tether, but it all worked out in the end."

Meg surveyed the darkened set with its colorful shag carpet and copious amounts of glitter until her gaze fixed on the wheel of misfortune sitting center stage, and the blank screen where the exposition fairy had once tried to educate her on camera. "So, a demon wants your soul with a contract, and the other guys—"

"They're called the Fehr. Your kind usually refers to them as angels," Hamilton interrupted.

"The Fehr wanna stop the demons then. That mythology checks out?" She waited for the Fey to nod. "Okay, I get those guys then, but what do *you* want? Fey in human stories are usually tricksters, so is this all just a game to you...or is it more than that?"

Hamilton shrugged.

"No, Charlie said that demons didn't eat souls. He said they fed off negative emotions. Assuming he's not lying...if demons feed off misery and angels probably get off on righteousness or something like that, then Fey..."

"Are you not entertained?" he asked with a wry smile. "We feast upon excitement, amusement, confusion, and chaos. My thanks to you for providing that in spades, and I'm certain that I shall be thanking you again one day."

"It can't be that simple!" But before she could say anything else, he gave her a salute and she ended up back on the beach, just in time to witness the leaders of Aquatica agreeing to bargains of their own with the fairy lord.

See you in one year's time, Meggle-Peggle. Hopefully you'll have learned something by then.

Then the beach faded into a sea of black. A taloned hand latched onto hers and she barely had time to grab onto her demon before reality exploded into a kaleidoscope of light. She watched helplessly as Vanth erupted into a fountain of pixels. She didn't even have time to scream, all she felt was the thud of her body landing on pavement.

"Doc, we've found them, I repeat, we've found the infidels. The ET is wounded."

"Bollocks!" was the last thing Meg heard before everything faded to black.

Chapter 40

The Bad Guys

N ow, you honestly didn't think you could rip a hole in the fabric of reality and there not be...consequences?"

Meg slumped her head and whispered, "I've been here before." She had once more woken up tied to a cold metal chair, with a one-way mirror behind her and a severely dressed woman directly in front of her. The redheaded stranger folded her hands and waited for a response.

"I don't know. I don't know anything," Meg confessed. "Can you please let my friend and I go?"

"A *friend*? Is that what you call it?" The interrogator pointed to the wall behind Meg. A moment later and a section lit up with industrial fluorescents, flooding Meg's side of the room with harsh light.

This time Meg managed to turn around without banging her knees on the table. "Same room, same scene, but...I can do things differently."

"What was that, Miss Reynolds?" the stranger asked.

Meg stared at the ashen figure splayed across an exam table, his silvery skin bleached from the last time she saw him in the same predicament. Rows of blackened chains strapped him down from head to toe.

Charlie, I need you to wake up right now!

A pair of men in clean suits decorated with ornate crosses slowly paced around the creature, poking the unconscious demon with silver sticks while a third figure wearing chain mail approached Vocharlian's head with Hell's version of wraparound sunglasses.

"Don't hurt him!" Meg cried aloud, even as her inner monologue yelled, *Vocharlian Variegatus, wake your ass up right now!*

Thick, black liquid oozed from his otherwise empty eye sockets. As the dude in chainmail drew closer, the demon hissed through interlocking black fangs as opposed to his former tiny needles. The scientist took one more step and the whole room flashed red.

"Hurry, the subject is—argh!" Meg could hear through an intercom. She didn't wait to see the fracas, and instead tipped her seat to go sprawling under the table—shielding herself from the lady in the room.

"I can do this. I can do this. *I can do this*," she chanted as fast as she could, wiggling her fingers in time with the song starting to play in her memories.

> *Let me be your armor,*
> > *Let me be your shield,*
> > *Let me take away the pain you feel...*

She sang with as much emotion as she could, even if her pitch fell slightly flat. *Charlie, please! Please let this work.*

Time slowed to a crawl. She heard the screams, the crash. Glittering glass cascaded from above. Energy surged from her wrist and streamed through her tether.

Her demon growled the next line, "*...Your armor. Let me be the light, that guides your way through darkest night.*"

"*Let me be your armor,*" Meg finished the chorus.

As the words flowed, memories returned—her head falling against Vocharlian's shoulder as they shared the earthorns. "*We learned this song and it's gonna save us now,*" she declared in her mind.

"Get that binding on him now, assholes!" the interrogator yowled.

Time rushed back to normal, a cacophony filled the air: screams, bangs, and the door to Meg's room slamming shut. A heartbeat later and boots slammed into the floor next to her, cracking the concrete with their jet-black spikes.

"Wow," Meg mouthed as she took in the armored demon with literal flames pouring out of his visor.

"They hurt you?" the demon growled before easily snapping her handcuffs.

She let him yank her to her feet and stared in horror at the guys in the clean suits splayed against the cabinets in the lab. "Did you...d-did you?"

"No—" he snarled, looking away. "Wanted to gut the fuckers, but I figured you wouldn't like that."

Meg raised her palm to him. "If I give you this, can you maybe be a little less...wrathful? We don't know who they are, and you're right I don't want to kill people."

"Fine," he snarled. "Let's try a little..."

The light under his visor shifted from scarlet to a soothing blue. Meg stifled her yawn, then took her demon's hand. As she let go, the hilt appeared in his grip.

Vocharlian let out his own yawn before the hilt transformed into a glowing club. "Bright side, we won't kill any of these dudes." He sighed. "Downside, we're probably gonna pass out before we escape."

He managed to burst through the interrogation room door with a single whack. They hustled into a sterile corridor, flooded with red emergency lights. A host of goons in black military gear rushed out of a nearby door. Vocharlian managed to pummel them each into submission, but each hit grew progressively slower and less impressive.

Meg fought another yawn. "Do you have a less angry...angry you can do?" she asked. "Maybe envy?"

"Nah, a jealous rage will just go to wrath," he moaned, now leaning against the wall. "Might be easier if I get angry...but I'll probably crush someone's skull with this new me..." He motioned over his broader chest and more powerful frame barely contained in his fancy armor.

"Yeah, you've leveled up for sure," Meg admitted. Her eyes lit up. "Hey, aren't you proud we escaped? Pride's a sin, isn't it?"

Despite them trying to both escape and deal with an impending slothalepsy attack, Vocharlian stopped to give his human companion some serious side-eye. "A pathetic half-breed like me? Nothing to be proud of there."

"Half-breed," Meg whispered. "Nothing wrong with being a mix—" She swayed and nearly crashed into the wall as the exhaustion caught up with her. "Hangry? Can we do hangry? No...you eat people when you get too hungry, don't you...?"

The demon swayed into the wall and slapped his jaw in a desperate attempt to stay awake. "Hits so much faster here," he complained between yawns. Meg stumbled and moaned as the goon-spewing door opened yet again.

"Hold up, team. I think the situation may be about to resolve itself," a cold voice said as the lights changed to cool fluorescents. Meg braced herself, then peered around her demon's wing to take in the full glory of their redheaded captor in her bespoke black suit.

Okay, it's a lady, so do your bow-chicka-wow-wow thing and get her to let us out of here.

Vocharlian cringed. *Yeah, I'm not into redheads. She's also a freaking stick, so...*

We're in danger!

"What can I say...worst demon ever," he confessed before turning his full attention to the redhead. He puffed out his chest and a touch of red crept into his gaze. "But I have a bitching set of armor and a big ole creature of the night stick that says I'm the one walking away from this standoff, lady."

Vocharlian stomped a few feet closer to the interrogator, the effect slightly dampened by another yawn. If the redhead was intimidated, she didn't show it. Instead, she nodded toward one of the many obvious cameras in the hall and more doors opened to a pair of guards carrying assault rifles.

"Guns? You brought guns to an infernal fight?" Vocharlian scoffed.

"You tell me. Is your armor bulletproof?" the redhead asked, still calm.

The demon scoffed, "My big, bad armor is way stronger than those peashooters of yours, Gingezilla."

The guards shifted their aim. Their captor didn't smirk or gloat. Instead, she pointed to the shadow ducking behind the demon's wings. "How about her? Where's her *big, bad* armor?"

His glare shifted to red. "You...wouldn't..." he snarled as more spikes jutted from his shoulders.

"Oh, I would, if only to see how fast Hellspawn can move. Maybe I'll learn how advanced this magician really is," the redhead explained. "But we don't want to test that, do we?"

Vocharlian growled, and the club transformed into a flaming sword. "I've got something to test, *bitch*."

"Hmm, impressive," the redhead said flatly. "But what we're really testing is willpower."

"What?" Meg asked, her voice cracking.

"It's a battle of wills between my highly trained and extremely skeptical men and a single, trembling witch who doesn't even know how she summoned a demon in the first place."

"I'm gonna wipe that smug—" The demon lurched a single step before Meg grabbed his arm and yanked him toward her.

"Wait!"

Despite her demon still burning with wrath, Meg needed to lean on him to keep from falling over. "Charlie, I don't feel so good, and I'm scared."

"I've got a flaming sword. We can take this—"

"Do the math, demon," the redhead warned. "You may strike me down, but the moment you do, everyone here will give their lives for righteous vengeance. You might also want to take a look at that fancy spell you've got going right now."

One by one his magical armor plates shimmered and faded from view. "Fuck," he snarled before turning to face his shaking summoner. "Is this you, woman?"

The stranger addressed Meg, as well. "It's tough, isn't it? When you know how your actions are impossible? When nothing makes logical sense? You're being watched, Miss Reynolds." She motioned to the cameras overhead again.

"What's happening?" Meg asked, grabbing her head.

The redhead continued, "Your actions are being seen by more and more people each passing minute, witch, and all of them know the truth that you've so conveniently forgotten. Magic doesn't belong in a world with science and logic. We have a set of laws that work equally for everyone. It's the only force in the universe...that's fair. They *know* this and their will is compounding with every breath they take." The stranger's face softened. "Please, don't hurt yourself, Meg. It doesn't have to be like this."

The last of her demon's armor fell away, but he still raised his flaming blade. "Meg, tell them to piss off and let's fight our way out of here. I believe in you, and these fuckers are just trying to get in your head."

"Charlie," Meg slipped around Vocharlian's wing and raised her hands in surrender.

"What are you doing?" he hissed. "Get back—"

If you can't shut up, I'm sending you to the Nowever.

He growled under his breath, but in her mind, Meg heard a huffy —*fine.*

"I'll call off my demon, if you lower the guns, okay?" Meg said, keeping her hands high in the air.

The redhead made a dismissive gesture, and the security detail lowered their weapons. Meg then nudged her demon until he handed the flaming blade to her. The moment her hands wrapped around the hilt, the inferno vanished in a puff of red smoke.

After a few awkward moments of Meg fumbling with a katana and trying to figure out where to store it, while the demon nearly tripped on his own tail, the redhead let out a deep sigh. "You two really have no idea what you're doing, do you?"

"Doc, they took out a whole team—"one of the guards started.

"And they didn't kill anyone, despite the fact that we are looking at an honest to goodness demon in our hallway," the redhead called Doc replied.

Meg's entire face lit up. "That's right! There is a demon here in this hallway, so as crazy as it sounds logic dictates that magic *did* happen. Magic does exist, so there."

"My dear, I never said that magic doesn't exist. I said that it *shouldn't*. You really need to pay attention to details if you're going to play with forces beyond your ability to control," Doc said ever so calmly.

"We get to shoot them now, boss?" the other guard asked. "You know, to protect the laws of reality and stuff?"

"Yeah, can we try to kill each other now or what?" the demon asked his summoner.

"I suppose that depends on you, doesn't it, Charlie? What *exactly* are your intentions for your summoner and for the people of Earth?" Doc asked, without a trace of irony in her voice. "Are you here as part of a hellish invasion? Perhaps you are here to overthrow governments? Organized religion? Anything like that?"

"Fuck no, that is way too much like work. I'm just here for five years of a break from Hell and to get the one soul required for my contract."

"Her soul then?" Doc asked, tapping her chin a few times before turning to Meg. "And what did you get out of this deal for bargaining your immortal soul? Are you looking for some sort of world-shifting power?"

Meg shook her head.

"Eternal life? Money, fame, and fortune?"

"No, nothing like that, and how would eternal life even work if I bargained off my soul?" Meg asked in return.

"It's never pretty, believe me. Idiots asked for it in the olden days when these sorts of things were more common, and it usually ended up with some sort of curse. You know, vampires, werewolves, and all that shit. We used to have to handle that mess," Doc sighed. "So, if it's not power...is it love? Dead relative? What *is* the deal?"

"I...I..." Meg stammered. "I didn't want anything, except an end to my food poisoning."

Silence fell over the room again.

"I...I didn't want to be alone either," Meg whispered.

"You do know that you could get a cocker spaniel instead of a demon if you needed a companion, *right?*" Doc asked. "Clearly, we are dealing with the most lopsided deal of the century and frankly, I think it's a low blow even for a demon."

"I beg your pardon," Vocharlian snapped, his aspect shifting to his envious green. "First off, you weren't even there, and you have no idea how bad the poor girl felt while praying to the porcelain god with all that dubstep blaring in her ears. Second, I don't even need *her* soul to fulfil the contract. We can find ourselves one grade-A arsehole that deserves to burn and *convince* him to take the deal before our time is up."

That made the redhead pause. "I see," she said, noncommittally. "Now I don't need to waste my breath with threats. You're a clever girl from what I can tell, even if a tad impulsive..." She eyed the demon.

"Err, extremely impulsive. You wandered where you shouldn't have, after playing with forces you didn't understand."

"So, you're gonna let us go?" Meg asked hopefully.

Doc shook her head slowly. "*But,* you wrecked our lab and smashed a few rather expensive doors. All things considered, there's only one thing left for you to do, don't you think?"

Chapter 41

The Aftermath

I can't believe this," the human-suited demon grumbled as he swept glass pebbles into a cheap plastic dustpan. He'd been dressed in some of the plain black clothes of the guardsmen, but even after all his enhancements in Aquatica, everything hung baggy and loose. He wore cheap plastic shades in lieu of his normal human form glasses. As his pants nearly fell while picking up the trash, he grumbled, "Even at my shittiest assignments, I wasn't a janitor."

"We made the mess. It's only fair," Meg replied from her own corner of the now brightly lit interrogation room.

"Not half an hour ago we were about to crack skulls and now she has us playing Sally Homemaker—"

"What was I supposed to do? Because believe it or not, I don't know if demons are bulletproof. Heck, they could have had magic bullets or silver bullets or whatever else they needed to take you down, and above all else, I know I don't want to be shot, okay? *Okay?*"

"Fine," he grumbled as he slogged through his next rounds of housekeeping. "All we're doing is delaying the inevitable, though. It's not like they'll let us go."

"Stranger things have happened. For now, I'm gonna take the time to stop and think for the first time in ages."

"Good plan, witch," Doc said, leaning in the demolished doorway.

"Look, I know we got off on the wrong foot, but we don't have to be enemies."

"Correct me if I'm wrong, but didn't you already explain to us that you lot don't think magic should exist? Dunno about you, but I'm getting a teeny conflict of interest vibe here, Miss Scary Lady."

"It's doctor, actually."

"Fine, *Doctor* Scary Lady. I would so hate to offend the woman that's threatening my companion here."

"I may deserve that," she replied. "Just like you deserve to go back to whatever Hell dimension spawned you but for some reason, our banishment rituals didn't faze you."

"Maybe it's because I was born in Essex," the demon quipped. He then tipped his glasses toward the redhead. "Or maybe it's because I'm just too powerful for you tossers."

"I'd love to know more about you, demon," Doc said with a strange smile.

"So you can figure out how to kill me?"

"In part, but I think you both have the wrong idea about who we are and what we do here. We're scientists, first and foremost. While we understand that magic needs to be eliminated for the good of humanity, it doesn't mean that we don't also want to study it, document it, and learn what we can use." She extended her hand toward Meg. "I'm Doctor Tyler and I'm the sect leader for the northeast branch of the Knights—"

"Oh, fuck me with a goat, it's the bloody Knights Templar here to go all Illuminati on our arses. I *knew* those fuckers were real."

"*Charlie!*" Meg snapped.

"We're not the Knights Templar, we're the Knights of Normalcy, a far saner secret organization dating back all the way to the Roman Empire."

Meg and her demon exchanged a look. "I beg your pardon?" the demon asked.

"We've had many names, including the Miletes Status Quo, but yes, the one that's stuck in modern times is the Knights of—"

"You're bloody cons!" Vocharlian said, barely containing his guffaws. As Meg didn't join in, he spelled it out. "Cons...K.O.N.... for the old Knights of Normalcy. Bloody Heaven, at least *I* still have a sense of humor."

"I giggled the first time I heard it too," Doctor Tyler confessed. "But as silly as we may sound, we serve a critically important function for this world."

"Making it tragically boring?" the demon offered.

"*Keeping it safe.* I can't expect you to understand everything all at once, but I am hoping that we can slowly open a dialogue here. I see that you had every opportunity to kill my men, but instead you're calmly helping to rectify our misunderstanding. I want us not to fear or judge the situation but rather start approaching each other with a bit of curiosity instead."

"Oh, I'm curious," Vocharlian laughed. "I'm curious as to how you expect us to believe this shite, right, Meg?"

Doctor Tyler kept her focus intently on the summoner. "Do you think it would be possible for us to talk without such a distracting presence?"

The demon muscled between the two women. "I may not be the brightest bulb in the socket, but I know divide and conquer when I hear it. Whatever you want to say, you can say it to the both of us."

The doc raised her hands in surrender. "I'm just trying to help a scared, confused girl out. You radiate some serious energy, Charlie, you know that right? Meg, has anyone explained to you about the way arcane and otherworldly energy works, how much it costs you every time this... friend of yours manifests without his extremely impressive human suit?"

It's a trap, Meg. She's being all conniving and I'm starting to wonder if she's just a pissblood hiding in her own damn human suit.

"I've heard the basics," Meg said flatly.

"Well, I hope it doesn't end up costing you too much. Anyway, I'll let you two finish up and then if you like I'll get you some lunch and we'll work on your release paperwork."

"Release? You'll let us go, just like that?" Meg asked, picking up on some of her demon's suspicions.

"Do you plan on causing any trouble? Casting any more rogue spells?"

"Not that I know of," Meg admitted.

"Well then, you'll be free to go."

"This is too easy, it's totally a trap and in a few hours we'll end up in a dungeon. I *guarantee* it," her demon warned.

"Well, you were kinda right, we did end up in a dungeon," Meg said as she stared at the avatars running across her monitor while she waited for the cut scene in her game to finish. She then leaned over her chair to see Vocharlian splayed on her bed, tapping his fingers against his knees with an annoyed look on his face.

"You can't just expect me to sit here all night. Lucifer's kittens, I'm supposed to be on Earth, not the eleventh circle of Hell. That one's boredom in case you couldn't guess. Come on, woman, after all we've been through, you want to play video games?"

Meg turned back to her screen. "Yeah, after all I've been through, I want a little normal for a change." She then plopped her headset on, cranked up a playlist in the background, and proceeded to fireball waves of mobs.

When she had finished clearing the final boss, however, she took a moment to do an online search across her server. While she saw several of the top raiding guild members online, one particular Knight of Valhalla—Vanth Mistweaver—didn't show up. Meg gulped. *Charlie, do you think those KON folks are bugging my house?*

More than likely, they seemed like efficient bastards. You ready to get into a little trouble?

I hope not, but I'm worried about someone we may have dragged into this mess.

"So, do you have super senses, things like that? Can you detect magic and stuff?" Meg asked as the pair tried to look as inconspicuous as possible while walking past the Boston Common.

Vocharlian, now the picture of Bostonian pride, kept fussing with his borrowed Red Sox cap. No matter how the demon moved, the shadow of the brim kept his eyes hidden. He then tugged at his drooping sweatpants. "Right now, all I have is super annoyance that I'm still borrowing your dad's hand me downs."

"When have we had time to go shopping?" She then stopped to get her bearings. "We were definitely in Beacon Hill when we left Vanth, but she found us sitting right over here, so maybe if we retrace our steps, we can make sure she's okay."

Meg surveyed the early evening crowds of picnickers and strollers, squirrels, and unfortunates snoozing under newspaper blankets. Nothing screamed danger until she noticed one guy with spiky blond hair and sunglasses lounging under an oak. Despite his casual supervillain look of yoga pants and a t-shirt, his face took Meg back to the standoff in the hall. "I think we're being watched."

"Hey, it's one of the KON blokes!" the demon called, followed by a cheeky wave. He then nudged Meg. "Almost didn't recognize him without an AK-47."

The guard gave them both a little salute before whipping out his phone.

Vocharlian tipped his cap to Meg. "Look on the bright side, if *you* can notice these guys tailing us, I doubt Pixie Stix is gonna get caught."

"Come on. It's a big place and they can't be everywhere."

However, with every step the pair took, Meg noticed someone looking their way. Whether it be a student pointedly looking up from their book or a corporate warrior pausing mid phone call, the atmosphere at the Common turned thoroughly voyeuristic.

"Why is this happening?" she whispered, as a kid looked up from his ice cream to stare at the pair. "What if they *can* be everywhere? I'm getting overwhelmed here, Charlie."

"First off, I'm still not Charlie," he grumbled, but with less bite than his previous protests. "And second, the scary doctor lady had a point, you can't just rip a whole in reality and not expect things to go a teensy bit bonkers, luv."

"I don't even know how I did it! Don't you think that's weird? Like, how could I *accidentally* summon a demon? What are the chances? Now I've got people after me, I've lost my job, *I'm pretty sure my raiding slot has been filled by someone else*, and I still have absolutely no idea how magic works despite living God-knows-how-long in some mermaid dimension. It's…"

"Please don't say insane," Vocharlian begged. "Give yourself a break."

"Don't you want to know how it happened? Heck, I've never even thought to ask. Do you know anything? How do people become summoners?" She stopped briefly for a breath. "Is it a genetic thing, or am I chosen by destiny? *Is destiny even a thing*?!? How can I possibly handle this situation if I don't even know what the situation is?"

Vocharlian shrugged. "I dunno, why not worry about now for a change? Does it even matter how we got here? I'd like to skip to us figuring out what kinda fun we can have fucking with those KONs who think they can mess with us."

"You're unbelievable. How can you not want to know how this all works? How it happened?" she asked as they exited the park at last. She paused and saw a figure in dark clothing slip into the crowd hurrying to cross Tremont St. "It can't all be an accident, can it?"

The demon, however, seemed more concerned with staring at a pile of boxes as they wandered away from the common and toward the narrower streets of Downtown Crossing. "Huh, they do say Nile and not Amazon," he noted.

"This is so messed up," Meg said as the hairs on the back of her neck stood on end.

"Yeah, still pretty sure it's supposed to say Amazon. Is that like a Boston thing? I'll admit, I never paid too much attention to Beantown before."

"*What*?!? We're being followed by some sort of magical men in black, and you're worried about online shopping?"

The demon shrugged and kept staring at the myriad of shops. The souvenir stands full of keychains, magnets, and cheerful stuffed lobsters looked right at home in front of familiar phone stores. However, as they passed a discount athletics shop, Vocharlian stopped and pointed to a pair of sneakers with a pointed check mark on the side. The ad in the window ordered the passersby to "*Simply Do It.*"

"That's what I'm talking about!" the demon cried. "It's supposed to be Nike and it's '*just do it,*' damn it! Someone is messing with us and I'm betting it's that Hamilton Hock wanker. Why can't you see that this world is just a wee bit off? He's got us locked in his mind mojo thing—"

Meg studied the advertisement, an image of a perfectly styled yet sweaty athlete in a black and white photo. "I don't know what you're talking about! It's been Victoria brand sneakers my whole life. They've done these ads since MJ and the Rockets won the NBA championships like a dozen times—"

"Oh no, I may be rubbish at American sports but even I know..." He trailed off as he noticed a flicker of pink reflecting in the shop window. He whirled to see something fluttering into an alleyway. "Hold that thought, I see something else wonky across the street."

"Wait!"

He stormed half-way toward the alley and immediately clutched his chest. The demon whirled around to see Meg teetering and clutching her temples. Vocharlian then looked heavenward and growled an accusatory, "If you're still fucking with her, Fey, I'm gonna figure out how to fly my arse right back to your studio—"

Charlie!

He ran to Meg and managed to steady her in time. "Hey, what's going on?" he asked as she shook against his arm.

"When...when's the last time we ate anything?"

"Oh...yeah, it's been a while."

He ended up leading her into a mini mall food court tucked into the recesses of the urban shopping district. More aberrant advertisements vied for the demon's already taxed attention, so by the time they had finally settled down to split a chicken teriyaki with extra meat, he was babbling like a caffeinated toddler.

"They always get it a little bit wrong, those Fey. They can use magic for illusions and shit, but they can never make a perfect copy of anything. I think if we keep following these flaws, then we are sure to find him!"

Meg glared over her glasses, waiting for her demon to shut up so that they could settle down to eat. Try as she might, she couldn't even raise her flimsy plastic fork while he went on and on about how the McRib was supposed to be a limited time offer only.

"We have bigger things to worry about than fast food!" she snapped.

Vocharlian raised a finger in protest. He then pulled out his disguised demonic device despite it being at only two-percent charge. "Just bear with me and look at this screen." He whirled around his search functions to show off the glorious history for Michael Jordan and the Chicago Bulls. However, the original Fell Enochian script left Meg scratching her head. Before he could whip through a few sneaker images instead, his device chose that moment to enter power saving mode. "Bollocks!"

Meg then whipped out her own device and produced a video titled "The Mandela Effect." It was the demon's turn to scratch his head. "No, that is ridiculous. It was Shaquille O'Neal in *Kazaam*. I know because it was nominated for a Luci Film award in nineteen-ninety-six—"

"Why are we still going on about this with everything else that is happening!" Meg snapped, slamming down her phone. "Can we just have a second this week that isn't totally insane?"

"Here we go with the whole insanity plea," Vocharlian sighed. "Let me know when you're done whining, so I can pay attention again."

"Maybe Doctor Tyler was right. You are just a horrible demon taking advantage of me! All you seem to care about is your stupid misre-membered memories, *swearing*, and innuendos. Oh, and banging fish gals!"

"Oy, I don't remember any fish fingering...not that Joan wasn't quite the catch. And if you're suddenly all jealous, I'm more than happy to sweep you off your feet and whip up a fresh baked soul so you can get rid of me in nine months or so—"

"I am *not* jealous," she snapped. "I am hungry though, and because of this stupid tether we're cursed with, I can't eat because you won't shut up and take a bite."

"Me? Me, shut up?" His voice rose enough to make a nearby table pack their trash and scuttle away. "Oh, that's rich from the girl who needed to babble on like David fucking Attenborough while we were about to get assaulted by the bloodsuckers from the black lagoon! I know you said we had to repeat ourselves like a million times down there, but how much of that was because you were faffing about and making goo-goo eyes at Captain Mackerel—"

"Pike! His name was *Pike*, and I never wanted him. Meanwhile you and Joan—"

He slammed his fist on the table. "There it is! There's the jealousy! Let's face it, you were only winking at the merman to play a little hard to get and get a rise out of me."

"You...are the worst," Meg sighed, burying her face in her hands.

"*I'm* the worst?" Vocharlian countered. "I dragged my ass out of Hell thinking I'd get a chance to avoid the drudgery of life down there, and maybe get to have a little fun with a witchy-witch in the land of chowder and terrible accents. But *no*...not this time. Instead of fun, I get a barmy bird constantly wondering if she's crazy and fretting about some terrible job she's lost or a bunch of strangers online and whatever raid she's missed. Oh, and she's just like, hey, let's listen to a bunch of clearly evil tossers who think magic should not exist—"

"I'm so sick of you! I never should have summoned you. You are just like the Charlie from under my bed. You are a monster!"

"Of course, I'm a monster, but I never—"

"Go...away," Meg whispered, her voice deadly calm. As he vanished in a puff of magenta sparkles, his arm tipped the edge of the Styrofoam container, sending their dinner sprawling to the floor. As the tears welled in her eyes, she could see the same blond guy from the Common leaning against one of the food court columns. She saw him mouth the word, "Sorry," before grabbing his phone and sauntering away.

"Oh dear, you've spilled your supper," a new, sympathetic voice said. Meg could see crisp black pants and sensible heels approaching her catastrophe of rice. "You poor thing, it looks like you need someone to talk to. Mind if I join you?"

Meg looked up to see none other than Doctor Tyler, still in her suit but minus her shades and severe updo. Meg motioned to the now empty seat. "Sorry..." she muttered, rubbing her eyes. "I...I don't know what came over me."

"Well then, it's a good thing I showed up, isn't it? I think it's time we talked about what your demon really is."

Episode Fourteen

Getting Back to Normal

Chapter 42

The Explanation of Everything

Iknow that the truth can be a bitter pill to swallow, Meg, but it's for your own good."

"You mean, I *am* crazy?"

"Crazy is not a word that should *ever* be used for all you've been through. Yes, you've been ill, ill to the point of hallucinating, but that's simply your body protecting your mind from the very real trauma you've been through. All I want you to do now is sit back, take a deep breath, and think logically about recent events. You're a brilliant girl, so all you need to do is calm your mind and let that brilliance shine," Doctor Tyler explained softly as the rest of the food court faded from Meg's focus.

Meg rubbed the base of her skull and winced as she hit a knot. "I hit my head when I was sick, didn't I? It...it would make so much sense, but I...but I did such strange things, and I think I can tell the difference between what's real and what's a fantasy. I mean Charlie... Vocharlian, he's..." She looked around the mall, to Doctor Tyler, and then down to the single serving of chicken teriyaki she'd ordered.

"Do you see anyone else here besides us, Meg?"

Charlie? Charlie, are you here? Come back now.

The good doctor stared expectantly across the table. Meg slumped her shoulders. "Bringing him back is always the tricky part."

The doctor didn't say a word. Instead, she slipped out a petite red notebook and scribbled a few notes. "Oh, you're a leftie too," Meg pointed out.

"Indeed, I'm terribly sinister," she replied with a tiny grin. "Sorry, even we professionals can lapse into humor as a defense mechanism. I hope you're not still intimidated by me. After all, I'm only here to help."

Meg shook her head a few times. "Why am I so uneasy?"

The doctor cocked her head. "Are you feeling anxious again? Do you remember your breathing? Come on, try it with me—one...two...three...four in, then—"

Meg let out a deep five count from her mouth. After a few more rounds, she could focus on the woman sitting patiently across the table. "No, I'm...*not* anxious, for the first time in what feels like a week. However, I don't remember much about you except being locked up..."

"Were you locked up?" Doctor Tyler asked. "Do you really think I locked you up? Just take another deep breath and think back to when you first met me."

Meg's hands slipped to her side. "We...were hurt."

The mall food court faded away, replaced by a different set of white walls. She looked down to see herself once more in an uncomfortable metal chair, but this one had a retro floral print on the seat cushion. The cold steel of an interrogation table had been replaced with a cheap office desk, and the wall of mirrors had morphed into a window overlooking a parking lot.

Meg shook her head again, a little more violently this time. "No, that's not what I remembered."

"Memory is a funny thing, isn't it?" Doctor Tyler asked sweetly, causing the hairs on Meg's arm to stand on end. "Sometimes what we *think* we've seen can actually be very different when we're calm, collected, and can take an objective look back at what we've experienced."

"I've...heard that before."

"Oh, where did you hear it?"

Meg slumped in her chair. Her attention wandered to a sign for Burrito Express.

Doctor Tyler gave her a moment to recover before pressing on with, "Don't worry, I'm not going to judge whatever you say. I know how stressful this past week has been."

"Stressful? Yeah, that's one word for it. I think ridiculous might be better."

"You want to take a moment, get something to eat? I can be here as long as you need, Meg—"

"Who are you!?!"

"I'm a doctor, Meg, and I'm here to help—wherever you need, whenever you need. If you want to be alone now, I can come back, but you seemed so upset leaving our session today..."

Meg stared frantically around the food court, finally zeroing in on the blond guy a few tables over, sipping his enormous drink as if he didn't have a care in the world. "Session? Who has bodyguards for an office visit?" she blurted out.

Doctor Tyler pointed toward the creeper in yoga pants and let out a deep sigh. "Are you talking about Billy? If his presence is upsetting you, I'll have him wait in the garage."

"Who *is* he?"

Doctor Tyler motioned the blond over. Meg took in the faded gym logo tee on his shirt. and he took off his glasses to reveal nothing more sinister than piercing blue eyes.

"Hey, how yah doing?" Billy asked with an easy surfer accent. "You lovely ladies need a ride or something?"

"He's your *driver*?" Meg asked, prompting Billy to laugh.

"It certainly feels like it. I'm her chauffer, personal trainer, chef, and cleaning service all rolled into one, but that's what I signed up for nearly a decade ago." He then flipped up his hand to show off a band of gold. "Oh, and I'm also the designated spider stomper and have been assigned permanent litterbox duties."

"What this man is trying to say is that he's my long-suffering husband, and he happens to be my ride. He also helps around the office, so I'm sure you've seen him everywhere, even when you don't want to."

"Yeah, she doesn't announce it much in the office, but I'm totally her kept man."

Meg studied him one more time but didn't see any guns at his side or anything more threatening than a gallon of soda in his grasp. Once more, her surroundings faded and she could see this Billy guy in the hall behind Doctor Tyler, only instead of a weapon, he had a steaming mug in his hands.

"He was in the office...that's where I remember him," Meg said softly, repeating it a few times to let it sink in. "Why is everything so fuzzy?"

"Hon, can you get us some waters, and take your time?" the doc asked. Once they were alone, she leaned in and gave Meg the most reassuring smile that she could muster. "You've been through so much, kiddo. Head injuries are no laughing matter. The good news is it looks like you're starting to get your bearings back. Are you feeling a little calmer, a little more in control?"

"You know what, I am...feeling better, but...but..." She stared at the empty tables.

"You're looking for someone? Who is it that you're looking for, Meg?"

"Vocharlian! I knew you'd be back. How's it going, Tiger?"

"Piss off," the demon replied as he splayed face first into a mud puddle, his gills spurting and kicking out filthy water. The demon burst from his undignified landing pad and roared until he managed to gargle up the remaining sediment. "I fucking hate this place!"

Mitch, meanwhile, leaned against the twisted tree at the heart of the Nowever, his usual grin strangely absent under his hood. He waited for the demon to hem and haw and flick the remaining muck from his extremities, all while the clouds broke overhead to reveal the swirling magenta sky of the realm. The demon eventually tilted his head back and gawked at the break in the perpetual cloud cover. "Well, we ain't in bloody Kansas anymore, are we?"

"That we aren't," Mitch replied somberly.

Thunder rolled in the distance. The demon squelched his feet a few times in the mud then stretched his wings before facing his half-angelic nemesis. The wind whipped around them both, and as the light filtered through the barren branches, a pair of brilliant gold and white wings materialized from the warlock's shoulders.

"I honestly thought you'd do better with your shreds of a humanity left flapping in that miserable shell of yours, but in the end, you were nothing more than a run of the mill demon," he said with a sigh.

"That might be the nicest thing you've ever said to me, mate." Vocharlian stared wistfully at his empty hand. *What I wouldn't do for my Fehr sticker right now.*

She's cut off from you. I hope you realize what that means.

"Get out of my head, wanker!" Focus blade or not, the demon shifted his stance to face the angelic asshole with his talons at the ready.

Although weaponless, Mitch didn't so much as flinch at the fearsome display. He chose instead to inspect the chips on his painted nails and kick a loose pebble out of his path. "I know you're frustrated, Tiger, but this little display won't get you anywhere."

"Slicing up your smug mug will make me feel better," the demon snarled.

"Then you're welcome to try, but no amount of blustering is going to save Meg. It's too late. They've already planted the seed of doubt—"

The demon lunged at Mitch. The half-angel flickered and sidestepped the attack without even looking Vocharlian's way. Teeth went flying as the demon's jaw clamped around the tree trunk. Vocharlian whimpered as inky blood spurted from his now crooked nose.

"Ouch, that would have hurt, if you'd managed to hit me."

The demon flipped him the bird before whirling around for a backhanded strike. This time he ended up with nothing but air as Mitch arched his back and dodged. "I'm guessing you're still upset with me."

Vocharlian continued his attack, hissing and snarling until Mitch fluttered his wings and lifted himself out of reach. The demon flapped his own wings a few times, until he lost his balance and ended up exactly where he began, face first in the mud.

"Remind me next time not to pick the most pathetic demon in all of Hell to save the world," Mitch said before flying off into the sea of clouds.

"Wanker." Vocharlian pounded his fist into the dirt. *Come on, woman, get me out of here. You hear me, Meg? Get me the heaven out of here!*

"I honestly thought I summoned a demon...in my bathroom," Meg confessed, now staring at an unopened bottled of water rather than a

pile of spilled teriyaki. Tears welled in the corners of her eyes. "Saying it
aloud sounds so crazy..." She paused at that word. "I mean ridiculous,
that I have to laugh, right? Am I supposed to laugh? Because right now,
I'm crying."

Doctor Tyler pulled a packet of tissues out of her pocketbook and
slid them silently across the table. After a solid nose blow, Meg asked,
"What kind of doctor are you again?"

"I have my doctorates in Anthropology, Archaeology, and Psychol-
ogy, so I can be a few different flavors depending on what you need. My
specialty is visions, dreams, and hallucinations, so the hospital gave me a
call."

"You think that I'm crazy, don't you?"

Doctor Tyler shook her head. "I think you've had an intense experience and I want to learn all about it, Meg. Do you remember us talking
about the importance of dreams and visions or is that still blurry? It's a
modern concept that seeing things is purely a mental illness. Often, it's
our subconscious reaching out to tell us something important. I'm here
to listen and to help you figure out what your inner mind is trying to
say."

"So...you think I'm letting my *inner* demons out? No, he was real, I
could see him, hear him, heck, he even smelled like cheap body spray. I
can't believe that I'd have a hallucination so real...and so weird."

Charlie, if you can hear me, now would be a great time to show up.

"If he's real, can you tell me someone who's seen him?"

"You! You saw him! You saw him in the hall...when...when you were
all scary and you had bodyguards and...and..."

This time Doctor Tyler pulled her phone out of her pocketbook and
slid it on the table. She opened a file to reveal a sleepy looking Meg
sitting across a desk, her eyes pointedly avoiding the camera. "*You
realize that you are being recorded, don't you, Meg?*" the doctor's
offscreen voice asked. The girl onscreen nodded furiously. "*Do you
know why you're being recorded?*"

"*Because I'm having trouble remembering things. Because I'm scared
that I'm going to go through another loop and forget the whole day and
think my nightmares are real. It's like I'm stuck on repeat, and I don't
know how to get out, and I'm just so...scared. Maybe if I can see myself
talking, maybe I'll remember and find a way to snap out of this.*"

Meg in the present shoved away from the table and hurried toward the ladies' room. The dribble of tears turned into a river, and she locked herself in a grimy stall, holding her own phone in trembling hands.

"So, are you looking up PTSD-related memory loss first or to see if there really *is* a Dr. J.M. Tyler in Boston?" Meg heard through the decorated bathroom door.

"Y-yes," Meg replied as she stared at her array of open tabs in her phone browser. The top page showed off an official headshot of one Dr. J.M. Tyler on staff at the Boston University Medical School.

"Now listen to me very carefully, Meg. I don't want you to see this as signs that you are crazy. Instead, I want you to know that you *are* getting better."

Chapter 43

When in Doubt, It Gets Worse

O h, it's getting worse out here, Tiger." The thunder shook the ground beneath the demon as lightning struck the tree at the heart of the Nowever. Sparks rippled from the top of his wings to the tip of his stubby tail. Vocharlian rolled to the left just in time to avoid what could only be described as a tornado of fire slamming down from the heavens into his former spot.

"Did you just try to bloody smite me?"

Mitch pointed to the heavens. "If I was going to smite you, would I miss?"

"Everyone has an off day," the demon grumbled before darting toward the hills for some cover. In his rush, he ended up at the door to Mitch's hut right as acid rain began to pelt his tender extremities.

"Let's take our cosmic bitch session inside, shall we? No point in getting disintegrated before one of us gets the last word in."

The demon turned to see a mix of sickening green and black clouds rolling along the horizon. Fire belched from a peak in the distance, followed by the aroma of rotten eggs. "Fire doesn't scare me."

Then the demon saw eight legs wrap around that same peak. As the massive arachnid clamped its jaws into the rock and began to slurp boiling hot magma like a morning coffee, Vocharlian pointed for the door. "I'm open to some indoor negotiations, yes."

"Spiders are what gets you? *Really?*" Mitch asked, holding open the door.

"That is a creepy-crawlie the size of Goddamn Godzilla! You are not slagging me on this, mate. Now let's hope this bungalow is up to code before we inevitably get stepped on."

The sorcerer and the demon perched on opposite arms of the sofa, both trying to deal with sodden wings. The drip, drip, drip of water plopped in a pleasant rhythm against the earthen floor. Mitch finally asked, "So, you want a towel? Cup of tea? Or should I just do the magic thing to get us dry? It's your choice."

"I don't need your Fehr magic touching me, wanker." Vocharlian then did his best impression of a cat and shook off the remaining moisture, making sure to get mud on as much of the furnishings as possible. He then sniffled and let out a sneeze. "I'll take the tea as long as you've got something proper and black and not that dishwater you yanks like to throw sugar and lemon in."

"Milk and sugar?" Mitch then snapped his fingers and both himself and his living room sparkled for a moment before reappearing shiny and clean. The demon snarled. Mitch declared, "I'll take that as yes to both."

Soon they were both right back on the arms of the sofa, each with a steaming mug in hand. The demon sniffed the cup and raised a brow. "You have Tetley in this dimension?"

"Something like that. I'm an earl grey man myself."

"Poncy tosser," he grumbled before they both took cautious sips. "You angelic types aren't one for poison, are you?"

"That's usually a Fell standby."

"I'm also English, and it would be rude to kill someone after he offered you a half- decent cuppa."

"Yeah, we should definitely wait till we're done to go back to killing each other," Mitch muttered, kicking his own boots against the floor. "Or..."

"Mate, if the next words out of your lips are some rubbish about how we need to team up and save Meg, so help me Satan I will find a way to punch you."

They sipped the rest of their tea in silence, instead taking in the rumbles of an oversized arachnid rampaging through their pocket dimension, rattling the very walls. As a loaf of bread went splat on the kitchen rug, Mitch let out the deepest of sighs. "That was a really good batch."

The hovel shook again, this time sending a vase crashing to the ground. "This isn't normal, is it?" Vocharlian asked.

"Define normal."

"I hate you."

"Well, that response is certainly on brand. If you must know, the bridge to this pocket dimension is in the process of collapsing, because we were too late, and they've already won."

The demon cocked his head. "Who's won?"

Mitch pointed to the TV, which popped to life to reveal Meg sitting in the middle of a different retro sofa, cradling both a tissue and her own cup of tea. "I can't believe this was all in my head," she said softly.

"No, no, no, no, you barmy bird!" Vocharlian yelled as he crawled over to bang on the telly. "How many times do I have to tell you that I'm bloody real?!?"

"Obviously you didn't tell her enough."

The demon flared his fiery eyes at the redhead stepping into view. "Fucking KONs! Oy, you seeing this?" A bluish shimmer floated out of the wall behind Meg, swirling around her face until an errant tendril would snake its way up her nostril. "Mate, that's—"

"Magic? I know. Did you really think an organization determined to protect the status quo at all costs wouldn't stoop to hypocrisy?"

"Fucking Satan's hunts! I knew they were up to something. Can't she see this?" Vocharlian asked as another tendril worked its way into Meg's ear.

"Maybe if she knew how to use her powers." Mitch sighed. "Even then, empathic manipulation is subtle and creeps up on the victim."

"Punch me!" the demon cried, throwing himself at the half-Fehr. "Stab my sockets or whatever you need to do. I'll snap her out of this shite in a second. It did the job before."

"It's too late for that I'm afraid." The warlock sucked his wings back in and flopped on the sofa. "This isn't a cocky Fey trying an obvious play, it's a master of manipulation subtly tweaking what she already wants to believe."

"You mean that ginger cu—"

The camera shifted to the adjacent room where Billy pressed his hands into the drywall, that same blue glow snaking from his fingers and his solid glowing eyes. "Fuck, I should have stabbed him when I had the chance!" the demon snapped.

"I'm normally not one to advocate violence, but that would've been a solution." Mitch let his hood fall back, his mismatched eyes staring at the ceiling. "I really thought it'd work this time."

Vocharlian stared at the magenta light flickering in the window. "Bloody Heaven, are we in another...?"

"The sensation of a time loop isn't unusual considering the head injury you've experienced, Meg. Don't worry, it's going to get better with time, *trust me*," the good doctor explained.

"Can I have a minute? I...need to walk or...clear my head..." She rubbed her temples and snorted a little. "You smell something?"

Doctor Tyler pointed to the peace lily on her windowsill. "Unless you think I need to freshen up my deodorant?" After they both chuckled awkwardly, she opened the door. "Take a walk if you need to. The bathroom is to the left, the coffee station is to the right."

Meg froze in the hall, alternating her stare between the tissue and her cup. "It's not a life-or-death decision, Meg," she chided herself, before wandering to the left and the lobby. Her shoe caught on a rogue bit of carpet and would have sent her sprawling if not for Billy whipping out of nowhere to catch her before she could so much as spill a single drop.

"Whoa there, you okay?"

A million words tried to spill out of her lips at that moment, but she settled for the weakest of "yeahs." Her focus then shifted to the TV hanging in the room where a guy in a plaid suit grinned at contestants clad in pastel outfits. The sheer volume of bleached blond hair set the scene as undeniably eighties, and the mix of blinking lights and shag carpet sent Meg's mind racing to the past.

"*Let's Make a Deal* is a guilty pleasure of mine. It comes on as a block with *Press Your Luck*, *Wheel of Fortune*, all the classics. Probably my favorite thing to watch when I'm sick at home during the day, how about you?"

"I...used to like *The Price as Right*, but it hasn't been the same since Richard Dawson retired." She trailed off as she saw the frosted tips on the host's toupee. "Was I watching this after I hit my head?"

"Our lucky winners have selected an all-expense paid luxury quest at one of our fine friends in Aquatica's eastern kingdoms!"

Meg stopped, breathed, and listened again. *"Our lucky winners have won an all-expense paid luxury vacation to Aqua-Suna resorts in Cancun!"*

Billy took her trash and chucked it in the bin. "Can I get you anything?" he asked softly. "You look a little stressed. Here, I'll put something easier on."

The program switched to fish drifting across a coral reef. Meg gasped at the octopus with blue rings slithering over the sand. A Welsh-accented voice began to explain the wonders of the eight-armed denizens of the deep before cutting away to a kindly looking woman in glasses and a wetsuit. Her name—Joan Garfield-Pike.

"I imagined it all," Meg gasped.

"What was that?" Vocharlian asked. The next crash sent him sprawling in front of Mitch's television. In the chaos, his wrath had faded to his default envy green.

The warlock sipped his tea and shrugged. "That's our current reality collapsing. Don't worry, you get used to it after a few million goes."

"You're completely mad. Have I mentioned that before?"

"Frequently," Mitch replied. He pointed to the white light shining through the windows. "Not for much longer though. I'm pretty good with barriers, but even I can't hold out forever."

Vocharlian shielded his sockets and approached the glass. He took in the mega-spider blasting through everything and the weather straight out of Revelation churning the fields of mud into a filth tidal wave. Only a gossamer curtain of light stood between the hut and annihilation. "Fuck me."

"There are worse ideas...considering our impending doom," Mitch said with a sigh. "It's probably all you're good for. After all, you're the single weakest iteration of an already pathetic demon in one of the saddest of all possible timelines. Did you know that your world doesn't even have the decency to go out with a bang, simply a self-inflicted whimper?"

"You're madder than her." Vocharlian extended his claws but held back as he saw the barrier flicker.

"You'll get your chance at revenge, never fear." Mitch looked at his watch then explained, "In an hour or so, I'll be drained, and you can get your cheap shot before we implode."

"Did you just say *implode* without a trace of irony in your voice?" Vocharlian asked before slumping on the floor. He rolled the scenario over in his head before his eye sockets lit up. "Oh, *I get it,* we're in another one of those stupid loops and Meg will wake up and everything'll be hunky dory." He slumped again. "Ugh, we'll start all over with the whining and the exposition, and she'll be the only one who remembers it until I get back here. I need a drink."

Mitch snapped his fingers and a beer appeared in both his hand and Vocharlian's. The demon sniffed it but found himself unable to seal the deal despite the intoxicating malty aroma.

"I told you poison is more a demon thing—"

"I can't—" Vocharlian growled, trying to raise the bottle again.

Mitch leaned forward and stared at the image of Meg onscreen. He pointed to her no longer having a drink of her own. "Holy Hannah, you're still tethered!" he exclaimed.

"*And?*"

Chapter 44

A Ray of Hope

Y ou sure I can't get you a drink or a snack?" Billy offered as Meg
continued to wander aimlessly around the cheery, if slightly
generic, office tucked into a brownstone in Brookline, Mass-
achusetts.

"No, I'm not hungry," she whispered even as her stomach growled.
"Can I just go home? I think it's all been too much for me."

"Of course, but remember, you're not—" Doctor Tyler started.

"Crazy?" Meg finished. "Then why do I feel so lost?"

"I guarantee you that some nice dinner, maybe a shower or two, and
a good night's sleep, and you'll feel right as rain. In fact, that's my
prescription as your doctor."

Meg looked her in the eyes. "Are you my doctor? I'm still not sure of
anything."

"You'll be sure when you get the bill," Billy muttered, prompting a
fresh death stare from his doctor wife. "Although I hear you have great
insurance, so it won't be too bad."

"Oh my God, my job!"

"Don't worry, we've already sent over the necessary note to your
HR. Your absence should be excused, and if you're worried about—"

"But I told Gina to...I went into work..."

"You haven't been to the office since Tuesday," the doctor explained calmly. "Do you need to double check that?"

"I...I just want to go home."

As she sat in the back of Dr. Tyler's car, she tuned out Billy singing along with the radio and instead logged into the HR portal for her job. Sure enough, her credentials still worked, and she saw time off requests logged for Wednesday through Friday.

"I'm...not fired?" She switched to texting. Every muscle tightened as she pulled up the contact card for "B. Roberts, aka 'Boss.'" Meg found the will to type in the innocuous phrase, "Sorry I was out," and waited with bated breath for her boss to correct her.

Just as she was muttering, "Maybe he doesn't recognize my number," the little dots lit up. "Here we go, ream me a new one for bringing in that consultant."

"Feel better soon, Reynolds."

"That's...it?" Meg asked. The dots didn't spring up again, leaving her to flop against the leather interior and stare at the scenery going by. For a moment she could see a shadowy reflection behind her own. What Meg couldn't see was the slightest trace of magenta in her hair.

"So, have you told any of your friends about your interesting experiences this week?" Doctor Tyler asked.

"Friends? I don't really have any friends."

"Come on, what about that girl you play with online? What was her name again? Have you talked to her at all?"

"*Vanth*," Meg said softly. "I must've imagined her too." She raised her voice just a bit as she shook her head. "No, I haven't talked to anyone."

"Okay, just know it's important for you to have support while you recover. You said this Vanth girl—"

"She's just a mage from a rival guild in *Eternaquest*, that's all. I've never even spoken to her!" Meg snapped. "Sorry, I don't know why I'm so testy."

"Head injuries can cause sudden outbursts of emotion. Take a few slow, deep breaths with me and I guarantee that you'll feel better."

A flicker of blue caught Meg off guard in the window, but as she slowed and deepened her breath, she did indeed start to unwind. The blue flashed again, but she could now see the Boston PD car whizzing by. "None of this was real, was it? What if I was just crazy?"

What if you get it right this time?

She clutched her chest and stared once more outside the window, searching every face in the crowd for someone a little less than human. *What if...*

"Did it stop or did the bloody spider just destroy everything that could make noise?"

Mitch's inhuman eye glowed for a moment. "Nope, the storm just calmed for a sec. We might have a smidge of hope, though. *Something* is still making our Meg doubt reality."

"You say that...like it's a good thing."

"Meg! We were worried," she could hear as she walked into her foyer. "Did you get something to eat or...?"

"Just a long walk. I lost track of time," Meg said flatly, staring more at her shoes than her mom waiting for her. She did let herself fall into a hug, taking in the unmistakable scent of her mother—a mix of vanilla body wash and scented detergent with a chaser of hairspray. "Sorry if I scared you."

"I'm used to you losing track of time. Now, do you need dinner? Your father did something with chicken that is theoretically edible or there are cans of soup—"

"I'm good," Meg lied. "Mom, have I done or said anything weird these past few days?"

Her mom led her into the living room, where her father looked up from his golfing magazine. Meg noticed her favorite blanket laying over one of the sectional arms, along with a TV tray still laden with empty iced coffee cups and water bottles. "Hey, Meggle-Peggle," her dad said, showing off his gap-toothed smile. "You wanna lie down here? I can put on *Azure Planet* or a movie. Whatever you like."

"I'm sorry I've been so out of it—"

"Nonsense!" her mother said, launching into a flurry of caretaker activities. Within seconds, Meg got tucked into the sofa, remote in her grasp, and a steaming mug of tea set on the tray. Every pillow was offered, as well as suggestions that there could be brownies if that would somehow make her feel better.

Meg settled into her spoiling, soaking in the attention of people that meant so well yet understood so little. Once she got sucked into watching a nature program, her parents quickly lapsed into their evening routines of reading or pulling up a tablet to review the never-ending slew of assignments to grade.

"Oh, you asked if you said anything weird," Meg's mother mused, tapping her stylus to her chin. "Right after the hospital...you talked about your old imaginary friend."

"Mish-gan?" Meg propped herself up to get a better read on her mom's face. "What did I say?"

"Not much, just that you saw him. You always had such a wonderful imagination, I'm not surprised."

"Was Mish-gan the dog?" her father asked. "You had so many friends."

"Spot was the dog, silly. Mish-gan was her best friend, the one that protected her from the monsters under the bed," Meg's mother corrected. "It gives me comfort to know that he came back to look after you when you were feeling poorly, kiddo."

"Yeah, it must be my memories getting a little jumbled," Meg said softly, while staring at the tea. "It's just my subconscious trying to tell me something, to protect me."

Then slowly, carefully she lifted the tea mug to her lips, but for whatever reason, she couldn't force herself to drink. "I wish everything would get back to normal."

"Normal! That's the ultimate enemy right there, Tiger," Mitch exclaimed as thunder rumbled in the distance. "Those KONs you met—"

"Knights of Normalcy, lamest supervillains ever," Vocharlian finished for him as he kept staring at the giant shape occasionally moving along the horizon.

"Not so lame. They win about ninety-nine percent of the time. You see, it's easy to get people to band together to fight something that seems violent or revolutionary or even just loud, but when you define something as *normal*, it becomes almost aspirational. Human beings are hard-wired to want to fit into a pack, so if you embody some standard that virtually anyone can adhere to, you're nothing to fear. You might even be called decent or some nonsense like that."

"Do you love the sound of your own voice? Is that your problem?" the demon asked, flicking out his claws once more. "Cause if that's the case, why don't you yak in a way that's actually useful and tell me what the fuck is going on?"

Mitch opened his mouth and the demon immediately pounced. "The short, *short* version, arsehole!"

"Told you, this reality is on the verge of collapsing, and when it does, we go poof."

"Big deal. We're in one of those loops, right? *Right?*"

"You see, there's a funny little thing about what you know as reality, Tiger. If you play a little too fast and loose with its laws, reality likes to slap you—"

"Been there, done that, heard the pimp slap speech before."

"I don't think you get it though, when this bubble collapses, it goes right back to the source," Mitch said solemnly.

Vocharlian cocked his head.

"Jesus, man, you really are one of the dimmest demons I've ever tried this with."

"And people say I use bad language," Vocharlian muttered. "Okay, sorcerous smarty-pants, spell it out for the idiots in the back. Just tell me what you mean for once."

"How about I show you?"

Chapter 45

Three Days, Five Hours and Fifteen Dimensions Prior Redux

This is not good," Vocharlian growled as he landed hard on a pile of bones. Scorch marks covered every exposed inch of flesh, giving him the appearance of tiger stripes along his arms. The runes on his breastplate glowed sickening green. "Really, *really* not good...and stupidly familiar."

"Fresh meat, fresh meat comes..." a sinister voice snarled from the shadows. Vocharlian snapped out his claws, red mist rolling out of his eye sockets. He scanned the edges of the refuse pit the soulforge had catapulted him into. Glowing red dots greeted him from every pool of darkness.

"You made your fucking point!" the demon cried out. "Hah, hah, so I end up here all over again."

He replayed his daring escape, complete with scraping his side as he slipped into the cave. "Come on, wanker, let's get this over with." This time, however, only the red glimmer from his eye sockets lit his way. "Oy, shit-for-brains...where are you?"

The cave shuddered as rocks crumbled away. "FRESH MEAT!"

All Vocharlian could do was gulp before the giant fist came crashing down on his head. "Fuck me," seemed as good a set of final words as any.

"I'm so gonna die," Meg whimpered, slapping her hand on the power button on her speaker before running to the bathroom. Her feet slipped on the rug, and she nearly planted face first on the john before throwing up every last morsel of her burrito.

"This is not lactose. This isn't even food poisoning. It's an alien, I'm sure of it," Meg moaned, leaning against her bathroom tile. She turned, pressing her cheek into the porcelain, all while clutching her favorite pink towel to her heaving chest. After a few more rounds of vomiting, she did her best to call out to someone, anyone, but only a terrible silence surrounded her heaving form.

The quiet minutes stretched into hours until she vomited again, more violently than before. Her head clunked against the shelf over the toilet. She collapsed. As her glassy eyes locked on the ceiling, the cold of the floor seeped into her skull.

Episode Fifteen

Atherosclerosis Is Irreversible, Or Is It?

Chapter 46

Soft Reset

E ver feel like someone walked over your grave?" Meg looked over her shoulder to her bed, as if expecting a response. She rubbed her eyes and yawned, but sleep didn't come, so she turned back to her computer, pushing to get in a few more of her daily quests. "I must have been really sick to miss these."

She went through the motions of placing items for auction, cleaning out inventory, and hopping from hub to hub to maximize all she missed out on her grind. Her pulse raced as she saw the messages roll in from other late night guildies who noticed her presence online.

"Zazzy, where have you been?"

What should have been a simple question renewed every ounce of panic that had been safely simmering in the recesses of her subconscious. Her fingers froze over the keys, even as she saw a pop-up that her DPS slot in the random dungeon queue had become available.

A message from her raid leader normally involved a fair number of tongue-tied struggles to get anything coherent in chat, but never to the point of complete lockdown. "I must have lost my raid slot for good. Heck, I'm shocked I haven't been booted from the guild," she mouthed, as her fingers remained locked over the keys.

You have been placed in the Regular Dungeon Daily Finder: 69 seconds remain.

"Sixty-nine, heh." She cocked her head. That single moment of uncharacteristic lechery snapped her into action, and while her mouth now stammered with a million potential comebacks, her fingers settled on typing out the blandest of, "Been sick."

"*That sucks donkey balls, Z. You missed all the drama,*" one of her other guildies explained.

"*Yeah, the Knights of Valhalla ghosted the server. Guess who is now the number one raiding guild on all of Dreamskull?*"

"What happened?" Meg typed.

"*Who knows, who cares? We're gonna get past Voldara this weekend and then the next two bosses are cake—*"

"*I heard their mage got recruited for some other mega guild, or maybe she just up and quit. You know how girls in raiding guilds can be—*"

"*I heard that Vanth chick was banging Apollo and Thor—*"

"Vanth," Meg said, quickly tabbing off the flurry of guild chat and searching the server for any trace of the Knights of Valhalla or Vanth Mistweaver.

No results found.

Meg pushed away from her chair, nearly tripping on the laundry she'd left on the floor. She surveyed the wasteland of cans and empty bags that littered her desk, the dusty mix of fandom plushies and plastic figurines lining any ledge not covered in unfolded clothes, and the mismatched posters plastering the walls between each blackout-curtained window. "Nothing has changed, just some raiders I didn't even know left the server."

She stared at a poster full of sea creatures surrounding a party of hapless adventurers to announce the *Terrors of the Deep* expansion for *Eternaquest*. She also took note of her collection of guiding pixies from all the *Legend of Link* games stuffed on her bookshelf. "Of course, it's all here. *It's all right here.*"

She pounded her thigh with her fist as each glance picked up a different beat from her nightmarish week—from slack-jawed monster statues to an anthropomorphic catfish figurine from a Japanese subscription box. "It's all in my head, it's all been in my head."

She pulled out her phone and pulled up her recent history. Sure enough, her searches went from looking for Dr. Tyler to a host of tips and tricks for *Eternaquest*, all leading back to a video showing the

Knights of Valhalla getting a server first Voldara kill on Dreamskull. "It makes perfect sense," she said with a sigh, before returning to her routine. "I saw...what I wanted to see."

What she didn't notice, as she re-entered her late-night queues with her guildies, was the video tucked three down from the server-first kill, a suggested selection all about the history and common misconceptions perpetrated by the Mandela effect.

"If I'd known that was all it took to shut you up, I would have summoned a beer ages ago," Mitch said as the demon remained parked in front of the television, his lavender stare locked on the frothy head of his untouched beverage. The wind had picked back up to wall-shaking gusts and the occasional thud reminding the boys that a giant spider was still out there. "Reality is hardening again, Tiger. I suppose it's to be expected."

"You assume I'm entranced by a beverage when I just saw myself get crushed? Crushed like a..." Vocharlian noticed himself eying the half-angel lounging nearby and shifted back to Envy.

"Oh, so you do remember? It's hard to tell how a mind will react to seeing a shift in their loop. Almost everyone goes right back into the fog. They write it off as a bad dream."

The demon didn't turn his way. "Well, I'm too fucking stubborn to fall for that anymore. Now if you'll excuse me, I'm gonna sit back and wait for my bird to get thirsty, have a drink, and hang around for this whole loop to blow over. Better luck next time, eh, mate?"

The demon heard the couch creak, as if Mitch was leaning in as he asked, "That's your plan, really?"

"I was raised English, at this point it's the response that makes sense. Once I get back here again, I'll remember all the repetitive bullshit and hopefully have a better response, but for now...I'm knackered."

Vocharlian stiffened as the half-angel warlock eased off the sofa and crawled next to him on the rug. The demon raised a brow as he saw the defeated expression on Mitch's face.

"Yeah, I don't think you quite...get it, Tiger. This isn't like the bubble Meg controlled in Aquatica. It's not one day that's going to be reset—"

"I'm not that daft. I remember it was all pink and fuckery when I first arrived. We'll snap back to that damn dubstep all over again, blah-blah-blah, summon poor Charlie, contract, shenanigans, much hilarity ensues..." Vocharlian trailed off as he saw the pained grin on Mitch's face.

"About that—"

The TV flickered to life again, showing Meg lying in her bed, earbuds tucked into her halo of hair, and her bloodshot eyes staring at her ceiling. Vocharlian shoved Mitch aside. "See that, she's going to listen to the world's worst song. Ooh, maybe she'll play one of the much better tunes I found her and do her summoner mojo. Then I'm gonna appear, say something obnoxious to snap her out of it, and then everything will be back to the way it was, Bob's your uncle!"

The demon's gaping grin fell a little as she had some instrumental ambient tracks queued instead of anything he recognized. "Come on, make me sing those terrible lyrics or something. Come *on*, I'll sing the bloody chorus if you just start it up! Meg, luv, do not make me start singing bloody dubstep on my own here." He turned to Mitch. "You've got magic, do a thing!"

"A *thing?*"

"Yeah, wiggle your fingers and make the song come up. She has to sing and dance to make her magic happen. I know if she can hear that rubbish, we're gonna come out just fine." He studied the increased cringe on Mitch's face. "Oh, for fucks sake, could you blurt it out, man? What is it?"

"I'm sorry to tell you this, Tiger, but you're on your last loop."

―――――――

Meg curled out of bed and rubbed her eyes, even her most soothing playlist being unable to send her off to dreamland. This time, instead of her computer, she padded downstairs to the kitchen and stared into the depths of her fridge like so many 3 a.m. zombies before her.

"Oh, you're still up?"

Meg nearly whacked her face on the door as she whirled to see her mom shuffling into the kitchen with a handful of mugs. They yawned in unison. "Yeah, brain still going even though the body is dead," Meg confessed.

"Story of my life at midterms. So...many...papers to grade." Dishes went into the washer, then her mom became lost in comparing boxes of herbal tea. "I want peppermint, but then I'm going to float to my bed. You want some tea, kiddo?"

"I...don't know what I want."

Her mom continued puttering about, until the draft from the fridge forced the older lady to walk over and nudge her daughter aside. "Perhaps you can make your decision without freezing the whole neighborhood first?" she teased. As she looked up and saw the puffiness around Meg's eyes, she pulled a hidden bar of chocolate from behind the containers of salad and shooed Meg to the table. She broke off a couple squares and went straight for the kettle. "What's on your mind?"

Meg stared at the tea in front of her. The tag promised sleepy times to come, but she couldn't force herself to take a drink just yet. Even the siren song of vegan chocolate didn't lure her into action, leaving her mom to nibble and stare out the window as the regular strength silence escalated into awkward silence over the next few minutes.

"Is your head still bothering you, or your stomach? I can get something else," her mom offered. "Water—"

"I'm fine," Meg lied. She went through the motions of blowing on the top of her mug. "It's just hot." Once she ran out of acceptable fidgeting and stalling time, she piped up with, "So, what all happened? I'm still...still so fuzzy."

"We got back from Grandma's, and it was terrible. You were passed out over the toilet and not making much sense, so we took you straight to the ER and found out you'd gotten dehydrated and hit your head. Oh, that reminds me, I need to talk to Alfie and see if his firm wants to take up your case. Those damn Poblano's restaurants got so many people sick and maybe we can get something for all your suffering..."

She went on for a while about the lack of care at the restaurant chain, and then the paperwork and the stress, until Meg chimed in with a weak, "I don't remember being in the hospital at all, Mom."

Her mom let out a deep sigh. "They said this would happen, kiddo. Head injuries are tricky."

"*Who* said? What happened? How did this even happen? Why can't

I remember the hospital? *Why?* It doesn't make any sense. Who was my doctor there?"

"I don't know. You know how it is in the ER. It was so much waiting, and the place was busy. I'm sure I can find the discharge papers somewhere if you need to see them. Meg, you seem very upset right now. Do we need to take you back?"

"No!" she nearly yelled. Her mom started reaching for her phone. "Ugh, sorry! Hey, are sudden emotional outbursts common with head injuries too?" Meg asked with a pathetic laugh. "I know it sounds crazy, but I feel like this whole week has been a blur."

"Well, no daughter of mine is crazy," her mom countered. "But, as always, you are being curious, and curious is a good thing." She yawned again. "If we remember in the morning, I'll get all the paperwork from Mass General out and you can read all the things, and if you have questions, I'm sure there's one of those terrible automated numbers we can call, right?"

Meg nodded and took her turn staring out the window, but she failed at that and became lost in their ghostly reflections in the glass. "I'm...sorry, Mom," she murmured.

"Sorry? You don't need to apologize for being sick. Plus, I made your father clean most of it up anyway."

"No, I'm sorry... I haven't done anything with my life."

Her mom ambled over and wrapped her arms around Meg. She leaned in so she could stare at her daughter's reflection and give her a patented motherly glare. "Well, you are young, and the best part of being young is that you have plenty of time to figure things out."

"Yeah, but I dropped out, and I disappointed you—"

She got interrupted by another hug. "Now, now, none of that. If you want to go to school again, we can make that happen. Stop fussing so much about things you can't change and worry more about what you can fix going forward. Ah, ah, ah, don't interrupt. If you're scared because it was a close call and you hit your head, it's perfectly normal, but don't worry about anything else right now. All you need to do is have a bit of tea, get some sleep, and everything will be better in the morning."

"Love you, Mom."

"Love you too, kiddo."

Her mom wandered right back to her office. Meg tried a few times to raise the cup to her lips, but each time before she took a sip, she got distracted by a flicker in her reflection. Finally, Meg gave up and shuffled into her mother's sacred sanctum where her harried parent kept checking one more email between yawns.

"I promise if you just lay down for a bit, you'll pass right out. You always do, kiddo."

"But, Mom, I—still don't know what to do."

"Well, you're not going to figure it out in the middle of the night. Now, be a good girl and let your mother be a hypocrite as she tries to make sense of quantum theory instead of taking her own advice. You need extra rest. Doctor's orders."

"Which doctor?"

Her mother pointed to the array of certificates on her office wall, including her PhD from MIT. "Doctor Mom, actually."

Meg's lip quivered as she took in her mom's workstation, equally messy to her own, but in a far different way. Her mother's office displayed so many awards and degrees, with her tchotchkes coming from travels far and wide rather than from online shopping. "When you were my age, you were finishing your post-grad in Germany."

Meg stared at the books, so many titles covering all manner of highbrow subjects. For a moment she could even see the pattern of light through water drifting over the stuffed shelves, but Meg quickly realized it was nothing more magical than a Caribbean screensaver flooding over her mom's lock screen.

Her mom pushed away from her desk. "You got into Harvard, remember that."

"And I dropped out. I couldn't...take it. I mean who was I kidding? I only went to law school because I wanted to be a public defender like He-Hulk—"

Her mom came over and touched her daughter's shoulder. "Kiddo, if you're that full of regret, then we'll do something about it...in the morning. Right now, there is nothing served by getting lost down memory lane. I know it's easy to keep asking 'what if?', but believe me, you should save your energy to ask, 'what now?' instead."

"You're right," Meg acquiesced, leaning in for one more desperately needed hug. "I can't help it, I just want to be able to change things, but I know...I know it's impossible."

Her mom walked her all the way back to the stairs, filling Meg once more with the relief that things might be getting back to normal. Indeed, she might have even plopped right onto her bed and fallen fast asleep if she hadn't heard her mom half-yawn, half-mutter the words, "It's not like you can change the past. Who do you think you are? Marty McFly?"

Chapter 47

Back to the Future

W hat the fuck are you talking about? I'm not on the last anything!" A bit of the fire had returned to Vocharlian's eyes as he took a cheap swipe at Mitch. The distracted Fehr barely managed to roll out of the way as the house still trembled, but a single ray of sunshine kept taunting them both from the window-panes. "I told you to make some sense."

"It's not like you'd understand it if I explained it."

"Try me!" the demon snarled between swipes. "While you're at it, tell me what you did to fuck with Meg in the first place. I might be an idiot, but even I can see that somehow this is all your fault."

Mitch froze, and for the first time, the demon landed a strike on the warlock. As the tips of his claws sliced a cheek, the kitchen wall cracked in two and his upper cabinets crashed to the floor.

"You idiot!" Mitch howled before returning the slap ten-fold. The living room wall gave way, sending the stunned and broken demon once more into the mud of the Nowever.

From this new vantage point, Vocharlian could take in the pure chaos of the Technicolor storms ripping apart the formerly monochro-matic wasteland. Beyond the raging clouds, he could see a swirling mass of purest black, a void that instantly made his blood run cold and the lights of his eyes flicker and dim.

He couldn't move as he watched that darkness expand. He couldn't even breathe. Mitch's boot landed squarely in his midsection, the force enough to knock the demon out of his nihilistic reverie.

"Don't stare at the end yet, we're not quite there," Mitch warned before dragging the demon back into the now-ventilated hut.

"You bleed red," Vocharlian said as he wheezed and looked at all the black goo dripping from his own face and onto his chest.

"And you wish you did," Mitch finished for him. "Believe me, I understand, and for what it's worth, I am sorry about what happened to you. You're the only version that had to go through—"

"Version? What the heavens are you going on about?" He tried his best to scuttle away from the warlock, but his wings fell limp and one of his legs now bent the wrong way. "Ow, I knew you couldn't resist getting me at least one time, you...you..."

Mitch closed his eyes, took a deep breath, and when they reopened, both glowed with a glorious white light. Vocharlian couldn't fight the wave of warmth that passed over him and while he still lay in a heap atop of the broken remains of a coffee table, at least he was no longer bleeding.

"I get it, it's no fun if you simply end it," Vocharlian whispered. "You gotta patch me up before I take my licks again, but don't you worry, I'm tougher than I look, and I know how to take it."

Mitch didn't say a word, he waved his hands and the demon floated to the intact bedroom section of the hut. When the half-angel followed, Vocharlian couldn't resist quipping, "Well, I guess you like 'em softened up first when you want a shag."

"I liked you better when you were giving up." Mitch took another moment to examine the demon's wounds before turning his attention to creating a thicker barrier around the room.

"I'm shite at giving up, too stubborn for my own good," Vocharlian said between wheezes. "I really hope I remember giving you that scrape next go. I'm gonna be insufferable about it...you wanker."

"I'm sure you would be," Mitch replied sadly. "You asked for answers, I guess I owe you a few."

"Fucking miracles, you really are part Fehr."

"What you call loops are more like bubbles in reality, tiny pockets where a single will defies the overriding soup, so that a little pocket of air and whatever else in there gets trapped inside. Some bubbles are tougher than others, but no matter what, they either eventually harden and become part of the grand custard that is the universe as we know it… or they pop. It's simply what happens every time this dimension gets stirred up. Most disappear before anyone ever notices."

"Custard? Did you really call the universe, custard?"

"What can I say, dumbing it down to your level is a challenge, but one I'm willing to accept."

"Does that make death a spoon scooping us out? Maybe there's a biscuit of God out there—"

Mitch burst out laughing. "You really are one of the better ones, at least for the laughs. Now, forget about the custard for a minute and focus on the bubbles. Inside these bubbles you can trap things, things that don't belong in a custard."

"Like bikkie crumbs?"

"Like demons, demons that aren't even hanging around the kitchen. Heck, demons that aren't from the same planet."

Vocharlian stared unblinking at the exhausted Mitch. "You lost me at alien custard, mate."

"Why do I want pudding?" Meg asked as she stared at the pile of paperwork that confirmed that she had been admitted for food poisoning and a possible concussion on a Tuesday and been discharged to her home safely on a Wednesday. She could piece together bits of a Thursday via her receipts and concluded that she most likely had a miserable, but completely boring week.

Her parents had disappeared to their jobs on campus, leaving Meg with a Friday off to give her one more long weekend before returning to work. No mystery messages awaited her, no strange noises went bump in the empty house, and above all, no demons appeared opposite her at the kitchen table. She slipped out her phone, but instead of pulling up the latest gaming news, she pulled up an online encyclopedia article on the cult classic of *Back to the Future*.

"Eww, that's his mom," she groaned, as she witnessed Eric Stoltz staring intensely at Lea Thompson. "Why am I even watching this?"

Lucifer's kittens, you are totally pulling a Marty McFly!

"I'm going crazy. That's the only explanation. I can't handle this."

But what if you can?

"Now I'm hearing voices. I need to call my doctor." Meg jumped to her feet. "No, I should go. I should go into town and see her."

Meg shook her head violently. "*No*, I need to go into town and see... I dunno, but I have to know if I'm missing something big. There is *something* that just doesn't belong, and I'm gonna figure it out. I'm not going to sit here for a change. I'm totally going to do something!"

"I guess what I'm saying is, I screwed up this time around, Tiger."

"I'm still stuck on the space pudding analogy debacle. You've got to give me a minute."

"I don't know if you have a minute, to tell you the truth. You see, this pocket is still unravelling, and once it does, everything resets," Mitch explained. "You'll go back to the moment you got yanked from your reality and no one will save her."

"She figured it out once, she'll figure it out again. Isn't this a riot, the demon has all the faith, and the angel boy is all quivery?"

Mitch neither laughed along nor slapped some sense into the demon for a change.

"You keep thinking that this is *her* loop, Tiger, and that it can go on and on forever." He tugged at the collar of his patchwork coat, pulling it back to reveal a section of his shoulder fading in and out of existence, right next to his heart.

"Well, you're gonna hold on for one more time, mate, it's as simple as that. Maybe next go we won't have some fucking Fey ruining everything—"

"You don't get it! Lord Hamilton's only showed up one time before, and that loop was...actually the closest to succeeding," Mitch said sadly. "I am tired, so indescribably tired. I don't think I've got another loop in me. Maybe I need to accept...that she's really gone...and you should too."

Vocharlian managed to prop up on his elbows. "Like heaven you are giving up, wanker. There is no way I've dragged my sweet arse across who knows how many dimensions—"

"Thirteen...oh thirteen plus one timeline," Mitch corrected.

"Yeah, this demonic Doctor Who has been through too much time and space just to get squished while my idiot companion dies in the goddamn loo! You are going to bollocks up, and we're gonna do one more loop. And this time, we'll get it right. I got her out of the fish porno in the making, so I guess I can drag your sorry arse out of this mess too. Whether you like it or not, I'm not going back."

Mitch hung his head. "I used to believe you, Charlie, but better versions of you have tried and failed. Damn it, I didn't even get a timeline with a full-powered demon this go around! You can't do a damned thing, and I'm sorry that I got you into this mess."

"What do you mean, other versions? What the *fuck* are you on about?!?" His eyes flared red, and he lunged at Mitch. For once, Vocharlian ended up slamming someone into a wall.

"All you are is hollow anger and rage—an empty vessel from a little boy left to die for his father's sins. You don't even have your human half anymore. You should have disintegrated the moment you arrived, but somehow Meg figured out how to give you a body, and it's probably destroyed her mind. You're the reason she's so weak right now, Charlie. It's all...your...fault."

"This is all my fault," Meg whispered as she rubbed her head while slouched on the train. Staring into the reflective windows only helped her continue her pity party. She tugged at her too tight t-shirt as it rode up. "I'm such a...a loser."

She tried surfing her phone for schools that would take twenty-something washouts, but then remembered the loans she was already repaying for her first attempt at a degree. Her cheeks flushed as the anger rose. "Of course, I'd want to escape from all this crap. It's...normal. I'm such a perfectly *normal* loser."

The bus pulled up to South Station and muscle memory took over. Despite it being closer to lunch, she still carried on the time-honored tradition of picking up an iced coffee. "Oh, and a water," she added before wandering outside to enjoy a mosey through town on this exceptionally average overcast day.

"What if...?" she whispered to the sky. "What if I just imagined it all?"

"It's close, I can feel it," Mitch said, the windows turning black as night. "There's always a tipping point, and your anger will get her there even quicker."

"How the heavens am I not supposed to be angry? I'm stuck in an imploding mud pit with a self-righteous wanker who keeps blathering about custard!"

"I'm sorry I ever used that stupid analogy. You run out of ideas after the first few thousand loops! Maybe I'm sick of ending up in the mud with a goddamned demon! Ever think about that? The only reason I put up with you is because of her. It's all...because of her." He slumped against the wall, his breathing heavy as his entire arm flickered out of view for a moment. He laughed. "Say, Tiger, if you wanna take your shot, now's a pretty good time. Any second it's gonna be the end, and I hate to tell you, you're not coming back here."

Vocharlian leaned against the other wall. "You can make it through one more bloody loop, wanker."

"Maybe... Maybe I can, but the truth is, I have no idea how a demon from a whole different timeline got snagged this go. All this time, no matter what I've tried, I've never been able to pull that off. You're just a blip, a wrong number, and, who knows, maybe in your timeline there's another damned Mitchigan Barnes trying his best to save his little Meg. Maybe he never got trapped in this damn loop to begin with. Maybe he was better than I was."

"Your name... It's Mitchigan? Like the state...but worse? Jesus and all the apostles and crap, I can't even bloody hit you. I just wanna laugh. As angry as I am, I don't think I want to waste my last moments ripping out your throat."

Everything dimmed as the final traces of light faded from the window. Even the brilliant red emanating from Vocharlian mellowed to a warm golden tone. "I say, I would like to know one thing. What is so special about Meg? Is she perhaps chosen by destiny? Are you coveting her powers, perchance? Could it possibly be that she is some long-lost greater Fehr changeling too?"

Mitch shook his head. "No, as far as I know she's just a human girl, born in Florida, I think. Got adopted, lived a quiet life with her teacher parents. Not even from some great magic bloodline, before you ask."

Vocharlian eased back into his envy aspect, bathing them both in a dull green glow. "Oy, she's got these amazing powers. That Hamhocks bastard was all over her too. He could see something. She's gotta be so special—so she'll do some hero thing or remember her secret attack in our darkest hour, and *everything will be fine*. That's what happens in epic adventures with demons and witches and obnoxious angel boys with terrible names. It's just what..."

Cold mixed with the dark, but the bubble didn't collapse around them quite yet. Mitch reached under the bed and pulled out the picture with the damning runes. He tossed it at the demon's feet. "I cast a spell I shouldn't, reality hit too hard, and I nearly lost all my powers. I got chucked through time and space and fragmented into so many worthless shades of myself. Just as infernals can restore themselves from negative energy, I needed something positive. I didn't need much, but I found one...*special* human who only thought of others instead of herself. I was careful. I was so, so careful to take the bare minimum to restore my magic, but in the end, something happened. The paradox that should have only punished me, lashed out at that little girl."

"You fed off her," Vocharlian growled. "And they say we're the monsters. Sure, I take my cut, but I'm honest about it. What were you, her guardian angel? Her—"

"I was her friend! I only wanted to be her friend. She had so much to give, and I needed so little of her reserves... I never thought that one tiny spell would ripple so far and so fast." He buried his face in his hands. "The universe, however, can usually be appeased by balance. If one half-Fehr entered the world, it could be evened out—"

"By half a bloody demon? You unbelievable cunt. All you had to do is *not* choose to pick on the poor kid and then none of this would ever have happened. You ever think of that?"

"Now who's being the unbelievable...what you said. Don't you think that's one of the first things I tried? The easy options all went first. I barely managed to create this loop after the damage was done. I can't undo my first mistake, so I kept trying to refine a solution...until I couldn't...I can't... It's getting hazy now in my head and it's getting dark. At least I can say, I tried, yeah, I tried pretty damn hard. I do wish I could have figured out how I ended up with you this go, cause...you are *definitely* the single worst demon I could have possibly found."

Vocharlian flipped him the bird. "Maybe I've got a power none of my screwed-up versions have, eh?"

"You literally lost the human half of your body and all your magic—"

"Wait, bizarro me has magic? That means I can get it too."

"No, you can get infernal powers, but you can't do anything remotely useful here because your soul is gone. You're horrible. Oh, and you don't have your other version's speed, or the flight, or say...the ability to summon your focus. You can't even talk to Meg to confirm that you are real. That means the paradox ritual the KONs cast on Meg will complete and she'll forget everything for good...*again*. As far as I can tell, your only gift seems to be pissing her off with pop culture references and being obnoxious."

Vocharlian seemed to consider those words carefully. "Maybe, but never underestimate the obnoxiousness of an Englishman! I'll tell you what, this Meg may be three skeins short of a jumper, but she's got a power somewhere in there and it *will* save us. You just wait. You just wait and see."

And then the lights finally went out.

Chapter 48

The Devil is in the Details

Meg stared at her phone, chewing on her lip as her last few searches came up empty. "I thought that song was called 'Let Me Be Your Armor,' but it doesn't exist for Assemblage 23. I must have the title wrong," she muttered as she kept dodging her fellow pedestrians. She'd made her way past South Station and into the endgame of her weekday commute. Monolithic skyscrapers towered overhead. "Or I'm just grasping at straws as I walk to my work...on a day I have off. I'm free and clear with a doctor's note, but what if someone I know goes out to lunch and sees me...and then thinks I'm not really sick? I don't look sick, do I...? And why am I talking to myself so much?"

"Oh, hello there," a gravelly voice said.

"I'm on the way to the doctor," Meg blurted out. She breathed a sigh of relief, however, as she saw that it wasn't one of her coworkers that had spotted her, but rather one of Meg's regular stops on her morning commute—the homeless lady with a friendly dog.

"Hope you feel better," the woman said before going back to rummaging through the pile of boxes stacked next to a dumpster.

"Oh yeah, I got an extra," Meg said, as she had countless commutes before. She handed over a bottle of water and gave the dog a pat on the head.

R.E. Carr

"Such a sweet, girl," the lady said, showing off a gap-toothed smile. Her eyes then lit up as she eyed an intact Nile-brand box left on a ledge. "Ooh, it's my lucky day."

"It can't be," Meg whispered as the can collector pocketed a bright orange staple remover from the stash. "I don't be—"

The lady then pulled out a succulent in a rainbow pot, one tiny leaf still clinging to life. She set it on a sill letting it soak in what little sun fought to get through the clouds. She then gave it a teensy splash of water before chugging the rest of the drink down.

"Wait!" Meg cried, darting over to get a closer look.

Meg picked up the pot and turned it around in her hands. She felt the chip on one side before turning it over to read "MR" in permanent marker near the drainage hole. "It came back," she said, pointing to the stubborn single leaf.

"People," her homeless guide grumbled. "Always throwing away perfectly good stuff. What a waste."

The lady and her dog went digging into the next pile of online shopping boxes. Another Nile branded box fell near Meg's feet.

"Should they say *Amazon?*" Meg asked. She didn't wait for a reply; instead, she bolted to the Common and to the myriad of carts selling lemonade to tourists and locals alike. Meg settled on a bench near a particularly bright stall, closed her eyes, and thought back to earlier in the week.

Life has just given you a big old tart as fuck lemon, so let's do the thing and get lemonade to make it all better. That's how it works, right?

"How the hell does any of this work?" she asked the sky. "Of course, spooky action at a distance!"

She pulled up her phone again, but instead of going to her regular playlists, she went deeper and dug into her listening history. "That can't be," she whispered, as she found her "Recently Played" to be empty. She then went to her social media and scrolled through ads—a mix of job sites and online schools even though she was gainfully employed.

Then came a bunch of Victoria images. "That should be...Nike."

Finally, she opened up MyTube and read the suggestions buried halfway down the app. *"The Mandela effect...* I looked up the Mandela Effect, because I was talking to a jerk who wouldn't accept the stupidest things. Oh my God..."

Memory...is a funny thing, isn't it? People think it's an indelible record, set in stone, but it's really just a soup of chemicals drifting in the savory pudding that is the brain.

"I've heard pudding before," she whispered, sticking out her tongue as she kept flicking through every program she could on her phone, every history, every cache, growling more and more as she found stuff inexplicably erased. "Pudding...and dubstep is what I need right now. I need one song. I really, really need one song," she begged.

Meg typed in the words "Princess Space" into her search bar. While she didn't see anything that jogged her memory, she started listening to their extremely generic back catalog. Most of the lyrics sounded written by AI, and every song featured some guest ethereal vocalist to complement the autotuned voice of the mysterious founder of the band—a British guy named Desmond Lowe. The moment she read his name, her fist clenched into a ball, and she could feel actual burning from the strange scars on her right wrist. "Well, who is this asshole?"

Vocharlian roared as a single name pounded through his skull. Red flooded the tiny remaining space, and he shook the fading Mitch awake. "Hey, Blizzard, I'm not dead yet, and you're not dead yet so get the fuck up! Do your fucking magic thing and get Meg that goddamn song! Jesus, I know why I heard it, why it makes me so *fucking* angry..."

"The Rage," Meg read as she retraced the history of the guy behind Princess Space. While this Desmond guy wore masks to concerts nowadays and pulled off the stereotypical hidden DJ shtick, Meg put all her years of hunting for obscure fandom knowledge to good use by finding a post-punk message forum. As she saw the skinny, spiky haired lead singer of a band that went absolutely nowhere, her guts twisted into a knot. *"Charlie."*

"What are you doing here, Meg?"

Meg choked as she heard a familiar voice behind her. She turned around to see Dr. Tyler standing right there. Billy waved from not far behind his wife.

"Are you following me, Dr. Tyler?" Meg asked. "I won't lie, it's kinda creepy."

The breeze changed, and Meg could pick up a sugary scent wafting on the air, mixed with lime and tequila. She couldn't see any pixies bounding to her rescue, but her phone vibrated.

Meg peeked at her notifications. Pho Certain-Boston informed her that, "Your order is ready for pickup."

"Did I order pho?" Meg muttered under her breath.

"What are you doing here?" Dr. Tyler asked again. "Don't worry, we're only here to help."

Meg noticed a flicker, a slight tinge of blue in Billy's eyes despite him being at least ten feet away. His hands kept repeating a tapping motion, as if he was creating some sort of rhythm while he almost imperceptibly mouthed some nonsensical words.

Meg put on her blandest, most zoned out face and turned her phone around. "Actually, I was picking up lunch. There's no decent Vietnamese in the suburbs."

Dr. Tyler let out a sigh of relief. At that simple motion, a few random strangers in the park chose that exact moment to disperse. "It's a funny coincidence. I was working downtown and happened to see you... that's all," she explained with a bland smile.

"Funny coincidence, yeah," Meg said. "Oh shoot, I better get my food and get back. If my mom doesn't find me on the couch, she's gonna totally freak out after this week."

Meg meandered along the Common until she found the address for her mysterious order on the edge of Chinatown—a large establishment adjacent to a karaoke bar and nightclub. Conveniently, one door led to both places. Inspiration struck, and instead of heading straight for the restaurant, Meg bolted left into the karaoke bar. There, a bored-looking clerk in a hoodie ignored the world and hunched over a laptop. As they shifted to get a drink, Meg could see a bit of a familiar user interface. "Oh, I play *Eternaquest* too."

"Good for you," the clerk muttered. "You gonna buy something?"

"Can I get a song...thing? Um, how does karaoke work? Is there a booth, or a room, or—"

The clerk didn't look up from their screen. "How many of you are there and how long do you want to sing? If you want booze, you'll have to show an ID to the waitress, assuming she ever gets off her break," they said, clearly loud enough to be heard through the door marked "Staff Only."

"Just me...maybe, and I don't know," Meg blurted out, looking quickly over her shoulder to see if she'd been followed. "Please tell me that you have dubstep."

"If it's on the internet, we've probably got it. The instructions are all on the TV, so go knock yourself out." The clerk cringed and launched into a string of expletives at the screen as their party tank ran right up to a boss.

"Please it's important, I need to know—"

"Not now! Ugh, go to room four and I'll set you up with whatever you want. Just let me focus cause I'm the healer this time and I'm dealing with scrubs."

"But—"

"Lady, I'm dying here, I will *literally* send you a free drink coupon if you shut up and leave me alone right now."

Meg saw the flicker of motion from the vestibule and wasted no time running up the stairs to find room four. It turned out to be shockingly easy with big numbers on every door. She struggled to find the English instructions on the system catering to a predominantly Vietnamese clientele. This room lacked bells and whistles, but it had a cracked leatherette sofa, a couple of mics, and a menu that did indeed look like it had any song you could possibly want.

M-A-G she typed in obnoxiously slow, using only the remote. "Come on," she begged, waiting for the suggestions to show her what she needed. "I know you are real. I know I can find you. Come on, *Charlie*. Come on, just show up right now!"

I-C

Still nothing by Princess Space showed up. Meg froze as she heard a bang and commotion downstairs. "Please," she begged. "I need a little more time. I just need a little bit more time."

The door to her room slammed shut, and for a moment she could see the tiniest shimmer over a poster for some boy band she'd never heard of.

As she typed in the D, the image of a guy in a tiger mask popped into view. Tears rolled down her face as she highlighted the song. Then came an even louder bang, and the door shattered into a million pieces.

"Wrong song—" she choked out before the bullet tore through her back.

Episode Sixteen

Killed Via Kindness

Chapter 49

Letting Go of the Past

W hy am I the only one who can see you, Mish-gan?" Little Meg asked as she put down her bright red crayon. "Is that because you're imaginary?"

Mish-gan leaned back to feel the sun streaming through a window on this glorious day. However, he kept his hood pulled up as well as a mask and gloves to hide any traces of skin. "Very clever, Meggle-Peggle, maybe I am," he whispered. "Maybe I'm tired, too tired to hold a physical form anymore." He then pulled off his right glove to show off that his hand consisted of little more than an outline.

"Maybe you're a ghost," Meg offered. "I'm haunted. Yippee!"

He wiped under his hood with his phantom fingers, doing his best to conceal any rogue sniffles from the girl still beaming at him. "Shouldn't you be afraid of ghosts?"

"If they were mean ghosts maybe, but it's you, Mish-gan, and you're my best friend." She then rummaged through her bookcase until she pulled out a collection of scary stories. As she gnawed on her lip, Mish-gan couldn't help but chuckle. Meg then asked, "Do we need to find your hand so you can go to Heaven or something? Or maybe it's a curse! Or *maybe* you're trapped by a wizard..."

As she went on and on, he took a moment to study her pile of drawings. Somehow this six-year-old version of Meg already had sketches of a big blue octopus, a coelacanth mermaid, and a stick figure in a plaid suit with pointy ears and a blond ponytail. Mish-gan smiled at the pig nose she'd added as well.

"Wait! I gots it!" She nearly dove across the table and flipped over a drawing of a unicorn to show off a triangular looking gray car with two colorful stick figures next to it. Rather than having a mall in the background, the car appeared to be parked next to a crude representation of the Tower Bridge and Big Ben. Meg then pointed to Mish-gan's hand. "You are like Mikey Fox, so you have to go back and then you can punch a bully and get your hand back in the future and then ride a unicorn."

She pointed out that her version of a DeLorean had both a rainbow horn on its hood and an Autobot logo. Her imaginary friend rubbed his head a few times before slumping into his seat.

"Mish-gan, are you okay? Are you too tired to play?"

"I'm very tired, my friend, but I'd like to know where you came up with this story."

"Well, I had a second juice box even though mommy told me not to and then I was watching my show, then I had to pee really bad, but Daddy was in the bathroom, um...so I went downstairs, and did my business, but I was too tired, so I took a nap, and then I dreamed it all up. I should tell Charlie about it!"

"Charlie?" this Mitch asked, his voice quivering. "Tell me all about this Charlie."

She pointed to under her bed. "He's hiding from the monster, shh."

"All this time, I tried to give you the best helpers, you know that?"

She had already gone back to her drawing. She sketched herself holding the hand of a boy in a patchwork hoodie, but this time her left hand held on to a cat-pig-bat hybrid thing with a huge smile and dinky little wings.

"Do you remember?" Mish-gan asked, pushing back his hood to reveal an Invisible Man layer of bandages and goggles. She answered him by drawing a bracelet around her wrist and the gray and black monster's. She then yawned.

"I'm tired again. I feel like I'm always tired, Mish-gan."

"Well, we've been playing an awfully long time, Meggle-Peggle. Maybe it's time for some rest."

She nodded and stifled another yawn.

"Hey, I want you to remember something for me. Can you do that?"

Meg nodded, set her crayons down, and folded her hands dutifully in her lap.

Mish-gan's voice broke a little and he looked away. "It's funny, we don't usually understand the importance of things when we first experience it... We also always think that we can fix everything."

"Sounds like we need super glue. Mommy says that can fix anything."

"I wish it could, I hope you know that."

"Is this like adult problems?" Little Meg asked. Her eyes lit up. "Or *magic* problems?"

Mitch looked out the bright sunny window again. "It's some big magic problems. Problems that are all my fault, and I keep trying to get a do-over to fix my mistake, but no matter how hard I try, I don't get it right."

"If you make a mistake, just say you're sorry," Meg said sweetly. "That's what you're supposed to do."

"Meggie! Time for lunch," her father called from the hall. Mish-gan flickered in and out of existence. The little girl reached for him, but her hand passed right through his arm.

"Even ghosts can say they are sorry."

"I am...truly...deeply sorry, Meg Reynolds, for..."

"Being my best friend?" Her eyes welled up with tears.

"No, no never that. I'm just sorry, that I tried too hard to fix my problems and I didn't think enough about what I did to you."

They both looked at drawings full of all kinds of mythical creatures, of hearts and laser beams and little kid fantasies, yet many of them featured what looked like an adult Meg fighting alongside all sorts of different monsters. "I love all our adventures," Meg finally said. "Will I get to have them when I grow up?"

Mitch shook his head slowly. "No, I'm afraid the world doesn't like it when grown-ups have imaginary friends."

"No, I don't want you to go! I'll take a nap and then we can play later. I wanna be your best friend when I grow up too!"

"Not this time, Meggle-Peggle. I'm...I'm sorry."

And then he vanished, leaving only one cryptic message. "Avoid the burrito."

"That is a really big dragon," Meg deadpanned as she stared at the pages of a coffee table art book splayed across the pile of other reduced titles.

"Yeah, it reminds me that we're going to get the server first tonight while your scrub ass guild wipes on the enrage timer, Zazz. Assuming we get done with the lame-o spook tour in time and the T isn't running behind," Quinn replied. The short, skinny geek in an anime hoodie rolled their eyes at row upon row of crystals. They then pointed to one particularly cheesy red one mounted in a skull pendant. "I'm pretty sure these are plastic."

The guy at the counter sneered at the browsing pair. "You break it, you buy it."

"Make sure not to breathe too hard on anything, Goth Girl," Quinn warned. This version of Meg sported an all-black ensemble, multiple piercings, and bright streaks woven through her mighty pile of curls. Quinn then pointed to the back wall. "Ooh, they have books of spells over there."

Meg took her time perusing the mix of souvenirs and new-age tat that filled Simon's Mystical Emporium of Salem, Massachusetts. Her companion groaned audibly as they read title after title and looked to the back matter to see just who wrote things like *Actualizing Harmony* and *101 Spells to Improve your Sex Life.*

"There are a lot of white dudes and Karens telling me how to cast magic here. Even the voodoo treatise has a pasty little fucker on it, and we know that ain't right," Quinn noted.

The pasty dude behind the counter cringed a little. Meg, meanwhile, walked down the history aisle and picked up a volume on local hauntings. "Hey, Quinn, they've got some ghosts over here."

Quinn pushed back their hood and gave some serious side eye to the clerk. "Lemme guess, more white bread for me to digest?" Still, they bounded over to get a peek at the latest and greatest tales of local haunting. "You do realize that books are totally last century, girl. If I need ideas for the podcast, I'll use the internet like a civilized person. Still, the internet does not have cheesy beaded curtains," they said, pointing to a room off to the back. "What do you think, seances or restrooms?"

Meg laughed for a moment, but something about her friend's last statement made her stomach turn. She then looked at another title about the haunting of children and froze.

Quinn picked up on the spacing out and gave her a one-armed hug. "Look, I get why you wanted to do a little light-hearted spoopy tour, girl-friend. For all the cheese, you know I believe that there is a lot of weird in this world that can't quite be explained. I believe you when you say that you saw a ghost as a kid."

Meg moved on to peruse the titles on reincarnation. "Everyone thinks they were Cleopatra or Joan of Arc," Quinn added ever so unhelpfully.

"What if you dreamed that you were *you* in a previous life?" Meg asked. "Like a you...that met a terrible end each and every time?"

"Then I'd say no more *Groundhog Day* marathons for you, chica." Quinn then flipped around their phone. "Guess who has two for one burrito coupons for Poblano's for a little pre-raid fuel."

This innocent enough token of gaming goodwill sent Meg swooning at the sight of the green and white logo. "I...don't think that's a good idea."

"If it's about that food poisoning scare, that was like in the garbage states, not here in ye old Commonwealth of Taxachusetts," Quinn reassured her. "Also, there is no better raid fuel than queso."

"Lactose intolerant," Meg countered as they reached the front of the bookstore. "I think I'll have leftovers instead. *Anyway*, you're gonna be so gassy from that cheese that you're going to be the mage that chokes, and the Knights of Valhalla are gonna be the scrubs tonight."

"Oh, so you can see the future now? Did you pick that up in..." Quinn picked up one of the discount titles to punctuate their point, "...*Premonitions and Portents* maybe?"

Quinn kept going on and on about the cheesy occult shop, but Meg had already zoned out. She stared across the narrow side street at a laundromat full of sudsy machines. Meg zeroed in on a TV with a cheesy game show showing on it. For a heartbeat, Meg saw herself onscreen, standing behind a podium, only she wasn't wearing contact lenses or any of her Goth trappings.

Quinn stepped in front of Meg and waved a hand in front of her face. "Earth to Meg, please say you're distracted, and this isn't like a seizure thing, cause it's my brother that's in med school, not me."

"Just give me a second, okay?" Meg started for the door, but her friend once more blocked her path.

"Hey, we haven't read the sex life book yet, am I right? I mean, it's gonna be a laugh and it might turn a couple of loveless geeks like us into regular Captain Pikes. Then again, if I saw a green girl, I'm pretty sure that would be my jam...or maybe a green guy. It's mostly the green that gets me going."

Meg kept staring off into space. "I—"

"Oh my God, there is a bubble tea place around the corner. They have lychee...your favorite," Quinn said, the dopiest of grins plastered across their face. "Bubble waffles too!"

"Bubbles...why do I keep thinking about bubbles today?" Meg asked. "And why is there suddenly a burrito too?"

As if on cue, she noticed a Poblano's commercial on the laundromat TV. She checked her phone and found out that despite never eating at the chain, her inbox had been spammed with ads for that two-for-one combo.

"Hey, are you two buying anything?" The guy at the counter seemed to have grown some cojones, possibly from the *How to be More Assertive* self-help guide he'd been reading.

"I dunno, you got anything not marketed for the tourists and suckers..." Quinn squinted and looked at the nametag on the dude's shirt. "Oh, you're Simon, and this is your emporium."

He then studied the pair just a little closer. "Wait a second, I know your voice. Are you on that podcast? Holy shit, you're Quinn Tran from *Queer Hauntings*! I'm a huge fan. Because of you I can't keep anything on Vietnamese ghost hunting in stock."

"*Sure*, can't keep it in stock," Quinn replied with a tight smile. They couldn't get another word in edgewise as Simon immediately bombarded them with questions, giving Meg an opportunity to return her attention to the laundromat. Just as she opened the bookstore door, her blood ran cold as she heard her friend explain, "Meg was a guest on the show, that's how we met, well...that and we share a deep connection over our love of MMORPGs and electronica."

"Ooh, what episode—?" Simon asked.

"I'm the burrito girl, okay!" Meg blurted out. "Yes, I'm the one that was warned against Mexican food by the great beyond. It's not quite the guy who thinks he has Satan's glory hole in his chinchilla farm, but I know it's a popular episode. Great to meet you, make sure you follow Q here on Flitter, they are super fun there. Now if you'll excuse me, I think I'm gonna take a walk to that bubble tea."

Meg did not walk around the corner to the bubble tea, but instead went straight across to Bubble Time Cleaners. "What am I doing? I should just..."

She trailed off as she now noticed one customer folding leopard print undies in plain view. Unlike the rest of the Monday afternoon clientele, this guy wore a suit and tie with sunglasses while getting his clothes clean. Something about his oily smile made Meg pause, and, for a second, the pink neon from the Bubble Time sign made her reflection shimmer with magenta light.

"Yo, Zazzy, watcha doing? Aren't we having the spoopy tour to celebrate the MyTube monetization dropping? Now I no longer have to work at my cousin's karaoke bar. I'm gonna hire you as a research assistant. No more call center gig!"

Meg remained frozen as Quinn prattled on. "There is literally a witch museum three blocks away and you're what, going to blow your PTO day to do laundry? Do you even have laundry with you, girl?"

"Give me five minutes. Can you go ahead and order me up a lychee oolong with strawberry jelly, and I'll catch up?"

Her friend's face fell just a little. "You don't get the mega skeeve vibes coming from this place? I'm pretty sure this is a front for a totally different kind of laundering, Meg. It's the kinda place where cute goth gals like you walk in but then end up on true crime podcasts instead of incredibly funny ghost ones."

"If you're that worried you can be my non-binary knight in shining armor," Meg said, giving her friend a wink before sliding into the laundromat. "Qui—"

The moment Meg stepped inside she noticed that while all the washers and dryers kept tumbling away, all the patrons had vanished save one—the stranger in the chintzy suit. She whirled around to see the side street hazy and empty, without a sign of her friend or anyone else.

"It's funny, I've always said that the greatest power of a witch is not what they can control, but rather what they can *perceive* and, my, do I love being proven right," the stranger said, grinning like the cat that caught the canary. "Nice to meet you...again."

Chapter 50

Spooky Actions at a Distance

I t's déjà vu all over again. What a heaven of a day," Vocharlian sighed as he watched the cubicle across the way. There, his arch-nemesis, Tez, slurped blood out of his World's Greatest Dad skull while closing out tickets left and right. "One day, I'm gonna make you suffer, mark my words, Mr. Employee of the Month."

"*Variegatus*! Variegatus, are you sleeping on the job again?"

The demon swirled his eye lights at his boss and motioned to his messy but drool-free desk. "You realize I have a condition—"

Lord Asafran, Vocharlian's pig of a boss, glanced toward the imposing portcullis of Demon Resources and took a deep snort before measuring his response. "I hope you realize that you are only here because I'm required to give you a two-month trial thanks to the deal your mother brokered with the Department of Envy, *but* if I catch you on your PD3 one more time while you're in your chains, I'm going to take the damn penalty and boot your skinny cambion ass out on the street. No more silver for you, and good luck finding any division that will take you no matter how famous—"

Vocharlian grinned as his boss's tirade got cut short by his succubi assistants moaning that he had an important message. "Saved yet again," Vocharlian chuckled, folding his claws behind his head as he watched the big guy get called away.

"Variegatus, you're fired!" Asafran bellowed.

"The fuck?!?"

"I...don't think I'm supposed to be here," Meg said as the chill ran down her spine. She whirled around and yanked on the Bubble Time door, but it locked, leaving her trapped with a guy oozing with cheap cologne.

"No, you're not. You're supposed to be at work, or off with your friends, or meeting some schmuck at a gaming store who's going to develop an instant crush on you," the stranger sighed. "*This time*, you were totally left on your own devices, free to wander around the Earth until your proverbial number comes up. It was supposed to be a gift from your little friend, one last chance to be free of all this mess before it all comes crashing down. I must say, I like this look on you...Meg."

"Who *are* you?" she asked, sliding her hand into her purse and wrapping her fingers around her keys.

"I'd say I was an old friend, but I'm certain a savvy Boston girl like you would see right through that. No, I'm more like a mosquito—useful to the environment, but ultimately annoying to people. The important thing is, however, *you* noticed me, even though *he* wants you to pass on by. Ever wonder why that is? Ever get a nagging feeling like you're meant for bigger and better things than playing video games and switching majors a dozen times?"

"Um, you don't *know* me."

"True and not true. Look, we haven't got much time, and if there's one thing I picked up at our last dance, it's that you're simultaneously both stupidly trusting and ridiculously hard to manipulate, so I'm going to try something new, just...for...you."

Meg raised a brow at the atrocious undergarments in his laundry, his greasy hair, and the shine on his crocodile shoes. "You look like a game show host."

The stranger smiled. "In another life perhaps."

Meg shook the door again.

"Tell me, Meg, if I told you right here, right now, that this world is a million times crazier than you give it credit for, what would you say?"

"It's feeling pretty weird right now," she said, whirling back to face the stranger.

"However," the stranger continued, "if you're willing to give up on the insanity, then you can have a long, safe, and relatively happy life. I'll even see to it personally, like your guardian...not quite angel."

"Are you propositioning me in a laundromat?" Meg asked flatly. "I'll admit, you're a little familiar, but every fiber in my being is telling me to run away."

"Yet you're not running away, *are you?*"

She stared into the void at the heart of a churning load of towels. "Ever have this terrible feeling, like someone walked over your grave? Now imagine feeling that every day of your life, since you were six years old and fell off the swings at the playground. I thought I saw someone else lying in the grass, someone who was hurt too, and ever since I asked if they needed help, then my whole life has felt...like a dream."

Meg slumped against the door. "I feel like everything I've done, I've done a thousand times before, and I don't know why. It got to the point where I started having therapy sessions with the monster I imagined was hiding under my bed, just because it was better than explaining things to total strangers. They would think I was crazy. I probably *am* crazy, and now I'm just spilling this all to you."

The blond leaned salaciously over his intimates. "And if I told you that you actually have lived a thousand lifetimes that all lead up to one crazy moment tomorrow night, what would you say?"

Meg watched suds shudder and pop in all the machines. An ad for Poblano's popped up on the television as well. "I'd ask you...does this have something to do with a burrito?" She laughed pathetically until she saw the stranger nodding, nary a trace of irony on his face. "Wait, my life really does hinge on a burrito? I haven't been crazy avoiding Mexican food for nearly twenty years? Are you a ghost too?!?"

"No, I'm just one failsafe put in place to make sure you get your happy ending. I wanted to set fire to every burrito joint in the greater Boston area, but I was told that might be a *trifle* excessive. I've had a while to plot and plan, but you know what, the one thing I never do is just blurt out the truth...so this time, I'm switching it up."

"I...I...don't—" Meg stammered.

"Meg, you didn't meet a ghost at the playground. Instead, you met a half-human, half-angel with a God complex who tried to go back in time and stop his own universe from imploding but totally screwed the pooch."

"*Excuse me?*"

The stranger waved dismissively. "He used you. Well, used your soul energy to make himself corporeal and you paid the price. Now rather than accept that you were going to die young, this half-angel decided to try and *fix* things."

"Fix? Fix how?"

"By balancing out the scales. It's a lot of advanced magic involving the reciprocal vortex created by him entering the plane, and I don't feel like explaining that, so let me give you the snappy, made for TV version." He then pointed to the screen and an animation of an angel falling down appeared on one side while a fiery pit opened on the other. "You see, babe, there is a single moment where *you* can bring a demon into this world."

"Me?" she asked incredulously.

"Yes, *you*, and if you survive long enough to complete a contract to feed a demon then theoretically reality should stop trying to kill you. Sounds crazy, yes? But as an ancient and extremely powerful neutral party, I can confirm that the theory is sound. The universe likes balance, you see."

"I don't see..." Meg tried to interrupt, but this stranger kept on going.

"Unfortunately finding a half-demon is difficult, and to be frank, most of them just ended up killing you. That's the sad truth of it all. The poor half-angel who got you into this mess is on his last legs, so he's burning out the final bits of his celestial power to give you as much time as he can. All you need to do now is be *boring* enough that the common will stops trying to snuff you out. I'll take care of the rest, babe."

"*Excuse me?*"

"You're welcome. You can go on and enjoy the rest of your life. I guarantee that if you avoid Mexican food for the next twenty-four hours, you'll gradually forget all about this and move on."

"*What?*"

"If you eat the burrito tomorrow, a demon appears in your down-stairs bathroom. No, that is not a metaphor for a change. Anyway, have an uneventful life, Meg Reynolds, and good luck."

"Dude, I can't believe you got fired," Dorp said as they sat together on Vocharlian's sofa. They kept a replay loop of their videogame playing to keep up appearances, but mostly shoved carrots into their gaping maws while they stared off into space.

"I beg your pardon?" the skinnier demon asked.

Dorp cringed. "Well, you have been fired from everywhere else...so I guess...yeah...um...no. Hey, it's not all bad, since you don't gotta go to work tomorrow, you can maybe hit up a little extra of this present I snagged for you from the recipe bank." He then pulled a silvery vial out of one of his many overhanging flaps of skin.

Vocharlian took one look at the vial and shoved it away. "I can't afford that right now."

His friend let out a heavy sigh and plonked the vial in the middle of the coffee table. "I didn't forget, it's the one-year anniversary of you-know-who too. It's on the house this time. Just don't get caught by Kruger though, because Lucifer knows you don't need that added to an already shitty week."

"You really are my best mate, *mate*, and don't you forget to floss. If your mom finds carrots in your teeth, then Kruger is the least of my worries."

His buddy gave him a pudgy thumbs-up before shambling his way back to the landing. Vocharlian picked up the vial and rolled it around a few times. "I really shouldn't, but then again, today has been utter shite."

Meg stared at the silver remains of the jelly at the bottom of her cup. Quinn looked over their phone and apologized, "I know I got strawberry oolong with lychee jelly, but you don't have to look like it's the end of the world. It's not the end of the world, is it, Goth Girl?"

"You'd probably think I was crazy," she whispered, still staring deep into the remnants of a mis-ordered drink.

"Considering I'm emailing a chick who claims to be running a zombie brothel in Pensacola, I think you're all right. Seriously, I'm putting you on the payroll to deal with the randos, Megsicle."

"Zombie brothel? That's a new one. It's almost as weird as that guy in New Jersey who claims that vampires are fighting a secret war with Bigfoot."

They both laughed and did their best to mix some small talk along with looking at their phones. Quinn facepalmed. "I'm such a douche kayak, aren't I? I can't believe I offered you a burrito tonight. Oh, the ADHD brain fog is ever so real. You're literally the burrito ghost girl and I..."

"Promise you won't judge me," Meg asked weakly. "Because I'm not sure I wouldn't even judge *myself* as a total whack job right now. Quinn, I might have left a little bit out about the burrito story. Tell me, have you ever watched *Back to the Future?*"

"There's no future between the two of us, Pookie," Vocharlian read off his text history. "I'm sorry, but this is the end. Don't worry though, you'll find your dream girl someday, maybe after a metric shit ton of therapy, but you'll get there. Goodbye."

"No bird, no job, not even any bloody bikkies in the tin," the demon moaned as he wandered around his kitchen. "Fuck...my...life!" he yelled into the void. "Let's see me get a lack of noise violation now."

He slammed the cupboard shut and meandered back to his room where his extra secret box already lay on top of his bed of nails. He propped his PD3 up so it could project on the far wall, and he swirled his eye lights at the FBI warning telling him that this content was copyrighted, and that pirating was illegal. "Whatever, what you gonna do, send me to Hell? Oh man, why do I keep talking to myself? Maybe Lashma was right, and I do need some therapy. Nahh, there is only one thing I need right now," he said as the movie started. The demon did a little dance, shuffling his talons through the carpet while his horns bopped to the tune of "Power of Love."

Vocharlian set up his emotion bong, kicked up his feet, and prepared the recreational Nostalgia for eye-socket absorption. He started with a few tiny drops then grinned and poured in half a bottle before grabbing a towel. "If I'm gonna go, I'm gonna go out in style," he said giving a wink to Marty McFly.

"Bring on the...oh bollocks!" he cried as the vapors knocked him out cold.

"*Vocharlian Milton Variegatus!*"

Vocharlian lurched upright. His ocular sparks reignited a bright red as he saw the silhouette of bull horns. "Fuck, this is not what it looks like," he blurted out, vapors spewing from his lips.

"Not what it looks like?" the bull-horned demon asked incredulously, stepping into the light. He pointed an accusatory claw toward the sizable water pipe. "Lucifer's kittens, have you been eyeballing emotions...again?"

"Kruger—" Vocharlian trailed off as he knocked over the bong by his side. He let out a pathetic hee-hee as the bigger, obsidian-skinned monster picked up and sniffed Dorp's vial. Vocharlian snapped, "It's just a little recreational emotion!"

"Recreational? *Recreational?* This could hold an ounce in here of pure, unfiltered Melancholy, and it's fucking empty!"

"Nostalgia."

"Excuse me?" Kruger raised one of his spiky brow ridges.

Vocharlian shook his head and slowly pushed to his feet. The smaller, slighter cambion stared right at his cousin's tie. Vocharlian shifted from wrath to the calmer envy and tried a pensive look for a change. "It's Nostalgia, not Melancholy, and if you'd ever felt a real emotion in your life—"

"Enough! I promised your mother when you came to this city that I would keep you clean, and here you have enough sentiment secretions to be charged with intent to sell." Kruger sneered. "Damn it, boy. Can't you just make it through a single month—?"

Vocharlian shuffled a bit. "Look, it's been a rough patch, cuz. Come on, I was thinking about Lashma—"

The lights in Kruger's eyes swirled sarcastically. "*Please*, it's been almost a year. You can't possibly still be holding out hope. Get over her, man. She moved on and so should you. Now as much as this pains me to do it, I have to turn you in. You need help."

"I lost my job too!"

"Oh, Vocharlian, just when I thought you couldn't get any more pathetic."

Vocharlian cracked his neck and narrowed his eye sockets into slits. "Damn it, Kruger, what do you want?"

The larger demon rubbed the points of his prominent chin.

Vocharlian let out a deep sigh. "You're a bloody lawyer, so let's make a deal."

"A deal, *hmm*." He surveyed the pitiable scene one more time. "I mean, it has been rough and at least you were watching something PG-13 and I didn't catch you trafficking pure wholesomeness again. You know what, asshole, I'm giving you a pass this time, but if I catch you again, I'm calling your mother."

"Hell Prime has frozen over and it's not even Christmas," Vocharlian muttered. He then tried for pensive again, and promised, "I'll try to do better, cuz."

Kruger's eyes lit up brighter. "You know, I have a pro bono shift at the Golgotha Bureau tomorrow—"

"Oh man, that's a shite assignment, *literally!*"

Kruger leaned in and licked his lips. "Well, since I did you a solid favor tonight, how about we *do* make that deal?"

Chapter 51

Decisions, Decisions

W ell, that's an existential crisis you don't hear every day," Quinn said, flopping back in their seat the moment Meg finished her laundry recap. "A strange man told you that if you eat a burrito tomorrow, you're gonna summon a demon and probably die. I'm seriously tempted to tell you to do that. Then we'll set up my camera in your bathroom. It'll be the podcast of the year."

"I knew I shouldn't have said anything." Meg gathered her purse and chucked her cup in the trash. "Now you think I'm crazy too."

She would have made her escape if not for a haunted Salem tour group filling the sidewalk. "Hey, don't put words in my mouth, chica!" Quinn called after her.

They ended up strolling to the waterfront so Meg could collect her thoughts and get some fresh air. She pointed one of her black-painted fingernails toward the boardwalk along the coast. "I have dreams about a kraken. Sometimes he stops a deep-sea war... Another time I dreamt he trashed the North End."

"Yeah, my dreams about tentacles are hella different." Quinn pulled their phone out and snapped a quick pic of Meg. "For posterity, you know, in case all hell breaks loose—"

"*Quinn!*"

"Think about it, if you *do* summon a demon, it would be the best show ever, way better than a zombie brothel." Meg turned and started to walk away. "Damn it, Summoner Girl, I believe you!"

Meg froze and turned around ever so slowly. "What did you call me?"

"*Goth* Girl... I said, I believe you." Quinn shuffled and stared at the gaps in the dock rather than Meg. After a long moment, they confessed, "You're not the only one who's ever had some wicked ass dreams...and you're not the only one who's had an encounter with real magic."

"Did you just say *real* magic?"

"Why do you think I have the podcast? I also have a ton of websites, message boards, forums...both on the regular and the dark web. Like ninety-nine point nine-nine...nine, nine, *nine* percent of all the stuff I encounter is total crap, but once in a fucking blue moon, I find the real thing. I just didn't know for sure about you until you noticed a glamour and were lured into it rather than walking away. Normies...they always walk away."

Meg looked back at the ocean. "And if I wanna be normal?"

"I know a guy that can make you forget just about anything. Rumor has it there's an even scarier dude out there that can manipulate emotions...and he kills people."

Meg's jaw dropped.

"Just magic people. You see, there's like this cult dedicated to getting rid of anyone or anything that disturbs their perfect ideal of normalcy, but I keep pretty good tabs on them."

"Because you're a witch?" Meg asked, blinking rapidly.

"I prefer technomancer, but yeah, I'm a witch, and you're definitely giving off some mojo right now. Something is about to happen, but if what your guardian creep said is true, something powerful is looking out for you, Zazz. So we just avoid anything with a tortilla for a few days and then you get a long, healthy life. Call me crazy, but that seems like a no brainer."

"Yeah, cause everything in my dreams is pretty weird...and horrible, and..." She looked at the water again. "And apparently in thousands of tries, I never managed to get it right. That's so...so pathetic."

"I'm gonna call out of raid tonight, because I think this calls for Auntie's spring rolls, a six pack, and so much more talking."

"Why did I hit so much at once?" Vocharlian moaned as his dim blue eye lights stared over the pond of fire near his apartment complex. He tried to focus on the job postings on his PD3 but found his gaze wandering to the couples promenading along the sputtering shores.

"Because you're an idiot?" Vocharlian heard as his best friend approached. He tried his best to shrink from Dorp's disapproving stare.

"All you had to do was not get caught by your evily-two-shoes cousin just one time. Judas, man! He's gotta know you're getting it from me." Dorp shoved a bag of greasy fried scorpions between them on the moping bench. "Now there aren't any openings currently in Gluttony, but I know a few people that owe me favors, and...are you even listening, dude? Come on, there are no free rides in Hell Prime. If we don't get you some silver flowing soon—"

"Was there anything extra in that Nostalgia, mate? You know, a little something-something to cut the sweetness. You catch my drift?"

Dorp clutched his chest so tightly that even his fourth chin jiggled. "You know I would never cut the shit I give to you, man, not after everything we've been through."

Vocharlian's normally slack jaw tightened up. "It's just...I dreamt about him for the first time in a long time, so I wondered if maybe some Trauma snuck in there."

"You mean...*him?*"

"I was hiding under the bed all over again," Vocharlian said softly. "The yelling and the banging wouldn't stop. I know these are the feelings that I'm supposed to embrace and that all that fear and hate is part of what will make me strong, but damn...all I wanted was to escape."

Dorp crunched on several scorpions before replying. "No man, it's definitely not supposed to do that. I mean maybe there was some cross-contamination from the emotional eating lab... No, I tested that batch. It was some of the best I've ever gotten my slime on."

Vocharlian shrugged and crunched on a couple of scorpions himself. "Well, maybe I'm just right and proper fucked up then, mate. It got weirder too. Right when I felt super low, there was this sweet little girl's voice—"

"Like in a family horror flick?" Dorp asked.

"No...actually sweet, like in the contraband shite. While I was hiding in my dream, this little girl told me that everything was gonna be okay. As mad as it sounds, I could swear it was a memory..."

"Yeah, that's a Nostalgia overdose. I'm cutting you off, dude."

"Don't worry, right after that I cleared my head with some specialized porn. Turns out, I have a thing for siren demons. Those fins...yeah..."

"Now you're sounding a whole lot better, Charlie," Dorp said, getting up.

"I *hate* that nickname," Vocharlian growled.

"I know, that's why I use it. I'll tell Mom it's dinner at my place again tomorrow, then I'll do my best to keep you from getting into even more trouble."

Please just give us more time.

Vocharlian shook his head and dug a finger into his ear. "You say something, Dorp?"

"Yeah, I'm gonna keep you out of trouble, so I'll see you as soon as I get out of work tomorrow—"

"Oh, no can do," the demon said, smacking his forehead. "I forgot. I need to do a solid for Kruger since he caught me freebasing emotions again. Whether I like it or not, I'm going to the Golgothan Bureau tomorrow, but don't worry, I'll be down for anything after such a fucking boring night."

Meg sat cross-legged on her bed, nestled amid her mountain of laundry while Quinn twirled idly in her computer chair. Quinn occasionally typed a few things into their laptop while Meg surfed social media on her phone. The silence stretched longer and longer until Quinn asked. "So, we gonna do anything?"

Meg shrugged, then made a conscious effort to slow her breathing, counting out each beat until she could finally focus. "No matter how hard I try, the anxiety is...yeah. I don't even know what to say right now."

"Are we to the big guns yet? Cause I've got some happy gummies with your name on them. Or we could rip through like all our dailies as a team, just like it's Sunday morning—"

Meg raised a brow. "*Or...you could cast a spell to calm me down. Is that a thing?*"

Quinn just sat there, tapping on the keys. "It's a thing, yeah, but it's not my thing." They waved their hand a couple of times over the trackpad and a handful of windows popped up on their own. "This is what I do."

Meg squinted to see nothing more wondrous than a search engine. Quinn continued. "You need to find some sort of obscure information? My aethereal spiders can find you what David Hasselhoff had for breakfast six years ago, or score you tickets to *Burr* on Broadway. Oh, would you like all your parking tickets gone? Can do that. I could even make the Talon of Thesis drop in the Howling Sands dungeon—"

"You're describing what a hacker can do. That's not magic, and wait...are you *cheating* in game? Is that why your gear is so good?"

Quinn clutched their chest. "You wound me, good lady! First, I don't cheat, I just nudge algorithms when I get really pissed off after a long grind on my alts. Vanth is one-hundred percent hard work. It's guild policy that mains are strictly for funsies, okay?"

"Wait is your guild—?"

Quinn cut her off. "*Second,* She Who Doesn't Understand Magic One Bit should not be ragging on the awesomeness in the room, because what I do is way more useful than turning a zippo into a fireball."

"You can do that with hairspray!"

"P'takh!" Quinn snapped, cracking their knuckles. "I get it, you want to behold the wonder of magic, but news flash, it doesn't work like that. Picture, if you will, that you are actually on stage..."

Meg's tongue swelled in her mouth and sweat beaded along her hairline. She slid deeper under her blanket as memories of school plays came flooding back with a vengeance.

Quinn backpedaled a bit. "Maybe don't picture too much. I know how active your imagination gets. Look, everywhere you go there is well...reality. You pick up a pen," they said, picking one up from the desk, "drop it, and it falls because we all know gravity is a thing. Now is gravity actually a thing, or does it exist because we all know that it does? These are the questions that the philosophy geeks wonder while I scrape their credit card info and use it to buy Bitcoin. The whys are still up in the air, but the important thing to know is—"

"If you slap reality, reality slaps back," Meg said softly. "I've heard that somewhere."

"There's actually a few games, tabletop and otherwise, that have that worked in. The sad truth is that the geek community and the arcane community have so much overlap that a lot of the stuff just seeps out. If you remember that limited run Witchcraft comic from like five years ago, that writer was totally a warlock."

"Didn't he die?" Meg asked.

"Yeah...about that, see if you're an idiot, like I said before, the boogeymen find you. Play stupid games, win stupid prizes. First, they'll try to cancel you, *ergo why that book only had six issues*, and if that doesn't shut you up..."

"Holy Hannah," Meg said. "It's that dangerous?"

"Now you know why I only put the most ridiculous guests on the show, and not my Auntie Kate who totally hunts ghosts in Patagonia right now. Argentina's a current hotspot and no one knows why—"

"So, I was ridiculous?" Meg pulled the blanket over her head. "Of course, I was."

"Lady, you told me that a ghost warned you not to eat a burrito."

"Okay, maybe a little ridiculous," Meg conceded.

"I've gotta be so careful, Meg. I don't want to be the next missing magi out there. Don't you get it? I told you about all this real magic shit now because I understand that what you went through was real...and because you're my best friend. I...trust you."

They took their time letting that settle in. Meg tuned out the fidgeting and muttering of her friend and instead focused within. She closed her eyes and immediately relived the laundromat followed by a highlight reel of every awkward conversation she'd endured since first grade. The countless hours sitting on couches, the tests, the worried looks from her parents all hit her like a truck until she got to the worst memory of all—her sitting in front of a doctor and declaring, "*I know that my imaginary friend wasn't real. He wasn't a ghost,*" so that she wouldn't be admitted to a hospital.

"I've failed a thousand times, that's a lot to take in," she whispered. "And magic seems to just get you killed."

Meg felt the tug. She acquiesced to Quinn pulling the blanket away, allowing them to curl up next to her. "Yeah, it's a stupidly dangerous life," Quinn admitted. "I'm lucky cause I grew up with it."

"Wait, your parents?"

Quinn laughed. "Are you kidding me? My dad's a dentist and most of the family runs the Pho Certain empire of New England. It's only my black sheep auntie and my bà nội who had the gifts. Don't worry, they are just as disappointed in me as my parents since I decided not to deal with ghosts unless they happened to be in a machine. I appreciate the symmetry of it all."

"So, all the ghost stories on the podcast...?"

"They're fake, yeah. I make sure never to use anything that can be traced back to anyone I know. Every once in a while, I'll find a lost witch among the trash in my inbox. Those I make disappear. It's gotta be done because if the KONs—Knights of Normalcy before you ask—"

Meg grabbed her chest and fought to breathe. Quinn held on a little tighter. "Hey, I get they are ridiculous.... Wait, you're not laughing at the stupid name, are you? Are you triggered?"

"I think they got me in a past...life? I don't know how to explain it. Is there magic for this or am I crazy?"

"You're buds with me, Zazz, so we already know you're crazy. I know there are some spells about reading genetic memories and stuff like that, but that's about actual past lives. You'd be shocked how many people really are related to Genghis Khan when you investigate that crap... Sorry, I'm on a tangent. Anyway, what you're describing are high-level theoretical spells that no sane magician would try to recreate. There's this one book on creating bubbles within reality to protect the caster from the overriding will around them, but that's like giving yourself a few minutes or maybe hours to get something right. Think of it like—"

"An instance in *Eternaquest*," Meg finished.

"I was just about to say that—*creepy*. Anyway, yeah, it's a limited time spell and even that can wipe you out for weeks. You're talking about, what, twenty years getting relived over and over? Even a full-strength coven of the best of the best couldn't pull that off, and if they did, I'm pretty sure it would get noticed..."

"Quinn, this is a terrible time not to finish your sentences!"

Quinn cringed. "Maybe that's why you failed each time. I'm not saying that's what *actually* happened, but it would make sense. A spell that powerful would be a beacon to every seer—*it's a special type of witch*—on the planet, and the KONs, they've got traitors on the payroll."

"So, I'm doomed...unless I agree to be boring? That's not a real choice! And if I give this up, I'm gonna forget everything, does that include you too? I don't have any other friends."

Quinn shut her up with another bear hug, surprisingly strong for their petite frame. "Girl, I'm still gonna be your friend... It'll just go back to pre-laundromat shenanigans. My bro Raj is an artist with a capital A, and one night of his ridiculously good pharmaceuticals and it'll be like you took the red pill and stayed in the Matrix all happy-happy. I promise."

Meg leaned into the hug. Quinn patted her on the head. "Doesn't a rave sound better than a demon?"

"Barely. I remember the last rave you took me to—"

"Since you remember it, I did it wrong. You love to dance though, and the DJ was like above average, but he did play way too much dubstep..."

As much as I would love to get out of here and for the love of all things unholy, shut off the damned dubstep! I am afraid that reality isn't going to move on this one, darling.

Quinn shook her dazed friend. "Meg? You look like you just got stabbed. Do I need...?"

"I'm okay, but do you think the flashbacks will go away if I avoid the burrito? I know it sounds ridiculous, but I'm really, really tired right now and I'm terrified. I want this to end. What if it's not the burrito, though? What if I summon the demon anyway? Do you even know how to summon a demon?"

Quinn pulled out their phone and the search screen popped up without any typing. Instantly a dozen results displayed, most from sites completely alien to Meg. "Don't worry, this is all on my private network. Make sure you don't search for too much magic stuff on your own phone, cause Big Boring Brother is always watching." Quinn scanned a bit. "Good news, it's impossible to accidentally summon a demon."

"Really?"

"Yeah, it's not like you can draw a pentagram with mustard and have a sandwich open a gate to Hell or something like that. The rituals require years of work and serial killer levels of sacrifices, so I think we're good, unless you have shit in your basement you've never told me about, Goth Girl."

Meg shook her head. "I get that a sandwich is out, but is there any way a burrito could...you know, open a portal to another dimension?"

"Not that I can see. Hmm, my next guess is what your Guardian Laundry-Man claims is true. Tomorrow night there is going to be an aftershock from what happened when you were a kid. If divine energy landed in one spot, the universe is gonna feel whiplash and eventually release a counterforce."

"In my downstairs bathroom?"

Quinn shrugged. "You said you fell off the swing when you were a kid and then there was this guy what...a few feet away? The reciprocal effect is going to be roughly the same distance from you *probably*. Your mom's the physicist, so all this quantum shit is more her jam, but I know just enough to be dangerous, so my working theory is stay away from people and places that you don't want to get exposed to Hell for a good twenty-four hours. That still doesn't explain the burrito...*unless*..."

Meg waited while Quinn's search engine went into overdrive. "Unless you finish your sentences maybe?"

"Oh...my...God...it's *not* the burrito!"

"So, the ghost and the Laundry Creep are what? Just messing with me?"

"Magic isn't like you see in the discount section at Simon's, girl-friend. And it's not like in our games where you just learn a spell and if you have enough energy, it goes off. Magic requires its wielder to exert more force of will upon the environment than the inertia of what is considered normal reality allows. Normally, you've got years of practice and the hormonal hell of puberty on your side to get things going, but if you experienced a singularly traumatic event that somehow let you combine all your brain waves at once, then—*pow!* You'd pop your thau-maturgic cherry. Throw in a cosmic weak point and whoop, there it is, a demon in your shitter! I mean it's crazy but if you were somehow engaged with music and thoughts and emotion.... Lady, do you have number two tune action happening on a regular basis?"

"What the hell are you talking about?!?"

The phone sprang to life again. Meg cocked her head as some beats began to drop from the speakers. Quinn winked and waved their hands then Meg's room speaker took over for the phone. "As cheesy as it sounds, I have this zone out playlist that I update and share from time to time to all my *Eternaquest* crew and friends. There is this one song that is so on the money that I had to investigate to make sure the band wasn't secretly in the circle—*that's real magic in case it wasn't clear*—but the band is full of normies..."

"Quinn!"

"Just listen to the song, okay?"

After an eternity of synth lines, a guy started singing lyrics of, "I get on with life as a demon..." piquing Meg's interest. By the time the chorus swelled, an ethereal female voice took over. Meg's jaw dropped.

Inspiration becomes a thought,
  Thoughts go into motion.
  Motion becomes a rhythm.
  Rhythm begets emotion,
  Emotion turns to song.
  The song invokes a spell...
  (And then the deed is done.)

"Did dubstep just tell me how to cast magic?" Meg asked.

Chapter 52

There Are No Accidents

Meg tried her best to sleep but woke up bleary-eyed and still in the same t-shirt and jeans as last night. At some point Quinn had gone home, leaving a note of, "We've got this, don't worry."

Meg then looked to the laundry she'd somehow forged into a body shaped mass to snuggle with. For a moment, she could see someone staring back at her. She reached in and pulled out a shirt at random and made a little "huh" as she picked her Union Jack crop top.

Five more minutes.

She looked at the shirt, then rubbed her ears to clean out the British voice that echoed in her brain. "Does the crazy end today?"

She rolled over and planted her hands on the rug. She leaned in and took a good, long look into the recesses under her bed. She shivered but found nothing more evil than a pair of knockoff designer boots waiting for her there. "It's okay. It's all gonna be okay," she reassured herself.

Her phone buzzed with the message, *"There's nothing under there."*

"Are you spying on me?" Meg replied.

"Not spying, scrying. It's your last day of the weird, so let's make it a doozy, OK?"

Said day consisted of a commute into Boston, water and plain bagels for breakfast, and a constant stream of tourist traps. "Why are we at Faneuil Hall again?" Meg asked.

Quinn pointed to the crowds lining up for overpriced seafood and beer. Cameras snapped pictures everywhere, and the pair could hardly find a place quiet enough to sit and talk. "Because of this. The more eyes on you, the more work the weird has to do to overcome it. We can still have fun, but all these normies are gonna be our insurance that nothing from Hell pops up to harass you, unless you count that mime over there. I'm pretty sure that's a nightmare sent to torture me."

"I've been thinking...a lot about the burrito. I think I get it now, because burritos often have cheese, it would make me sick..."

"And if the Poblano's listeria outbreak just happens to be gracing Beantown today then you'll get hella sick. I'm pretty sure if I got the squirts bad enough, I'd beg anyone for help."

"And then listening to music?" Meg prompted.

"Listening activates different parts of your brain and if you were singing along or somehow dancing... Yeah let's not think about that image any longer, but you get what I mean," Quinn explained. "*If* you could hit a zone where all parts of your brain were in sync and you were desperate and in pain enough to wish for anything to help you, then a weak spot in reality could become a hole. Ghost dude—"

"His name was Mish-gan," Meg interrupted. "He said that he'd been helping me before, but this time he was letting me go to have a nice life. Maybe that means *he's* the one that found the demon and then there won't be one tonight, or...or...I dunno. I'm weighing out my options here."

"Whoa, hold the proverbial phone here. What do you mean weighing your options? Did we not go over the probable death, not to mention the potential *releasing a demon* scenario? You told me last night that an actual angel got you stuck in this mess and is now sacrificing himself to give you a normal life. I also pointed out that I'd still be your friend and take care of you. There isn't a discussion, right?"

Meg's lip quivered.

"*Right*, Megsy?"

"I know. I keep hearing in my head that I failed. I failed so much. But when I fell asleep, I know it's gonna sound crazy, but I had this one...nagging...thought."

It was Quinn's turn for lip quivering action. "And what might this dangerous little thought be?"

"What if I finally get it right?"

"Make it stop!" Vocharlian roared as he clutched his head. His breastplate surged with Fell light from the moment he'd entered the conference room. Vocharlian's eyes flashed an unending rainbow of colors—cycling between red, blue, violet, and green with rare blips of black and gold to change it up.

Although the gelatinous lady by his side quivered, she stared blankly at her more solid companion. "Make *what* stop?" Shishi the Golgothan asked.

Vocharlian slammed his fists into his eye sockets, rattling the gray matter in his skull. Shishi slithered toward him, getting slightly closer to the central soulflame as well. The cambion, however, thrashed violently as the words rattled in his throbbing head. "Jesus Christ, you can't hear her?" he whined. No sooner had his mouth opened than a rush of words poured out of him.

"You're not alone, Charlie. I want you to know that no matter what, you're not alone, even if you can't see me or hear me anymore. I'll always be there," the demon said in a voice not his own. "I'm sorry, but I don't think I can do this."

"Um, excuse me?" Shishi's eye-blobs swirled with confused black sparkles. Vocharlian coughed and gagged. He dropped to one knee as his guide shambled his way. Before she could reach him, a klaxon sounded as a double-reinforced portcullis raised over the conference room door. Shishi gasped. She pointed a dripping digit toward Vocharlian's glowing armor, just before the pure Fellfire of the soulforge erupted from the central brazier.

"No!" Vocharlian's eye-lights shifted to red, and he used all his wrath-given speed to snatch one of the conference chairs and scoop the blob up as best he could. Unfortunately, in his gallantry to slide Shishi to safety, he took a step too close to the raging inferno. Black and green flame poured straight into his back. "Oh...bollocks," he managed to spit out before the conflagration consumed him.

"I don't think I can do this," Meg said as she stared at the silver-foiled cylinder lying on her kitchen table.

Across the way, Quinn let out a sigh of relief. "Now you're coming to your senses. I can feel the arcane pressure change starting in that powder room. You want me to put on a movie or something? We could totally use a distraction." They got up and made a beeline for the living room. "I'll double check the wards too!"

Meg stared at her reflection—at the glasses she had to wear because she'd slept in her contacts, at her frizzing hair, and at the smeared eyeliner and lip-stain that no amount of scrubbing had managed to take off. Her ears perked up at the first strains of "Hip to Be Square." "Of course, Quinn had to pick that one."

She eyed the trash, then the chicken roll-up of doom. "What was I even thinking?" Meg asked the girl in the glass.

What if you get it right this time?

"What?"

What if...you get it right for a change?

"And you just believe me?" she asked as the dream unfolded one last time.

I'm twenty-thousand leagues under the deep blue sea with a semi every time I look at a fit freckled fish lady. Also, I've got this hunch we're about to be attacked by lesbian vampire mermaids, so really, who am I to doubt anything at this point? For fuck's sake you are totally giving me the full Michael J. Fox experience so let's get your parents to kiss or whatever we have to do and save the day!

Meg closed her eyes and for a moment she could see a face-off between a demon and a giant with one glowing eye. Her heart raced as she could see a terrifyingly familiar winged figure begging for his life.

Where are you?

The giant raised its enormous foot.

"Oh my God, if I don't do this, what happens to him?" Meg gasped. "What if it's not all about me?"

"You, say something, chica? Come on, it's movie time and hopefully the tear in reality is about to pass, so we can have a popcorn and Chinese food geek night. Meg? *Meggieeeeeeee?*"

"Fuck me," Vocharlian moaned as he cowered in the darkest recesses of a cave full of obsidian blades. He clutched his knees to his chest, wings draped sadly over his shivering form. Even the runes on his charred breastplate were beginning to dim. "I'm scared. I'm bloody scared."

He'd avoided the first stomp, and the cyclops had turned his attention to devouring a few filth-eaters. However, as the chill soaked into the cambion and he saw nothing but a starless sky overhead, he took little comfort in his reprieve. "Are you out there?" he asked softly. "I don't know why, but I didn't think I was supposed to be alone."

Another one of the rat-like creatures met its end, so the demon curled even further into the corner. More blades sliced into his tender new wings, and the breastplate made it difficult to hide. "Some armor you turned out to be. Thanks, Mum."

The boneyard rattled from top to bottom. Vocharlian let out a deep sigh as he saw not one but two more of the hungry giants rise out of the pit. "FRESH MEAT!"

Vocharlian jammed his elbow against the wall, knocking free a sorry excuse for a knife. "I guess if you gotta go, you might as well go out with a fight. If only I had..."

He trailed off as he saw something carved into the rubble ahead. "Just in case she changes her mind," Vocharlian mouthed. He scrambled over and found a hunk of plastic nestled in a crack. Earbuds dangled tantalizingly from the tiny device. Without thinking he shoved them in and pressed the power button. "Only two songs? What the...?"

"...Hell," Meg whispered. "I can do this."

Inspiration becomes a thought,
Thoughts go into motion...

Motion becomes a rhythm.

Rhythm begets emotion...

"What the hell is this nightmare? Can't a bloke die in peace?" the demon snarled as the synthesizers assaulted his eardrums. He didn't have time to yank it away, as he had to find a rhythm of his own and scramble for his life. Red surged in his eye sockets. "Fuck me! I'm gonna die!"

"Oh my God, I'm gonna die!" Meg cried as she lurched over the toilet. "I'm such...a..." She stopped moaning to force herself to sing along with the chorus.

> *...Emotion turns to song.*
> *The song invokes a spell...*
> *(And then the deed is done.)*

Tears rolled down her eyes as she fell away from the porcelain throne in defeat. Even though she heaved, she managed to yank the shower curtain to the side but saw nothing more threatening that her collection of poufs and sensitive skin body washes.

"Meg!" Quinn banged on the door. "What the fuck is going on, Meg?"

"Damn it, I'm making a choice!" she snarled as she slapped her filthy hand on the back button for her music player. This time she sang as loud as she could, vomit be damned, and she made a point to twirl her fingers in a pathetic rendition of a dance.

> *Inspiration becomes a thought,*
> *Thoughts go into motion.*
> *Motion becomes a rhythm.*
> *Rhythm begets emotion,*
> *Emotion turns to song.*
> *The song invokes a spell...*
> *(And then the deed is done.)*

Still nothing, so she slapped it again, and again until somehow, she screwed up and one synth line switched to another. As she lay helpless against the cold tile, her cheek blessed with the relative comfort of the fuzzy bathmat, tears poured out in earnest.

This song lacked the clear arcane instructions of the Princess Space track, but Meg couldn't help but sniffle and sing along once the chorus came around for a second time.

"Let me...be...your armor, let me be your shield..." she choked out as the numbness crept along every extremity. She tried so hard to push to her hands and knees, but the mix of sweat and sick turned out to be just too slippery. In that moment she resigned herself to smashing her face straight into unforgiving tile.

"*Let me take away the pain you feel,*" and entirely new voice sang along, and a furry palm cushioned her, mere moments before her fall.

"*Your armor,*" they sang together as each one protected the other from a grisly fate. The lights flickered and the phone went dead but the demon and summoner could still sing...

"*Let me be your armor.*"

Meg stared deep into a pair of hollow, burning red eye sockets and ignored the wings, the claws, and the rather jagged array of horns on the monster's fearsome face. "Is that you, Charlie?"

The red faded to a soft green glow. The strange creature helped Meg to her feet.

"Pardon me, luv, but have we met?"

THE END

Obligatory Post Credits Scene

Iknow I said you were boring, but do you think we could have had a little bit of the old banter and figuring out how all our powers work before we ended up twenty-thousand leagues of fucked up?" the demon asked as he stared at an army full of bloodsucking fish.

"You're the one who let me redline the contract, Charlie," Meg replied with a tight grin, trying her best not to gulp too much and throw off her gills. "This is what we have to do to pay off the Fey."

"I dunno, I think vampire mermaids are the coolest thing ever," Quinn said, rocking their Vanth avatar to float effortlessly in a bubble while Meg and her demon had to get soaked to the bone, "not to mention Joan. I think she's into you, Spike."

"Can we table my demon's sex life until after the big fight?" Meg snapped. She then flicked her wrist and tossed her focus over to Vocharlian. Both his eye sockets and the hilt burst with scarlet flames the moment his talons made contact, prompting his witch to give him some serious side eye. "Remember, we only have to buy the deep-sea crew enough time. It's not going to turn into a sushi platter."

Her demon pouted, but he shifted to the same blue as the sea and the death blade became a slightly less deadly club. "Fine...we'll do it your way, but they'll be a time where it's gonna get nasty and I'll have to actually reap a soul. You know that...right? Dudette?"

Meg stared at the insanity as far as the eye could see and nodded. "Yup, I got it. After all, this is the path I chose."

Keep In Touch

If you'd like to know more about R.E. Carr, you can check her out at:
www.rachelecarr.com
www.facebook.com/totalrecarr
On Twitter: @totalrecarr
Instagram: @totalrecarr
Also, if you liked what you read, or heck, even if you didn't, feel free to leave a review on Amazon, Goodreads, or wherever you'd like. Thanks!

Acknowledgments

The author would like to thank the spectacular team at Falstaff Books for believing in her even when she, herself, did not. An extra special shoutout goes to the editing team of John Hartness, Alexandra Christian, and Melissa McArthur who made this manuscript make sense. The author will also give additional praise to the all-mighty Hartness for adding yet another *Authors & Dragons* author to his publishing Infinity Gauntlet.

Special thanks go to the Bite Club of loyal beta readers as well: Walter, Nick, James, RH, Nicole and Emelie. Sorry for all the damn homonyms and jump cuts!

Oh yeah, thanks to Logan Peterson as well for actualizing a demon being summoned via a burrito in cover form.

Last but not least, the author would like to thank the gracious Tom Shear of Assemblage 23 for allowing her to use his classic hit "Let Me Be Your Armor" in this work, rather than solely relying on AI and spite to generate some lyrics to inspire the interdimensional hijinks. His music and lyrics have certainly kept the author going through good times and bad and she wouldn't be published today without the support beautiful songs can provide.

About the Author

R. E. Carr likes to split her time between the alien (well, resident alien) she married, her two adorable offspring and the vast army of characters who constantly argue in her brain. She uses her past life as a video game reviewer to remind herself just how awesome it is to be writing novels now.

Rachel writes because she knows so many people and places that never quite made it into this version of the universe. It's her duty to let them out. Writing also gives her mind a certain peace and calm rarely felt in this multi-tasking, wired world.

Also By R.E. Carr

Rules Undying

Four

Six

Ten

Point One Five

Zero

One

The Download Files

The Download

The Source Code (coming soon)

False Icons (with Rick Gualtieri)

Second String Savior

Wannabe Wizard

Halfhearted Hunter

Deviant Dark Dryads (coming soon)

Friends of Falstaff

CPSIA information can be obtained
at www.ICGtesting.com
Printed in the USA
BVHW040800180822
644918BV00001B/1

9 781645 541691